T

Just as we w[...]
commotion in [...] voices raised in
alarm, then little Alisette, barefoot and in her
nightgown, came flying into the dining room. "I
saw him," she cried, nearly hysterical. "I saw him
riding a horse right up to the door. *My father's
here!*"

I stood, clasping Alisette's hand and drawing
her to my side. She must have been dreaming
again. Poor fatherless child . . .

Suddenly, the door flew open, and a man strode
in from the night. He pulled off a brimmed cap to
reveal thick dark hair. As his green gaze touched us
all, I noticed a scar running across his forehead
and down his temple to his left cheek. Except for
the scar, he was the picture of the master of Sea
Cliff House, come to life. . . .

No one moved; no one spoke. The man's gaze
fastened on me, then he smiled and strode toward
me, looking at me so intently that I felt I was
drowning in his sea green eyes.

Before I could turn away, he swept me into his
arms and kissed me. Far from gentle, his kiss was
so hungry and demanding that I all but swooned.
He tasted of brandy, and the sea, but most of all I
felt the oddly pleasurable warmth of his male body
pressed so closely against mine.

The kiss ended, and he held me away from him,
staring into my eyes. "My dear wife," he murmured. "I'm home at last."

ROMANTIC SUSPENSE WITH ZEBRA'S GOTHICS

THE SWIRLING MISTS OF CORNWALL   (2924, $3.95)
by Patricia Werner

Rhionna Fowley ignored her dying father's plea that she never return to his ancestral homeland of Cornwall. Yet as her ship faltered off the rugged Cornish coast, she wondered if her journey would indeed be cursed.

Shipwrecked and delirious, Rhionna found herself in a castle high above the roiling sea—and in thrall to the handsome and mysterious Lord Geoffrey Rhyweth. But fear and suspicion were all around: Geoffrey's midnight prowling, the hushed whispers of the townspeople, women disappearing from the village. She knew she had to flee, for soon it would be too late.

THE STOLEN BRIDE OF GLENGARRA CASTLE   (3125, $3.95)
by Anne Knoll

Returning home after being in care of her aunt, Elly Kincaid found herself a stranger in her own home. Her father was a ghost of himself after the death of Elly's mother, her brother was bitter and violent, her childhood sweetheart suddenly hostile.

Elly agreed to meet the man her brother Hugh wanted her to marry. While drawn to the brooding, intense Gavan Mitchell, Elly was determined to ignore his whispered threats of ghosts and banshees. But she could *not* ignore the wailing sounds from the tower. Someone was trying to terrify her, to sap her strength, to draw her into the strange nightmare.

THE LOST DUCHESS OF GREYDEN CASTLE   (3046, $3.95)
by Nina Coombs Pykare

Vanessa never thought she'd be a duchess; only in her dreams could she be the wife of Richard, Duke of Greyden, the man who married her headstrong sister, Caroline. But one year after Caroline's violent and mysterious death, Richard proposed and took her to his castle in Cornwall.

Her dreams had come true, but they quickly turned to *nightmares.* Why had Richard never told her he had a twin brother who hated him? Why did Richard's sister shun her? Why was she not allowed to go to the North Tower? Soon the truth became clear: everyone there had reason to kill Caroline, and now someone was after *her.* But which one?

THE EMERALD SHADOWS OF SEA CLIFF HOUSE

JANE TOOMBS

ZEBRA BOOKS
KENSINGTON PUBLISHING CORP.

ZEBRA BOOKS

are published by

Kensington Publishing Corp.
475 Park Avenue South
New York, NY 10016

First printing: November, 1991

Printed in the United States of America

Chapter 1

Through a curtain of sea mist, I stared from my carriage at the black-hooded figure standing silhouetted against the gray and lowering sky. The crash of the wild waves against the rocks drowned any cry from the few seagulls wheeling overhead. Perched on the edge of the carriage seat, I took a deep breath, clenching my gloved fingers tightly together.

Had I been too hasty in agreeing to come to Sea Cliff House? I'd convinced myself I'd be able to contain my fear of the sea, but I hadn't anticipated this dark figure on the cliff's edge with its black cape swirling in the wind. Though I didn't believe in apparitions, the unmoving figure sent a chill along my spine.

"Waiting for the *Sea Dragon*," Armin Brown, the carriage driver, called down to me. "Day after day she waits there."

What was he saying about sea dragons? I shivered, hugging myself, my eyes on the black-garbed woman until the horses rounded a curve and the dark figure was lost to my sight.

"Mrs. Peter couldn't see the ship if it did sail past," Armin went on. "She's well nigh blind."

I straightened. Again I'd allowed my imagination to overcome my common sense. I could almost hear Sister Samara's chiding voice. "Keep your feet on the ground, Esma, where they belong; keep your mind on what is real, away from flights of fancy."

Mrs. Peter must be the elder Mrs. Nikolai, grandmother of Alisette, the sickly five-year-old girl for whom I'd been hired to care. Mrs. Peter Nikolai must walk to the cliffs every day to watch the sea for the arrival of her son's ship, the ship Armin had called *Sea Dragon*.

"Some folks think Captain Stephen won't never come back," Armin chuckled unpleasantly, "and there's them who wish he wouldn't. Been five years and more, it has. Many's the things that change in five years."

I said nothing. The Nikolai carriage had met me at the stage station in Eureka, California, and Armin had first stared at me as if I were some kind of freak of nature, then questioned me as though he were the one passing on my ability for the post—he'd even asked my age. Twice! I'd been relieved when he finally began pointing out the sights of Eureka on our drive along the south coast into the highlands where Sea Cliff House was located.

Though I'd answered his questions and listened to his discourse on Eureka politely, I'd been careful not to encourage him in any way. I didn't set myself above him—I'd soon be working for the Nikolais as he already did—but I didn't take to him, even though he was good-looking enough, with shrewd brown eyes and hair as dark and curly as my own. His manner hinted he knew unwholesome secrets.

Catching sight of a peaked tower thrusting above the redwoods, I tensed in anticipation of my first sight of the Nikolai mansion. That was what

Sister Samara had called it, a mansion.

"Remember, wealth means nothing compared to the condition of your soul," the sister had cautioned. "Indeed, the love of money is the root of all evil. Keep a pure heart." She'd fixed me with her gray eyes. "And a level head."

Heart pounding with excitement, I stared from the carriage window. Since I was five, I'd lived at the Sisters of Charity Orphanage in the hills outside Fort Bragg, California, the last two years at their nearby hospital where I'd been trained as a nurse. In all my eighteen years, this was my first trip beyond Fort Bragg, my first time away from the protective hovering of the sisters. I'd worked at the hospital but never before had I been on my own.

I can do it, I assured myself. I will do it. Then the carriage turned and the magnificence of Sea Cliff House filled my vision. My mouth dropped open.

Why, it was as big as a hotel! The tall, peaked tower I'd seen above the trees sat dead center atop the third floor with two shorter, domed cupolas at the ends of the wings to either side. An arched veranda graced the front of the mansion. From an enclosed second-floor balcony, circular windows on each side of an imposing two-story portico above the veranda stared down at me like large, round, suspicious eyes.

The mansion awed me and disturbed me at the same time. I shrank from its isolation, perched as it was on the edge of the cliffs, several miles from Eureka, with no near dwellings. I felt it loom forbiddingly over me, a place of loneliness and secrets under the lowering sky.

Armin's voice recalled me from my flight of fancy. "'Tis all built of redwood," he said, reining in the horses in front of a double set of stairs rising to the entrance. "Top to bottom, all redwood."

7

He helped me dismount, then, walking slightly behind me, carried my traveling bag up the stairs. The gloom of the afternoon deepened under the veranda's overhang so I could barely make out the design of the crest on the pair of brass knockers ornamenting the massive double doors. A dolphin? No, the face was a man's. Surely, though, that was a fish's tail. A merman? What an odd fancy.

Armin raised one of the knockers and let it fall, once, twice. The door opened quickly, as though someone had been waiting on the other side. I gazed at a middle-aged woman dressed in black and wearing a white apron. Her brown hair peppered with gray was pinned to the top of her head in a tight bun. She fixed me with a penetrating look, her eyes lingering on my face.

"Miss Esma Drake, isn't it?" she asked finally. Hardly waiting for my nod, she bade me enter, adding, "Armin, take Miss Drake's bag to the Ivory Room in the east wing, if you please."

Armin grinned at the graying woman as though they shared some unspoken agreement. "With pleasure, Mrs. Yates." He ambled toward an archway leading off to the right.

"I'm the housekeeper." Mrs. Yates looked me up and down once more, then nodded. "We'll soon get you settled in."

"Thank you."

Had my words revealed my inner sigh of relief? Mrs. Yates appeared to have accepted me, at least for now. I knew from my work at the hospital how newcomers to the staff were often hostilely received. It would be much easier to work in the Nikolai mansion if the housekeeper approved of me.

As I followed Mrs. Yates toward the curving staircase, I tried not to stare as I glanced about the spacious foyer. A silver chandelier with sparkling crystal prisms hung at the foot of the staircase, and wall lamps with matching prisms hanging from their chimneys gleamed softly to either side of a gilt-framed mirror. I caught a glimpse of my flushed face underneath my plain brown hat and glanced hastily away; the image of Esma Drake looked out of place amidst this luxury.

Climbing the stairs, I couldn't help noticing the housekeeper's black bombazine gown had a small bustle, unlike my own brown serge. The sisters hadn't encouraged what they called fripperies, and, besides, I hadn't the money to try to be fashionable.

At the top of the stairs I noticed a door with a gleaming brass knob and lock. Ornate carvings of mermen and mermaids frolicking amid sea foliage decorated its panels. Remembering the tower, I wondered if that's where the door led.

The Ivory Room proved to be on the second floor near the end of a long right-hand corridor. When we passed the back stairs, Mrs. Yates pointed them out. "As Miss Alisette's nurse, you're permitted to use the front stairs, but the back ones are more convenient to the kitchen. Be careful, though, they're steep." She glanced over her shoulder at me as she led the way into the bedroom.

My heart warmed by the housekeeper's courtesy, I stepped into the loveliest room I had ever seen. "Oh!" I gasped, my hand flying to my mouth.

Mrs. Yates's eyes fixed on me and her eyebrows rose. "Is something wrong?"

"This is to be my room?" I managed to say, staring at the exquisite black lacquered chests with their decorative inlays of ivory and the pale green wallpaper that shimmered like silk.

"It doesn't suit?"

9

"It's beautiful! So much more than I ever expected."

'Mrs. Peter thought you should be near the child and this room is the most suitable. Miss Alisette is across the hall."

It occurred to me as it had several times before that no one from the Nikolais had mentioned Alisette's mother, neither when I'd been offered the position nor at any time since. Yet Stephen Nikolai's wife, Cecile, lived at Sea House, Sister Samara had told me.

"You've just the one bag?" Mrs. Yates asked.

I stiffened with embarrassment. "Yes," I admitted.

"Didn't they tell you you'd be dining with the family?"

"No. I'm afraid I own nothing suitable for that."

Again the housekeeper scrutinized me, more critically this time, until I grew restless under her gaze.

"Something will have to be done," Mrs. Yates said finally. "In the sewing room are some lengths of gold faille Mrs. Stephen rejected. Gold would look well with your hazel eyes and dark hair. Molly, that's Armin's wife, is a more than passable seamstress."

"But I couldn't—that is, I have no money to—"

"Mrs. Peter will expect you to be properly clad. I'll arrange for Molly to sew you a gown. In the meantime, you'll have a tray with Miss Alisette in the evenings. She'll like that."

"I'd be quite content to eat with the child every evening, Mrs. Yates. I don't expect—"

"What's proper is proper. There are rules here, Miss Drake. As soon as I can arrange proper clothes for you, you'll dine with the family." The note of finality in the older woman's voice warned me that any further protest was not only useless but might antagonize the housekeeper.

My stomach fluttered as I contemplated taking meals with the Nikolais. The nuns had trained me well enough in table manners but in so grand a mansion as this there was certain to be etiquette of which I knew nothing. My chin rose a little. I'd do what I had to do as best I could. Crossing to the windows, I looked out.

"These rooms in the east wing don't have a sea view." Mrs. Yates sounded almost apologetic.

"I prefer to look at the gardens," I assured her, knowing that hearing the waves crash against the cliff would keep me awake at night, not because of the sound but because I'd be reminded how near to me the threatening sea was. "How lovely the June roses are."

"The coast mist seems to suit them."

"You can have the one I picked. Here." Both of us turned toward the door as a wiry black-haired child in a bedraggled pink frock sidled into the room. She held a golden rose out to me.

"Thank you." As I took the bloom, I noticed a blood-encrusted scratch on the child's hand.

"Miss Alisette!" Mrs. Yates scolded. "You've gone and slipped outside again when no one was looking, haven't you? Just look at your dress."

Alisette thrust out her lower lip. "I only wanted to smell the roses."

"Why don't you help me find a vase for this beautiful flower?" I asked Alisette. "Then we'll both wash up."

"You don't look dirty," the girl said, her dark eyes examining me.

"Manners, miss," Mrs. Yates reminded her. "Miss Drake's come a long way today and no

11

doubt she needs a bit of a rest. You come with me."

"Oh, please, I'd like Alisette to stay," I interjected.

The girl, meanwhile, had pulled a peacock feather from a slim vase of green crystal and offered the vase to me.

"Miss Alisette—" Mrs. Yates began, shaking her head. She sighed and looked at me. "Don't begin by spoiling the child, she's a handful already."

"I'd like Alisette's company," I persisted. "We'll get acquainted."

Mrs. Yates shrugged as if to indicate she'd done her best, nodded to me, and walked to the door. As she left the room she turned back to say, "Sonia will be up later with the trays. Mrs. Peter won't be wanting to see you till tomorrow. I'll let you know when she's ready."

"Mrs. Yates calls my grandma Mrs. Peter," Alisette volunteered after the housekeeper was gone. "Grandma's name is really Katherine. She's named after a Russian queen, Catherine the Great, only she spells it with a *K*. She says that's why Grandfather married her, because she had a Russian queen's name. Grandma says I'm partly Russian, too, only not all because Mama isn't. My mama's name is Cecile and she's pretty."

"I'm certain she is. You're a pretty girl yourself." I slid the stem of the rose into the vase I'd filled with water from the pitcher atop the commode and set it on the stand next to the walnut four-poster bed. "It was very thoughtful of you to pick a rose to welcome me, Alisette."

A series of expressions flitted across the girl's face, finally resolving into a scowl. "Everyone thinks I look like a raggle-tag gypsy 'cause I heard them say so. And I picked the rose 'cause I wasn't supposed to."

"You gave it to me, that's what counts. Now I

think we're ready to wash our hands and faces." I touched Alisette's tangled hair. "And make ourselves as neat as we can before we eat."

Alisette jerked away from my hand. "I hate to have my hair brushed."

"You can brush mine first, then I'll do yours. That's fair."

The child eyed me dubiously. "You're *Miss* Drake so that means you aren't married."

I nodded. "I've taken care of lots and lots of children, though. Girls and boys, both. Ever since I was ten years old. You see, I grew up in an orphanage, a place for children who don't have a mother or father. The older children took care of the younger ones."

"Babies, too?"

"Sometimes."

Alisette looked wistful. "I wish I had a baby to take care of. Rosie's sister Kate has a baby. Sometimes I get to hold him when Kate visits in the kitchen. His name is Russell and he's got blue eyes and he smiles at me. Kate lives in Eureka so she doesn't get to visit Rosie a lot."

I assumed Rosie must be the cook. "Maybe someday you'll have a little brother or sister of your own," I said.

Alisette shook her head. "Mama says she's not going to have any more babies even if my father does come home. She says one was enough, even if I wasn't a boy."

I chided myself for forgetting that Alisette's father, captain of the *Sea Dragon*, hadn't been home since before she was born. The poor child had never known her father.

It seemed to me, though, that either people had been talking far too openly in front of this child, or Alisette had overheard more than she was supposed to.

13

"Grandfather's ship sank and he drowned," Alisette went on. "My father's ship didn't sink. His ship won't sink; I don't care what they say."

"I'm sure the *Sea Dragon* is still afloat," I said hastily. "It hasn't sunk."

"She."

I blinked. "She?"

"My father's ship. Grandma says ships are shes, like girls and ladies."

"I'll try to remember. I don't know much about ships."

"I can teach you. Grandma's told me lots and lots."

"Good. You can teach me about ships, and I'll teach you what I know about reading and writing and numbers."

"That's fair," Alisette said, echoing my earlier remark in such a solemn manner that my heart went out to her. The child had yet to smile. In some ways Alisette reminded me of a new arrival at the orphanage, wary and sad, yet hungering for loving attention.

I could see my job was to be somewhat different than I'd expected after listening to Mr. Tisch, the lawyer who'd journeyed to Fort Bragg in May to inverview me about this position. He'd made certain I was qualified to deal with fits, since he'd been told Alisette was subject to them. Since I was well aware that "fits" covered everything from a true convulsion to a fainting spell, I tried to find out more, but either Mr. Tisch had been instructed not to tell me, or he didn't have any other information.

Watching the little girl, I could see no obvious symptoms of illness. True, the child was pale and thin, but she seemed energetic enough to get herself thoroughly mussed up, an encouraging sign.

14

Alisette's illness was the reason a nurse had been chosen, a nurse with enough education to teach the basic skills of reading, writing, and arithmetic. I smiled at the child, drawn to her.

"After we're all tidy, maybe you'd like to show me your room," I said.

"And my ships, too," Alisette agreed. "They're just like the big Nikolai ships, with names and sails and all. I've got *Sea Bear* and *Sea Wolf* and *Sea Dragon.*"

"Do they really sail?"

"They would, only I don't have any place to sail them."

"I thought I saw a pond in the rose garden."

Alisette nodded. "There's goldfish in it. I can't go there, though. I'm not supposed to leave the house 'cause I might get sick and have a fit."

My brow creased. Not go outside? Not at all? There must be some mistake. I wouldn't question the child but wait and ask Mrs. Yates.

Alisette glanced at me slyly. "I do go out sometimes, anyway."

Like today, when she'd picked the rose. Better not to discuss the matter now. "I can't wait to see your ships," I said. "Let's hurry and wash, then brush our hair."

Molly, the seamstress, appeared the next morning after breakfast with a tape measure and several yards of gold faille. Alisette watched me being measured for a new gown.

"This gold color does suit you, miss," Molly said.

"My mama likes to wear blue," Alisette put in. "Uncle Gerald says blue makes her eyes look heavenly. I wish *my* eyes were blue."

Molly, a small, thin sallow woman, shot a quick

15

appraising glance at me before gathering up her pins, as if to see how I felt about what the child said. "That'll be doing it, miss," she told me. "If I can fit it on you once I'm started, that's all I need."

"Thank you, Molly, you're very quick. I've never been much of a seamstress, try as I might. The nuns gave up on me years ago. I admire your ability."

Molly reddened, smiling at me in embarrassed pleasure at the compliment.

After she'd gone, Alisette slid from the bed where she'd been perched and stared into my face. "Your eyes are a funny color," she said. "Sort of a greeny-gold."

"That's called hazel."

Alisette sighed. "Mine are plain old brown. Like muddy water, Mama says."

I swallowed the hot words of protest that rose to my lips. What mother would say such a thing to her child? "When I was little," I finally told Alisette, "I once was given a velvet muff exactly the color of your eyes. It was the softest and prettiest thing I ever owned. I cried when the muff got so tattered the sisters made me give it up. When I look at your eyes I think of that muff and it makes me warm and happy."

Alisette gazed uncertainly at me, the hint of a smile brightening her face.

Before I had time to say anything more, Mrs. Yates appeared at the door.

"Mrs. Peter wants to see you now, Miss Drake," the housekeeper announced.

I moistened my lips nervously as I smoothed my dark green gingham, the gown shabby from too many washings. What if Mrs. Nikolai didn't like me? I'd already grown attached to Alisette and badly wanted to stay at Sea Cliff House.

When Alisette trailed after us, Mrs. Yates shook

her head. "Off to the kitchen with you, miss," she ordered. "Sonia's to mind you there until Miss Drake is finished talking to Mrs. Peter."

Alisette scowled but, under Mrs. Yates's watchful eye, started down the back stairs.

"Is it true Alisette's not supposed to leave the house?" I asked the housekeeper as we walked along the corridor toward the main staircase.

"Well, the doctor did say the sea wind wasn't good for her. The truth is, no one has the time to watch her properly since that scatterbrained woman from back East left her without giving notice. Frightened of the child's fits, she was. More interested in making eyes at Mr. Gerald than watching over Miss Alisette properly, anyway. We didn't cotton to her and she knew it."

"Then I could take Alisette into the rose garden on a mild day? It's almost June, the weather's not harsh."

"Best to ask Mrs. Peter."

"I'll do that."

We didn't descend the stairs but turned into the corridor to the left, passing through a small gallery displaying gold-framed oil paintings. Eyes as green as the sea stared down at me from one of the portraits, and I paused to look closer at the handsome black-bearded man dressed in a bemedaled white uniform.

"That's Captain Alexi, the first of the Nikolai family to leave Russia to live in America. Captain Stephen is the very image of him."

The glint of laughter in Alexi Nikolai's eyes, so at odds with the hard, determined jut of the bearded chin, added a reckless charm to the portrait.

A handsome man and, I suspected, a ruthless one. He'd emigrated to a new country where he'd founded a family and began amassing the Nikolai

17

fortune, according to Sister Samara, who approved of ambition in men.

"He was Russian Orthodox, of course," Sister had said, "and I understand he built Sea Cliff House next to a Russian church that's now in ruins. I've been assured, though, that the present family is of our faith."

Alisette's great-grandfather. Long dead. And her grandfather had drowned.

"Alisette has never seen her father."

I wasn't asking a question, but Mrs. Yates replied, "It may very well be she never will."

I shivered slightly at the portent of the words, recalling a song the old Irish gardener at the orphanage used to sing:

Down at the bottom of the wild green sea
Down at the bottom where the fish swim free
Many a ship has found her home
Many a sailor has left his bones
Down at the bottom of the sea. . . .

"Do you think something's happened to Stephen Nikolai's ship?" I whispered.

Mrs. Yates blinked. "To *Sea Dragon?* How would I know? Captain Stephen's had five years to return and he has not, that's all I'm saying. Time we stopped dawdling here. Mrs. Peter will be wondering what's keeping us."

Mrs. Nikolai lived in a suite. A tall, slender woman, she stood at the window of her sitting room dressed in a black silk gown fashionable ten years before, her gray head bowed. Outside the window I could hear the crash of waves against the nearby cliff and knew the rooms in the west wing must face the ocean. Thank God my room did not.

18

"Good morning, Mrs. Peter. I've brought Miss Drake."

Mrs. Nikolai turned toward us at the house-keeper's greeting. "Come closer," she ordered.

Mrs. Yates pushed me forward, and I remembered the carriage driver, Armin, telling me the mistress couldn't see well.

I walked up to Mrs. Nikolai, saying, "I'm Esma Drake," and stopped directly in front of the gray-haired woman.

Mrs. Nikolai reached out her hand and touched my cheek for an instant. "You have a pleasant voice."

"Thank you, ma'am." I was at a loss how to go on.

"Have you met Alisette?"

"Oh, yes. She's a lovely little girl." I forced myself to stop, I mustn't waste my employer's time by babbling on about how much I liked the child.

Mrs. Nikolai's smile transformed her thin face, showing traces of the beauty she once must have had. "Alisette is my one joy."

"I—I'd like to take her into the rose garden on sunny days, if you approve," I said. "We might sail some of her ships in the goldfish pond if that's all right."

"Of course. Fresh air never hurt anyone. I'm sure you'll take precautions to keep her from becoming chilled."

"Yes, ma'am."

"She needs love and attention. When Stephen comes home he'll see to it his daughter is happy, but for now it will be up to you, Esma Drake. That's why you're here. Do you understand?"

"I understand. I'd like to know a bit more about her illness so I'll be prepared to—"

Mrs. Nikolai cut me off with a wave of her hand.

19

"Alisette is not ill."

I swallowed. "No, but I've been told she some-times has—problems."

"Dr. March is a fool and a charlatan," Mrs. Nikolai said sharply.

Mrs. Yates touched my arm. When I glanced at her, the housekeeper shook her head and I realized I mustn't keep on about Alisette's illness.

"We'll talk again," Mrs. Nikolai said. "I feel you're someone I can trust."

"Oh, yes, I hope to be, I'll try to be," I said earnestly. "I want Alisette to be happy, just as you do."

Mrs. Nikolai's dark eyes focused on me, and it was hard to believe she couldn't see me. "I'll hold you to that. Make her happy, a child deserves hap-piness. We grow up too soon."

Once we were outside the door, Mrs. Yates whispered, "Mrs. Peter doesn't like to be reminded anything's wrong with Miss Alisette. I should have warned you."

"Exactly what kind of fits does Alisette have?"

"She goes to gasping and wheezing and shaking all over. Seems as though she can't get her breath. Scares the poor tyke nigh to death. The rest of us, too. The last time, she was taken so bad we all thought she was sure to die. That's when Mr. Gerald convinced Mrs. Peter we needed a trained nurse to replace that foolish woman from Boston. Before that, Mrs. Peter wouldn't hear of bringing a nurse here."

"Couldn't Alisette's mother have gotten a nurse here sooner?"

Mrs. Yates shook her head. "Mrs. Stephen leaves all decisions to Mrs. Peter."

I was none too sure that was the right thing to do. Not where her daughter's health was con-cerned.

As we approached the gallery, a bedroom door opened and an attractive auburn-haired woman in a magnificent blue silk dressing robe stepped into the hall and fixed her eyes on Mrs. Yates.

"I thought I heard your voice," the woman said. "Sonia's simply impossible, you'll have to do something about her. When she brought my tray a few minutes ago, she slammed it down any old way and all but ran from the room. What kind of a maid does that?"

"I'm sorry, Mrs. Stephen." The housekeeper's voice was cold. "Sonia's supposed to be keeping an eye on Miss Alisette, and I imagine she's flustered."

"That's no excuse. Hasn't that nurse arrived yet?"

"This is the nurse, Miss Esma Drake."

I stepped forward. "I'm pleased to be taking care of your daughter, Mrs. Nikolai," I said.

The woman shrugged, her pale blue eyes flickering disdainfully over my worn dress. "Well, but you don't seem to *be* taking care of her, do you?"

I flushed. "I'm sorry. I was—"

"Mrs. Peter asked to see her," Mrs. Yates broke in. "If that's all, we'll be getting back to our duties."

"I don't like my breakfast slopped onto my tray. No matter what the excuse." The pale eyes glared at Mrs. Yates.

"I'll see it doesn't happen again." The housekeeper's voice was even chillier than before.

The door closed abruptly. We continued along the corridor, Mrs. Yates muttering something under her breath that I was just as glad I couldn't hear.

Alisette's mother was beautiful, I thought, while at the same time Sister Samara's words echoed in my mind: "A charitable heart is worth

21

far more than a pretty face."

Mrs. Stephen Nikolai didn't show much evidence of a charitable heart, but these were early days and who was I to be judging her? She certainly did have a pretty face, framed by that glorious deep red hair. I fingered my own dark curls, rebelling against their confinement in a bun at the back of my head. I glanced down at my drab dress, recalling the iridescent sheen of Cecile's silken robe.

I did try to keep a charitable heart, but at the moment I couldn't help wishing for a more attractive exterior. You mustn't be envious, I admonished myself. Think of your good fortune in being asked to work at Sea Cliff House and finding your charge such an appealing child. Reflect on the good and give thanks.

Outside my door, Mrs. Yates stopped. "Before we go downstairs I'd best mention Mr. Gerald. Mr. Gerald Callich, he is, who works at the Nikolai shipping office in Eureka. He lives here at Sea Cliff House by Mrs. Peter's wish." She frowned, eyeing me. "It wouldn't do to allow Mr. Gerald to become too friendly, if you understand what I mean."

I stiffened. "I know my place."

"I don't doubt that. Nevertheless, a word to the wise is never amiss." Mrs. Yates headed for the back stairs.

After a moment I followed her, musing about how little experience I'd had with men. It amounted to none, except for occasionally taking care of them as patients in the hospital. Sick men, those were, and usually old. Sometimes young men had tried to talk to me when I went on an errand into town with one of the sisters, but a withering glance from the nun always nipped those attempts in the bud.

Once a delivery man had caught me unawares in a hospital storeroom, pulled me to him, and kissed me on the mouth. I hadn't enjoyed the experience, fighting free as quickly as I could.

If a man with reckless green eyes and a jaunty black beard kissed me, would I feel differently? I smiled ruefully when I realized who I was picturing. Little danger of that happening. Alexi Nikolai was many years in his grave.

"Mrs. Yates, Mrs. Yates!" Alisette bounded up the steep stairs toward us. "Miss Drake! Guess what?"

"I can't imagine," the housekeeper said.

"Tell us," I suggested, putting a hand on Alisette's shoulder.

The little girl grasped my hand, squeezing it in her excitement. "Armin was down at the docks and he heard," she paused to catch her breath, "he heard *Sea Dragon* was sighted sailing into San Francisco Bay."

Mrs. Yates put a hand to her breast. "Mercy!"

So *Sea Dragon* wasn't at the bottom of the Pacific Ocean, I thought. Nor Stephen Nikolai.

"Does that mean my father's coming home?" Alisette's voice was shrill with joyous hope.

"For good or ill, I'd say it does." There was no joy in Mrs. Yates's voice.

For good or ill? I hugged Alisette to me as I pondered the enigmatic words. Surely Stephen Nikolai's return could only bring good to Sea House.

Chapter 2

Alisette was so keyed up over her father's imminent return I knew she'd never be able to settle down for her afternoon rest without some exercise in the fresh air. Following lunch, I persuaded her to put on a sweater and took her into the rose garden with her replica of *Sea Dragon*. Under the warm spring sun, surrounded by the scent of roses, we sailed the little ship a dozen or more times across the goldfish pond, causing a flurry of panic each time among the fish.

"Why do the goldfish run away and hide?" she asked. "My ship won't hurt them."

"They probably think the ship's a great big fish and they're afraid it—I mean she—means to eat them."

Alisette laughed. "That's silly."

I nodded. "But the goldfish don't know that."

"I don't like to scare them." She plucked her ship from the water, set it carefully beside the tiled rim of the pool, and looked up into my face. "Do you want to see my special place?" she asked.

"I'd like to very much."

"First, you have to promise you won't tell. 'Cause they wouldn't like me going there."

"Your grandmother says it's all right for us to be

outside if the weather's warm and we wrap up well," I reminded her.

"Yes, but she didn't say I could go just anywhere, did she?"

I wondered what Alisette had been up to without anyone being aware. "I don't think your grandmother would mind us going to any nearby place that isn't dangerous," I said carefully. "You know what dangerous means, don't you?"

"Walking by the edge of the cliffs is dangerous. I don't ever go close to the edge."

I repressed a shudder at the thought of the waves splashing high against the rocks. I didn't intend to walk along the cliff edge, either.

"Rosie told her sister it's haunted," Alisette said.

Startled, I stared at her. "The cliffs are haunted?"

She shook her head. "My special place. I asked Uncle Gerald what haunted meant, and he said it meant somewhere with ghosts, except there aren't any ghosts, not really. What are ghosts, Miss Drake?"

I'd made up my mind before I came to Sea Cliff House to be as honest as possible with Alisette because I believed children's questions should be answered as best as one could in accordance with their age. Now that I was confronted with explaining ghosts to a five year old, I chose my words with care. "Some people believe a part of a person—the spirit, maybe—sometimes stays behind after a person dies and they call that part a ghost."

Alisette's brow puckered, then cleared. "Like Grandpa Peter. He drowned dead a long time ago, but Grandma Katherine says he tells her things from under the water."

What was I to make of that, for heaven's sake? It was enough to make the hair on my nape prickle. Deciding we'd had enough talk of ghosts, I said, "Is this special place of yours very far?"

Alisette shook her head and pointed south toward the tall cypresses planted so close together they formed a hedge, to the south. "It's over there, right by the old church."

The trees blocked my view, but I remembered Sister Samara mentioning there'd once been a Russian church near Sea Cliff House. "We'll have to walk around," I said.

"I know a secret way." Alisette took my hand and led me toward the cypresses. When we neared them, she pointed. At the base of the hedge was a child-sized hole in the greenery.

"I don't think that's big enough for me to get through," I protested.

"You could crawl."

I thought of what an undignified picture I'd present to anyone looking from the house windows, but I couldn't resist the appeal in Alisette's eyes to go her "secret way." Hoping the rose beds would help to conceal me from view, I hiked up my skirt and got down on my hands and knees, easing my way through the opening. Once on the other side, I stood up quickly, brushing dead needles from my clothes as I looked around.

Perhaps fifty yards away was a small and dilapidated frame church sitting askew on its foundation. Despite the church's decay, a bell still hung in the pointed dome of the tower. I hoped Alisette's special place wasn't inside the church, for the building looked dangerous and I didn't want to be forced to forbid her to play there. Beyond the sagging roof of the church rose the tops of pine trees.

"We go in back of the church," Alisette said, emerging from the hole to stand beside me. "Let's run."

I tossed dignity to the sea wind as, hand in hand, we raced across the rocky ground, skirting the

26

ruins. I stopped abruptly when I realized we were entering a tiny graveyard.

"Come on!" she urged, tugging at my hand. "We're almost there."

I let her lead me between sea-weathered granite and marble grave markers to a small crypt with a rusty padlocked chain across the door. A marble angel the size of a six-month-old baby stared sadly down at us from the crypt's top. Her eyes were blank stone, but a prickle between my shoulders made me wonder if seeing eyes secretly watched us.

"Alexandria's in there," Alisette told me. "She's a Nikolai, just like me." She pointed. "See?"

Carved into the marble was the name Alexandria Catherine and the dates of her brief life: March 15, 1842–March 30, 1847.

"She's just five, like me," Alisette said.

"I didn't realize you could read well enough to decipher the marker," I said brightly, trying to banish the chill that had come over me.

Alisette blinked. "I can't read many words. I guess maybe her ghost told me her name and how old she is. Sort of inside my head."

I shivered, glancing around uneasily, wanting to gather up Alisette and hurry away. No doubt the girl had learned the name and the dead child's age by hearing someone at the house speak of little Alexandria, but I couldn't rid myself of the feeling someone watched us, yet there was no one in sight.

Something rustled through the weeds beside the crypt, and I suppressed a startled squeal. A snake? Whatever made the noise, it was hurrying away from us and so posed no threat. I pulled myself together, knowing I mustn't frighten Alisette or let her see I didn't care for her "special place."

"What a pretty little angel," I said as calmly as I could, raising on my tiptoes so my reluctant fingers reached a cold marble wing.

"Alexandria likes it and I do, too. I'm going to have an angel just like hers on *my* grave."

It curdled my blood to listen to her, nor could I tolerate another moment of those unseen eyes that watched the two of us from God knew where. "Thank you for showing me Alexandria," I said, hoping my nervousness didn't show in my voice, "but it's time to go back to the house now."

To my relief, Alisette came along with no fuss, chattering away as we hurried home. "Alexandria liked you, Miss Drake, I could tell. I like you, too. I hope you never, ever leave."

I smiled at her. She couldn't be blamed for believing a dead child spoke "in her head" when her own grandmother talked of hearing from her drowned husband. What was Mrs. Peter thinking of to expose the girl to such an eerie tale?

To forbid Alisette to visit the graveyard again would make her all the more determined to go. I made up my mind to wean Alisette from her morbid fascination by keeping her busy, not only with lessons but with games. And perhaps there were other children who might be asked to the house with whom she could play. I'd find out. Once Alisette made friends and had other things to think about, she'd gradually lose interest in Alexandria and forget about the crypt guarded by the angel.

While Alisette napped, I sat in the rocker in my room, still unnerved by what had happened and wishing I had some yarn so I could keep occupied by knitting. Being busy would give me less time to indulge what Sister Samara assured me was an overactive and not always healthy imagination. When someone tapped on my ajar door and Sonia poked her head inside and smiled, I sprang up in relief. "Come in," I invited.

She eased into the room. "I better not get caught.

Mrs. Yates already yelled at me once today. On account of *her*—Mrs. Stephen. But I got a few minutes free and I thought I'd take the chance and get acquainted." She handed me a small bundle wrapped in cotton cloth. "It's some embroidery work I got for a gift. I thought you might like to have it since I'll never do it—I hate needlework."

Sonia was a pretty woman in her late twenties, fair-haired and blue eyed. I liked her smile and wasn't at all averse to making a friend. I thanked her for the gift.

"Don't get me wrong about Yates," she went on. "The old gal ain't so bad even if she does keep an eagle eye on us. Rosie's all right, too. Armin," Sonia grimaced, "you got to watch. He thinks he's God's gift to women. I don't know how Molly puts up with him. You met Mr. Gerald yet?"

I shook my head, beginning to wonder what he was like. Alisette called him Uncle Gerald and evidently liked him, yet Mrs. Yates had warned me about him. Why did Sonia wonder if I'd met him?

She studied me for a moment, taking in my old gingham gown and seemed about to say something but didn't. "How do you like the place so far?" she asked finally.

"It's a bit overwhelming. I've never lived in a house like this. A mansion." I didn't mention how gloomy I found the long corridors, or that I'd prefer to live in a house that wasn't perched on the edge of a cliff with the ocean, green and treacherous, waiting below. To say nothing of the graveyard next door.

"I'm waiting to see what'll happen when Captain Stephen gets here." Sonia's smile wasn't as pleasant as the one she'd greeted me with. "*She'll* have to change her ways, that's for sure."

I knew she meant Stephen Nikolai's wife but wasn't certain at what exactly Sonia was hinting.

"Some of us aren't blind and deaf—or dumb to what's going on," Sonia added, "no matter what Mr. Gerald thinks."

I was torn between wanting to be friendly with Sonia and not wanting to listen to gossip. Evidently my expression gave me away because she laughed.

"You're an innocent, that's plain to see," she told me. "Never mind, you'll learn. We all do, sooner or later. But you might as well know right now that not everyone in Sea Cliff House is happy about Captain Stephen's return. You might even say some'd rather he'd drowned like his father."

Leaving me shocked at what she'd said, Sonia slipped from my room. I puzzled over her words. Was she trying to tell me Gerald Callich and Mrs. Stephen were more than friends? I shook my head. Even if that's what Sonia had meant, I had no intention of forming judgments by listening to others. Actually, what any of them did wasn't my business anyway. I was here to take care of Alisette.

I recalled how Armin, on the drive from Eureka, had also hinted there'd be trouble if Captain Stephen returned. Whether it was any of my business or not I couldn't help but wonder why.

Alisette was cross when she woke from her nap, as children are wont to be. Once again she was the recalcitrant little girl I'd first met. She didn't want her face washed nor her hair brushed.

"I'll have a fit if you make me," she threatened, scowling.

I raised my eyebrows. "I didn't realize you could cause yourself to have a fit," I said, rather pleased that the subject had come up. When people tried to keep problems a secret, more harm than good usually came from it.

"I can if I want to."

"Why anyone would want to make themselves

30

have a fit is beyond me," I told her. "But if you'd rather do that than play the new game I was going to teach you—"

"What new game?"

I shrugged. "My hair is brushed and my face is clean. I see no reason to play a game with someone whose hair is in tangles and who has grape jam smeared on her chin."

Alisette's hand flew to her chin. "I don't either have jam on my face!"

I nodded my head at her vanity table. "The mirror doesn't lie."

She couldn't resist turning to look at herself and made a terrible face at her image. "I'm ugly."

"*I* don't think so. But I admit you'd look better without jam on your chin."

Lured by the promise of the game, Alisette was finally convinced to wash her face and let me brush her hair. I had the feeling no one had ever bothered to play games with her and, when she was quickly entranced by a game every child in the orphanage knew, tic-tac-toe, I was sure of it.

"Maybe my father will play this game with me." Her tone was doubtful, telling me Alisette didn't expect much from adults.

"I think he'll have to get acquainted with you first," I said, wanting to spare her possible disappointment. How did I know what Stephen Nikolai would be like? "After all, he's never seen you, just as you've never seen him."

Her brow furrowed. "Do you think he'll like me?"

"I'm certain he will." I tried to sound as positive as possible. The longer I was in Sea Cliff House, though, the less sure I was that anyone cared about Alisette. "I liked you right away, didn't I?"

Her smile lightened her somber little face, and

31

she remained in a good humor through supper and until she went to bed for the night.

I fell asleep immediately, only to find myself lost in the green depths of my terrible, recurring nightmare. . . .

Water closed over my head. I couldn't breathe. There was no surface and no bottom, only a world of green water. Faces appeared and disappeared, voices spoke but no one came to my rescue. I struggled to cry for help but could not as I drifted away from the voices into green oblivion . . .

I woke to darkness, shaken and trembling, unable to believe for long moments that I was safe in a bed. I desperately wished to light a lamp for the comfort of seeing its flame, but didn't give in to the urge.

Sister Samara had explained to me how I'd been brought to them in Fort Bragg by a farmer who'd found me wandering, delirious and alone, in his field during a pouring rain.

"More than likely abandoned by them there gypsies that passed through there," the old farmer had told her. "No good ever come from gypsies."

The doctor had diagnosed pneumonia and hadn't expected me to live.

"Wee child that you were, you fought to live," Sister Samara told me. "I'm not one to give up, and so I prayed and fought along with you, and here you are, strong and healthy, learning how to save other lives."

Sister, who'd never believed I was a gypsy, had confided something else to me shortly before I'd left for Sea Cliff House. "We were sent a sum of money by a person we never saw or knew, with instructions the money be used to educate you and, later, to train you as a nurse. That's why we've kept you here so long, we wanted to do the best we could for you."

32

I'd pressed her for more information. She had none, though she suspected it was someone who'd noticed me among the orphans at some outing or other and was impressed by me but had no desire to adopt me. My benefactor remained a mystery to us both. I knew I'd be grateful to the end of my days for what that person had given me. Most of the female orphans left the home at fourteen, hired to work as servants. I'd been luckier than most, my unknown benefactor had given me a better chance by having me trained as a nurse.

My training had brought me here to Sea Cliff House. I was no longer a child, afraid of the dark or of a nightmare—I didn't need a light. Still, I wished there weren't so many mysterious creakings and rustlings in this house. Above these unidentifiable night noises, I thought I could hear the faint whisper of the sea beating against the cliffs.

I tried not to think of Mrs. Peter standing on the promontory as I'd seen her when I arrived, her billowing cape giving her the look of a great, dark bird. Had she been waiting for her son's ship as Armin had said, or was she listening for a drowned man's voice from beneath the waves? A chill ran along my spine.

The dead do *not* speak to the living, I told myself firmly. Because of her grief for her husband, Mrs. Peter imagines she hears him. Just as Alisette, because she's lonely, imagines the child in the crypt talks to her. Don't let *your* imagination run wild just because you're alone in the dark in a strange place.

A louder, closer creak made me sit up in bed, hugging myself and staring toward the door. A dim sliver of light slanted into the room from the oil lamps in the sconces on the corridor walls. Someone was opening my door!

33

I tried to ask who was there, but only a whisper of sound emerged from my lips. The door opened wider, and a figure in white darted across the room and flung itself onto my bed. A small figure.

"Miss Drake!" Alisette cried.

I let out my pent-up breath in relief as I reached for her.

"I dreamed the house fell all to pieces with you in it," she said into my ear as she hugged me tightly.

"The house is still here," I assured her, "and so am I." I stroked her hair and patted her back, but it was several minutes before she stopped shivering and released her frantic hold on me.

"Can I sleep in your bed?" she pleaded. I thought I detected a slight wheezing when she spoke, and I hoped she wasn't coming down with a cold. Everyone would be certain she'd become ill because I'd taken her outside.

Not wanting to make a habit of having her sleep with me, but knowing from my own experience how shreds of a nightmare could cling and continue to frighten, I said, "You may stay with me this one time."

Alisette sighed and settled in under the covers. Sooner than I expected, she was fast asleep. Her presence in my room, as well as the light slanting in through the partly open door, made me forget my foolish night fancies, and I fell asleep, too.

I woke to a pale gray dawn. Alisette slept on and, listen as I might, I heard no trace of a wheeze in her breathing that morning. I rose and, as I donned my robe, I noticed that damp tendrils of sea fog trailed across my windows. Lifting Alisette into my arms, I returned her to her own bed. She partly woke but closed her eyes again when I murmured that everything was all right.

Molly brought me the completely finished gold

faille gown before noon, prompting Mrs. Yates to announce I'd be dining with the family that evening. As I praised Molly's skillful needlework and marveled at what a quick worker she was, I quivered inwardly, certain I was bound to make a fool of myself at the dinner table. After Molly left, I again told Mrs. Yates I'd really rather eat with Alisette as I'd been doing.

She frowned at me. "You'll do what's right and proper." Her brusqueness told me that my appeal was in vain.

Because the fog didn't lift, I kept Alisette inside and made a game out of learning numbers, happily discovering her quickness of mind. The girl was a joy to teach. After her nap we explored the walnut-paneled library on the first floor, a dark and gloomy room. There we found a globe of the world, and I showed Alisette the United States, California, then the state's northwest corner, where we lived.

"Where's China?" Alisette asked. "Grandma says my father sailed home from China."

Not waiting until I pointed to China on the globe, she began skipping around the room. "I can't wait, I can't wait," she chanted.

Alisette, at least, would welcome Stephen Nikolai with open arms.

Never had a day passed so swiftly. Before I knew it, it was time for me to dress for dinner. Molly's gown fit beautifully. Since I didn't own a bustle, the dress wasn't made to accommodate one, but Molly had fashioned a bustlelike series of pleats that made it appear quite in the mode. At my request, Molly had made the neck of the dress high, and her careful ruching along the front of the bodice added a decorative flair. In truth, I'd never owned such a fine gown.

Sonia came to see how I looked and insisted on

loosening my bun and gathering a portion of my hair in back with a length of gold ribbon so curls spilled down onto my shoulders.

"Much more fashionable," she proclaimed, admiring her work in the mirror.

I had to admit I was surprised at my transformation. Inside I was still plain Esma Drake, but my mirror image showed a young lady of fashion, and I didn't quite know what to make of her.

When I descended the front stairs a bit early—I dreaded being late—I saw a handsome fair-haired man looking up at me from the foyer. He must be Gerald Callich, I told myself. Uncle Gerald, as Alisette called him, though he was no true relation to her.

He bowed slightly as I reached the foot of the stairs. "You must be Miss Drake," he said, smiling. "How charming you look this evening."

"Thank you," I managed to say, rather flustered by the admiration in his blue eyes. How kind of him to remember my name and greet me with such courtesy. I couldn't help but notice how agreeably his dark dinner jacket contrasted with his blond hair. He was, I thought, not much over thirty.

"Gerald!" The call came from the top of the stairs, Mrs. Stephen's voice. "I need your arm, Gerald."

Did I imagine his annoyed frown? It came and went so swiftly I wasn't sure. He nodded politely to me and climbed toward Mrs. Stephen. I didn't wait for them to descend but walked to the drawing room where, Mrs. Yates had informed me, the family gathered before dinner.

"For a glass of sherry," she'd said. "Not that you'll be taking any such. Fruit cordial is my recommendation."

To my relief, I wasn't the first to arrive since Mrs. Peter was already there, seated on a settee before the fire. Conscious of her poor vision, I murmured my name as I entered.

"Do come and sit next to me, Esma," she said. When I obeyed, she patted my hand. "I do hope you don't mind me calling you by your first name?"

I didn't and told her so.

"I do it because I feel we're already friends," she said.

I warmed to her. She might have eccentric habits, but she made me feel welcome. When Gerald and Cecile came in, he spoke to me again, but, after one appraising glance and a slight nod, Alisette's mother ignored me. She did the same once we were seated in the dining room, four people around an ornate walnut table meant to seat twelve.

The head of the table remained vacant. Mrs. Peter sat to the right with me next to her. Opposite Mrs. Peter was Gerald, with Cecile across from me.

I didn't mind being ignored, since I was concentrating on not making any mistakes in etiquette, carefully watching Mrs. Peter for cues on using the alarming variety of silverware to either side of and above my plate. Once Sonia, who was serving, winked covertly at me, and I had to struggle not to dissolve in nervous laughter.

I've always had an excellent appetite, and I ate my way more or less successfully through beet soup, cold fish, and rack of lamb served with peas and potatoes, and also coped with various side dishes of pickles, spiced peaches, and buns warm from the oven, gradually relaxing enough to enjoy the well-prepared food.

Conversation hinged on Stephen Nikolai's return. Gerald thought he might be home by tomorrow, but Mrs. Peter thought it might take

37

longer, perhaps to spare herself disappointment in case he didn't arrive as early as Gerald expected. Cecile didn't comment.

Just as we were finishing dessert, a delicious cherry cobbler, there was a commotion in the foyer. I heard Mrs. Yates's voice raised in protest, and then Alisette, barefoot and in her nightgown, came flying into the dining room. She hurried to her grandmother's chair.

"I saw him, he's riding a horse right up to the door!" Alisette cried, clutching her grandmother's arm. "My father's here!"

Mrs. Peter stood, her face expectant, and I stood, too, clasping Alisette's hand and drawing her to my side. Gerald rose and hurried to offer Mrs. Peter his arm. Only Cecile, her beautiful auburn hair gleaming in the light from the chandelier, remained seated. Not knowing what else to do, I followed Mrs. Peter and Gerald from the dining room, holding tightly to Alisette to make sure she didn't dash outside in her eagerness to greet her father.

We waited in the foyer where Cecile finally joined us. My gown, proud as I was of it, couldn't compare to her ruffled creation of pale blue silk and lace. Her expression, cool and detached, showed no indication of the excitement she must be feeling. Perhaps she was saving her warmer emotions for a less public reunion with her long-absent husband.

Alisette hopped up and down in impatience as we all watched the front door, so I took care to keep a good grip on her hand. Mrs. Yates, Rosie, and Sonia appeared and stood waiting expectantly, too.

Suddenly the door flew open and a man strode in from the night. He pulled off a brimmed cap to reveal thick dark hair, curling below his nape, and a trim black beard. As his green gaze touched us all, I noticed a scar running across his forehead and down his temple to his left cheek. Except for the scar, he was the picture of Alexi Nikolai come to life, complete with Alexi's air of ruthless charm.

We all seemed held in a trance. No one moved; no one spoke. Once more Stephen Nikolai glanced from one to another of us, then his gaze fastened on me. I stared at him as he smiled and strode toward me—no, it must be toward Alisette. But why, then, did he keep looking at me so intently that I felt I was drowning in his sea green eyes?

Before I realized what he intended, he swept me into his arms and kissed me. Far from gentle, his kiss was so hungry and demanding I all but swooned from the unusual and thrilling sensations racing through me. I was vaguely aware he tasted of brandy and smelled of the sea, but most of all I felt the strangely pleasurable warmth of his male body pressed closely against mine.

The kiss ended and he held me away from him, staring into my eyes. Even if I'd known what to say I couldn't have spoken if my life depended on it.

"My dear wife," he murmured, "I'm home at last."

Chapter 3

Stephen Nikolai's words, greeting me as his wife, fell into a shocked silence. No one in the foyer either moved or spoke until at last Alisette reached up and tugged at his sleeve.

"How come you kissed Miss Drake?" she demanded.

His eyes sought mine in a mute question and, though I still couldn't speak, I managed a tiny nod. With my senses in wild disorder from his embrace, I did remember my name, if nothing else.

"Stephen?" his mother asked plaintively. "It is you, isn't it?"

I thought I saw a flash of panic in his green eyes before he turned to her.

"Come closer to me," she urged, "for I'm nearly blind."

Stephen hesitated for a long moment before he walked to his mother and put his hands gently on her shoulders. She smiled and reached to touch his face, frowning when her fingers encountered the scar.

"You've been hurt!" she cried.

"In Hong Kong," he told her. "I'm afraid it affected my memory." He glanced sideways at me.

"I apologize to Miss Drake. Since she was holding the child, I assumed she must be my wife. You see, I remember nothing of my life before I was injured in Hong Kong." His gaze swept the room. "I regret to tell you that you're all strangers to me."

"Oh, Stephen, no!" his mother exclaimed. "You poor boy, what you must have gone through."

"Why didn't you send word to us earlier?" Gerald asked.

"I kept hoping I'd regain my memory," Stephen replied.

Cecile said nothing, but her pale eyes narrowed as she watched Stephen. Alisette grabbed my hand again, holding fast. My fear that Stephen was upsetting her gave me back my voice.

"This is your daughter, Alisette, Captain Nikolai," I said as evenly as I could. "She's counted the seconds until your arrival."

He knelt to bring himself to Alisette's level. "Do you have a hug and a kiss for me?" he asked her.

She squeezed my hand hard, then let go and took a tentative step toward him. He held out his arms, and she glanced back at me. When I nodded encouragingly, she threw herself into his arms, hugging him around the neck.

"Your beard tickles," she complained, drawing back.

He glanced swiftly at me, the corner of his mouth twitching, and I flushed, remembering the soft brush of his beard against my face.

Holding Alisette in one arm, he rose and, carrying her, he at last confronted Cecile. It crossed my mind that he was using the child as a shield, but I thrust the thought away. What a trial this must be for him! Once I heard what had happened to him, I readily forgave him for what he'd done to me. My

41

embarrassment amounted to nothing compared to the anguish he must be feeling.

"I'm sorry I don't recognize you," he said to Cecile, "but I assume you're Alisette's mother."

"And your wife." Her tone was chilly.

He raised his eyebrows but said nothing, his gaze shifting to Gerald. "And you're—?"

"Gerald Callich, the Nikolai shipping agent and general manager of the mill."

Stephen shifted Alisette into his left arm and held out his hand.

Gerald shook it, saying, "We were friends, you know."

"The trouble is, I *don't* know," Stephen said. "I lay for days in a Hong Kong hospital, unable to move or speak. I didn't even know my name until my first mate found me and identified me. For some reason, I didn't lose my knowledge of the sea and ships, only of past events and people. The British doctor who took care of me there called it amnesia and told me I might never regain old memories. I realize it'll take time for us all to get used to my lapse."

"You didn't ever see *me* before right now," Alisette said to her father.

He smiled at her. "And now that we've met, I'll never forget you." He seemed more at ease with her than with anyone else.

Alisette, intent on helping her father, pointed at the servants, still standing in a row. "That's Mrs. Yates, and that's Rosie, she's our cook, and that's Sonia."

Stephen nodded to them and they greeted him, calling him Captain Nikolai.

"Sonia's new, dear," his mother told him, "but you did know the others. Goodness, I never thought to ask if you've had your dinner. Rosie,

42

Sonia, some food for the captain, please. We'll return to the dining room and keep you company while you eat."

Watching Alisette squirming in Stephen's arms, I saw my chance to escape. "I'll take Alisette upstairs, ma'am," I said to Mrs. Peter. "It's past her bedtime."

"I don't want to go to bed," Alisette whined.

"If you don't, you won't be rested enough to show me around the grounds tomorrow," her father said. "I was counting on you to tell me where everything is because I've forgotten."

Alisette frowned, looking at him doubtfully.

"Make up your mind," he told her. "Either kiss me good-night and go up to bed with Miss Drake or stay here and I'll ask someone else to show me around tomorrow."

Alisette settled for the kiss and bed. As I tucked her in she said, "Why didn't my father kiss Mama like he did you?"

I'd been afraid she was going to ask something of the sort, since Alisette didn't miss much. "You heard him tell us he didn't know one of us from another because he's lost his memory."

"I mean after he found out who Mama was."

I didn't have a good answer. "Once he made the mistake, it was too late," I said lamely, unable to come up with anything better.

Luckily, she accepted the explanation. "I'm glad he likes you," she said.

I kissed her good-night and left her room. Without intending to, she'd unsettled me all over again. How would I ever sleep tonight? I needed a magic potion to induce my own amnesia so I wouldn't be able to remember anything that had happened after Stephen Nikolai walked in the door.

43

Where would he sleep? I wondered as I sat brushing my hair before going to bed. In Cecile's room? And, if he did, why should it upset me to think of them together? They were man and wife. They had a daughter.

Somehow, though, I thought he'd choose a room apart from Cecile, a room of his own, at least for the time being. She could hardly seem like his wife if he didn't recognize her.

On the other hand, he'd greeted me very ardently, thinking *I* was his wife. Setting the brush aside, I brought the back of my hand to my mouth. He'd kissed me the way a famished man would greet food. Remembering brought back the inner warmth, the thrilling excitement of his embrace, and I closed my eyes, giving myself up to the pleasure of the memory. I found I could even recall the way he tasted and the scent of the sea that clung to him. . . .

I took myself severely to task. It would never happen again. Stephen's kisses would be reserved for his wife. As they should be. What was I thinking of, falling into a reverie over a married man? Even if his wife was a stranger to him, it didn't alter the facts.

When I got into bed I spent a long time tossing and turning in my fight to keep Stephen Nikolai from my mind. I heard the grandfather clock on the upper landing strike one before I finally fell asleep.

I woke to bright sunlight and Alisette bouncing on my bed. "I thought you'd never wake up," she said. "You have to hurry so we'll be all ready to show my father around."

Despite my resolve not to think about him except as Cecile's husband, my stomach fluttered at the thought of seeing Stephen again.

44

"You'd enjoy it more without me, with just you and your father," I said hastily. "Besides, he didn't invite me."

Alisette's chin jutted out, giving her the mutinous look with which I was already becoming familiar. "I *want* you to come with us."

Since I was hired to look after her, I could hardly refuse a reasonable request from Alisette. There was no reason I shouldn't go along with them—no reason but my own private one.

"We'll ask your father what he wants to do," I said, half of me hoping he'd want to be alone with his daughter, and the other half hoping he'd invite me. I'd already decided to wear the most presentable of my shabby gowns, a dark blue twill that had been my Sunday "best," just in case.

Ten o'clock found the three of us, Alisette, her father, and myself strolling in the rose garden.

"I sailed my *Sea Dragon* in the fish pond," Alisette told him, "but she scared the goldfish. Does your ship scare fishes in the sea?"

"I don't think so," he said, "because the ocean is very deep, and they swim so far below the ship they probably don't even see her."

"That's good," Alisette told him. "Miss Drake didn't even know ships are shes. I'm going to teach her about them."

Stephen smiled at me. "I'll help."

I hadn't said a word to him beyond "good morning," but his smile was so enticing I couldn't help smiling back.

"Do you 'member about the church?" Alisette asked him.

He shook his head. "I'm afraid I don't remember anything."

"Not even who the President of the United States is?" Alisette demanded, having just learned

45

herself about our President. Before he could answer, she added triumphantly, "He's President Garfield and he lives in Washington, D.C."

"I can see Miss Drake has been teaching you as well as you teaching her," he said. "Now what is this church I should remember?"

"Grandma Katherine says it used to be Russian something."

"Orthodox," I put in.

"Anyway, it's falling down now," Alisette said. "'Cept for the bell. Rosie told her sister the church is haunted, and if ever bad trouble comes to Sea Cliff House, a ghost will rise up and toll that bell."

Stephen glanced at me, eyebrows raised, and I shrugged. Alisette had heard entirely too much. I'd have to speak to Rosie. Not that I believed for a minute in haunted churches or ghosts who tolled bells. Still, the memory of the unseen watcher yesterday made me shift my shoulders uneasily.

"Your own imagination," Sister Samara would have chided.

"I'll show you the church," Alisette offered. "It's that way." She pointed. "You can't see it from here, just the tippy-tops of the trees in back of it. Miss Drake says they're pine trees."

"Then I expect they are," Stephen said. "But we'll save the church for another day. I'd like to walk along the cliffs now."

Alisette looked at me, then back at her father. "Grandma Katherine goes there, but she told me it was dangerous and I couldn't."

"She's right," Stephen agreed. "It's much too dangerous a place for you to go alone. But today I'm with you and so is Miss Drake. You can walk between us and we'll hold your hands."

Alisette went along with this willingly enough, and I was too ashamed to admit to my own reluctance. Maybe I'd be all right if I didn't look down at the sea.

Before we left the rose garden, Stephen took a pocket knife and cut a pink rose for Alisette, then a crimson one for me. As I took it from his hand, his fingers touched mine and, startled at the tingle I felt from the contact, I closed my hand convulsively around the stem of the rose. A thorn pricked my palm and I grimaced, giving an involuntary murmur of pain.

"A thorn?" he asked, taking my hand.

He blotted the drop of blood on my palm with his handkerchief. Flustered, I pulled my hand away, not meeting his eyes. The rose fell to the ground.

"I didn't mean to hurt you," he said, bending to pick up the rose and offering it again. The flower's sweet scent beguiled me.

"You didn't," I muttered as I took it carefully from him. "I hurt myself."

"In some of the South Sea Islands," he said as he put his handkerchief away, "there's a belief that if you let anyone have even one drop of your blood, that person gains power over you forever. It's an interesting superstition, don't you think?"

I gazed into his sea green eyes and found his intent regard more disturbing than his words. I found I could neither speak nor look away.

"Come on, let's go," Alisette cried, catching at my hand.

Stephen had so unsettled me that I came to the very edge of the cliffs before the familiar flutter of panic began rolling my stomach. Waves crashed against the wall of rock below us, flinging spray halfway up the side of the cliff face. So violent was the pounding that I fancied I could feel a tremor vibrating from the rock through the soles of my

47

shoes. I'd vowed not to so much as glance at the sea, but now that I had, I was transfixed with awe and terror.

Stephen pulled me back, keeping one hand on my arm while gripping Alisette firmly with the other. "Don't stand so close," he said, his voice pitched to carry over the sound of the waves. "It's not safe."

I swallowed, still half-mesmerized by the rhythmic throb of sea against rock. While the waves frightened me, they also beckoned me. I could almost feel the damp caress of the spray and taste the salt on my lips. Somewhere in its blue-green depths, the ocean hid a secret, unrecoverable.

"Miss Drake!" Stephen shook my arm.

I blinked, dragging my gaze from the sea to focus on him.

"You look as though you've seen Alisette's ghost," he said. "What's the matter?"

"I don't—It's the waves," I stammered.

"You're afraid of the sea?" He sounded disappointed in me.

I stiffened my spine. I wasn't proud of my fear, but what business was it of his how I felt about the ocean?

"The waves are scary," Alisette told him, and I was relieved to have him turn his attention to her.

"I see I have my work cut out for me," he said. "No Nikolai has ever been afraid of the ocean. It's our livelihood and our love." Presumably he was speaking to Alisette, but he glanced sidelong at me.

"I'm not a fraidy-cat!" Alisette insisted.

"Good!" He lifted her high in the air, lowered her into his arms, hugged her, and set her on her feet once again, keeping hold of her hand. "Then you'll enjoy coming aboard *Sea Dragon* with me."

48

"Can I really, truly?" Alisette jumped up and down with excitement.

"As soon as I can arrange it, I'll take both you and Miss Drake onto the ship."

"Oh, but," I protested, "surely you'll want your wife to be with you."

"Mama hates *Sea Dragon*," Alisette put in. "She told Uncle Gerald she hoped it would sink to the bottom of the sea and stay there."

Stephen frowned, and I turned away hastily so he couldn't see my shock. What a terrible thing for Cecile to say—especially in Alisette's hearing. Did everyone in Sea Cliff House assume the child was deaf? Or did they think she was too young to understand?

"Shall we continue on our tour?" I asked with false brightness, hoping to forestall any further revelations by Alisette.

"You sound like Miss Postern," Alisette accused, scowling at me.

"And who was Miss Postern?" Stephen asked.

"She was here before Miss Drake," Alisette said. "She talked silly, and she only pretended to like me."

"So be grateful we have Miss Drake now, she's not a bit silly and she likes us all. Don't you, Miss Drake?" Stephen grinned at me.

How could I say no?

"What does Sea Cliff House look like from a ship?" I asked, changing the subject.

"If you remember, we sailed past late on a foggy afternoon. All I could glimpse was a tall tower." He glanced down at Alisette. "I wondered if a princess lived in that tower."

She shook her head. "No one ever goes there. Grandma Katherine locked the door to the stairs after Grandpa Peter drowned, 'cause that tower

49

was his special place."

We'd turned away from the sea, and Alisette, holding her father's hand, led him back the way we'd come. The end of the west wing, facing the sea, was barely five feet from the cliff edge, making a narrow passage indeed. Though there was room to walk past to the front of the house, I had no desire to try it. I wondered why the Nikolais had built so close to the edge. Or perhaps they hadn't, perhaps as the years passed the cliff had eroded from the onslaught of sea and weather. Since I was living in the house, that wasn't a possibility on which I cared to dwell.

The gardens were all near the east wing because to the west the rockier ground and the unbroken sweep of the sea wind tolerated only a few twisted, stunted cypresses and pines. We visited the stables, set well back from the cliff behind the east wing, a mortared stone wall twined with ivy separating them from the grounds. Armin and Molly's cottage was next to the stables. I saw no sign of her, but Armin was in the stable grooming a handsome chestnut gelding.

"Thanks for having my horse waiting for me in Eureka," Stephen told him.

"I been exercising Bosun regular all the time you been gone, Captain," Armin said. "He's some horse, all right."

Stephen agreed, then examined the rest of the stalls. I trailed after him and Alisette, seeing a gray mare and the two black carriage horses.

"No pony?" Stephen asked Armin, who shook his head. Stephen looked down at Alisette. "Every child needs a pony, that's what I think."

"'Specially me," she agreed enthusiastically.

Turning to Armin, Stephen asked, "Would you see if there's one for sale in the area and let me know?"

Armin nodded. "Think I know where we can get a pony."

"Do you ride, Miss Drake?" Stephen said to me. I shook my head regretfully. The Sisters of Charity had only a wagon horse. Like them, I'd always walked wherever I had to go.

"I'm glad you've come home, Papa," Alisette said, clinging to his hand, her eyes bright.

He went down on one knee, ignoring the straw on the stable floor. Looking into her eyes, he said, "I am, too."

"There's some as thought you weren't never coming home, Captain," Armin put in.

Stephen glanced up at him. Looking from Armin to Stephen, I was struck by the similarity of their coloring—except for the eyes one might have thought they were related. But, of course, dark curly hair was common enough—I had it myself.

Stephen rose. "There were times I wondered if I ever would come home," he said, as much to himself as to Armin.

"That's some scar you got," Armin said. "I hear tell you got hurt so bad you don't recollect folks and all."

"I'm afraid I don't. I didn't even know Bosun until a dockhand told me he was my horse."

Armin shook his head. "I sure would hate to forget my family." He shot me a quick glance, and I knew he'd heard what happened on Stephen's arrival, how he'd mistaken me for his wife. "And maybe there's worse. It'd be a helluva thing not to know a friend from an enemy."

"I'll have to hope I don't have any enemies." Stephen spoke lightly.

"Can't count on that. A family like yours, living around these parts all these years, is bound to make enemies."

Stephen gave Armin a hard look, but Armin just

smiled slyly and shrugged. "Stands to reason, don't it?"

As we walked back to the house, I pondered Armin's enigmatic remarks about enemies. Did he know of an enemy? If so, why wouldn't he tell Stephen?

"It's quite a place, isn't it?" Stephen said as we neared the front of the mansion.

Since Alisette didn't respond, I felt I had to. "It's magnificent."

"What did you think when you first saw the house?"

"I was awed. And a bit uneasy."

"Why uneasy?"

"You'll think I'm silly, after all. It's those round windows. Don't they look like eyes staring down accusingly?" As soon as the words were out of my mouth I was sorry I'd said them. Especially in front of Alisette.

Stephen stopped and gazed at the house. "I have to admit there's something unfriendly about the windows. What do you think, Alsie?"

Alisette looked up at him in surprise, mostly, I thought, because he'd given her a nickname. She glanced at the house and lifted her thin shoulders in a tiny shrug. "They're just windows."

"Thus speaks the innocent child." Stephen smiled at his daughter as he spoke, but when his gaze shifted to me I saw his eyes were somber.

"You don't mind if I have fits sometimes, do you, Papa?" Alisette asked suddenly.

He raised his eyebrows. "Fits?"

Alisette looked at me in appeal.

"Apparently she has some sort of seizures occasionally," I said, "but not since I've been here."

"Miss Postern wouldn't let me leave the house 'cause she thought it brought on my fits," Alisette said. "But I sneaked out anyway."

Stephen put an arm about his daughter's shoulders. "Never mind what Miss Postern thought. Sea air's good for the constitution. And nothing in this world could make me dislike you, Alsie."

Sincerity rang in his voice, and his words made my eyes prick with tears. Alisette's papa would never tell her that her eyes looked like muddy water or let her welfare rest in another's hands. Not while he was around.

But how long would it be before he sailed away again?

As we walked up the drive toward the entrance, I discovered how much it hurt to think of Stephen gone from Sea Cliff House.

Once inside, Alisette and I went off to my room for more learning games. Mrs. Yates had told me there was a schoolroom on the third floor of the east wing, but I wasn't ready to use it yet. I wanted Alisette to think of numbers and letters as fun first.

After she was settled for her afternoon nap under her red and white morning star quilt, I went down to the kitchen to have a word with Rosie. I found her kneading bread dough, the room filled with the pleasant yeasty aroma.

First I told her how much I enjoyed her cooking. "You certainly have a way with cherry cobbler," I added. "Yours is the best I ever tasted."

Rosie, plump and freckled, with graying brown hair, beamed at me. "I'm glad you liked it," she said. "That other one was always complaining. A real picky eater, she was."

I took her to mean Miss Postern. Which gave me an opening. As carefully as I could, I led up to Alisette. "I'm afraid little pitchers have big ears," I said, finally arriving where I wanted to be. "I don't mean to accuse her of eavesdropping, it's just that she's underfoot a good deal and hears more than is good for her. From everyone."

Rosie bridled, as I feared she might. "I'm sure I don't say anything I shouldn't in front of the child."

"Of course you don't. Not if you know she's there. What's troubling me is that she's overheard talk of ghosts and hauntings."

Rosie's face cleared. "Goodness me, you mean those tales about the old church. Why that won't harm her, she's bound to hear them sooner or later, because everyone around here knows the story. My sister and I were just speaking the other day of how we loved the ghost stories Grandma used to tell us when we were small. Children like scary stories, you ought to know that."

"Up to a point. But Alisette is a Nikolai, and the church is right next door to Sea Cliff House."

Rosie chuckled. "Bless you, miss, Miss Alisette isn't a bit afraid of that old church or the grave-yard. Every time she runs off, that's where we find her."

I was getting nowhere with Rosie, that was plain.

"Some say it's old Alexi himself who's supposed to rise when the time comes to toll the bell," Rosie said, as though I'd asked. Despite my misgivings, I listened eagerly. "Never mind his ship was lost with all hands in the China Sea. I say 'twon't be Captain Alexi, he's too far away. But there's plenty other Nikolais ready and waiting in their graves." She spoke with relish, her sinister words in marked contrast to her round, placid face.

"It'll take a ghost to ring the bell," she said, "for there's been no rope to it for many a year. I'm sure I won't be around to hear it toll. Sea Cliff House has stood for nigh onto forty years, and it's good for a hundred years or more, that's what I say. Them in their graves'll have a long wait." She chuckled. "Not that they got anything else to do."

Fascinated against my will, I asked, "Doesn't a strong wind ever ring the bell? I imagine the storms here can be fierce."

Rosie shook her head. "Nothing's going to ring that bell unless the day comes when Sea Cliff House is doomed." Her voice became a chant. "When that happens and only then will a Nikolai rise from his grave. He'll float up to the bell tower of the old Russian church and there he'll toll the bell. Its ring will be the death knell of Sea Cliff House, once and for all."

Chapter 4

As the days passed, try as I might, I found it impossible to avoid Stephen Nikolai's company. I could hardly blame him for wanting to become better acquainted with his daughter but, since Alisette was my responsibility, the result was that the three of us were often together. This didn't pass unnoticed. On the third Monday after his arrival, Sonia stopped me on the back stairs.

"We hardly ever get a chance to talk these days," she complained, smiling slyly. "Captain Stephen keeps you too busy."

"There's nothing improper—" I began indignantly.

Sonia's smile widened. "Did I say there was?"

I had to admit she hadn't.

"I do believe you see more of him than his wife does," she went on. "Did you know he hasn't visited her bed since his return—not once?"

I was aware he and Cecile didn't share a room, but Sonia's information was new to me and my heart leaped. What happened between Stephen and his wife was none of my business, or Sonia's either, but I couldn't help being glad to know they were still estranged, wrong though that emotion might be. As wrong as the rapid hammer of my pulses every time he smiled at me.

"Could be the captain wishes for someone else in his bed." Sonia's sidelong glance left no doubt she meant me.

I could only hope the dim lighting on the stairs concealed my flushed face as I mumbled, "I don't think you ought to say such things."

"After all, he *did* kiss you," she persisted.

I needed no reminder of that terrible, wonderful moment; it was a memory I'd cherish all my days. Just the same, it was none of Sonia's affair how I felt about Stephen. Raising my chin, I said, "It's only natural Captain Stephen would want to spend time with Alisette. She's in my care, and that's the beginning and the end of my association with the captain."

"If you ask me, it'd be even more natural for him to bed his wife after all those months at sea." Sonia cocked her head, eyeing me. "Don't you agree?"

My face felt as hot as fire as I sought words to silence Sonia. I was unaccustomed to such frank speech, but that wasn't what bothered me—it was wondering what went on in a marriage bed and being uncomfortably certain I couldn't bear to imagine Cecile snuggling close to Stephen under the concealing covers.

They're married, I reminded myself. Man and wife.

"You're blushing," Sonia accused. "Haven't you ever—?" She paused. "No, you're a real innocent, you are. I keep forgetting the nuns raised you. I'll bet the captain's kiss was the first time a man ever touched you."

"I've been kissed before!" I didn't add that I'd hated the one other time.

Her gaze flicked over me curiously. "Hidden

depths, have you? Good. Nothing I'd like better than to see Princess Cecile founder and sink. Serve her right."

I tried one more time. "I have no interest in Captain Stephen other than caring for his daughter."

Sonia laughed. "You might believe that but *I* don't. I've seen how you look at him. And how he looks at you."

How does he look at me? I longed to ask, but I bit the words back, at the same time resolving to do a better job of masking my emotions when I was in his presence. I had no right to Stephen Nikolai, no right at all.

It would take time for him to reacquaint himself with his wife, but undoubtedly he would. He must have loved Cecile once, loved her enough to marry her.

But why did he smile so beguilingly at me? And why couldn't I resist those smiles?

"Miss Drake!" Alisette called from the second floor hallway. "Miss Drake, where are you?"

Welcoming the excuse to leave Sonia's disturbing company, I hurried up the stairs.

"We have to hurry," Alisette scolded when I reached the top. "My new pony's waiting." She chattered on about the pony as I hurriedly donned a hat and pulled on my gloves. Then, to my surprise, she added, "Papa says I'm to be fitted for a riding habit, and you are, too, so you can ride with us."

"But I told your father I don't know how to ride," I protested.

"Papa's going to teach us. He says it's easy 'cause the horse does all the work if you learn how to tell him what you want him to do. It's kind of like captaining a one-man ship, Papa says."

Though I'd never seen Cecile ride, I suspected

she did. Stephen ought to be asking his wife to ride with him and Alisette. But my rebellious heart warmed with pleasure that he wanted me along instead.

The pony was a plump white gelding named Sir Toby, and Alisette fell in love with him at first sight. I did my best to keep my attention focused on her and the pony rather than on Stephen Nikolai but, despite my best efforts, my glance too often strayed.

He was dressed in brown nankeen riding pants, black boots, a white linen shirt under a sack coat with a bright blue patterned neckerchief. He'd swept his wide-brimmed black hat off when we appeared, but now wore it slightly tilted to the left, giving him the dashing look of a vaquero. I'd never seen a handsomer man.

His glance caught mine. "Green, I think," he said. "A sea green."

"Pardon?" I stammered.

"For your riding habit. Unless you object. Alsie insists on hers being red." A smile lit his eyes and curved the corners of his mouth. "Perhaps you can persuade her that burgundy is a practical shade of red."

I nodded, unsettled by his choosing a color for me. Sea green, like his eyes. How could I object? Especially when his smile sent strange tinglings along my spine.

"Can I sit on Sir Toby?" Alisette pleaded. "Just for a minute? I won't fall off, I know I won't."

The pony wasn't saddled and Alisette's Kate Greenaway dress of striped flannel wasn't at all suited for riding, but Stephen lifted her onto Sir Toby's bare back, holding her there.

"I wish I could ride like a boy," she said, doing her best to fling one leg across the pony's back so she could sit astride.

"You're not a boy," I pointed out. "If you were to learn to ride like one what would you do when you grew up? Ladies ride sidesaddle."

Alisette scowled. "I don't want to be a lady. It won't be any fun."

"You might be surprised," Stephen said, easing her off the pony and holding her in his arms. "I'm sure Miss Drake quite enjoys being a lady. In any case, I've already ordered your sidesaddle."

Alisette slanted a glance my way. "But I won't look nice like Miss Drake does when I'm a lady 'cause I'm ugly. Mama said so."

In the silence that followed I noticed Stephen's eyes narrow in anger. While I sought words of denial, he held Alisette away from him, pretending to examine her.

"I can see you're a Nikolai," he said decisively, "so you don't have to worry. Your mama must not realize that Nikolai girls always grow up to be beauties." After giving her a hug, he set her on her feet. "And right now I think you're the sweetest little girl I ever met."

Alisette beamed, all thoughts of riding astride forgotten. "I'm glad you came home, Papa," she said.

Stephen's smile faded. "Yes," he said somberly, "I'd put it off long enough. It was past time."

Later that afternoon I saw him accompany his mother when she went for her daily walk to the cliff's edge. Ordinarily she insisted on walking alone, but evidently her son's company was more important than her solitude. He seemed devoted to his mother and his daughter, if not his wife.

"Grandma Katherine is glad Papa's home, too," Alisette told me, coming to my side to look down from the window.

And so, God forgive me, was I.

The next day it rained and the wind blew, send-

60

ing waves splashing so high and hard against the cliffs that I could faintly hear the ominous sound even in my east wing bedroom. By midmorning Alisette had tired of all the learning games I could devise and fretted restlessly because her papa hadn't come to see her and because it was too wet to visit Sir Toby in the stables. By the time Molly appeared to measure us both for riding outfits, Alisette couldn't stand still.

"Your papa wants you to have a riding costume," I reminded her. "How can Molly make you one if you won't let her take your measurements?"

"I don't care." Alisette's voice was sullen. "He went off without saying good-bye to me."

Casting about for something to interest her, I remembered how the little ones at the orphanage loved surprises. "If you hold still for Molly, I have a surprise for you this afternoon," I said, hoping something would occur to me by then.

"What kind of a surprise?"

I lowered my voice. "A special, secret one."

Her face brightened, and she quieted enough for a hasty wielding of Molly's tape measure.

"Are we going to the tower?" Alisette whispered after Molly finished with both of us.

When I shook my head, I noted that her face showed both disappointment and relief. Since no one ever visited the tower since Peter Nikolai's death, likely the tower was forbidden to me and to Alisette as well. But her mention of it gave me an idea and later, while Alisette was finishing her lunch, I took Mrs. Yates aside.

"Is it possible for me to take Alisette to one of the attics?" I asked. "She's restless, and it occurred to me she might like to explore someplace in the house she's never been."

"As you know, the east-wing attics are the servants' quarters," she said. "As far as the west-wing attics go, there's naught but old clothes and furniture stored in them. I do my best to see they're kept clean, but there's bound to be spiders and maybe a mouse or two."

"A few cobwebs won't harm us, and I've seen many a mouse in my time."

Mrs. Yates pondered the matter, finally saying, "Well, I can't see any harm in giving you a key to the west-wing attic. Mind you lock the door and return the key when you come down."

I went off with her to get the key and when I returned Alisette was scowling. "You were whispering with Mrs. Yates," she accused. "Telling secrets. Just like Mama and Uncle Gerald do. No one ever tells *me* a secret."

I motioned her to come closer, saying, "I'll tell you one now."

Eyeing me mistrustfully, she sidled over and I bent to whisper in her ear. "We're going someplace you've never been before."

"Where?"

"As soon as you wash your face and hands, you'll find out."

The door to the attic stairs was a long walk from our rooms in the east wing, the attic being over the west wing, the sea wing where Mrs. Peter had her suite. Alisette's face lit up when we stopped and she saw me insert the key in the lock.

"The attic!" she cried. "That's the secret place."

She scrambled up the narrow, twisting stairs only to stop at the top and wait for me to join her. I soon saw why. The gray light coming through the two tiny windows did little to alleviate the gloomy dimness of the room, making the hulking outlines of draped furniture unpleasantly menacing. Overhead, various castoff articles, unidentifiable in the gloom, hung from hooks set into the unfinished roof braces.

I lit the lamp I'd brought along and held it up, seeing a scattering of trunks among the furniture. Dare we open one to see what treasure might be stored inside?

As if reading my mind, Alisette, who'd been pressed against my side, suddenly stood straight and pointed at a black trunk with brass trappings to our left. "It's in that one!" she cried. "The trunk with the anchor on top."

"What's in there?" I asked.

"I don't know. She told me there was a present for me in the trunk with the anchor on top. I didn't know what she meant until right this minute. Open it, please, Miss Drake."

"Who told you?"

"Alexandria. In the graveyard." Alisette's voice was impatient as she tugged at my hand, urging me toward the trunk.

I stared down at the embossed brass anchor on the lid and tried to dispel the chill creeping over me. I didn't think Alisette was making up a story from whole cloth, yet how could I believe a dead child had spoken to her?

"Hurry up!" Alisette demanded.

As I knelt in front of the trunk something brushed across my face and I gasped before realizing it was only a cobweb. My hands trembled as I set the lamp onto the floor. Slowly I reached for the brass clasp and froze as I heard a rustling in the darkened far reaches of the attic. Alisette grasped my arm, her eyes wide with alarm.

Taking a deep breath, I said, "Mice," and prayed I was right.

"I'm not scared of a little old mouse." The quaver in Alisette's voice belied her words.

Mustering my courage, I forced myself to touch the clasp. For some unknown reason, I felt a marked reluctance to detach it, lift the lid, and confront the contents. I found myself hoping the trunk would be locked.

It was not. Both Alisette and I held our breath as the lid creaked open. A musty, dusty scent mixed with traces of camphor filled my nostrils. Alisette leaned over the side, scrabbling through what looked to be neatly folded children's clothes—small dresses, bonnets and tiny shoes. Then her hand closed on what appeared to be a sword hilt.

"Help me lift this," she said. "It's heavy."

Feeling it might be dangerous to allow her to handle a sword, I told her I'd lift it out by myself. It *was* heavy, and I laid the sword on the floor in front of the trunk while we examined it. I made no effort to remove the blade from the tattered, rotting leather scabbard that encased it.

Alisette touched the golden double eagles on the hilt. "Was this Captain Alexi's sword, do you think?" she asked.

"It looks very old. Those eagles mean the sword came from Russia. Why don't we ask your grandmother about it?"

She nodded, losing interest, and resumed rummaging through the remainder of the trunk's contents.

"Here she is!" Alisette held up a bedraggled rag doll with a tattered red-checked dress, faded yellow yarn hair, and black button eyes.

The sight of the forlorn doll made my mouth go dry and my heart pound. The world whirled around me alarmingly, and I clutched at the lid of the trunk to keep my balance. The lid slammed down, narrowly missing my fingers. I sat back on my heels. Alisette, crooning over her find, paid me no heed as I fought to recover my wits.

I was certain I'd never seen the doll before and yet something about it frightened me. Was that because the dead Alexandria had told Alisette where to find it? Had the doll belonged to Alexandria? Such wear and tear suggested it was ancient.

I tried to speak, failed, swallowed to moisten my dry throat, and tried again. "Did you know the doll was inside the trunk?"

"As soon as I touched her I knew she was my present from Alexandria." Alisette smoothed the yarn hair tenderly. "I'm going to keep her forever and ever."

I shivered, wondering if Alexandria had once said those same words. The doll had lasted past its time while the child had died too soon. I reached for Alisette and hugged her to me. If I could prevent it, the same fate would never overtake Alisette, she would grow up to be one of the beautiful Nikolai women, just as Stephen had promised she would.

I recovered enough to return the sword to the trunk and told Alisette it was time to leave.

"My doll's name is Estelle," Alisette insisted as we descended to the second floor, "and I'm going to show her to Papa as soon as he gets home."

Estelle. Wasn't that the name of Stephen's young sister who'd drowned years before? I wondered if I should suggest another name to Alisette but decided not to. Once she made up her mind, she clung tenaciously to her purpose.

I didn't realize I had yet to discover just how stubborn she could be.

When it was time for Alisette to go to bed, she announced that I might make her get into the bed, but I couldn't make her go to sleep.

"I'm going to stay awake until Papa comes home," she said determinedly. "I want him to kiss me good-night and then I'll show him Estelle."

Nothing I said could persuade her differently,

65

so finally I decided to read to her until she, whether she wished to or not, drifted off. She fought sleep and it was after nine when her eyelids at last drooped shut. I lowered my voice and read a few more pages to make certain she'd truly lost the battle.

With Stephen absent, I hadn't been commanded to dine with the family and therefore had eaten an early supper with Alisette. There was no reason for me to go downstairs, so I decided to retire myself.

Like Alisette, I didn't fall asleep immediately. Every time I closed my eyes, the image of the tattered rag doll returned to disturb me. Why, I didn't know, since the doll itself was not in the slightest degree sinister. When sleep finally did conquer me, I seemed to be whirled at once into the familiar and terrible nightmare.

Green water closed over my head. I couldn't breathe. My world was green, my world was water. Blurred faces came and went, none heeding my terror-stricken cries. I was doomed. . . .

Someone touched me, held me, a voice spoke soothing words, and I knew this wasn't part of my dream. I saw a face hovering close to mine, and the smell of the sea filled my nostrils. . . .

"Wake up, Esma," Stephen's voice said urgently. "Wake up!"

He was with me! Not in my dream but in my room, I could see him clearly in the wedge of light coming through my open door from the hall. He sat on the side of my bed, holding me in his arms as I clung to him in confusion, the shards of nightmare terror still haunting me.

"Are you all right?" he asked. Did I imagine it or did his lips brush my temple?

"I—I think so," I managed to say. But I wasn't. Though I was rapidly recovering from the dream, his nearness made me feel weak all over again in a thrillingly different way. My pulses pounded and I could scarcely breathe. I blushed when I realized I was still clinging to him and eased the frantic clutch of my fingers.

Slowly, carefully, he released me, easing me down against the pillow before rising. Becoming aware how revealing my white batiste nightgown was, I hastily pulled the covers up to my neck.

"I apologize if I startled you," he said, "but when I passed your room after putting Alsie to bed, I heard you cry out and came in to see what was wrong."

"You put Alisette to bed?" I echoed. "But I did that hours ago!"

He smiled. "She didn't stay there. I found her asleep on the settee in the front hall."

"I might have known! She insisted she meant to stay up and wait for your return. I'm afraid I was remiss for not checking on her. She must have roused and crept downstairs."

He touched my lips with his forefinger. "Ssh. No need to apologize. Alsie is a true Nikolai—we're bound to have our way, no matter what." His gaze held mine. "Be warned."

Before I could gather enough breath to reply, he added, "Good night, Esma." Then he was gone, closing the door behind him.

The warmth of his touch lingered on my lips and his masculine scent stayed with me as I pondered his words. Why was he warning me? So I'd keep closer watch on Alisette? Perhaps, but what I'd seen in his eyes led me to believe there was more to the warning.

You must beware of me because I'll have my way despite everything, is what Stephen had meant.

What did he want of me?

67

Sonia's words crept insidiously into my mind. "He doesn't lie with his wife; he wants someone else in his bed."

Heat flamed inside me. I well knew what a sin it was for an unmarried woman to lie with a man—and worse, a married man. Yet I couldn't deny the turbulent emotions coursing through me. I would never commit such a sin, no matter how tempted, but, oh, how I longed to feel Stephen's arms around me once more and his lips against mine.

Pressing my heated face against the coolness of my pillow, I tried to banish all thought of him—and failed. When I slept at last, the dreams came again but this time they were woven around a bearded man with dark curls, green eyes, and a scar across his left temple.

The next morning I admonished Alisette for leaving her bed during the night, but my heart wasn't in the scolding. She was as enchanted with Stephen as I, so how could I blame her?

The rain persisted and, as the day went on, once again she grew restless.

"We'll go into the library where the globe is," I told her, "and trace the course of Nikolai ships from California to the Sandwich Islands and onto China."

This appealed to her. Holding the doll Estelle under one arm, she scampered down the staircase ahead of me. I'd recovered enough from my strange aversion to the doll so that the sight of it no longer upset me.

Alisette hurried to the library door, pulled it open, and paused on the threshold. When I reached her side, I realized why she'd stopped. Stephen sat at the great oak desk, papers before him. He wasn't alone. Perched charmingly on the edge of the desk, one slippered foot swinging, was Cecile, becomingly gowned in her usual blue. One hand rested on her husband's shoulder as she frowned across the room at the intruders, Alisette and me.

"Pardon me," I murmured, starting to withdraw.

Alisette had no such scruples. "Papa," she said, "we want to use the globe."

"Later," I told her, reaching too late for her hand—she was already into the room, heading for the desk. I had no choice but to go after her.

To my surprise, Cecile smiled at me. "Why, of course you may show Alisette the globe," she said sweetly. "Stephen and I have other things to keep us busy." She slid off the desk and took his hand, gazing down fondly at him. "Don't we, dear?"

He glanced up at her, shrugged, and rose. Cecile let go of his hand and tucked hers under his arm, leading him toward the door. He grinned fleetingly at Alisette, but not once did he look at me.

"You know what Papa told me last night?" Alisette asked after they were gone.

I shook my head, endeavoring to pay attention to her and ignore my own upset. Stephen and Cecile were man and wife. I had no right to be jealous of the attention they paid to one another. I would *not* be.

"He said Estelle looked woebegone," Alisette continued. "What does that mean?"

Take a good look at me and you'll know what the word means, I felt like telling her. Naturally I said nothing of the sort. Forcing a smile, I said, "Woebegone means sad and forlorn."

"But Estelle isn't sad, not any more, 'cause now she's got me."

Maybe he thought she was woebegone because her clothes are so old and tattered. We might make her a new dress from Molly's scraps, what do you think?"

69

Alisette gazed at the doll for some time. "Estelle wants a new dress," she said finally, "but first we have to take her to the graveyard. Alexandria might not know who she is in new clothes." She glanced at the rain-swept windows. "I guess we can't go today."

I sighed inwardly. Refusing to go along with Alisette's belief in Alexandria would likely make her all the more insistent that the dead girl really did speak to her. I felt the best course was to say nothing and try gradually to wean her from such an unhealthy preoccupation by filling her days with normal activities.

That evening I dined with the family. Having made up my mind not even to glance at Stephen, I held to my resolve. Unfortunately, I couldn't help but notice the languishing looks Cecile bestowed on him and the way she fluttered around him. Nor could I ignore her magnificent satin gown, cut low to reveal the milk white skin of her throat and upper breasts. With her auburn hair piled high, she had never appeared lovelier.

I was grateful when Gerald Callich took pity on me and engaged me in conversation. He was even courteous enough to pretend interest in my replies, and I began to think him an extremely kind gentleman.

"I have never seen that color worn more becomingly," Gerald told me over the meat course. "Gold suits you."

I was, of course, wearing the same gold gown, and his compliment pleased me.

"I'd enjoy seeing a golden topaz necklace around that lovely neck," Gerald went on, "with the gem the exact color of your eyes."

"Thank you, but that's unlikely," I told him, smiling.

"Don't be too sure. Beautiful women have a way of attracting precious stones."

Since I wasn't entirely certain what he meant, I didn't risk a reply. Still, true or not, no woman resents being told she's beautiful, and I warmed to him.

"I understand you and Alisette are learning to ride," he went on. "Perhaps one day you'll allow me to escort you."

"I suspect Alisette will make a good horse-woman far sooner than I."

His blue eyes assessed me. Was that a gleam of admiration I saw or was I imagining things? "Nonsense," he said. "Anyone as graceful as you should have no trouble mastering the finer points of riding."

I shook my head at Gerald's lavish praise. Cecile's high trilling laugh shifted my attention to her and I inadvertently caught Stephen's glance. To my amazement, he was glaring at me.

I stared down at my plate, wondering what on earth I'd done to deserve such a glower. When I risked another look, he was leaning toward Cecile, murmuring to her. I bit my lip.

"Are you always with Alisette?" Gerald asked. "Surely you must have some time to yourself."

"I don't need time to myself," I said. It was true. I had no family, no one to visit except the sisters, and the convent was too far away to make the trip.

"Perhaps you'd be willing to make some time for me," he said.

I stared at him blankly, unable to believe my ears.

His laugh was rueful. "Your surprised expression tells me I've made a blunder. I didn't mean to alarm you. I expect I should have gone about this differently, so I'll start over. I find you a fascinating woman, Miss Drake, and if you have an hour to spare now and again, I do hope we can become better acquainted."

"Why, I—I imagine that's possible," I stammered, taken aback but flattered by his interest.

Only after I was alone in my room did I recall Mrs. Yates's admonition about not becoming too friendly with Gerald Callich. Very well, I'd heed her words, but occasionally conversing with him could do no harm. And Gerald's company might serve to take my mind off the man I must never, under any circumstances, be alone with again.

I must never forget that Stephen Nikolai belonged to another woman.

Chapter 5

Though the following day was misty, I decided the weather had improved enough to take Alisette to visit the pony in the stables. After patting Sir Toby's nose, feeding him a sugar cube, and telling him how she'd found her doll, Alisette insisted we walk to the graveyard.

"I have to show Estelle to Alexandria," she said and would not be dissuaded.

I did refuse to go the secret way through the hole in the cypress hedge, because I knew the trees and shrubbery were wet. To my surprise I found a well-defined path from the grounds to the ruined church. I wondered who else besides Alisette came this way. Alisette's grandmother? I'd never seen her go anywhere but onto the cliffs.

As we skirted the old church on the way to the tiny cemetery behind it, I thought I heard voices, and the hair rose on my nape. As usual, Alisette had run ahead of me so I couldn't tell if she'd heard anything or not. Ghosts don't exist, I told myself firmly as I hurried to catch up with her, it's the wind blowing through the broken windows. But I couldn't quite believe it. The truth was I preferred not to be anywhere near the church or the cemetery. The pine grove farther on looked far more appealing.

I took Alisette's hand more for my own comfort than anything else, and together we threaded between weathered gravestones to the crypt guarded by the marble angel.

Alisette held up the rag doll. "See, Alexandria, I found your present just like you said." Her words seemed to hover in the damp air. "I named her Estelle and we're going to make her a new dress so she won't look woebegone."

I repressed a shudder when Alisette cocked her head as though listening. After a moment she shrugged and turned away. "Let's go back and ask Rosie for hot chocolate," she said to me.

I retreated from the graveyard with relief. As we came around the church, I saw, ahead of us, a dark figure slipping through the mist. My steps faltered. What, who, was it? What should I do? Alisette, murmuring to her doll, didn't look up.

I caught a glimpse of bright hair and my pent-up breath eased out. Cecile. What she'd been doing here I had no idea, nor did I care. It was enough to know I saw a real, live person. I shook my head, annoyed at myself for even momentarily believing in ghosts. Cecile had been in the church; it had been her voice I'd heard earlier. Praying?

No, I'd had the impression there were two voices. Had she met someone inside the ruins? Why? A secret assignation? But with whom? Surely not Stephen—she'd have no reason to meet her own husband in secret.

Cecile disappeared into the mist without noticing us, and no one else came into view as Alisette and I made our way along the path toward the house.

After I changed Alisette's damp outer clothes, we drank our hot chocolate and then repaired to the schoolroom on the third floor. I laid out a pencil, a scissors, a packet of pins, a long sheet of

74

butcher's paper Rosie had given me, and the scraps of material I'd begged from Molly.

"Do you know how to make a dress pattern?" I asked.

Alisette shook her head, her eyes bright with interest. We divested the doll of her tattered gown and pinned the dress onto the paper where I showed her how to trace the outline. She was busy cutting along the pencil lines when I became aware that someone watched us. Glancing at the door, I encountered Stephen's green gaze.

"Don't let me disturb you," he murmured.

As if I could help it! I hoped he'd never realize how the mere sight of him distracted me beyond reason.

"Papa!" Alisette cried, abandoning her work and running to him.

He caught her in his arms and swung her up into the air, then hugged her before setting her on her feet. "Armin tells me you visited your pony today," he said to her.

"I showed him my doll before we went to the graveyard," Alisette said. "I don't know if Sir Toby liked her, but Alexandria did." Her brow creased. "At least I think so. I don't always understand what she means. I told her I named my doll Estelle, and she said to remember I could always trust Estelle."

"Alexandria?" Stephen looked at me, raising his eyebrows questioningly.

I answered reluctantly, certain he'd be irked at my humoring Alisette's fantasy. "Alexandria Nikolai is buried in the little cemetery behind the ruins of the Russian church. She's—ah, Alisette's friend."

"She's five, just like me, Papa," Alisette put in. "I guess she's a ghost, but she's very nice."

He blinked, frowning.

Alisette stared at him hopefully, but when he didn't speak, disappointment curved her mouth downward.

"I've never conversed with a ghost," he said finally, "but when I as a boy I had a friend no one else could see. He was an old one-legged sailor with a parrot perched on his shoulder, and he used to tell me stories of adventure and of the sea."

"Really, truly, Papa?" Alisette asked, beginning to smile.

He nodded. "His name was Pegleg Louie."

Alisette took hold of his hand and led him to one of the small chairs. "Sit down, Papa," she begged, "and tell me a story like your friend told you."

Wordlessly, I offered him the one adult-sized chair in the room, but Stephen shook his head and settled his large frame onto the child's chair, his long legs thrust out in front of him, crossed at the ankles. Alisette tugged another little chair close beside him and perched on the edge of the seat, gazing hopefully at him.

"Won't you join us?" Stephen invited, his eyes on me.

Thinking I'd feel uncomfortable sitting on the teacher's chair while Stephen used a small one, I, too, chose a child's seat, placing it next to Alisette.

"No, over here," he commanded, indicating a spot to his other side and slightly in front of him.

I obeyed, though it brought me closer to him than I preferred.

"Once upon a time in the Sandwich Islands," he began, "there was a beautiful dark-haired princess named Auria."

"How old was she?" Alisette interrupted to ask.

Stephen slanted her a mock frown. "No questions until after the story's told," he warned. "Princess Auria liked to swim in the ocean, and when she was a little girl she made friends with a

76

porpoise who came to frolic in the waves with her every day. Porpoises are sea animals who never harm people." He went on to explain about them to Alisette, who'd never seen one.

After a time I grew engrossed in his story of the beautiful princess who thought nobody loved her. When the evil queen set her adrift in a leaky boat, I gasped, and Alisette abandoned her chair to sit on the floor by my side, her hand gripping mine as we waited tensely to hear if poor Auria was doomed.

". . . so the little boat sank," he went on. "The night was moonless and dark. Though Auria bravely swam, she couldn't see the shore and soon tired. As she started to slip under the waves, she felt something solid beneath her, lifting her. It was her friend, the porpoise, come to save her."

Alisette gave a great sigh of relief and so did I. Auria's triumphant return on the back of the porpoise to a cheering crowd of her people and the banishment of the evil queen seemed an anticlimax to me, though Alisette hung on every word.

"That was the best story I ever heard," she told her father. "Wasn't it, Miss Drake?"

"Your father is an excellent storyteller," I admitted.

"I'm sure Miss Drake found the moral of my tale," he said.

"What's a moral?" Alisette wanted to know.

"Something you learn from a story. Ask Miss Drake what she learned from this one."

Alisette's inquiring gaze shifted to me.

I hesitated, then ventured, "The value of friendship, perhaps."

Stephen looked at me. "I'd say the story warns that one should never underestimate the power of love."

I could neither look away nor find a reply. I felt I was drowning in the green of his eyes and there

77

was nobody to rescue me. *The power of love.* The words seemed to echo in my head.

"I'm glad we don't have any bad queens around here," Alisette put in, "'cause I don't know how to swim."

"You will," Stephen said, turning his attention to her.

It was then I heard footsteps descending the stairs and realized someone must have been listening outside the open door. Though I hurried into the hall, I was too late to see who it was. Stephen, intent on Alisette, paid me no mind.

"Molly told me she'd have your riding habit finished by tomorrow," he told her. "If the weather improves, we'll begin your riding lessons then."

"And Miss Drake's too," she reminded him.

"Yes, Miss Drake's, too." He spoke brusquely, as though regretting having made the offer to include me. "Now you'd best return to your work—I have to go into town."

After he left, I continued to show Alisette how to make a doll's dress, but my mind wasn't on the project. Why, I kept wondering, had Stephen so abruptly switched from warmth to coolness? Not toward Alisette, of course, but toward me. It was as though he'd opened a door and invited me in only to slam the door shut in my face before I could enter.

At dinner he didn't once look at me, devoting himself to the beautifully gowned Cecile who fawned over him. I tried to concentrate on Gerald's lively conversation but was glad to return to my room when the meal ended. Taking up the embroidery Sonia had given me, I vowed not to waste another moment's thought on Stephen Nikolai.

But when someone tapped on my door, my heart

leaped in hopeful anticipation. After my breath-less, "Come in," brought Sonia into the room, my disappointment proved to me how foolish I was being.

As usual, Sonia was primed for gossip. Since she knew far more about the goings-on in the house-hold than I, the conversation was mostly one-sided.

"Did you see that gown Cecile had on tonight?" she demanded. "I swear you could see her nipples. Mrs. Yates sniffed so hard in disapproval you'd think she was coming down with pneumonia. She's doing her best to bring the captain to heel."

"Mrs. Yates?" I asked in some confusion.

"No, you goose, I mean Mrs. High and Mighty, the captain's wife. He might like the view, but he's not in any hurry to dance to her tune. Oh, he smiles and all, but he don't touch her. Take it from me, if a man don't touch you, he don't want you. I'm the one who makes the beds, and I can tell you he's not come to hers yet, nor she to his." Sonia giggled. "She could've tried for all I know, but he keeps his door locked."

I shouldn't be glad, but I was. It occurred to me to mention that I'd seen Cecile by the church ruins but, before I'd made up my mind, Sonia changed the subject.

"Another thing I noticed." She frowned at me. "Mr. Gerald's getting mighty friendly with you. What d'you think of that?"

"I think he's most kind to take any notice of me."

Sonia's smile was lopsided. "As the hen said to the fox, before he carried her off. That's a man no woman can trust, you hear?"

I bridled. "As far as I'm concerned, Mr. Callich has behaved like a perfect gentleman."

"Well, don't expect to cry on *my* shoulder when

you find out different." Sonia rose abruptly and, without saying good night, stalked from my room.

I puzzled over what she'd said, uncertain why she was miffed at my response to her comments about Gerald, but my thoughts inevitably circled back to Stephen. Why couldn't I put him from my mind once and for all? Obviously he didn't feel the same way, but it was as though his homecoming kiss had put a spell on me, binding me to him.

Molly had the outfits ready on the morrow but the weather didn't cooperate, remaining chill and misty. Alisette, disappointed, refused to settle to any one occupation, constantly dashing to the window, vainly hoping to see the sun break through the clouds.

Nothing I suggested suited her and finally, as a way to let her blow off steam, I decided we'd take a walk outside. Even if she couldn't ride Sir Toby, she could visit him in the stables. I made up my mind we would *not* return to the graveyard, though.

After leaving the stables, I began a lively game of tag. We chased one another through the gardens until we were both panting for breath and, from brushing against the wet shrubbery, thoroughly soaked.

"It's into a hot bath for you," I told her as we entered the house. "I wouldn't mind one myself."

Alisette had her bath, and I was helping her into dry clothes when Cecile marched into the bedroom. Curtly dismissing Sonia, who was draining the water from the zinc-lined tub, Cecile turned to me, her eyes narrowed in anger.

"What do you mean by taking my daughter out in this kind of weather?" she cried. "Are you trying to kill her?"

Taken aback, I stammered, "Mrs. Nikolai, I only—"

She didn't let me go on. "You know very well Alisette can't endure dampness and cold, and if you don't know, then what kind of a nurse are you? Just look at her, she's shaking all over with chill."

Likely because she's only half-dressed, I was tempted to retort. I turned to pull a woolen petticoat over Alisette's head.

"Look at me when I'm speaking to you!" Cecile's raised voice was shrill.

Shifting Alisette so I faced her mother, I continued to dress her, determined that, whatever happened, the child wouldn't have to wait around without her clothes on.

"Well?" Cecile demanded of me. "Have you nothing to say?"

Alisette burst into tears. If I had intended a reply, I forgot it because, mixed with her sobs was an ominous wheeze. Cecile heard the wheeze, too.

"See?" she said, on a triumphant note. "You see what you've done to my little girl? I must call the doctor immediately or it'll be too late." She rushed from the room.

Alisette gasped for air while her face drained of color until even her lips were pale. Tremors coursed through her, and if I hadn't been holding her, she would have slumped to the floor. The bubbling wheeze she made frightened me but at the same time reminded me of how one of the orphan babies sounded when he had the croup.

Remembering what the sisters had done for him, I hastily pulled the morning star quilt from Alisette's bed, wrapped it around her, gathered her into my arms, and carried her down the back stairs to the kitchen. I hurried to the stove where Rosie, as usual, had a tea kettle steaming.

"Please bring me a stool," I said as calmly as I

could and, when Rosie obliged, I perched atop it, arranged Alisette on my lap, and moved the kettle until the spout puffed its vapors toward us. Carefully keeping far enough away to avoid burning the child, I draped the quilt over both of our heads to trap the steam. Though I wasn't sure this treatment would be of any benefit to Alisette, I knew it wouldn't harm her.

"Don't be afraid," I murmured to her. "I'm holding you, I won't leave you." I kept talking quietly, telling her about the baby boy at the orphanage whose croup was improved by steam. Gradually her trembling stopped and, though she continued to wheeze, I fancied her breathing wasn't so labored.

I don't know how long we sat there inhaling steam before Cecile stormed into the kitchen with a short, gray-bearded man I took to be Dr. March.

"What on earth are you up to? Are you a halfwit?" Cecile demanded of me, snatching the quilt from our heads. I felt Alisette tense in my arms and stroked her damp hair soothingly.

"What's the meaning of this, young woman?" Dr. March asked, his pale eyes accusing. "Who gave you permission to do such a thing?"

I gathered myself to answer, but no sooner had I opened my mouth than Stephen strode into the kitchen. "What the hell's going on?" he growled.

Cecile and the doctor both spoke at once and, while they sorted things out, I whispered in Alisette's ear, "Your papa's here, he'll make everything right." I wasn't at all sure he could or would, but I desperately wanted to reassure her.

She sighed and relaxed against my shoulder.

"Never mind," Stephen ordered, raising a hand to stop both Cecile and Dr. March. "Explanations can wait." He moved closer to me and bent over to examine Alisette.

"How's the sweetest girl in the world?" he asked her.

"I'm—having—a—fit," she gasped.

"If you can talk about it, the fit must be pretty well over," he told her firmly. "How's about me carrying you up to bed?"

She held out her arms in answer, and he scooped her from my lap, quilt and all, and strode from the room with Dr. March trailing after.

Before following, Cecile fired a parting shot. "You can begin packing, Miss Drake. We've had quite enough of you."

Mrs. Yates and Sonia, who'd joined the group in the kitchen, remained behind with me and Rosie.

"If you ask me," Sonia muttered, "all that screeching and hollering would make any kid sick."

Though I didn't say so, I agreed with Sonia. While I wouldn't go so far as to say it had brought on Alisette's attack, I knew Cecile's angry scolding of me in front of the child hadn't helped.

"No one did ask you, miss," Mrs. Yates said tartly to Sonia. She crossed to me and laid a hand on my shoulder. "Don't you begin packing just yet," she said soothingly. "Let Captain Stephen have his say."

I rose from the stool and mumbled, "I'll be in my room." How I managed to get the words out without crying, I'll never know. By the time I reached the back stairs, my eyes were blurred with tears.

How could I bear to leave Sea Cliff House and Alisette? I refused to add Stephen to my list of regrets. Mrs. Yates was wrong to think he'd stand up for me. Once he heard Cecile's accusations and the doctor's negative report, he'd be only too glad to see the last of me.

I stumbled into my room and flung myself into

the rocker, sobbing. I hadn't meant any harm to Alisette; I'd never in the world knowingly do anything to hurt her. Was I to blame for her attack? She hadn't seemed a bit sick while we were playing tag or while she was in her bath. Still, it *was* cold and damp outside. Perhaps my steam treatment was wrong, too. The doctor had thought so. Filled with remorse I rocked and cried until no more tears came.

Drying my eyes, I rose, sniffling, found my carpetbag at the bottom of the wardrobe and set it on the bed. I was reaching under the bed for my slippers when the door burst open. Stephen stood framed in the opening, his face dark with anger.

"What do you think you're doing?" he demanded.

"P-packing," I stammered.

He reached the bed in two strides and flung the carpetbag into the corner of the room. "You're not leaving. Alsie needs you; you're to remain here."

I gaped at him, hardly able to believe my ears. Finally I managed to ask how she was.

"Much better. She was recovering from the attack even before that fool of a doctor saw her. Pompous ass! Couldn't bring himself to admit you might have done exactly the right thing for Alsie even when the child herself insisted the steam made her breathe easier. I kicked him out; his pontificating was making her worse. As for her mother—" Stephen paused and drew in a deep breath. "She's overwrought," he said at last, "and in no condition to deal with Alsie's attack. I convinced her you were not to blame. In any case, I understand you were hired by Alsie's grandmother. Your dismissal is up to her, not to my— my wife."

Agitated as I was, I noticed how reluctant he was to refer to Cecile as his wife.

84

"I'm sorry I took Alisette outside in such bad weather," I said.

"Nonsense! A little mist never hurt anyone. The girl needs fresh air and exercise. What she doesn't need is hearing a lot of nonsense about fits."

"She didn't actually have a fit," I said, recovering some of my confidence. "She had trouble breathing. Now that I've thought it over, her attack resembled what Sister Samara taught me was called asthma. It's something like croup in babies. Steam inhalation and quiet is recommended until the attack is over."

He smiled at me. "Exactly what you did for her."

I thought he'd played a part in Alisette's rapid improvement as well. I knew she'd believed me when I told her that her papa would make everything all right.

"I came to fetch you," he told me. "I left Alsie with Mrs. Yates, but it's you she wants."

Suddenly aware—and ashamed—of my disheveled hair and tear-reddened eyes, I stared down at my shoes. "Give me a moment to tidy myself and I'll—"

He stopped me by putting a finger underneath my chin and tilting my face up. "Damn it, you've been crying." Without warning, he gathered me to him, and his lips covered mine.

His kiss was anything but gentle, his mouth demanded and took. Dazzled and dazed by the fiery sensations rocketing through me, I was more than willing to give him anything he wanted and more; I wished the kiss to go on forever.

He tasted of something dark and strange and wonderful, a man's taste, Stephen's taste. No wine could be more intoxicating, no sugar confection more sweet. The hard strength of his body thrilled me and my hands gripped his shoulders to hold him close. At this moment I knew I belonged where I was, in his arms, that I was meant to be his and his alone.

He released me so abruptly I staggered, and his hand shot out to steady me. "Esma," he said huskily, "I—" He stopped, shook his head, and took his hand from my arm. "Alsie needs you," he muttered. Turning on his heel, he was gone.

Pulse pounding, my head in a whirl, I tidied my hair, washed my face, and crossed the hall to Alisette's room. Mrs. Yates, with an I-told-you-so nod, rose from the chair beside the bed.

"I'm glad you're staying on," she said as she walked to the door. "I'll have Sonia bring up a tray for the two of you."

I thanked her and took her place at the bedside. Alisette, propped up on two pillows, the rag doll clutched to her breast, murmured, "Papa said you'd never go away. You won't, will you?"

"Never," I vowed, smoothing a strand of hair from her forehead while I fervently hoped nothing would happen to make me break my promise.

Alisette soon fell asleep and, as I kept my vigil at her side, my thoughts revolved around her father. The emotions he roused in me were wrong, I knew. Sinful. Yet how could I prevent myself from feeling as I did when his look and his touch made my senses reel?

Had he been going to tell me he regretted the kiss? *I* didn't. Wrong though it was, I would treasure the moment like a precious jewel.

Still, nothing could change the fact he was a married man. I must curb my desire for his touch; I must avoid him as much as possible. How could I belong to him when he already had a wife? Alisette's welfare was my first concern, and I'd do well to remember that.

In the morning, Alisette seemed in perfect

health. The weather, as if celebrating the fact, cleared, and our riding lessons with Stephen began. Luckily, staying on the placid gray mare assigned to me proved difficult, so I was forced to give my full attention to it. But the fact he was teaching me as well as Alisette didn't go unremarked in the household.

"Anyone can see the captain has an eye for you," Sonia told me after the first week of lessons. "Cecile's green with envy."

"He's merely teaching me so Alisette will have a companion with which to ride," I protested.

She laughed. "Sure, and the moon's made of goat's cheese."

Mrs. Yates offered no comment, but her disapproving eye told me I wasn't behaving properly as far as she was concerned.

Cecile ignored me completely—nothing new—but was even more attentive to Stephen, and every time I saw her touch him, a harpoon of jealousy stabbed through me. I couldn't bring myself to ask Sonia if they ever shared a bed because I feared I couldn't bear hearing that they did. Certainly if Cecile had her way, they would.

Gerald Callich, during this trying time, proved a great support. Without the aid of his conversation at the dinner table, I couldn't have survived the evening meals. No matter how I tried not to watch Stephen, I was aware of every move he made and every word he spoke, though never was a word of his directed at me.

"I can't help but observe that the captain evinces a certain interest in you," Gerald told me one evening in mid-July, after detaining me following dinner and leading me onto the balcony off the front parlor.

"I'm not sure what you mean," I said coolly.

He smiled thinly. "No, you wouldn't be. Sailors, of course, are notorious womanizers."

"Please," I said frostily, "I don't care to hear Captain Nikolai criticized."

"I beg your pardon. I'm sure you realize he *is* a married man."

"And what could possibly cause me to forget that?"

Gerald's blue eyes assessed me. "I don't mean to antagonize you, Miss Drake. Because you were raised in, ah, protected surroundings, I do feel a certain obligation to watch over you that I hope you won't take amiss."

My annoyance fled. How could I object to his kind interest in me? "I appreciate your concern, Mr. Callich, but I do believe I am capable of taking care of myself."

"Would it distress you to hear I've grown rather fond of you in these past months?"

I blinked. Distress me, no. Surprise me, yes.

Gerald laughed. "I see I've startled you."

I flushed, unsure what to say.

"A charming blush," he told me, taking my hand, "from an altogether charming girl." Before I realized what he meant to do, he pressed my fingers to his lips.

Later, as I made my way up the stairs to my room, I realized I'd appreciated the romantic gesture, but I'd experienced no corresponding leap of pulse, no catch of breath. Whereas, if Stephen had kissed my hand, I would have felt the touch of his lips to the farthest corners of my being.

Chapter 6

After several weeks of daily riding lessons, Stephen announced that Alisette and I were proficient enough to ride without him. I concealed my disappointment at losing his company, but Alisette, not one to hide any emotion, pouted.

She cornered him at his paper-strewn desk in the library after our first ride without him. "I missed you, Papa," she complained. "It's more fun with you along—isn't it, Miss Drake?"

"Your papa is a busy man," I said.

"All he's doing is looking at papers," she countered.

"These papers tell all about Nikolai ships," he told her, "and our sawmill, as well. One day you'll have to learn the family business, as I'm trying to do."

Momentarily diverted, she craned her neck to look at the papers on the desk but quickly gave it up. "I guess I don't read good enough yet," she said.

My heart went out to Stephen as I realized his amnesia must extend to the Nikolai holdings, too, and he was literally having to learn the family business all over again. I tried not to pry, but I couldn't help but notice many of the jottings were in red. Since I'd helped with the orphanage accounts, I knew red ink meant a debit.

Surely, though, the Nikolais, with a sawmill as well as ships to carry the finished lumber to market, needn't worry about money.

Sawmills abounded in Eureka. I'd seen six when Armin drove me from town to the mansion, and he'd told me there were over twenty in Humboldt County, all busy and prospering. "With all them redwoods yet to cut, there's room for even more mills," he'd said.

Alisette put her hand on her father's arm. "Maybe later you can come to the schoolroom and tell us another story."

He shook his head. "I can't, Alsie. I'm leaving in an hour, and I'll be away for several days. But I promise I'll have a surprise for you on Friday."

"What is it?" she cried.

"That's my secret. Run along with Miss Drake and learn to read better so you can help me one of these days." He looked only at Alisette as he spoke.

I masked my hurt that I'd become simply Miss Drake to him and no longer the Esma he'd held in his arms and kissed so ardently. At the same time, I knew I should be glad he was behaving properly, since there could never be anything between us.

"Friday's three whole days away," Alisette informed him, having counted on her fingers. "That's a long time."

He smiled at her. "Two and a half days, to be exact. Don't fret, Friday will come sooner than you think."

Seeing that she was prepared to argue, I took her hand. "Your papa has told us to run along, and that's what we'll do. This very minute."

Alisette had learned that when I gave an order in a certain tone, she'd best obey or suffer my disapproval plus a restriction of privileges. Dragging her feet, she let me lead her from the library. As we reached the door, Stephen called after us.

"Oh, Miss Drake, I'll expect you to accompany Alsie and me on Friday."

My heart soared as, glancing over my shoulder, I murmured my agreement. But he still didn't look at me.

"Where do you think Papa will take us?" Alisette asked as we climbed the stairs. "Will we go riding?"

"I don't know any more than you do, and we won't find out until Friday."

"It'll be fun," she said gleefully, her pouting forgotten. "It's always fun when Papa's there. I hope he never, ever sails away again."

He would, eventually, leaving both Alisette and me to mourn. But I refused to think about it, wanting instead to savor the anticipation of what Friday might bring.

As usual, the rag doll, resplendent in her new blue calico gown, had to be brought to the third floor to sit in the schoolroom with us. Alisette ate and slept with Estelle beside her and had grown so attached to the doll that she could hardly bear to leave it behind when we went riding. Only my warning that Estelle might fall off the pony and be lost persuaded her the doll was safer in the house.

With the loving care Alisette lavished on the doll, I was surprised when, after her evening bath, she couldn't find Estelle.

"She ate supper with me," Alisette insisted. "Where did she go?"

I couldn't recall when I'd last seen the doll so, despite Alisette's words, I ran up to the school-room to look, but Estelle wasn't there. Sonia and Mrs. Yates were enlisted to help search. The doll was nowhere to be found.

"I can't go to sleep without her." Alisette's

lower lip quivered as, sitting on her bed, she gazed accusingly at the three of us. "Where is she?"

Cecile's sudden appearance startled every one of us—she almost never came to her daughter's bedroom. "What's all the commotion?" she demanded, standing framed in the doorway, wearing a lace-trimmed blue dressing gown. "Is my daughter ill?"

"Mama, my doll's lost." Alisette burst into tears.

Cecile hurried to the bed and put her arms around her daughter. "You poor dear," she crooned. Fixing a stony blue gaze on me, she said, "You know Alisette is prone to sneaking off when she's not watched. Doesn't she always go outside? Have you looked there?"

"But, Mrs. Nikolai, I was with her—" I began.

Cecile cut off my words. "Not while she napped, I'll wager."

Unfortunately, she was right. I had no way to be certain Alisette hadn't slipped from the house when she was thought to be napping. Though she hadn't run off lately, it was always possible she had today and was afraid to own up. For the life of me I couldn't recall if the child had the doll at supper as she claimed.

"There, there, dear," Cecile said soothingly to her daughter. "Miss Drake will find your doll for you." Again that implacable gaze fixed on me. "Won't you, Miss Drake?"

I could hardly bear to listen to Alisette's heartbroken sobs. "I'll do my best," I promised.

"Since you seem to have searched the house," Cecile said imperiously, "I suggest you look outside in the places where Alisette would be likely to go. Obviously, that's where the doll is."

In my room, I donned a brown shawl I'd knitted at the orphanage, hurried down the back stairs, begged a lantern from Rosie, and let myself out through the side door. The two places Alisette might have visited were the goldfish pond and the cemetery. I hoped with all my heart I'd find the doll by the pond.

I did not.

The day had been fair, but the fog always waiting off shore had crept in with the darkness, and tendrils of mist wavered among the rose bushes. My nerve faltered when I thought of entering the graveyard, gloomy at the best of times, with the fog thickening among the tombstones.

But how could I return without the rag doll?

I sent up a quick prayer, raised the lantern, and set off for Alisette's shortcut through the hole in the cypress hedge.

The only sound as I approached the church was the mournful moan of the foghorn at the entrance to Humboldt Bay, several miles to the north of Cliff House. Armin had pointed out the conical brick lighthouse to me while we were in Eureka.

"A fixed light she be, not one of them revolving ones," he'd said. "Got a steam horn, too, for all the good it does when the fog settles in. Many's the ship wrecked along this coast. Treacherous, it be. The Nikolais found that out, to their sorrow." I hadn't liked his triumphant laugh.

Fog or not, I wasn't a hapless ship sailing blind. I was on dry land, I knew where the cemetery was, and I had a lantern. The dead were at rest, they wouldn't harm me. I had nothing to fear; I'd find the doll and hurry back to the house.

But I couldn't control a shiver as I passed the ruined church. To keep my too-active imagination under control, I began counting the seconds between hoots of the foghorn. Twenty-eight, without variation, though I found the horn blasts alternated in length from four to eight seconds and told myself it must be a kind of identification code so a ship, enshrouded in fog, would know which port they were passing.

Concentrating on the horn, I hurried past the church and into the graveyard. There, the mist was thicker, and I could no longer see the lights of the house. With my vision limited to scant feet on all sides, I had to slow my pace to a snail's crawl to avoid running into tombstones.

A scraping sound to my left set my heart hammering, and I froze. What had I heard? Though it was impossible to identify the sound, I told myself someone from Sea Cliff House might have come to help me search.

"Is—is anyone there?" I quavered.

There was no answer. I took a few steps, stopping when a creaking began to my right. I swallowed, quelling my impulse to scream and run. If I panicked, in this fog I was as likely to run away from the house as toward it. Or worse, past the house and over the cliff into the sea. The mysterious noises, I reassured myself, must be branches of shrubbery brushing against the gravestones. Taking a deep breath, I raised the lantern and inched on, resisting the urge to keep glancing behind me. All the minions of hell could be on my trail, and I wouldn't be able to see one of them for the fog.

"There are no ghosts," I muttered under my breath. "The dead stay in their graves until Judgment Day." I knew the words to be true, and yet I found that what was believable in daylight was harder to accept when one was alone in a cemetery on a fog-shrouded night.

Distracted by my fears, I nearly passed by the small crypt that held Alexandria's remains. Standing several feet to the left of it, I stopped and looked around. What was that spot of blue on the ground close by the crypt? Could it be the doll's calico gown? I lowered the lantern and, by its

94

feeble light, saw with relief that my search was over—Alisette's rag doll lay in front of the crypt.

In my eagerness to retrieve the doll, I didn't watch where I was going and stumbled over a broken grave marker, dropping the lantern and falling headlong. As I went down, something brushed against me, snatching my shawl from my shoulders, then slammed into the ground beside me, smashing the overturned lantern. I screamed into the darkness.

A man shouted from a distance. "Miss Drake! Esma, are you all right?"

"Over here," I cried, still frightened. Though certain he must be Stephen come to my rescue, I feared a renewed attack before he reached me. "Hurry!" I begged. "Hurry!"

I rose to my knees and called frantically until I saw a dim light shining through the fog and heard footsteps pound toward me. Moments later, a man appeared in the mist, the lantern he carried haloing his light hair.

Gerald Callich!

Only then did I recall Stephen wasn't at home.

"Thank God I've found you!" Gerald exclaimed, kneeling beside me, lantern in hand.

I clutched at his arm as we both stared at the marble angel on the ground beside me, my shawl caught on its outstretched arm. Its fall from the top of the crypt had decapitated the angel as well as smashed my lantern. I shuddered and turned away. If I hadn't tripped and gone sprawling, it wouldn't be the smashed lantern under the fallen angel, I'd have been its victim.

"A close call. You'd have been seriously injured if that angel had hit you," Gerald said as he helped me to my feet. "Can you walk?"

"I—I think so," I stammered, leaning against him, my legs wobbly. "The doll," I said when he started to lead me away. "Bring Alisette's doll." I pointed toward the crypt. "That's why I came here."

He scooped up the doll and handed it to me. "Cecile told me you'd gone after a doll. You should have asked me to come with you. Do you want the shawl, too?"

Shuddering, I said, "No, leave the shawl. I could never bring myself to wear it again. Whoever would have thought the angel would come loose from its perch?"

"Even marble cracks in time."

Upset though I was, I noticed he spoke as though his mind were elsewhere.

We walked on in silence, our pace necessarily slow because of the fog. "Miss Drake," he said, finally. "Esma. I know how terribly shaken you must be after such a narrow escape. Believe me, I realize this is a poor time to talk, but we must."

"Talk?" I echoed, not understanding.

"I'll do the talking, all you have to do is listen. I called you Esma because you're not really a stranger to me, I've known you for several years— four to be exact."

"But I—I never met you until I came to Sea Cliff House," I protested.

"That's correct. Didn't the nuns tell you how it came to be that you were trained as a nurse?"

"Sister Samara said a mysterious benefactor—" I paused as an inkling of the truth came to me. "You?" I asked, incredulously. "Are you the person who paid for my training?"

"I'm a man who looks ahead," he told me. "I always have and I always will. My lifelong duty has been to look after the interests of the Nikolai family—in all ways. It was obvious soon after Alisette was born that she needed special care, and I soon noticed the women hired to tend her were

96

either inadequate or refused to remain at such an isolated spot as Sea Cliff House.

"We needed a young woman who was well-trained as a nurse, a young woman who didn't object to a quiet life. I thought of orphanage girls and went looking for a likely prospect. I found you and arranged the rest."

I was struck dumb by his revelation, my near-fatal accident pushed to the back of my mind as I tried to come to terms with what he'd said. When I found strength returning to my legs, I ceased to lean on him, though I kept hold of his arm for guidance.

"I don't know what to say," I managed finally.

"That's just it. I don't want you to say anything. Not to anyone. This is our secret, yours and mine. For Alisette's sake. Cecile loathes interference of any kind in her life, and if she ever discovered what I've done, she'd be so furious she'd make my life— and yours—a misery. One way or another, she'd force you to leave Sea Cliff House. You know how much the child needs you; you must remain here at least until Alisette has a chance to grow out of her sickly temperament."

My mind whirled with confusion. Gratitude for what Gerald had done for me warred with my reluctance to hide his generous act from the Nikolais. At least from Stephen. I disliked keeping unnecessary secrets. But I suspected Cecile would behave exactly as Gerald said. She'd taken an aversion to me from the first and had already tried to send me packing once. Without Stephen's intervention, I'd have packed and left weeks ago.

The one undeniable fact was Alisette's need for me. I'd come to love her, and I knew she depended on me. How could I not do everything in my power to stay with her as long as she needed me?

I saw the lights of Sea Cliff House shining dimly

through the fog and realized that before we reached it I must give Gerald some assurance I'd keep his benevolence a secret.

"I won't tell anyone," I said in a low tone. "But I must thank you from the bottom of my heart for aiding me to learn how to help Alisette. You're a kind and wonderful person to go to such trouble and expense for others."

"I don't expect praise. As I said before, I take the long view. I did what I did for myself as much as for anyone else."

How modest he was, disclaiming any altruistic intent. As we climbed the steps to the front door, my opinion of Gerald rose to new heights.

The first thing I did after entering the house was to return the doll to Alisette. All I wanted to do once I saw her contentedly settled for the night was collapse into bed. Unfortunately, Gerald had told Mrs. Yates—there was no sign of Cecile—about my near brush with death, and she insisted nothing would do for me but a hot bath followed by a cup of her own special soothing herb tea. While the water for the bath was being prepared, she wormed every detail of my ghastly trip to the cemetery from me, little as I wished to recall the experience.

"Why, that angel's been on that crypt forty years or more," she said. "Sea Cliff House wasn't built until 1841, but I've been told the Russian church was here much earlier, long before Eureka was a town." She sighed and shook her head. "That salt sea air corrodes everything. What a blessing you weren't hurt."

By morning, I'd recovered enough to be grateful the angel hadn't fallen earlier and harmed Alisette. I took it upon myself to tell her about the angel, because I knew she'd hear about my misadventure from others and I wanted her to know the

98

unvarnished truth. But when I questioned her about her clandestine trip to the cemetery, she denied going there.

"I didn't visit Alexandria yesterday," she insisted. "I didn't take Estelle there. Somebody bad did. A bad man."

She seemed so positive I couldn't bear to accuse her of lying. Like any child, she did tell an occasional fib, but it was possible she'd wiped the visit from her mind after hearing what happened.

"Now we know for sure the cemetery really isn't a safe place to wander around in," I pointed out.

"Alexandria takes care of me," Alisette said. "And she likes you, too. She didn't let you get hurt by her angel."

Maybe not, but I'd certainly been frightened nearly to death. For the time being, though, I decided to drop the subject and, Alexandria or not, do my best to make certain Alisette stayed away from the graveyard.

Later that day, the shocking news of President Garfield's death from an assassin's bullet made my mishap in the cemetery seem unimportant. Since I'd begun to teach Alisette about the capital of our country, I told her as simply as possible that President Garfield had died and another man, President Arthur, had taken his place.

Being only five, she was more interested in what time we were going for our daily ride and if I had any idea what her papa's Friday secret could be.

I didn't care. It was enough to know I'd be with Stephen, wrong though the feeling was. "We'll have to wait and see," I told her for what seemed like the hundredth time. But I was as eager for Friday to arrive as she.

When I looked from my window at dawn on

Friday, mist drifted in the gardens but, by mid-morning, it had dissipated under the warmth of the mid-September sun. Though Stephen hadn't arrived the evening before in time for supper, I knew he'd returned home, because Alisette had taken it upon herself to find out. Her eagerness to see him made her hard to keep amused, so I was relieved when Mrs. Yates climbed to the schoolroom with a message from him.

"He wants you and the child in riding costume," she announced. "You're to meet him at the stables."

Alisette shouted in glee and rushed for the stairs. As I started to follow her, Mrs. Yates held up her hand. "I hope you're not getting ideas," she said.

"I'm not sure what you mean," I told her, not quite truthfully.

"Captain Stephen has a wife," she said bluntly. "See that you keep the fact in mind."

To my distress, I flushed as I fumbled for words, at last mumbling, "I'm quite aware he's married," as I edged past her and fled down the stairs to join Alisette.

Walking to the stables I told myself over and over that I'd be as prim and proper as possible in Stephen's presence, but at the sight of him, every thought fled from my head. He wasn't wearing his riding clothes; he was dressed in the dark blue uniform he'd worn the night he'd first arrived, complete with a brimmed captain's hat, and I was struck once again by his close resemblance to the portrait of Captain Alexi in the west-wing gallery. But Stephen was even more handsome, despite the scar.

He greeted Alisette by sweeping her off her feet and hugging her but paid little heed to me. As he set her on Sir Toby, she began chattering.

"Papa, you're warning your captain's clothes," she said. "Are we going to your ship? To *Sea Dragon?* Is that the surprise? I've never been on a ship. Does the deck go up and down? What—?"

"One question at a time," he protested, laughing. Assisting me to mount, he swung onto Bosun's back before telling us, "*Sea Dragon's* finally out of dry dock and afloat at the wharf by the sawmill. Do you really want to go aboard her, Alsie?"

"Oh, yes, Papa!"

"And you, Miss Drake?" His glance was impersonal.

"I'd like to very much, thank you," I told him, pleased to hear how distant and cool my voice sounded.

"I hate it when you talk like Miss Postern," Alisette put in.

Stephen's green eyes glinted with amusement as they briefly met mine before returning to his daughter. "Lucky for us she's *not* Miss Postern, right, Alsie?"

Alisette made a face. "I hope she never comes back. I hope Miss Drake stays for ever and ever. Don't you, Papa?"

He looked at me again, the amusement replaced by an emotion I couldn't name, one that darkened his eyes and sent a tingle along my spine. "Yes," he said, so softly I barely heard, "forever."

My heart turned over and I gave up on prim and proper. Was it so wrong to enjoy being with Stephen? My pleasure in his company harmed no one. Or so I told myself.

"Visiting *Sea Dragon* is only part of the surprise," Stephen said, speaking to both me and Alisette. "The two of you have an unreasoning timidity about the sea that I intend to conquer."

"By tossing us overboard?" I asked, smiling,

101

suddenly so carefree that not even the sea seemed a threat.

"Nothing quite so drastic," he assured us.

"What will we do, Papa?"

He shook his head. "I'm saving that part of the surprise. Respect for the dangers of the sea is one thing, fear of the water another. No one should fear the sea—especially a Nikolai."

"I'm not 'zactly scared, Papa."

"Good. How about you, Miss Drake?"

I couldn't bear to admit to my deep dread of the green waves. "I've never had much to do with the ocean," I said evasively.

"Then it's past time you did." He spoke decisively.

Fearful or not, I trusted him; wherever he led me, I'd do my best to follow.

The Nikolai mill, with its yards and rollways of logs, sprawled over almost an entire block at bay-side. Once I saw *Sea Dragon* moored to the wharf, though, my interest focused on the ship.

"Landsmen call everything that sails the seas a ship," Stephen said, once we stood on the wooden planks of the dock. "They're wrong. Besides ships, there are barkentines, barks, brigs, brigantines, and schooners, all differing in size and masts and rigging. *Sea Dragon* is a true ship, as any sailor could tell you at a glance." He gazed with loving pride at the sleek, trim three-masted vessel towering over us.

I admired the handsome red and gold dragon figurehead below the bowsprit. Alisette had told me red and gold were the Nikolai colors, and pennants in those colors flew from the masts.

"She's lots bigger than *my* ship." Alisette's tone was awed. I understood how she felt.

A piping whistle sounded. "Captain coming aboard," a sailor called from the deck, and a gangplank clattered into place.

Once we were all aboard, Stephen pointed out the new mast. "We lost one in a storm off the Sandwich Islands. She broke clean off. We're waiting now for new sails to replace the old ones."

His tour of the ship with us was quick but thorough, and he patiently answered Alisette's questions in as much detail as she could understand. I was most interested in the captain's quarters, for I wanted to be able to picture Stephen in them after he sailed away from Sea Cliff House.

When we'd seen all there was to see, Stephen led us to the rail overlooking the bay and lifted Alisette into his arms so she could see.

"Humboldt Bay provides safe mooring," he said, "but there's a problem getting into the bay—a sand bar across its mouth. The bar's down that way." He pointed to the southeast. "She shifts and changes all the time so ships coming in or out of Humboldt Bay need a pilot to guide them around the bar into harbor or out to sea. The best pilot I ever saw lives right here in Eureka: Hans Buhne and his tug *Mary Ann.*" Pointing again, he added, "There's the *Mary Ann* now, towing a lumber schooner in."

"I don't have a tugboat for my ships," Alisette said.

Stephen smiled at her as he set her on her feet. "Then it's lucky the goldfish pond doesn't have a sand bar. Of course, if you *do* happen to get a tug, maybe we can make a sand bar."

Engrossed in Stephen, not once did my terror of the water overcome me, at least not until we left the ship and Stephen pointed to a rowboat tied to a mooring post, bobbing up and down in the water. "There's the rest of my surprise," he said.

I stared at the wooden ladder leading down to the little boat and swallowed. He didn't expect me

103

to climb down and sit in that tiny craft, did he?

He did.

Alisette showed no hesitation but, despite my resolve to follow Stephen no matter where, I balked.

"It's so small," I quavered.

"Don't you trust me?" he asked.

How could I say no?

"If you do exactly as I tell you, you're perfectly safe," he assured me and held out his hand to help me into the rowboat.

Once I was seated on the board in the boat's center, Stephen cast off the rope and shoved against the mooring post, sending the boat adrift. I closed my eyes.

"Esma, it's only the bay, and it's as calm as a frog pond. There's no danger." Stephen's voice was gentle and persuasive. "Open your eyes."

More thrilled that he'd called me Esma again than reassured by his words, I obeyed.

"What are you afraid of?" he asked.

I saw that nothing but the truth would do. "I have nightmares about drowning. In waves. Tall green waves."

"Look around," he commanded as he dipped in the oars and began rowing. "Do you see any waves large enough to frighten you here?"

Reflected sunlight glinted off the barely rippling waters of the bay while underneath me the boat rocked gently. "No," I said as calmly as I could, denying the rapid beat of my heart as I found myself surrounded by water.

"I'd never put you in danger." His voice was soft, the words sweet to my ears. Yet I could barely control my fear.

"*I* think it's fun," Alisette piped up. "Will you teach me to row, Papa?"

"You need to grow a bit, to gain more muscle,"

he told her. "Then I will."

"I bet I could do it," she persisted. "It looks easy."

He smiled at her, shaking his head. "As a boy, I used to be just like you, certain I was capable of anything." The smile faded, a cloud passed over his face. He shifted the oars and stared back at the wharf, his eyes fixed on *Sea Dragon*.

"And this, God help us, is the result." He spoke to himself rather than to either of us.

The somber tone of his voice quelled even Alisette, for she asked no questions.

He looked so unhappy that, without thinking, I leaned forward, reached across, and laid my hand on his.

He blinked, coming back from some unknown land only he inhabited. "There's you, though," he said, gazing straight into my eyes. "I met you."

"And you met me, too, Papa," Alisette reminded him.

The corners of Stephen's mouth quirked as his gaze shifted to her. "How could I forget the sweetest girl in the world?"

Trying to fight my way free of the spell he'd cast over me, I murmured, "Don't worry, Alisette will never let you forget her."

"I have the feeling *you* won't, either," he told me and began to row again, leaving me pondering exactly what he meant, so wrapped up in his words that my fear of the sea receded into the far recesses of my mind.

There was certainly no chance of my ever forgetting him. I knew now, beyond the shadow of a doubt, that I was hopelessly in love with Stephen Nikolai. And would be as long as I lived.

Chapter 7

I woke with a hand shaking my shoulder and sat up abruptly. In the vague grayness of predawn, Sonia stood over my bed. "What's wrong?" I cried in alarm. "Is Alisette—?"

Her finger to her lips stopped me. "Alisette's still sleeping. As to what's wrong, you ought to know."

I blinked at her, confused.

Sonia shook her head. "Sometimes you act like you left your wits back at that orphanage. You go off together all day, you and the captain, and you ask me what's wrong."

"It wasn't just me and the captain," I said indignantly, "Alisette was with us."

"He takes her along to cover up spending time with you, that's how the rest of us see it. All except the old lady—Mrs. Peter. She don't pay any heed to what goes on around her." Sonia plumped down on the bed. "Esma, how can you be such a goose?"

"I haven't done anything wrong."

"Nothing wrong?" She laughed without humor. "When I saw him kiss you in this very room? You know what comes after kisses, don't you?" Leaning forward, she peered into my eyes. "No, I guess you don't. Not yet, anyway. So I'll tell you. Next thing, he'll be creeping into your bed at night. Even a nun-raised innocent like you ought to be able to figure what happens then. Either you get caught and sent packing as a slut, or you get with child and *he* gets rid of you. The captain's a Nikolai, and from old Alexi on down they got a reputation around here for fathering bastards they never take care of.''

Her blunt words set my face aflame. There'd be nothing shameful between Stephen and me, and I meant to tell her so.

Before I could, she added, "Ever take a good look at Armin?"

I couldn't help but recall how I'd noticed a certain similarity between him and Stephen. "Armin is a Nikolai?" I asked faintly.

"I heard from someone who ought to know that Mrs. Yates's sister was Armin's mother. Years back she was a maid here, a looker by all accounts, and she caught Captain Peter's eye. She died when Armin was born."

I bit my lip, unable to refute what she said when the truth was so evident in Armin's Nikolai features. "But at least the family did hire Armin to work here," I put in.

"Not till Captain Peter's ship went down. Mrs. Peter's eyesight started going after her husband drowned, and it was then Mrs. Yates convinced her to hire Armin, never mentioning he was a bastard of the captain's."

"Does Armin know who he is?"

"Sure he does. Everyone does except Mrs. Peter."

"And Stephen."

When she raised her eyebrows, I explained. "His amnesia."

"He might have lost his memory, but he's got eyes in his head." Sonia rose. "I got to get cracking

107

or Mrs. Yates'll have my hide. I just wanted to warn you that Cecile's fuming over that trip of yours yesterday, and she's out for blood. Your blood." She reached the door and half-turned to add, "I wouldn't stand under any more marble angels if I was you."

Sonia slipped from the room leaving me staring after her, shocked by her implication. I couldn't believe Cecile had somehow arranged the accident with the angel.

Although she *had* forced me to go outside to search for the rag doll. And everyone in the house knew Alisette's favorite place was Alexandria's crypt. As for the doll being missing, Alisette still insisted she'd had Estelle with her at supper and "somebody bad" took the doll when she wasn't looking.

Her own mother? After all, Cecile didn't like me and wanted me gone.

No, I couldn't believe Cecile would actually try to harm me. Yet the fact I'd thought for a moment she might left me uneasy.

Sonia's other comments unsettled me further. The way she'd spoken of Stephen slipping into my bed sounded so tawdry. I shook my head. Though it might be true—how I hoped it was!—that he enjoyed my company, he was too fine and noble a man to stoop to back-stairs seduction. Even if I'd countenance such deviousness.

But as I washed and dressed, Sonia's words echoed in my mind. "Everyone knows the Nikolais father bastards . . ." Obviously Captain Peter had. And Stephen *was* a Nikolai.

I saw neither Cecile nor Stephen during the day and, in view of Sonia's warning, I went down to dinner that evening with some trepidation, wondering what Cecile intended. Surely she was enough of a lady not to make a public scene.

I tried to look at the situation from her point of view, that of a wife, and despairingly agreed she had a right to be angry with me as well as with Stephen. According to Sonia, Cecile's husband had so far refused to share her bed, and he did spend more time with me than he did her. What was I to do about changing what was happening? I couldn't find an answer.

In the parlor, Gerald introduced me to a burly, sandy-haired man named Jock Ferguson who, he said, would be staying at the house for several weeks. I greeted him with polite enthusiasm, thinking that his presence at the dinner table would restrain Cecile.

"Mr. Ferguson is a San Francisco engineer who specializes in sea walls and breakwaters for harbors," Gerald told me. "He was on a business trip to Eureka, and I asked him to have a look at the cliffs here and give us an opinion."

"The house *is* set very close to the cliff edge," I commented.

"Ay, 'tis." Mr. Ferguson had a Scottish burr. "I've yet to discover how much of a problem that might prove to be. Depends on the ocean currents hereabouts, y'see, and the prevailing winds. Then there's the composition of the rock. Some kinds of sea can gnaw away on for hundreds of years with maybe a wee bit flaking off now and again. Other kinds crumble and fall with every storm."

I was interested in his explanation and also in the fact that he was here at Gerald's behest. Gerald did more than his share for the Nikolais, I thought. He was truly concerned with not only the business but with every aspect of their lives. As he'd told me, he took the long view. His bringing Mr. Ferguson here might very well save Sea Cliff House for future generations of Nikolais. I smiled warmly at him, knowing that *I* was certainly beholden to him.

At the dinner table, Mr. Ferguson sat between Mrs. Peter and Cecile and, though he was courteous to the older woman and responded with cautious interest to Cecile's coquetry, I noticed his eyes followed Sonia every time she came into the room. From her sidelong glances at him, I decided she'd noticed, too.

I was seated between Stephen and Gerald. Prudence made me address most of my remarks to Gerald. When I did venture to speak to Stephen, he replied in monosyllables. Finally I said, "It was far thinking of Mr. Callich to invite an engineer to inspect the sea cliffs."

Stephen glanced at me, scowling. "Far thinking? Or meddling?" His words were pitched loudly enough for Gerald to hear, and I winced.

"It seems to me he's worked hard for the Nikolais," I said reprovingly.

"Always on hand when the men were away at sea, at least." An undercurrent of challenge hid among the slightly too-loud words, obviously aimed at Gerald.

Gerald had the sense to pretend not to hear. What on earth was the matter with Stephen? He was all but picking a fight at his own dinner table.

I hoped no one else had noticed but, looking at Mrs. Peter, I saw her blind gaze fixed on her son.

"Stephen," she said, "I find I'm a bit fatigued. Would you please see me to my room? You will excuse me, Mr. Ferguson?"

Stephen didn't return to the table. After the meal, Gerald drew me into the parlor. "I couldn't help but notice your embarrassment," he said in a low tone. "Don't pay any heed to the captain, he's not himself." He shook his head. "A real tragedy, his amnesia. Imagine forgetting your entire past— your childhood, people and places you love, the

110

very events that made you who you are. He bears up well, considering." As he spoke, he toyed with something he'd taken from his pocket.

I smiled approvingly at Gerald. He was so understanding. I almost told him that I, too, had no past I could remember besides the orphanage; I remembered nothing that had happened before then. But my attention was caught by what he was doing and I gasped.

"Why, that's a dagger!"

"Do pardon me." Gerald hastily slid the wavy-bladed knife into its sheath and returned it to his pocket. "I didn't mean to startle you. Please believe me, I wouldn't alarm you for the world." He was clearly agitated.

"I never before saw such an odd dagger," I said, hoping to put him more at ease.

"It's a family heirloom, a Malay kris. I use it to open letters at the mill, and I'd quite forgotten I had it in my pocket." He smiled ruefully. "Sometimes when I'm nervous I tend to play with the kris and, at the moment, I must admit to a certain trepidation. You see, I mean to ask you to go riding with me."

I stared at him in amazement. Go riding with him? Surely he meant Alisette and me.

"I'm busy during the week," he went on, "as are you, but perhaps one of these Sundays you'll find the time."

"I'm sure Alisette would enjoy that," I said primly.

"She's a lovely child, but, much as I'd enjoy her company, I'd prefer to ride without her. In other words, just the two of us, you and me."

I was flattered that an attractive man like Gerald sought my company. Nevertheless, I replied, "My time is not my own, as I'm sure you're aware."

"I'm also sure Mrs. Yates wouldn't mind

111

keeping an eye on Alisette while she naps."

"Mrs. Yates doesn't approve of the help being too friendly with the family."

"Ah, but you forget I'm 'help,' too. And I'm sure Mrs. Peter wouldn't mind our riding together. So, you see, you have no excuse. Unless you don't care for my company."

Help or not, Mrs. Yates had warned me to keep my distance from Gerald. Not that I meant to say so. "I do enjoy talking with you," I assured him truthfully. "Dinners wouldn't be half so pleasant without you at the table."

He caught my hand. "Then I'll look forward to riding with you next Sunday, weather permitting."

I could think of no graceful way to refuse. I owed Gerald more than I could ever repay, and I quite liked him, besides. "If Mrs. Yates agrees to watch Alisette," I conceded.

He pressed my hand and released it. As I turned to leave, I came face-to-face with Stephen, who stood glowering in the parlor archway, blocking my passage. For no good reason, I felt guilty.

"Excuse me," I murmured, endeavoring to edge past, angry with him but more at myself for feeling guilty.

For a moment I thought he didn't mean to step aside, then with a twisted smile, he said, "No, excuse *me* for interrupting your tête-à-tête." He moved back and, with an elaborate flourish of his arm, gestured for me to pass.

Head high, I sailed past him, hoping I might reach my room without any more untoward encounters. It was not to be. Cecile lay in wait near the top of the stairs.

"I don't want you in this house another day." Her voice was low and venom filled; her blue eyes glittered angrily. "Do you understand?"

"Alisette needs—" I began uncertainly.

"My daughter has nothing to do with this. She survived before you came, she'll survive after you leave. Pack and get out. Tonight."

Whether Cecile realized it or not, Alisette *did* need me, and I had no intention of summarily deserting her. Knowing that she didn't have the authority to dismiss me, I gathered my courage. "I don't mean to defy you," I said as calmly as I could, "but Captain Stephen reminded me I was hired by Mrs. Peter, and he told me I was not to leave unless she asked me to."

Cecile clenched her fists and I stepped aside, half believing she meant to strike me.

"I won't have you here." She spit the words at me. "I'll get rid of you. One way or the other."

When I finally reached the privacy of my room, I was trembling. Cecile didn't merely dislike me, she hated me! The realization of her intense hatred was more disturbing than her threats. As far as I knew, no one had ever hated me before.

"But I've done nothing wrong!" I cried aloud.

Except maybe for allowing Stephen to kiss me in this very room. Then again, how could I have stopped him when I didn't know he intended to kiss me?

My eager response to his kiss was wrong, perhaps. I sighed and slumped into the rocker. Loving him was wrong, but I couldn't help myself. I could and would try, though, never to come between him and Cecile again, in any way. Whether I liked her or not and even though I didn't trust her, she *was* his wife.

I was in bed, though not asleep, when Sonia looked in on me, coming to sit on my bed.

"The captain and his wife had a terrible fight," she said with relish. "She screeched like a dozen gulls. Didn't get her anywhere 'cause he walked

113

out on her. Then she started in on Mr. Gerald. He had an awful time calming her down." Sonia's lip curled. "He's a master of sweet words, he is."

"Mr. Callich is a fine man," I put in. "He thinks of the family before he thinks of himself."

"In a pig's eye," Sonia muttered.

If only she knew all Gerald had done for the family!

"Poor Mr. Ferguson," she said. "With all the carrying on, no one had time for him." She smiled slyly. "Except me."

"He watched you at dinner," I admitted.

"I may meet him in town on my half day, like he asked. I haven't made up my mind."

I stared at her. She and Mr. Ferguson had barely met and surely hadn't had the chance to do more than exchange a few words. All this on such short acquaintance?

As though reading my mind, she said, "Esma, honey, when a likely man shows up, you got to act quick or the chance is gone."

"But you don't even know if he's married!"

"Well, he *says* he's not. You can't trust a man to tell the truth, but I'll believe him for now. I got to take some risk. Anyway, you're a fine one to talk. It don't seem to bother *you* that Captain Stephen's married." She rose and flounced from the room.

The next morning Mrs. Peter sent for me. Because of Cecile's threats the previous evening, I entered Mrs. Peter's suite fearfully, more than half-convinced Cecile had convinced her mother-in-law to dismiss me. She was standing by one of the windows facing the sea, her back to me, and, if I hadn't known better, I'd have been sure she was staring down at the wild waves. With her regal bearing, I thought, she might have descended from the Russian queen Alisette said she was named after.

114

"Esma," she said, turning and walking toward me, "now that you've been here several months, what do you think of Sea Cliff House?"

Whatever I'd expected, it wasn't this question. Taken aback, I sought for a polite way to tell the truth.

"It's a fine and gracious home, ma'am," I said at last, "and the gardens are lovely."

She smiled a bit sadly. "Yes, of course, but how do you like living here?"

"I never dreamed I'd live in half as grand a place."

"You find the house cheerful, then?"

I bit my lip. "Not exactly, ma'am."

"Come, child, speak up. Tell me the truth."

"Well," I admitted, "I find it rather gloomy." Listening to the crash of the waves against the cliff, clearly audible through the closed windows here in the west wing, I added, "And too close to the sea."

"Mr. Ferguson said something similar about our proximity to the cliff edge. He seems very knowledgeable. I admit I hadn't considered the matter until I spoke to him."

I breathed a sigh of relief, because I feared I'd been too outspoken.

"It was kind of Gerald—Mr. Callich—to persuade Mr. Ferguson to visit us," she continued. "Gerald has been so helpful to me. To us all. I've known him since he was a boy. His father was once my husband's partner in the mill." She sighed. "How long ago that seems. Now both Peter and Gerald's father are dead. I linger on; sometimes I wonder why."

"Alisette is very fond of you," I said, hoping to cheer her. "She's always quoting her grandmother."

"The child is fond of you, too. You've been good

115

for her. And having her father home has worked marvels."

"She believes the sun rises and sets in him," I said fervently.

Mrs. Peter was silent a moment, inclining her head as though observing me, though I knew she couldn't really see me. "Will you walk with me along the cliffs this morning?" she asked.

Her abrupt change of subject as well as her request rendered me momentarily speechless. Walk along the cliffs? I'd rather scrub every floor in the house on my hands and knees ten times over. But of course I couldn't refuse.

"Certainly, ma'am," I told her.

"We won't bring Alisette; I've asked Mrs. Yates to keep an eye on her while we're gone." She turned to a tall chest, opened a middle drawer, took out a brilliantly patterned Chinese shawl, and offered it to me.

"Gerald tells me you lost your shawl when the angel fell in the graveyard. I want you to have this to replace it."

"Oh, but this is too—" I began.

"Always accept a gift graciously," she admonished.

I swallowed, feeling the expensive smoothness of the silk under my fingers, the rich colors dazzling my eyes. I'd never owned anything so beautiful. "Thank you," I managed. "It's very kind of you."

"I feel you have been a gift to us, and I'm so grateful you weren't injured in the accident."

A few minutes later we were outside the house, walking toward the cliffs, she in her long black cloak while I wore the gorgeous Chinese shawl. Mrs. Peter, I learned, didn't need to be guided; only occasionally did she touch my arm with her gloved fingers.

I sought for a topic to keep my mind off my fears of the sea. "Is it possible," I asked, "that you know a child of Alisette's age in town with whom she might play occasionally?"

"I'm sure some of my old acquaintances must have grandchildren," she said after a pause, "but I'm afraid I've lost touch with the people I knew in Eureka, with everyone but those in Sea Cliff House. Perhaps not too wisely."

"It was just a passing thought," I said hastily, not wishing to distress her.

"It's true every child needs a playmate. I once had hopes Alisette would not be an only child but—" She broke off and shook her head.

We continued in silence along the cliffs, barren near their edge except for here and there a stunted cypress or pine. The only tree of any size was a lone pine standing well back from the edge, and I wondered how it had been able to grow so tall with the sea wind constantly blowing.

The crash of the waves grew louder and louder, the sound conjuring up echoes of the green-water terror of my dream. I will not be afraid, I told myself firmly. Nothing can happen to me, I'm perfectly safe with solid ground under my feet.

As we neared the edge, the ground—actually rock—I walked on vibrated underfoot with each wave that slammed against the cliff, feeling not so solid, after all, but I gritted my teeth and went on. Mrs. Peter came here every day and had for years; the cliff would *not* suddenly crumble under me.

She didn't speak, nor did I. All my will was concentrated on putting one foot in front of the other, in continuing on with her. I watched my feet, not the ocean, and when she stopped, I did. We'd reached the narrow promontory where I'd first seen her with the water lashing the point and sea side of the cliff. Standing behind her, rigid with

117

fear, I fixed my eyes on her, afraid to look at the pounding, punishing sea.

Mrs. Peter cocked her head, listening. I remembered Alisette telling me the reason her grandmother came here, and I shuddered. Did she really expect to hear her dead husband's voice speaking to her from the bottom of the sea?

"I don't understand," she said so softly I barely heard her over the waves. I knew her words weren't meant for me but for another, and a chill ran along my spine. If I looked over the cliff edge as she was doing, would a seaweed-shrouded face be visible under the water?

"'The alive are dead,'" she murmured. "'and the dead, alive.' I understand your words, Peter, but your meaning is far from clear."

She was speaking to her long-lost husband as though he stood beside her! After a time she turned away and, thankfully, we began the journey back to the house. Mrs. Peter said nothing more until we reached the steps.

"I expect you think I'm an addled old woman," she said.

"No, oh, no!" I exclaimed.

She reached and, unerringly, touched my face. "You're a kind girl, Esma. There's too little kindness in this world." She started up the stairs, paused, and added, "But you really ought to overcome your fear of the sea. Perhaps you should try a daily walk along the cliff, staying away from the edge until you've gained enough confidence to go closer."

"Yes, ma'am," I mumbled unhappily, aware I'd have to do as she told me because she'd undoubtedly ask me later how her plan was working.

Before leaving her in her suite, I thanked her again for the gift of the shawl, then hurried off to find Alisette.

She was in the kitchen helping Rosie make cinnamon buns. When I came in she was setting aside her own little panful to raise.

"I'm making these for Papa," she said, "but you can have one."

"I'm sure they'll be delicious," I told her.

We climbed two flights of stairs to the schoolroom, but Alisette wasn't ready to settle down to learning her numbers.

"I saw you with Grandma Katherine," she said. "Did you hear Grandpa Peter say anything?"

"I think he speaks only to your grandmother," I said carefully.

She nodded. "Like Alexandria and me."

Certain no good would come of pursuing the subject, I distracted her by suggesting an afternoon tea party in the garden for the two of us and her dolls, adding, "But not unless we finish this lesson."

As it turned out, we had an unexpected visitor at the party in the person of Mr. Ferguson.

"Seeing young ladies at tea makes a man feel he's back in Glasgow," he commented as he surveyed the diminutive table and the four small chairs occupied by Alisette, me, Estelle, and a porcelain doll named Susan.

"You may join us, if you like," Alisette informed him, playing the role of the proper young lady to the hilt. "'Course all the chairs are taken so you'll have to sit on the grass."

"I don't know when I've had a nicer invitation," he told her, winking at me as he lowered himself to the ground beside the table.

With grave concentration, Alisette poured tea from her child's teapot into one of the tiny cups. "Sugar?" she asked.

"Just a wee touch of milk, thank you, lass."

Alisette obliged, handed him the cup of tea and

119

offered the plate of sandwiches shaped like various flowers. "Rosie says you came to fix Sea Cliff House so it won't fall into the sea," she told him.

Before answering, Mr. Ferguson swallowed his doll-sized sandwich in one bite and emptied his cup in one sip. "Did she now? Well now, lass, 'tis not so simple a matter as fixing the house. The house is fine. 'Tis the ocean waves that are the problem—the waves and the rock that make up the cliff. But don't worry that bonny wee head of yours, old Jock here's bound to find a cure, just wait and see if I don't."

He rose, setting the cup on the table. "Thank you kindly for the refreshment, Miss Nikolai. And good day to you, Miss Drake."

Alisette barely waited until he was out of earshot before demanding to know what *bonny* meant. As I told her, I pondered Mr. Ferguson's words. I took them to mean he'd found a problem—perhaps the cliff was composed of the crumbling type of rock he'd mentioned—but also a solution. A sea wall? A breakwater? Either would have to be massive to contain the violence of the waves along this section of the coast.

The next afternoon, while Alisette napped, instead of strolling in the pine grove behind the cemetery, as was my wont, I gathered my courage and ventured onto the cliff, determined to give Mrs. Peter's cure a fair try. Keeping well back from the edge, I walked toward the promontory but not onto it, for the land narrowed there to a spear point, and I'd be too close to the edge: it had been all I could do to endure the moments I'd spent there the day before with Mrs. Peter.

I returned from my walk, if not triumphant at least pleased I'd managed without undue panic, vowing that tomorrow I'd venture a teeny bit nearer to the edge.

As the days passed, I gradually inched closer to the cliff edge until, on Saturday, I decided I'd be brave enough to actually look down at the sea. Hadn't I grown accustomed to the sound of the crashing waves and the tremble underfoot? Surely I could also come to tolerate the sight of the foaming whitecaps above the green water.

Nothing could be kept a secret at Sea Cliff House, and Alisette had learned of my daily walks from Rosie. Naturally, she was unhappy because she couldn't come with me. In keeping with my decision to be as honest as possible with her, I explained why I waited until she napped.

"If I overcome my fear completely, I promise I'll take you with me for a walk along the cliffs," I finished. "But we'll have to wait and see. Meanwhile, since you're asleep when I walk, you aren't missing anything, are you?"

Though she looked far from convinced, she stopped teasing to go with me.

Saturday dawned misty. By the afternoon, though, I had to admit the mist had burned off enough to see where the cliff ended, so I'd be safe enough venturing forth. Since I feared if I didn't keep to my routine, I might find myself back at the frightened beginning when I resumed my cliffside walks, I decided to brave the weather.

I started out bravely enough, occupied by my thoughts. I'd been fretting all week over the fact I never saw Stephen anymore except at the dinner table—when he was home. He'd taken Alisette again to visit *Sea Dragon,* but not me, and he seemed to be spending a great deal of time at the mill.

This is how it should be, I told myself firmly. The less you see of Stephen, the better for everyone concerned. Sooner or later he must reconcile with Cecile and once again become her husband in more than name. That was only right and proper. You have something of your own to look forward to—tomorrow you're going riding with Gerald.

But I couldn't stop myself from wishing I'd be with Stephen instead.

As I neared the cliff edge, my pace slowed and everything fled from my mind except the worry I wouldn't have the courage to go close enough to look down at the water. Considering the lingering mist, I wouldn't be able to see the waves—would that count? I decided it would. It was the act, after all, not what I actually saw. With trepidation, I inched forward, closer and closer.

Without warning, I was struck between the shoulder blades and, unable to catch myself, sprawled forward, my head and shoulders hanging over the edge of the cliff, suspended in space. I screamed as I struggled in vain to pull myself back. With nothing for my frantic hands to grip, inexorably I slid over the edge toward the angry waves below.

Chapter 8

Unable to stop myself, I plunged headfirst over the edge of the cliff, knowing I was doomed. Below the green water waited to enclose me in a final embrace. When my clutching fingers closed over wood, I grabbed onto it desperately and, suddenly, I was hanging by one hand instead of falling. With a wild lunge, I caught what I held with my other hand. Now both hands grasped what I realized was the meager trunk of one of the twisted pines that braved the sea spume and the wind. I was saved! But for how long?

The stunted tree grew from a crevice in the cliff, and I had no way of knowing how long it could bear my weight or how long I'd have the strength to cling to it.

"Help!" I shouted, but my voice seemed lost in the mist.

From above I thought I heard shrill screaming. I feared it was only a gull, but with all my heart I prayed it was someone who'd seen me fall.

It was then I recalled I *hadn't* fallen—I'd been pushed, shoved over the edge of the cliff to drown. Fear dried my throat. If my would-be killer waited at the top, I had little or no chance for rescue.

My shoulders ached with the strain of clinging

to the tree trunk—how much longer could I hold on? Pebbles and dirt spattered my face when I looked up, and I feared they came from the tree gradually being uprooted from the pressure of my weight. Mist hid the top of the cliff.

The old Irish gardener's song went round and round in my head: "Down at the bottom of the wild green sea . . ." Would my bones, too, rest on the sea bottom?

I would die without Stephen ever knowing I loved him.

"No!" I cried. "I won't die." Whether or not danger waited above I once more shouted for help. Again and again.

No one responded. My fingers grew numb; my voice became too hoarse to continue calling. Soon, I knew, I'd lose my grip and that would be the end. I'd drown, exactly as my recurrent nightmares foretold. Despair filled me.

"Esma!" Did I really hear Stephen's voice or was it only in my head?"

"Esma!" The call came again. "Answer me!"

"Stephen?" I mumbled, only half aware.

"Louder!" he ordered.

My senses sharpened. "I'm here," I shouted.

"Keep talking, I'll locate you by your voice."

I knew my life depended on making enough noise for Stephen to find me in the mist, but I feared I was about to burst into tears in relief at knowing he was at hand and ruin my chance to be saved. I could think of nothing to distract myself except the old Irishman's song, and so I began to sing.

When I reached, "Many a sailor has left his bones," Stephen's shout came from directly above me.

"I've found her!"

Something scraped along the cliff to my left.

"I've let down a rope, Esma. Can you reach it?"

I could see the rope close by to my left, close enough to touch. But I didn't dare try. "I'll fall if I let go of the tree trunk."

He swore. "Never mind, I'll climb down. Hold on!"

If only I could!

Rocks and pebbles clattered past me, and then suddenly Stephen ws beside me. "I'm going down just past you. When I'm almost underneath, I'm going to hike up your skirts and put your legs around my waist as though I'm carrying you piggyback. After I do, you must let go of the tree, grab my shoulders, and hold tight. Do you understand?"

"Yes."

He did as he'd told me, then said, "Let go and hold onto me, Esma."

It was far more difficult than it sounded. My fingers refused to move, seemingly glued to the trunk.

"Let go!" Stephen ordered. "For the love of God, Esma, let go."

Finally I summoned up enough will to release my deathgrip on the tree and grasp Stephen's shoulders. Closing my eyes, I buried my face againt his back. Stephen was here. I didn't know how he'd get the two of us up the cliff, but whatever happened I wasn't afraid now that he was with me.

With my additional weight overbalancing him, he couldn't climb up the rope attached to his waist; he had to climb the cliff face. So slowly it didn't seem as though we were moving, he inched upward, searching for invisible toeholds and fingerholds in the face of the cliff while below us the waves slammed against the cliff in rage at being cheated of my bones.

When at last we reached the top, he ordered me to crawl over him until I was safely away from the edge. Numbly, I obeyed. As I huddled on the ground watching him, a tiny figure flung herself at me, sobbing. I hugged Alisette to me, never taking my eyes from Stephen as he heaved himself over the edge, crawled a few feet toward me and collapsed to lie gasping on the ground.

When he could, he rose to his knees and shouted, "Armin? Where the hell are you?"

Armin materialized out of the mist, leading the chestnut gelding.

"Right here. I went for Bosun like you said."

"Christ, you could have traveled to Eureka and back in the time it took. It's no thanks to you Esma's alive." He climbed to his feet and glared at Armin. "Or that I'm alive either, for that matter."

"I came as fast as I could." Armin's voice was sullen. Unbidden, Sonia's words came to my mind. *"He's Peter Nikolai's bastard."*

I remembered when Armin drove me to the house for the first time, remembered how he'd seemed to relish the possibility that *Sea Dragon* might have sunk with all hands lost. Did Armin hate his legitimate half brother, Stephen, the Nikolai heir, and wish to see him dead?

He'd have no reason to want me dead, but quite possibly it might make no difference to him whether I lived or died. I shivered.

"Oh, Miss Drake," Alisette sobbed, "I thought you'd drowned like Grandpa Peter."

My concern for her partially overcame my shock and fright, enabling me to rise and draw her to her feet. "You shouldn't be out without a coat or even a sweater," I said inanely.

"I followed you," she whispered.

"The horse is no damn use now," Stephen told

126

Armin. "You may as well take him back to the stables." As Armin turned away, Stephen moved closer to me, putting his arm around my shoulders, urging both Alisette and me toward the house.

"I hoped to have Bosun pull you up by turning the rope around the tree I anchored it to." He pointed to the only decent-sized tree in sight, the pine I'd noticed before, set back from the cliff edge. "Bosun would have had to pull me up, too, as it turned out. Easier by a long shot than climbing."

"You saved my life," I told him.

"No," he said, "the honor goes to Alsie." Reaching down, he scooped her up and settled her into the crook of his left arm, putting his right arm around me once again. I leaned against him feeling wonderfully safe and protected.

"I called to you as soon as it happened, Papa," she said, "'cause I saw you. I was hiding so Miss Drake wouldn't find me."

"Apparently Alsie wasn't napping. She'd sneaked away to surprise you," Stephen said. "I happened to be nearby and—"

"You were following Miss Drake, too," Alisette put in.

He smiled at her, "Maybe I was, at that."

"Thank God for the both of you," I said fervently.

"Then you're not mad at me?" Alisette asked.

I leaned over and kissed her cheek in answer, wishing I had the right to kiss her father as well.

By the time we reached the house, Armin had already spread the news. Mrs. Yates took charge at once, shooing us all, Stephen included, up the stairs with orders to change immediately into dry clothes. Hot drinks would be sent to our rooms, and we were to swallow every drop.

"You wouldn't want to get pneumonia on top of what else happened, would you?" she demanded.

Alisette, after her father put her down in her room and left, lunged at me, clutching my leg. "Don't go!" she cried. "I want you to stay here."

"Now, now," Mrs. Yates chided her. "I'll tend to you. Miss Drake needs to change her own clothes and rest."

Alisette began to cry, holding to me all the harder.

"Never mind,." I told Mrs. Yates, alarmed by the wheeze in Alisette's breathing. "I'll bring her clothes into my room, and we'll both change there."

She shrugged and went out.

Some minutes later both Alisette and I were clean and dry and snuggled under the quilt on my bed with pillows propped under our heads, sipping hot chocolate, the rag doll between us. Lassitude crept over me, a weakness so great I could scarcely put down my cup.

Alisette set her cup carefully on the tray beside the bed and edged nearer to me. Leaning even closer, she whispered in my ear.

"It was Mama."

Groggy and only half aware, I raised my eyebrows, not understanding.

"She pushed you," Alisette whispered. "I saw her. I was afraid to tell Papa."

Before I had time to be stunned by what she'd said, she began to wheeze in earnest. I came alert, pushed aside all other concerns, and gathered her into my arms.

"You don't need to have an attack," I said soothingly. "You saved me. I'm here safe and sound, and you're safe with me. I love you and your papa loves you. We'll never let anything bad happen to

128

you. Safe, you're safe, and everything's all right."

I kept murmuring all the comforting words I could find, finally singing a lullaby with which I used to put the orphanage babies to sleep, nonsense words with no real meaning. I didn't even know where I learned them:

"Bhayu bhayushki bhayu
Bhayu detochke moyu—bhayu . . ."

Alisette relaxed in my arms, her breathing quieted, and her eyelids drooped shut. I eased her onto the pillow and slid down beside her, thankful she'd avoided a full-fledged attack. Though horrified at what she'd told me, the aftereffects of my terrible experience had caught up with me. I was too exhausted to do anything but fall into a deep sleep.

I woke to a tap on the door. It was Sonia with a tray for Alisette and me. After setting the food on a small bamboo table, she drew the curtains over night-dark windows.

Glancing at the still-sleeping Alisette, Sonia said, "Didn't I warn you to be careful?"

I put my finger to my lips, determined not to discuss the accident with Sonia while Alisette was with me. Not that I meant to tell her what the child had said. A shiver ran along my spine as I remembered.

Sonia shrugged. "I'll be back."

While I roused Alisette, Sonia arranged chairs by the table for us and then left.

I didn't feel hungry but, wanting Alisette to eat, I began sipping the hot chicken soup with pretended enthusiasm. My appetite returned with the taste of Rosie's savory broth, and we both finished our soup and did justice to the bacon and cheese sandwiches.

"I wish you could always eat supper with me," Alisette said wistfully.

I was glad to see the color had returned to her face. While nothing could make her forget what she'd seen, at least she'd managed not to have an attack, proving to me that not only could her asthma sometimes be brought on by her emotions but also that she could learn to control the attacks.

I didn't want to think about what she'd witnessed. I'd been too near death to want to relive the experience. And what was I to do about what Alisette had confided in me? Hard as it was to believe Cecile would push me, I knew the child wouldn't lie about such a dreadful happening.

"Alisette," I said, when I'd set the tray and the used dishes outside my door for Sonia's convenience, "We must talk." I sat in the rocker and pulled her onto my lap.

"You remember what you whispered to me?" I asked.

I felt her tense. "Yes." Her voice was very small.

"Well, I've thought it over and I think your mother must have meant only to scare me, and she was as frightened as I when I went over the edge. I'm sure she's sorry."

I wasn't sure of anything of the sort, but Alisette desperately needed to be reassured. No matter how neglectful Cecile was to her daughter, Alisette loved and admired her.

Alisette, not looking at me, didn't say anything.

"So," I went on, "here's what we'll do. You and I are going to keep this a secret between us."

"All right." I felt her relax a little.

"We won't tell anyone, not even your papa. And you must not mention to your mother that you saw her. Nor will you and I speak of it again to each other."

"I won't tell!" she said fervently.

"Good. Now it's time for you to get into your nightgown and for me to decide what bedtime

130

story to tell you and Estelle."

"We'd like the one about Princess Auria. You know—the story Papa heard from Pegleg Louie." Alisette nestled against me, playing with my fingers. "When I thought you fell in the ocean, I prayed a porpoise from the Sandwich Islands would come and save you."

"Instead, you and your papa saved me." I hugged her. "Now we're all safe and sound."

But after Alisette was asleep in her own bed with Estelle clutched protectively close, I had to face the fact that I might be safe for the moment, but I still had Cecile with which to contend. I couldn't believe she hadn't meant me to die, and I feared she'd try again if I didn't leave Sea Cliff House. What was I to do if I wanted to remain here?

If I claimed she'd pushed me, she'd deny it, and Alisette would be forced to say she'd seen her mother's murderous act. Even then Cecile probably wouldn't admit the truth; I could almost hear her insisting I'd put words into the child's mouth. Would anyone believe me? And what would happen to poor Alisette, caught in the middle of the furor?

No, I couldn't publicly accuse Cecile. How about privately? Would it stop her if I told her I knew she was responsible for my fall? I didn't think so. She'd know very well that without a witness I couldn't prove anything.

Once in bed, I found myself wide awake, still pondering what to do and more than a bit nervous on top of that. What if Cecile crept into my room while I slept?

Don't be a ninny, I scolded myself. How could she harm you? Somehow I couldn't see her trying to smother me or wielding a dagger—guile was her weapon. She might try to poison me, but I'd be watchful about what I ate or drank from now on.

131

And I'd pay special attention to who was behind me.

Of course I could always leave. If I were ready to abandon Alisette. But how could I abandon her? I tossed and turned, unable to find a solution, while at the back of my mind crouched the fear that, if I did fall asleep, my nightmare waited with renewed menace, considering my near escape from death.

Finally I sat up, lit the lamp, propped myself on the pillows, and picked up a compilation of English and Scottish ballads, hoping to distract myself by reading. I'd borrowed the books from the downstairs library in hopes I'd find one or two I could recite to Alisette.

I opened the book at random and the title "Kissin'" caught my eye. Whether appropriate for Alisette or not, it interested *me*. I whispered the words aloud:

> "Some say kissin's ae sin
> But I say, not at a';
> For it's been in the warld
> Ever sin' there were twa.
> If it werena lawfu',
> Lawyers wadna' 'low it;
> If it werena haly,
> Meenisters wadna' dae it;
> If it werena modest,
> Maidens wadna' taste it;
> If it werena plenty,
> Poor folk couldna' hae it."

I noted that the author was anonymous, like so many of the old ballads. I smiled as I stared at the lines until they blurred and I saw Stephen's face instead. Kissing him hadn't felt in the slightest sinful: the kiss had been the most wonderful event in my life.

Without warning, the door opened. I gasped as Stephen stepped inside, shutting the door behind him.

"I couldn't go to bed until I made certain you were all right," he told me, advancing to the side of the bed.

"I—I'm fine. I was just—just reading." How breathless I was! I knew he shouldn't be in my room and yet I was so delighted to see him I couldn't summon words to tell him to leave.

He lifted the book from my grasp, glanced at the open pages, and grinned. My face flamed.

Putting the book aside, he sat on the side of the bed and took my hand. All trace of a smile left his face as he looked into my eyes. "I know now I couldn't bear to lose you," he said softly.

My heart pounded at his words. He did care for me!

"If I could only tell you—" He stopped and shook his head. "Esma, trust me. Somehow everything will come right with time."

I was willing to trust him, but how could things come right when he was married?

"You're so very sweet," he said huskily. "So very lovely."

As I gazed up at him, mesmerized by the warm glow in his eyes, I moistened my suddenly dry lips with the tip of my tongue. With a groan he reached for me, gathered me into his arms, and kissed me.

I was lost the moment his lips met mine.

I learned lips were only a part of a lover's kiss as Stephen's tongue invaded my mouth, warm and caressing, infusing me with a liquid fire that melted my very bones. The silken curls of his hair tangled in my fingers. I couldn't get enough of touching him.

He trailed burning kisses along my throat and

upper breasts and then, after the ribbons of my nightgown yielded to his touch, he put his mouth to my bared breast. I moaned with a pleasure so exquisite it was almost pain. I pressed him closer.

I murmured that I loved him. I wanted him to know, I wanted to give myself up to him entirely, I wanted him to go on and on and never stop. His hand slipped beneath my gown, caressing me in secret places until I felt I would die with rapture.

"Stephen," I whispered, "oh, Stephen."

I'd never dreamed being in a man's arms would be so wonderful, but now that he'd shown me, I was also certain no man but Stephen could ever make me feel this wonder. Together we floated in a magic realm between heaven and earth. There was no yesterday or tomorrow, there was only this sublime moment, our moment.

"You're beautiful," he breathed, "so beautiful. Only you."

He eased down beside me, pushing the bed-covers aside so there was nothing between us except the thin batiste of my gown and the clothes he wore. I thrilled when he held me against his hard man's body, clinging to him with eager ardor. I longed to be even closer, to somehow become a part of him.

I drowned in his deep, passionate kiss. My arms wound tightly about him. Nothing had ever tasted so good as his mouth, his tongue. Nothing ever would.

"I want you, Esma." His voice was low, husky, his warm breath teased my ear.

"Yes," I murmured, knowing I could deny him nothing.

Suddenly he thrust me away, swung around, and sat on the side of the bed, feet on the floor, his back to me, his head in his hands. Unable to bear the loss, I rose to my knees and leaned my head on his shoulder.

"Stephen?"

"I can't do this to you," he rasped. "I must not. Don't touch me, Esma, or I won't have the will to leave you."

"I don't want you to leave me."

"Oh, God," he groaned. "Do you think *I* want to?" He eased me back among the pillows gently but firmly, pulled the covers to my chin, then got to his feet.

"We must never be alone together again," he said, "for I can't trust myself not to take advantage of your innocence."

"But I love you!" I cried.

He closed his eyes in a brief grimace of pain. "Don't say those words to me when I'm fighting not to touch you. You have no idea how much I long to hold you, hold you forever, and never let you go. I should never have come to your room. God help me, I won't from now on. Good night, Esma."

I stared at the door he'd closed behind him, hardly believing he was gone. My entire being throbbed with my need for him, with an ache only he could soothe. Why had he left me so abruptly?

The knob turned, the door edged open. I held my breath, my heart beating faster in anticipation. He'd come back!

Sonia's blond head poked inside the room. "I saw him leave," she whispered, slipping all the way in. "Didn't I tell you he'd come to your room?" She sauntered to the bed and stared down at me. "Well?"

I grew conscious of my disordered hair, and I thanked heaven the covers hid me, remembering I was naked to the waist.

Sonia sat on the edge of the bed. "More than kisses this time, I'll bet." She smiled.

Under Sonia's assessing eye, I felt soiled, and I grew angry that she'd come to spoil what had been so beautiful. "He came to ask if I was all right after my accident." I hoped my frown and sullen tone would make her decide to go away.

"Sure he did. And I'm the Queen of Sheba."

I gathered myself to make a scathing remark, but before the words rose to my tongue, Sister Samara's face flashed before me and I could hear her saying, "Marriage is a sacrament that no man or woman should defile."

Hadn't I done just that? Defiled Stephen's marriage? How could I blame Cecile for what she'd tried to do to me when I well knew what had driven her to attempt murder? It was my fault. Though I hadn't deliberately tried to lure Stephen away from his wife, I certainly had done nothing to stop him from making love to me.

"Oh, Sonia," I cried, sitting up and clutching my gown around me. "I can't stay here. I must leave now, tonight!"

"Are you crazy?" she demanded. "What's the matter with you?"

"It's all my fault."

"I suppose next you'll tell me it wasn't an accident, that you jumped off the cliff on purpose."

I stared at her, aghast. "I'd never do such a thing!"

"Don't you think I know it, you goose? You weren't at fault because Stephen climbed into your bed, either. It was his. Men being what they are, it had to happen sooner or later."

"No, I mean it's my fault for coming between a man and his wife. Cecile has a right to hate me."

Sonia rolled her eyes. "Tell me, what rights does an adulteress have?"

136

"An adulteress?" I didn't understand.

"Cecile's a first-class bitch, and don't you forget it. What makes you so sure she's a wronged wife? The fact is, Cecile don't deserve a loving husband. I saw her with my own eyes in the ruins of the church making love with Gerald. And you can be sure it wasn't the only time. She and oh-so-helpful-to-the-family Gerald have been lovers for over a year. The last thing she wanted was for the captain to come sailing home. Grow up, Esma."

I gaped at her. Cecile and Gerald? But almost immediately, I sensed it was true. Alisette's innocent prattle and Mrs. Yates's hints about Cecile and Gerald had prepared me to accept what Sonia said. Hadn't I come across Cecile in the ruins once myself and wondered if she had an assignation there?

"Why should Cecile care if the captain keeps to his own room?" Sonia went on bitterly. "Gerald's always available." She spat his name.

I was shocked. "Surely they're not still—?" I broke off, unable to say the words.

Sonia shrugged. "Cecile's not one to deny herself. Nor is he."

She spoke with such venom I couldn't help but wonder if, at one time, Sonia had fancied Gerald.

While I didn't doubt what Sonia had told me, I began to wonder why Cecile would care what Stephen did if she were in love with Gerald. Would she care enough to try to murder me? Unless, of course, she wanted the full attention of both men. Was it possible she'd noticed Gerald's recent interest in me and resented it?

"I'm supposed to go riding with him on Sunday," I muttered without thinking.

"With the captain?"

I shook my head, sorry I'd opened my mouth. Sonia smiled knowingly. "So Gerald's after you,

137

too, is he? Watch out, that's my advice. He don't play fair.''

My mind whirled in confusion. What should I do? If I left Sea Cliff House, how would Alisette fare without me? Cecile had insisted her daughter would survive, but surviving was not the same thing as growing up strong and happy.

Stephen would look after Alisette, but he'd soon sail off and the child would be left behind. As for Gerald, he might care enough about Alisette to see to her welfare but not like I would. She needed me.

"Come to think of it," Sonia said, "Gerald's going after you could be to pull the wool over the captain's eyes. See, if the captain thinks Gerald's pursuing you, he won't catch on about Gerald and Cecile."

I supposed it was possible. So much had happened to me in the past few hours that my mind seemed as misty as the weather outside. I couldn't trust any thought to come clear.

"I'll postpone my decision about leaving," I said at last.

"There you go." Sonia patted my cheek and rose.

"One more thing," I said, feeling myself flush. I plowed on, face aflame, not wanting to discuss my private life but determined she wouldn't leave with the wrong impression. "We didn't—that is, Stephen and I didn't—well, we—"

"You're still an innocent, is that what you're trying to say?"

I nodded. "And I don't intend to ever be with him alone again."

She shook her head. "You know what they say about good intentions. I've been down that road myself." She opened the door. "Pleasant dreams, Esma. Let's hope we don't wind up in hell together."

Chapter 9

The next morning, Sunday, I awoke, started to stretch, and groaned. My desperate clinging to the trunk of that tree on the cliff face had left my arms, shoulders, and upper back so stiff and sore that movement was painful. I'd noticed a slight ache before I fell asleep, but nothing like this.

With slow and careful maneuvering, I was able to wash and dress, but I knew I could never manage even so placid a mount as the gray mare. I'd be forced to postpone riding with Gerald.

Rather than being unhappy, I was relieved. What Sonia had told me on her late-night visit had left me convinced I'd be wise to stay away from Gerald as well as Stephen.

As usual on a Sunday, Mrs. Peter, Alisette, and I shared the Nikolai carriage while Armin drove us into Eureka for early mass at St. Bernard's. Either Mrs. Peter hadn't been told of my accident or, more likely, didn't care to discuss what had happened in front of Alisette because she made no mention of it.

"Mrs. Yates has made me aware that you should have some new gowns made up," she told me. "I'm terribly sorry I didn't inquire earlier into the state of your wardrobe. It was most remiss of me; I should have realized that as an orphan you'd have no money for clothes. I've instructed Mrs. Yates to help you choose the yardage for two dinner dresses, a suit for Sundays, and four day dresses. She's also to assist you in shopping for the necessary underclothing, shoes, gloves, and a new hat. Please let me know if you require anything more."

I was stunned by her generosity. So many clothes! "I really don't need—" I began, then stopped, recalling her admonition about accepting gifts graciously. "Thank you," I said. "You're very thoughtful."

She smiled. "I'm sure you're always neat and clean, but a young woman needs to be able to dress attractively, and I'll enjoy making that possible for you."

"Miss Drake told me she used to have a velvet muff," Alisette put in. "It was brown, just the color of my eyes. Maybe we could find her another muff like that, Grandma."

"The color of your eyes?" Mrs. Peter said to her. "What a lovely brown shade that muff must have been. By all means choose a muff, Esma, and consider it a present from Alisette."

Alisette beamed at both of us. "Miss Drake isn't real pretty, like Mama," she told her grandmother, "but it makes you feel good to look at her."

Tears came to my eyes at her words. I couldn't have asked for higher praise.

Mrs. Peter patted the child's head. "Looking at her and listening to her has certainly done *you* some good."

"Papa says I'm the sweetest girl in all the world." Alisette's tone was complacent.

Mrs. Peter raised her eyebrows. "Your papa doesn't know you as well as Miss Drake and I do. I'm fond of you Alisette, but sweet is not the word I'd pick."

140

Nor I. Sweet was too bland and prissy a word for the energetic, bright, sometimes naughty but always loveable little girl who was in my care. But obviously Alisette treasured her father's description of her.

As always when we drove into town, the yellow gravel spread on some of the streets caught my eye. Stephen had told me the gravel had once been ship's ballast, hence the odd color. I found it rather attractive.

"How many people live in Eureka?" I asked Mrs. Peter.

"Thirty-five hundred or so, I believe. The town has certainly grown from the original twelve houses in Eighteen Fifty. Of course, Captain Alexi came into the area before the town had even one house. There's an old journal of his somewhere— written in Russian, of course—that claims Humboldt Bay was first entered in Eighteen Hundred Six by a Russian sea-otter hunter named Slabodchikov."

Alisette began chanting the Russian name, apparently enjoying the sound.

Reminded of the sword we'd found in the attic, I asked about it.

"I haven't thought about that old Russian sword for years," Mrs. Peter said. "My husband believed it had been given to an ancestor by one of the early czars. He liked to pretend it was Peter the Great, the czar he was named after, and, perhaps, it was."

She lapsed into silence, no doubt recalling happier days when her husband still lived. I looked from the carriage window at the rows of frame houses, small and close together by the docks, larger and with more spacious grounds farther away. The town was built on very flat land

141

near the bay with the red bluff to the south the only high ground until the headlands where Sea Cliff House stood.

Eureka seemed a pleasant town, and I thought I'd much rather live here than at the Nikolai mansion. Not that I'd leave Sea Cliff House, not as long as Alisette needed me.

After church, Alisette and I went up to the schoolroom where, along with Estelle, we took turns asking questions and giving answers from the worn child's catechism I'd brought from the orphanage. When boots on the stairs warned of a male visitor, my treacherous heart began to beat wildly in anticipation of seeing Stephen.

"Good morning, ladies," Gerald said as he entered the room. "Not studying on a Sunday, I hope."

Concealing my disappointment, I shook my head. "We're merely learning the catechism by heart."

"I heard about your accident yesterday, Esma," he said. "Thank God you were rescued. Are you all right?"

"Yes," I said, "though I'm afraid the experience has left me too stiff and sore to ride today."

"I'm sorry to hear of your discomfort." Gerald turned to Alisette. "When Miss Drake recovers, perhaps the three of us can go on a picnic. How does that sound?"

"Oh yes!" Alisette agreed.

"I'm sure you won't mind if I take her for a stroll in the garden today while you nap. All right?" He kept his attention fixed on Alisette.

"I guess so." She wasn't enthusiastic. Alisette hated to miss anything.

"Good! Then it's all settled." He smiled at her and then at me.

I resented not having a chance to accept or refuse, but I could hardly say so in front of the child.

"I'll see you later in the garden," he told me and retreated.

"You don't look like you want to stroll in the garden with Uncle Gerald," Alisette observed.

Hastily, I smoothed my frown. "I don't mind," I said, more or less the truth. What I hoped was that Cecile wouldn't mind.

Exactly what had motivated her attack still puzzled me. I wished I understood why she hated me so. Was it because Stephen paid me more attention than she liked? Or because Gerald was courteous to me at dinner? These reasons didn't seem enough for her to try to kill me. This morning in church I had said a prayer for the three of us— Stephen, Cecile, and me.

Wanting to forestall any more comments by Alisette, I said, "Let's begin again with the first question. Who made the world?"

"It's Estelle's turn to answer," she said.

Estelle was still with her when I tucked Alisette into bed for her afternoon nap.

"Sing me that song with the funny words," she begged. Realizing, after a moment, she must mean the nonsense lullaby, I told her I would if she closed her eyes first.

Once I was certain she slept, I eased from the room, collected my hat, gloves, and the Chinese shawl, and descended the front stairs. Letting myself out the door, I walked slowly around the house to the gardens surrounding the east wing.

Gerald stood by the pond, one foot on the coping, apparently studying the goldfish. When

143

he saw me, he straightened and tipped his hat. He was soberly dressed in a dark gray frock coat with matching trousers, the somber color setting off his fair hair. Any woman would consider him an attractive man.

"Have you ever pondered the uselessness of goldfish?" he asked by way of greeting.

"But they're so colorful," I objected, "and so graceful to watch. Surely something that gives pleasure to the eye isn't useless."

He shrugged. "I might have agreed with you once. Now I'm afraid I demand a bit more of living creatures than merely being attractive." I sensed a hidden meaning in his words, one I wasn't eager to explore. Superficial conversations were safer.

"The sun is pleasantly warm for a change," I said. "I'm so glad the mist has left us for the time being."

"Did you really trip and fall yesterday?" he asked abruptly.

Did he suspect I'd been pushed? I hesitated, hating to lie but unwilling to tell the entire truth. "The first I knew I was hanging in space," I said evasively, shivering at the memory. "I'd really rather not talk about it."

"I'm sorry. You see, after the accident with the angel, I couldn't help but wonder." His gaze probed mine.

I wondered myself, but I didn't want to discuss either accident with Gerald. Searching for a diverting topic, I said, "I understand from Mrs. Peter that your father was Captain Peter's partner in the mill."

"My father owned the mill!"

I blinked at the intensity in Gerald's tone, unable to think of a suitable reply.

"Peter Nikolai bought him out," Gerald added

144

after a short pause. His clipped tone didn't encourage the subject.

"I see," I said, wondering if we'd be able to find any topic that suited us both.

Gerald offered his arm. "Shall we walk?"

I nodded, laid my fingers on his coat sleeve, and we strolled between the roses in silence, inhaling their sweet fragrance.

"You don't see at all," Gerald said at last. "How could you when you never met Captain Peter? Ruthless is the kindest word I have for him. Like their green eyes, ruthlessness carries over from one generation of the Nikolais to the next. It's no secret that Captain Peter ruined my father."

"Yet you still work for the family."

"Through Mrs. Peter's intervention. I had no choice; after my father died I had to support my mother somehow. The captain didn't care what became of us, but Mrs. Peter did. She's a wonderful woman—but then she's only a Nikolai by marriage. I've tried to give her good value in return for her kindness."

"She speaks very highly of you."

"When she asked me to come and live at Sea Cliff House after Captain Peter went down with his ship, at first I refused. But then I saw she truly needed me, and so here I am." He smiled at me. "Like you, I'd prefer not to dwell on the past. Let's look ahead to the future."

"And what do you foresee for yourself?"

"Ah, that's a secret I'm not ready to reveal to anyone. As for you, I predict a rosy future. You'll prosper and be happy beyond your wildest dreams."

I smiled. "I quite like your fortunetelling."

"It's no more than the truth."

A current of seriousness ran beneath his banter.

145

Surely he didn't actually believe in foreseeing and such superstitions.

I caught a glimpse of Armin slipping through the gate in the wall separating the grounds from the stables and, though I didn't mean to, I stared at him. Having heard Sonia's account, I could see his Nikolai features quite clearly, though, in my opinion, somewhat debased.

"So you've heard," Gerald said.

I turned to him, eyebrows raised, embarrassed to have been caught gaping at Armin.

"There can be no other reason for your sudden interest in that lout," he said. "Someone's told you he's Captain Peter's by-blow."

I nodded, a bit shamefaced.

"His working at Sea Cliff House is another example of Mrs. Peter's kindness. The captain wouldn't have anything to do with the boy, but after his ship went down, she listened to Mrs. Yates and brought Armin here."

"Then she—knows?"

"She doesn't miss much despite her blindness."

The sun was warm, easing my aches, and I always enjoyed talking to Gerald because he seemed so understanding. Unfortunately, I couldn't shut away the possibility Cecile was watching us from one of the windows, watching and plotting her next move. This made me uneasy and prevented me from taking pleasure in the fine weather and Gerald's company. I was also not entirely comfortable about Alisette's health.

"I'd better check on Alisette," I said.

"Mrs. Yates is perfectly capable."

"Yes, but Alisette started to have one of her spells last night. I don't like to be away from her too long." It was the truth.

He shrugged. "I can't complain of *your* usefulness—though, alas, not to me. I have to agree the child does need you. I know you'd prefer to have Alisette with us at our future meetings and, while I'd rather have you to myself, I'm willing to concede the point. For the time being, at least."

Gerald was *so* understanding. I squeezed his arm in thanks before saying, "I really must go to her now."

I tossed my hat and gloves on my dresser and hurried into Alisette's room. Her bedcovers were badly rumpled, and Estelle lay sprawled on the floor, but there was no sign of Alisette. I called her name. No answer.

I drew my breath in alarm. Had she suddenly taken ill? Mrs. Yates might have hurried her to the kitchen for the steam treatment. Rushing down the back stairs, I burst into the kitchen, startling Rosie, who was rolling out pie crust. There was no one else in the room.

"Where's Alisette?" I demanded.

"Isn't she in her bed?" Rosie asked.

I shook my head. "Where's Mrs. Yates?"

"Mrs. Peter called for her, and she sent Sonia to listen for the child. Have you asked Sonia?"

"I haven't *seen* Sonia."

Rosie frowned. "Probably lollygagging with that Mr. Ferguson somewheres. Chances are Alisette's with the pair of 'em, seeing and hearing what she hadn't ought to see and hear at her age."

Why hadn't Alisette taken Estelle with her? I wondered. Ever since the rag doll had been lost in the graveyard that one time, Alisette carried her everywhere. She'd never leave her beloved doll tossed carelessly on the floor. Tendrils of fear curled along my spine.

Where was Alisette?

Before I checked Sonia's room, I hurried to the

library, just in case Alisette might have been looking for her father and found him there. The library was empty.

I ran back upstairs and found Sonia's room empty. On my way to Mr. Ferguson's room, I noticed Cecile descending the front staircase. Alisette was not with her. When I reached Mr. Ferguson's door, I knocked and, when there was no answer, tried the knob. The door was locked, making me almost certain Sonia was inside with him. I called her name, waited, and called again.

"Sonia, do you have Alisette with you? Answer me!"

After an eternity, the lock clicked and Sonia edged the door open enough to peer at me. "Would I be stupid enough to bring her in here?" she muttered angrily.

"Then where is she?"

"In bed sound asleep, the last I saw her."

"She's not there now. You were supposed to be watching her!"

"Christ, you might know something would happen. She's run off again I suppose."

"You've got to help me find her, Sonia. Now!"

"All right, all right. Give me a minute." She closed the door, leaving me waiting impatiently in the corridor.

When she finally came into the hall, Jock Ferguson was behind her. Both of them looked somewhat disheveled.

"Y'say the wee lassie's gone missing?" he asked.

"I can't find her."

"Can I be of help?"

I thought a moment. "Could you search the gardens and the old graveyard by the ruined church? Alisette likes to play in those places."

He nodded, glanced at Sonia, then said to me, "I'll be off, then."

148

As he strode toward the staircase, I said to Sonia, "You take the upstairs, including the schoolroom, and I'll search downstairs." There was no use berating her for her negligence; the important thing was to find Alisette and make sure she was all right.

As I went from one of the downstairs rooms to the next, looking in each, I tried to think where Alisette might have gone. She knew I was in the garden, so she wouldn't have been searching for me. She wasn't with her mother. Had Stephen taken her somewhere?

I heard Cecile playing the piano before I reached the music room and recognized the tune as "Greensleeves." I glanced in as I passed and saw Gerald with her, leaning on the curve of the grand piano as she played. Alisette wasn't in the room.

When I came into the kitchen again, Mrs. Yates and Sonia were there with Rosie.

"You didn't find her?" Mrs. Yates asked.

I shook my head. "She didn't go to visit her grandmother, then?" I asked.

Mrs. Yates shook her head. "Do you suppose she took it into her head to go exploring in the west-wing attic again?" she asked.

"I thought the attic was kept locked," I said.

"It is. But last week I sent Sonia up to give the place a quick clean." Mrs. Yates frowned at Sonia. "Did you lock up when you left?"

"I most certainly did." Sonia's tone had the defiant ring of someone who felt she was in the wrong.

"Go and make sure," Mrs. Yates ordered. After Sonia left the kitchen, she muttered, "I knew from the first she was trouble, but Mr. Gerald wanted her here, so what could I do?"

In spite of my worry over Alisette, I was startled by her words. "Mr. Gerald?" I echoed.

149

"Sonia was his housekeeper before he came to live at Sea Cliff House. At least that's what he called her." Mrs. Yates's expression left little doubt she thought Sonia had been something quite different.

I dismissed any speculation about Gerald and Sonia. We had to find Alisette!

"Do you think Captain Stephen might have taken Alisette with him?" I asked.

Rosie answered for her. "I don't see how. Armin himself told me the captain rode off alone. In a black mood, he was, according to Armin."

Her speaking of Armin reminded me of Sir Toby. Perhaps Alisette had gone to visit her pony. I hurried outside to look for her at the stables. But she wasn't there, and Armin denied having seen her. On my way back to the house, I met Jock Ferguson returning from the cemetery.

"Nary a sign of the wee lassie," he reported as he walked with me toward the side door.

The clatter of hoofs stopped me before we reached the house. I turned, saw Stephen riding up the circular drive toward the front entrance, and waved frantically. He swerved Bosun toward us.

"Alisette's missing!" I cried when he was within earshot.

He reined in and looked down at us. "For how long?"

"Over an hour, by now," I said. "Mr. Ferguson's looked in the church ruins and she's not there."

"Nor in the graveyard or the gardens," Jock Ferguson added.

"She—she didn't take Estelle with her," I told Stephen, my voice trembling. "Her rag doll. She never goes anywhere without the doll."

Stephen dismounted. "Would you take him to the stables for me, Ferguson?" he asked.

"Ay, Captain." Jock swung into the saddle and rode off.

"Have you searched the house?" Stephen asked me.

I nodded, fighting back tears. This was no time to cry.

"How did it happen no one was watching her?" he asked.

I bit my lip, feeling desperately guilty. "She was napping. I took a walk in the gardens. Mrs. Yates thought Sonia was keeping an eye on Alisette but Sonia was—busy elsewhere. When I went to Alisette's room, she wasn't there, and her doll was sprawled on the floor." I looked at Stephen earnestly. "She'd never go off and leave Estelle on the floor. Where can she be?"

Stephen laid a gentle hand on my shoulder. "It's not your fault, Esma."

"But it is!" I cried. "I never should have left her."

He gave me a not-so-gentle shake. "Keep your head, don't waste time blaming yourself. What do you think could have happened to Alsie?"

"I don't know!" I wailed.

"If anyone can find her, you can. Calm down and go over every possibility." His hand on my elbow, he began leading me toward the house. "The first thing to do is call everyone together and mount a systematic search."

Within minutes, Stephen had gathered us all, including Molly and Armin, into the parlor, assigning each of us a specific area to search. Even his mother was to go over her own quarters carefully.

"It's all Miss Drake's fault," Cecile insisted when he came to her. "She can't be trusted. I knew it from the first."

"It's no more her fault than yours," Stephen

151

said, a tinge of bitterness in his voice. "If you paid the slightest attention to your daughter this wouldn't have happened But this is no time for blame—we have work to do."

I was given the west wing and so I accompanied Mrs. Peter up the stairs. As we passed the tower door, it struck me no one had mentioned the tower. Of course it was kept locked and no one ever went there. Still . . .

"Does Mrs. Yates have a key to the tower?" I asked Mrs. Peter.

"Not so far as I know. I believe my husband's key is the only one in existence, and I keep that hidden. Alisette would have no access to the key."

"It's the only place we haven't already looked," I said.

"But the child's afraid of the tower. She'd never go there alone."

I suspected Mrs. Peter was right, and yet I persisted. "Would you mind giving me the key, so we can be sure?" I asked.

Mrs. Peter hesitated. "I promised him no one would ever visit the tower while I was alive," she said finally. "How can I break that promise?" I knew she meant Captain Peter, and I was stumped. How could I find an argument to overcome a promise to the dead?

"Alisette is his granddaughter," I said at last. "If he were here, wouldn't he look in the tower for her?"

Mrs. Peter touched my arm. "You may be right. God knows Alisette is an inquisitive and adventurous child. I mustn't refuse you my key if there's a chance she may have found another key and somehow locked herself inside the tower."

Once the large brass key was in my hand, I persuaded Mrs. Peter not to accompany me to the tower since I sensed she was too distraught to make the effort. The fact the tower was to be opened, coupled with Alisette's disappearance, was too much for her.

When I faced the mahogany door with its detailed carvings of mermaids and strange sea beasts, a sudden dread crept over me, a feeling that what lay behind the door was better not disturbed. My hand shook as I tried the knob. The door as I expected, was locked. I fitted the key into the polished brass lock but found it difficult to turn. Surely a five year old wouldn't have the strength to unlock the door. Yet I didn't turn back. I'd never forgive myself if I didn't look everywhere for Alisette, no matter how unlikely the place.

The massive door creaked open, and I peered up at a dark, spiral staircase. Dim light slanting down from above revealed folds of cloth dangling from a metal step halfway to the top. I took a deep breath and, clutching the key firmly, started climbing. As soon as I let go of the door, it swung shut, making me feel trapped, key or not. When I reached the cloth I picked it up and found myself holding Alisette's morning star quilt. Until that moment I hadn't realized it was missing from her bed. She surely wouldn't have dragged the quilt with her. But that meant someone else had. Who? And for what sinister reason?

"Alisette!" I cried, my voice quavering with fear.

"Miss Drake?" Her voice came hesitantly from high above. "I'm scared, Miss Drake!"

"I'm coming, Alisette," I called, winding around the spiral as rapidly as I could climb.

I found her huddled on a window seat in the dusty, moldy-smelling round room at the top of the stairs. She sprang up when she saw me and ran into my arms.

Hugging her to me, I quickly scanned the

sparsely furnished room. A round Oriental rug in glowing deep reds and blues covered the floor, but other than a brass telescope, the cushioned window seats, and a small round brass table badly in need of polishing, there was nothing else in the room.

"The bad man brought me here," Alisette whispered, as though afraid he were waiting below.

"What bad man?" I asked.

"The same one who took Estelle and put her in the graveyard." She clutched me tightly. "Is he gone?"

"There's no bad man here now," I said soothingly. "Did you see him?"

She shook her head. "I was taking my nap. Then I was all wrapped in my quilt so I could hardly breathe, and he was carrying me. Then I was on those funny steps, and I crawled out of the quilt and tried to open the door. It was locked. I was afraid to yell 'cause he might've come back. So I climbed up here. I was scared, Miss Drake."

"You were very brave," I told her.

With her clinging around my neck, I cautiously made my way down the spiral staircase. At the bottom I found myself again reluctant to open the door, wondering if danger waited on the other side. Knowing my fears to be groundless, I pushed through the door, carrying Alisette.

The first person I saw was Stephen, rushing up the stairs two at a time.

"Papa!" Alisette cried, reaching toward him.

He took her from me, holding her close.

"A bad man locked me in the tower," she told him. "But Miss Drake came and got me."

Mrs. Yates, bustling along the hall from the east wing, joined us. After asking the housekeeper to let the others know Alisette had been found,

154

Stephen carried his daughter to her room where she immediately clutched Estelle to her chest.

Alisette's answers to her father's questions revealed no more than she had told me. Actually, she wasn't even certain the "bad man" *was* a man, since she hadn't caught even a glimpse of the person who'd abducted her. She was convinced, though, it had to be the same person who'd stolen her doll.

"'Cause he doesn't like me and Estelle, Papa, he wants to scare us. Can't you make him stop?"

"When I find him, I'll see to it he never scares you again." Stephen's voice was grim.

Sonia brought up a tray with hot chocolate and raisin cookies for Alisette, and while she was setting it next to the bed, Stephen took me aside.

"What could be the point of locking Alsie in the tower?" he asked in a low tone. "She may have been frightened, but she wasn't hurt, and we were bound to find her before she came to any serious harm."

"I don't understand it at all," I admitted.

"Thank God you thought of looking there as soon as you did."

"Papa," Alisette called to him, "Estelle and I don't want to sleep alone tonight. We want to sleep with Miss Drake."

"Is that all right with you?" he asked me, his eyes holding mine for a long, lingering moment, their message as clear as if he'd said the words aloud: *I wish I could, too.*

Chapter 10

The next morning Mrs. Yates told me that Mrs. Peter had invited Alisette to her suite and would be keeping her there until after lunch.

Not knowing exactly how to spend this unexpected free time, I made up my mind I wouldn't huddle in my room in fear of what Cecile might do. Forewarned was forearmed, and she wouldn't catch me napping again.

The sun had burned away all traces of fog, so it was a beautiful morning, a day to be outside. While I didn't feel like strolling along the edge of the cliffs, there was no reason not to take a walk. Perhaps the sun would clear my head of the dark cobwebs left by Alisette's unexplained abduction.

With the Chinese shawl over my shoulders, I set forth, walking along the cliffs but nowhere near the edge. While I found it troubling to believe anyone at Sea Cliff House would be so cruel as to frighten a child, there'd been no sighting of any stranger. In any case, a stranger wouldn't be able to obtain a tower key.

There was no question in my mind that Cecile had pushed me over the cliff. I half-believed she'd also planted the doll by Alexandria's crypt and then sent me after it, though I didn't see how she could have toppled the angel at precisely the right moment. Nor could I imagine her wrapping Alisette in the quilt and locking her own daughter in the tower.

Who had, then? I reviewed the household, trying to set my prejudices aside and deal strictly with facts. Neither Gerald nor Stephen could possibly have taken Alisette—Gerald had been with me and Stephen off riding Bosun. Mr. Ferguson and Sonia were likewise exempt, having been with each other. Such was also the case with Mrs. Peter and Mrs. Yates. If Cecile was innocent, that left Rosie, Molly, and Armin.

What motive would any of those three have? To my mind, only Armin might have one, and his remained nebulous. Was it simply to alarm and upset the Nikolais in revenge for being sired and then cast off by Captain Peter? Unlikely. Still, Armin *had* gone to the house at the right time. I'd seen him myself.

As if thinking of him conjured up his presence, I caught sight of Armin leaning against the pine whose trunk Stephen had used for the rope. Whether he was guilty of locking Alisette in the tower or not, I was wary of going near him, so I turned and began to retrace my steps, only to see, to my dismay, a blue parasol bobbing towards me. Underneath the parasol, I knew, was Cecile. Unless I turned my back to her and resumed my original direction, there was no way to avoid our meeting. If we must meet, I preferred it to be face-to-face rather than have her at my back, but I certainly wasn't happy about encountering her. No matter how sternly I lectured myself, I remained a bit afraid of Cecile.

"I've been looking for you," she said when she was several feet away. "You may fool everyone else, but I know you did it."

157

I raised uncomprehending eyebrows. What was she accusing me of now? Wishing I could simply sail on past, I knew, as an employee, I couldn't. Reluctantly, I stopped and waited for her to explain.

"How could you deliberately lock an innocent child in that dreadful tower?" she demanded, folding her parasol and pointing its sharply pointed end at me.

"You can't believe *I'd* ever harm Alisette!" I protested, shocked.

"Don't play the innocent with me. You did just that. You locked my daughter away, then pretended to find her just to further your sinful suit with my husband." Raising the folded parasol like a club, she advanced on me. "I'll make certain you're punished, see if I don't!"

I backed away. "Please believe me, Mrs. Nikolai," I said, "I did nothing of the sort."

"Don't lie to me." On she came, her face distorted by rage. "I know your sort. Meek as milk on the surface but as scheming as they come underneath. You can hoodwink my husband and Gerald, but not me." She swiped viciously with the parasol, narrowly missing my head. "I warned you to leave Sea Cliff House, but you refused. Now take the consequences!"

Retreating from her onslaught brought me closer to the edge of the cliffs, putting me in additional danger. I tried to change direction and edge past her, but she forestalled me, now lunging with the parasol as though handling a fencing foil. The sharp point caught in my shawl and yanked it from my shoulders. Cecile tossed the shawl aside and pursued me.

Seeing I couldn't escape, I realized I must save myself before she drove me over the cliff. There was no reasoning with her: whatever I did would have to be quick and direct. As a child, many was the game I'd played with sticks at the orphanage when we pretended to be dueling with rapiers, but this was no game, this was in earnest. And, while she had the parasol, I didn't have so much as a stick.

I began to dart this way and that in an irregular fashion, not only to avoid her thrusts with the parasol but to keep her guessing which way I'd move next.

Cecile cursed at me, calling me vile names. She flung false accusations with every lunge of the parasol. The woman's mad, I thought, appalled and frightened almost out of my wits.

Desperate to save myself, I waited until the parasol was fully extended toward me, then swooped forward, clenched my fingers around the slippery silk and yanked sharply. Caught unawares, Cecile, with her death grip on the parasol, lost her balance and sprawled face down onto the ground. I immediately released the parasol, dashed past her and ran for the house without looking back.

By the time I reached the front door, I knew I had to either tell Stephen the entire truth, not only about today but about Alisette seeing her mother push me, or else leave Sea Cliff House immediately. It wasn't safe for me to remain here otherwise. Or, perhaps, even after I told him.

Unfortunately, he wasn't at home. Nor was Gerald. Reluctant to do nothing and fearing Cecile would be back at any moment, more furious than ever, I finally knocked on Mrs. Peter's door. She bade me enter.

"Esma," she said after I'd greeted her, "how nice of you to visit us. Perhaps you'll have lunch with Alisette and me."

"Thank you, but first I must speak to you on a

159

matter of utmost importance. Is it possible for Alisette to play in your other room for a few minutes?"

The urgency in my voice apparently convinced her, because she led Alisette into her bedroom. "You may play with the music box while I talk to Miss Drake," I heard her say before she shut the connecting door.

This must have been a seldom-granted favor, for Alisette made no protest.

"If Captain Stephen had been home," I said when Mrs. Peter returned, "I would have spoken to him instead of coming to you. I'm sorry to upset you, but his wife has threatened to kill me. A short while ago she attacked me with her parasol on the cliffs. Under the circumstances, perhaps it's better if I leave Sea Cliff House."

"Oh, no!" She reached for my hand, grasping it between both of hers. "No, you mustn't leave. I realize Cecile has been disturbed of late. We all have been; the house itself is uneasy. Even my husband's spirit is troubled, sending me warnings I cannot understand.

"Stephen's not himself. He hasn't been since his return, I don't know why. It's more than his unfortunate amnesia. My hands feel his face and tell me he's Stephen; he speaks and I hear Stephen's voice. He's my son, but he's changed inwardly. The house feels the difference along with me. The house is aware something is amiss."

Her words made me shudder. If I came to think of Sea Cliff House as a being with a life of its own, I'd not be able to remain in it another moment.

"I don't mean to frighten you, Esma," she told me. "I know I must seem strange, but I depend on you as I can on no one else. Having you in the house makes me feel more secure. And to imagine what would happen to Alisette without you chills

160

MORE PASSION AND ADVENTURE AWAIT... YOUR TRIP TO A BIG ADVENTUROUS WORLD BEGINS WHEN YOU ACCEPT YOUR FIRST 4 NOVELS ABSOLUTELY *FREE*
(AN $18.00 VALUE)

Accept your Free gift and start to experience more of the passion and adventure you like in a historical romance novel. Each Zebra novel is filled with proud men, spirited women and tempestuous love that you'll remember long after you turn the last page.

Zebra Historical Romances are the finest novels of their kind. They are written by authors who really know how to weave tales of romance and adventure in the historical settings you love. You'll feel like you've actually gone back in time with the thrilling stories that each Zebra novel offers.

GET YOUR FREE GIFT WITH THE START OF YOUR HOME SUBSCRIPTION

Our readers tell us that these books sell out very fast in book stores and often they miss the newest titles. So Zebra has made arrangements for you to receive the four newest novels published each month.

You'll be guaranteed that you'll never miss a title, and home delivery is so convenient. And to show you just how easy it is to get Zebra Historical Romances, we'll send you your first 4 books absolutely FREE! Our gift to you just for trying our home subscription service.

BIG SAVINGS AND FREE HOME DELIVERY

Each month, you'll receive the four newest titles as soon as they are published. You'll probably receive them even before the bookstores do. What's more, you may preview these exciting novels free for 10 days. If you like them as much as we think you will, just pay the low preferred subscriber's price of just $3.75 each. *You'll save $3.00 each month off the publisher's price.* AND, your savings are even greater because there are never any shipping, handling or other hidden charges—FREE Home Delivery. Of course you can return any shipment within 10 days for full credit, no questions asked. There is no minimum number of books you must buy.

4 FREE BOOKS

TO GET YOUR 4 FREE BOOKS WORTH $18.00 — MAIL IN THE FREE BOOK CERTIFICATE T O D A Y

Fill in the Free Book Certificate below, and we'll send your FREE BOOKS to you as soon as we receive it.

If the certificate is missing below, write to: Zebra Home Subscription Service, Inc., P.O. Box 5214, 120 Brighton Road, Clifton, New Jersey 07015-5214.

FREE BOOK CERTIFICATE

4 FREE BOOKS

ZEBRA HOME SUBSCRIPTION SERVICE, INC.

YES! Please start my subscription to Zebra Historical Romances and send me my first 4 books absolutely FREE. I understand that each month I may preview four new Zebra Historical Romances free for 10 days. If I'm not satisfied with them, I may return the four books within 10 days and owe nothing. Otherwise, I will pay the low preferred subscriber's price of just $3.75 each; a total of $15.00, *a savings off the publisher's price of $3.00*. I may return any shipment and I may cancel this subscription at any time. There is no obligation to buy any shipment and there are no shipping, handling or other hidden charges. Regardless of what I decide, the four free books are mine to keep.

NAME

ADDRESS _____ APT

CITY _____ STATE _____ ZIP

TELEPHONE
(   )

SIGNATURE _____ (if under 18, parent or guardian must sign)

Terms, offer and prices subject to change without notice. Subscription subject to acceptance by Zebra Books. Zebra Books reserves the right to reject any order or cancel any subscription.

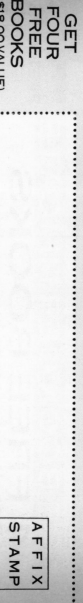

GET
FOUR
FREE
BOOKS
(AN $18.00 VALUE)

ZEBRA HOME SUBSCRIPTION
SERVICE, INC.
P.O. Box 5214
120 BRIGHTON ROAD
CLIFTON, NEW JERSEY 07015-5214

me. I'll see to Cecile; she won't trouble you again."

Mrs. Peter spoke as though she believed Cecile would listen and obey. I had my doubts.

"You must, of course, tell Stephen as soon as he returns," she went on. "In the meantime, you and Alisette will remain in my suite."

I relaxed a little; I was safe for the time being.

Sonia had just rolled in a serving cart with our lunch when Mrs. Yates came hurrying breathlessly into the room.

"Lord help us, Lord help us," she gasped, wringing her hands. "It's terrible. Terrible." I'd never seen the housekeeper so agitated.

"Get hold of yourself, Mrs. Yates," Mrs. Peter said firmly. "What has happened?"

"Oh, ma'am, it's Mrs. Stephen," the housekeeper cried.

"Remember, Alisette is here," Mrs. Peter warned.

Hand to her mouth, Mrs. Yates stared at the child, then glanced at me and quickly averted her gaze.

"Did something happen to my mama?" Alisette demanded.

Mrs. Peter frowned. "When I know, I'll tell you. Right now I want you to take Miss Drake into the bedroom and show her the music box."

"I don't want to."

"You will do as I say, and you will do it immediately." There was steel in Mrs. Peter's voice.

Alisette scowled, but she slid off her chair. I was already standing, and I took her hand, hurrying toward the bedroom. Once inside with the door shut, Alisette picked up a porcelain music box. A charming and delicate representation of two dancers, a woman and a man dressed in old-fashioned finery, adorned its lid and, after she wound the key, the dancers revolved to music. Between the tinkling of the box and the noise of

161

the waves below, it was impossible to hear voices from the other room.

"That's a lovely tune," I said. "What is it?"

"'The Blue Danube Waltz,'" Alisette told me, her attention clearly not on the music box. "Do you think my mama's all right?"

Recalling my last sight of Cecile, sprawled on her face, I tensed in alarm. Had she been seriously hurt?

"I hope she's all right," I said, truthfully enough. Despite her enmity toward me, I didn't really want Cecile to come to harm. "Your grandmother will tell us soon."

"Mrs. Yates said it was terrible," Alisette persisted as the dancers revolved and the music tinkled on.

I put my arm around her shoulders, and she leaned against me. "I love my mama," she said.

"Of course you do. And she loves you."

"Sometimes Mama says she wishes I'd never been born."

"She doesn't really mean that. When they're tired or cross, quite often people say things they don't mean."

"Do you think Papa loves me?" Alisette asked hesitantly.

"I'm sure he does. Look at the way he picks you up and hugs you. And who else calls you Alsie and thinks you're the sweetest girl in the world?"

She smiled. "I guess he does love me, all right."

"Maybe someday he'll dance with you like the two on the music box," I said, searching for something to take her mind off her worry over her mother. "Shall we practice so you'll know how?"

Although I'd never waltzed in my life, I managed to interest her in trying to dance with me as the music tinkled, and she was giggling at our

162

efforts when her grandmother finally opened the bedroom door.

Mrs. Peter knelt and beckoned to Alisette. The child's laughter faded, and her eyes grew round with fear as she walked slowly to her grandmother. Mrs. Peter put her hands on Alisette's shoulders. "I'm sorry, dear, but your mother is dead," she said bluntly. "I'm afraid she fell off the cliffs." Wrapping her arms around the child, she hugged her close.

I stared at her, shocked. Fell off the cliffs! Cecile? But how could she?

I didn't hear the details until much later, after I'd finally gotten Alisette to fall asleep in my bed. It was Stephen who told me after beckoning me into the hall.

"I thought you should know we've recovered Cecile's body from the cove just past the promontory," Stephen said, his face strained and drawn. He placed his hands on my shoulders. "I want to tell you I place no credence in Armin's story."

I stared up at him apprehensively. "Armin's story?"

"He insists he saw you and Cecile quarreling on the edge of the cliffs and that you shoved her over."

I gasped in horror. "No! Never!"

"I knew he was lying."

I bit my lip. "There's some truth in what he says. She—she attacked me with her parasol." How lame the truth sounded. "I grabbed at the parasol to save myself, and she did fall to the ground. The last I saw of her she was lying face down near the edge, but not close enough to fall over. And I certainly didn't push her over." Even as I disclaimed responsibility, guilt overwhelmed me. I pictured Cecile rising, stunned by the fall, stumbling to the edge and falling to her doom.

163

I pulled away from Stephen and covered my face with my hands. "I must leave here," I said brokenly. "How can I stay?"

He gripped my shoulders again, his fingers digging in. "You can't leave! With her mother gone, Alsie needs you more than ever."

I knew he spoke the truth. I couldn't turn my back on the child, not at a time like this. I'd have to somehow come to terms with my guilt. While I hadn't pushed Cecile over, I feared I was to blame for her death. But why had Armin lied and said I pushed her? What did he have against me?

"I'm so confused," I told Stephen. "I am sorry your wife is—"

"I couldn't think of her as my wife," he interrupted. "Cecile was a stranger to me and, though her death saddens me, I won't pretend to be a bereaved husband."

I was taken aback by his frankness.

"I spoke the truth when I said Alsie needs you," he went on, his green eyes dark with emotion, "but so do I, Esma, so do I."

Again I broke free of his grip. "How can you speak of such things?" I demanded. Shocked, I glanced around to make certain no one had overheard.

He sighed. "Tell me you'll stay on. I don't know what I'd do without you. What Alsie would do."

I felt he'd tacked Alisette's needs on to win me over. Still, I knew he was right. She'd be desolate enough over her mother's death without losing me, too. I must remain at Sea Cliff House, at least for the time being. For her sake. Not for Stephen's. The way I felt at the moment, I couldn't bear to think of us, of Stephen and me. Not when I couldn't absolve myself of responsibility for Cecile's death.

"I'll stay." I didn't look at him as I spoke. "I

must get back to Alisette, she's very restless." Without another word, I slipped through my half-open door and closed it behind me.

As I kept vigil beside the sleeping child, I prayed for guidance. Later, as I lay beside her, I tried to wipe away the memory of the many times I'd wished Stephen wasn't married to Cecile. If only I could take the wish back and have Cecile alive and healthy once more.

I still loved Stephen. I would until the day I died. But I could never forget or forgive myself for my part in his wife's accident. The ghost of Cecile would stand between Stephen and me forever.

The first of the new gowns Molly made for me was black, for mourning, because Alisette insisted she wouldn't wear a black dress unless I did. So I wore black to the funeral, feeling guiltier than ever by appearing to mourn for a woman who, in life, I'd had no reason to like.

During the days following the funeral, Alisette dogged my every footstep, as though afraid if she took her eyes off me, I'd disappear. After several weeks of this, with my strong approval, Mrs. Peter took steps to wean Alisette from my side.

"I've found a little girl for you to play with," she announced to Alisette in my presence. "Her name is Margaret Plains. She lives with her grandmother, Mrs. Plains, and they're coming to tea. I expect you to amuse Margaret while she's visiting. Next week, you and I will take tea at Margaret's home in Eureka."

"And Miss Drake, too," Alisette insisted.

"No, child. Miss Drake is not invited."

"Then *I* won't go."

"You and Margaret will have a better time without me," I said hastily. "You wait and see."

165

Alisette glowered at both her grandmother and me. "I don't have to like Margaret," she muttered.

"You will make me very unhappy if you don't try," Mrs. Peter said.

On the afternoon of Margaret's first visit, I found it a relief to be away from Alisette for a few hours. Much as I loved her, I needed time to be alone, just as she needed time away from me, so I blessed Mrs. Peter's thoughtfulness. I worried, though, that Alisette, pouting because she couldn't have her own way, might misbehave at the tea.

Since the day, though overcast, was mild, I decided I'd walk in the gardens while Alisette was occupied. For a time I stood beside the pond, watching the goldfish swim lazily to and fro. How enviable their uncomplicated life seemed at that moment; they needed to do no more than show off their beauty and grace.

I'd put off writing my monthly letter to Sister Samara because of all the frights and the final tragedy. I couldn't bring myself to put everything that had happened onto paper, especially to her, so I tried now to compose a letter in my head that would satisfy her without too much sinning by omission.

"Cherish truth in your heart," she'd always advised. "Lying to others is wrong, but lying to oneself is the greater sin."

What was the truth in my heart? I studied my image floating on the pond's surface and regretted that the innocent girl who'd come to Sea Cliff House had vanished. Not merely as a result of new clothes and a more fashionable coiffure, but also because I'd learned the pain of love and the burden of guilt.

The truth was I loved Stephen, but, through my own fault in leaving Cecile helpless on the ground, I had forfeited any chance of happiness with him. As my eyes blurred with tears, his image appeared beside mine in the water. I was so accustomed to seeing his face in my mind that I didn't understand he was actually beside me until he spoke.

"Will you stay a moment and talk?" he asked.

Not looking at him, I blinked furiously to remove any trace of tears. "I was thinking of going in," I said.

He touched my arm, not letting his hand linger. "You run off every time I appear. Why?"

"Once we agreed not to be alone together," I reminded him.

"That was before—" He broke off. "I promise to behave," he said.

The words he hadn't said echoed in my mind. Before Cecile died. Couldn't he understand that, for me, she might as well still be alive?

"Captain Stephen, I prefer not to be alone with you," I said firmly.

"I remember when you called me just plain Stephen." His voice was soft, his gaze compelling. "When you whispered my name over and over."

My knees went weak at the memory.

"Esma, it's no sin to seek happiness," he said. "You and you alone can make me happy."

Gazing into the sea green of his eyes, I could almost believe it was possible for us to be happy together. Recalling the joyous rapture I'd felt in his arms filled me with an aching warmth that made me long for his kiss.

How could I resist the compelling bond between us? I so yearned for his touch that it was all I could do not to sway toward him.

"We must meet somewhere else," he said urgently, "away from these unfriendly windows staring down at us. Away from Sea Cliff House and all its gloomy secrets."

167

Stephen's words surprised me. While it was true the house made *me* uneasy, he was, after all, a Nikolai and Sea Cliff House was part of his heritage.

Trying to disentangle myself from the enticing web he wove around me, I ignored my pounding heart and said, "We must not meet anywhere." I was aware my voice lacked conviction.

"Come with me to *Sea Dragon*."

I shook my head, not trusting myself to speak, unwillingly picturing his snug quarters on the ship and the two of us wrapped in each other's arms in the bunk where he slept.

"Esma, don't turn away from me," he said.

"It's my fault!" The words burst from me. "Cecile would be alive today if I hadn't grabbed her parasol the way I did. Oh, why did I leave her on the ground? If only I'd waited, if I'd helped her to her feet, she wouldn't have stumbled over the edge. I'm to blame and nothing anyone can say will change it. How can we ever be happy when I'm guilty of causing her death?"

"No one blames you but yourself."

"Armin does. He lied about what he saw, but he knows it was my fault."

"I haven't trusted Armin since the first time I saw him holding Bosun's reins, there on the dock. He's a conniving wretch."

"He's your own half brother," I said.

Stephen scowled. "Not mine!"

I stared at him in surprise. "But he's obviously a Nikolai."

Stephen blinked. "I'm sure you're right," he said after a moment. "The damned amnesia's to blame. Plus my unwillingness to claim such a untrustworthy lout as any kind of a relative. Please don't believe anything Armin says."

I wanted to share my suspicions of Armin with

Stephen but hesitated lest it seem I was accusing Armin in retaliation for his accusation against me. In any case, I had no proof he was the "bad man" who locked Alisette in the tower.

"Forget Armin," Stephen told me. "Why can't you understand that Cecile's death, while tragic, wasn't your fault. Or anyone else's. It was an accident."

Didn't he realize I could never forget what had happened?

"I must go in," I murmured. He reached a hand toward me, then let it drop, glancing toward the house.

"I'll not give you up easily," he warned as I walked away.

Seeing the Plains carriage still in the drive, I knew that Alisette would be with her grandmother and the visitors yet, and so I made my way to the kitchen, greeted Rosie, and slipped up the back stairs to my room. I had scarcely settled myself in the rocker when Sonia tapped on my door and entered without waiting for permission.

"Can you keep a secret?" she asked. Again, not waiting for me to say yes or no, she chattered on. "It won't come as any surprise to you seeing as how you caught me with Jock." She reached inside the bodice of her brown dress and pulled out a chain with a man's ring on it. "He gave me this."

A large golden yellow stone was set in a heavy gold ring. "It's very attractive," I said.

Sonia held the ring in her hand, admiring it. "Jock tells me the gem's a cairngorm, from the mountains of Scotland. It's a sort of pledge."

"Of marriage, you mean?" If so, I was glad for her.

Sonia shrugged. "Who can tell? What it means is he's coming back. At least I hope so."

I knew Mr. Ferguson, having completed his

169

examination of the cliffs and the sea currents, had returned to San Francisco the previous day.

"He seemed quite taken with you," I assured her.

"Yeah, but with men it's out of sight, out of mind." She bit her lip. "I maybe shouldn't't've given him a sample. Don't you go doing that, Esma. Don't you let a man have his way with you, or, like as not, he'll turn his back on you."

I had no intention of letting any man "have his way." Although I was certain if the man were Stephen, he would never turn his back on me.

"Mr. Ferguson would prize a ring from his homeland," I told Sonia. "Since he gave you the ring, it must mean he prizes you, too."

Sonia stared at me for a moment, broke into a wide grin, threw her arms around me, and hugged me. "You're a friend indeed, Esma. You almost make me believe he *will* come back."

"Have faith," I urged.

"I don't have much anymore, but I'll try. How about you and the captain? I saw you talking to him in the garden.

Sonia didn't miss anything. I wondered how many others had also seen us.

As if I'd asked the question aloud, Sonia added, "And I saw that bastard Armin sneaking around spying on the two of you. Better watch out for him."

"Armin claims I pushed Cecile over the cliff," I said. "I wish I could understand why he's lying."

"He's got something up his sleeve, you can count on it." She frowned. "Did you ever think he might be lying to cover up? That he's accusing you 'cause he pushed her over himself?"

I gaped at her. The thought had never crossed my mind. Little as I cared for Armin, I could certainly imagine no reason for him to kill Cecile.

170

"I can't believe he'd do such a terrible thing," I protested.

"You never heard about him being questioned by the sheriff when that girl from town turned up missing, did you? Molly was scared to death, so scared I figured she knew something that made her believe he might be guilty. That was over a year ago, and it all blew over. But they never did find the girl. In my opinion, Armin's a bad one and don't you ever forget it."

Chapter 11

As the days passed, Alisette began to look forward to her weekly visit with Margaret Plains, a sturdy, sandy-haired girl just her age. I was happy to discover that Margaret, unlike Alisette, showed no tendency toward the fey. If she also showed little imagination, Alisette had more than enough for the two of them. I welcomed the chance for my charge to play with another child—a real, live girl and not an imaginary spirit she'd conjured from the grave—even more than I appreciated the few hours to myself.

I thought that renewing ties with her old friend Mrs. Plains had also proved good for Mrs. Peter, for on the days she took tea at the Plains' home in Eureka, she didn't visit the promontory.

By the first of October, no one in the house seemed to remember that Cecile had ever existed; even Alisette rarely mentioned her mother. But Cecile and the way she'd died haunted me, and I continued to do my best to avoid Stephen, except, of course, at the dinner table, where I had no choice. There, I depended on Gerald's conversation to keep me from having to talk to or look at Stephen, though this resulted in my having to fend off invitations to go riding with Gerald.

172

On the second Thursday of the month, Mrs. Peter stopped me in the upstairs hall on her way to the staircase. Alisette was already down in the entry, impatiently awaiting Armin and the carriage that would take them into Eureka.

"Mr. Callich is a fine young man," Mrs. Peter told me.

"I'm sure he is," I said, wondering why she'd brought him up.

"He told me you keep refusing him when he asks you to ride with him. I was sorry to hear that. Is it perhaps because you fear I might not approve of an employee associating with a member of the household?"

"Not exactly," I said hesitantly.

The truth was that, as much as I admired Gerald, I had no desire to further my acquaintance with him. No doubt my continuing guilt over Cecile contributed to my apathy, but that's how I felt. Besides, rightly or wrongly, Stephen occupied my every thought. I had no room in my mind or my heart for any other man—even as kind and thoughtful a man as Gerald Callich.

"I have no objection whatsoever to you riding with Gerald in your free time," Mrs. Peter said. "It would do you good." She smiled. "Besides, a young woman must think of her future."

I could hardly believe my ears. Good heavens, was she matchmaking?

"Thank you," I managed to say, unhappily aware she'd now expect me to accept Gerald's next invitation.

Maybe I should. What harm could it do? For all I knew Mrs. Peter could be right, an outing with him might do me good. As for matchmaking, she was on the wrong track. Though Gerald would make some woman a considerate, charming husband, he was not for me. I loved the one man my

173

guilt would never let me marry—even given the unlikely possibility of his asking me.

I stood on the porch waving good-bye to Alisette as the carriage pulled away. Tempted by the bright sunshine and mild day, I decided to spend my free hours outdoors. Several times I'd walked with Alisette to the small pine grove behind the cemetery, enjoying the scent of the trees and the whisper of the wind through their branches. To say nothing of a very saucy bluejay who'd scolded us thoroughly for invading his territory.

This seemed the perfect day to bring a book and an apple, prop myself against a pine trunk, and read. I might even make friends with the jay by offering him the apple core.

If I slipped out the back way, taking Alisette's shortcut through the cypress hedge, chances were no one would notice me going. By no one, I meant Stephen, for I knew I must keep away from him.

Everything worked as I'd planned. Choosing a spot in the midst of the small grove, I laid an old quilt retrieved from the ragbag onto the fragrant pine needles, sat down, and opened *Castle Dangerous,* a Sir Walter Scott novel I'd borrowed from the house library.

Sister Samara hadn't completely approved of Sir Walter Scott. "It's not a sin to enjoy light reading now and then," she'd commented, "but a wise and pious girl doesn't waste her time on dross when pure gold is at hand, such as books about the lives of the saints. Or the Bible."

I treasured the little Bible she'd given me as a farewell gift and kept it on my night table. Unfortunately, I wasn't as pious as she'd have preferred. Or as wise. I doted on Sir Walter Scott and read him every chance I had. I couldn't help but thrill to the perils, loves, fortunes and misfortunes of the Scottish nobility in their gloomy old castles. His

174

stories kept my mind from my own misfortunes in equally gloomy Sea Cliff House.

I soon was engrossed in the book, so enthralled that I reached for the apple without taking my eyes from the printed page. A hand closed over mine. I gasped, dropped the book, and looked up. Stephen stood over me.

He eased down onto the blanket beside me and glanced at the book as he handed me the apple. "Though you really ought to give it to me," he murmured.

"Give you the book?" I asked in some confusion.

"The apple. To tempt me, as Eve tempted Adam. I assure you I'd eat every bite and ask for more. Much, much more."

My heart thudded wildly at his nearness, and the soft caress in his voice bemused me until I couldn't think what to do or say. I could only drown in his green eyes.

"Ah, God, Esma, I've longed for this moment," he murmured, catching my shoulders and turning me until I fit into his arms.

I was aflame even before his lips covered mine. Every thought fled from my mind; reason deserted me. There was only Stephen, the fiery magic of his kiss, the caressing brush of his beard on my face, and the anticipatory thrill of what might follow. His male scent mingled with the pine smell, intoxicating me. Before I knew what I was doing, my fingers were tangled in his hair, holding him to me.

"I need you so," he whispered in my ear, his warm breath making me shiver in delight. "Love me, Esma, or I can't go on."

"I do love you." I breathed the words against his lips. "I can't help myself."

His kiss deepened, and my very bones melted in

the sweet fire consuming me. Soon the buttons of my bodice yielded to his agile fingers and then, somehow, I was naked to the waist and once again I felt the aching wonder of his lips on my breast. Clinging to him, I begged him never to stop.

"Never," he said hoarsely. "I'll never have enough of you."

His caresses became more intimate, his fingers finding secret places.

"Do you know you have two tiny moles, here and here?" he murmured, touching them with the tip of his tongue.

I trembled in need, wanting more and more until finally when we lay in each other's arms with no garments between us, I thought I'd die from the exquisite feel of his bare flesh against mine.

"I love you, Esma," he murmured. "I have from the first moment I saw you."

With tears of joy in my eyes, I pressed my mouth against his neck, tasting his skin, savoring the slight salty tang that was his and his alone. His caresses grew bolder, more demanding, and I moaned, pressing against him.

"Stephen, oh, Stephen," I whispered.

He slipped his knee between mine, gently easing my legs apart and raised above me, his eyes dark with the same need that flamed through me. For a second I felt a strange, almost painful pressure, and then it passed. I was overcome with a multitude of indescribably wonderful sensations that mounted and mounted as we moved together until, like a wild sea wave, all feeling crested, tossing me into a miraculous realm I'd never dreamed existed.

I cried out, holding him tightly against me until he began to move again, faster and faster, sending rivulets of delight through me. He groaned, gripping me tightly and then collapsed, as spent as I was.

"You're mine now, Esma," he said. "You'll never belong to any other man."

As if I wanted to! I gloried in the knowledge he loved me as I loved him.

"Does that mean you're mine, too?" I asked shyly.

"From the instant I saw you I've been yours," he assured me.

We lay quietly in each other's arms for long, contented moments. I had never been so happy in my life.

"Much as I'd like it, we can't stay here forever," he said at last, sitting up and looking down at me.

Until that moment I hadn't thought about being undressed, but suddenly I realized I was naked and I flushed, covering my breasts with my hands. He took my hands in his, bent, and kissed the tips of my breasts, causing my breath to come short.

"You're beautiful," he told me. His lips brushed the two moles near my collarbone. "Everything about you."

Though his words and his touch gave me great pleasure, I couldn't overcome my shyness and, as quickly as I could, I sat up, turned my back, and began pulling on my clothes. Even after I was fully dressed, I still couldn't bring myself to face him.

"Sit down, Esma," he said gently, "and we'll share the apple."

I obeyed, watching him covertly as he opened a jack knife and sliced the apple in two.

"This half is for you," he said, handing it to me. "The other half is mine." He tipped up my chin, forcing me to meet his gaze. "You and I are like the halves of this apple now, only becoming whole

177

and complete when we're together."

Mesmerized by his words and by the warmth in his eyes, I couldn't speak. All I could manage was to moisten my dry lips with the tip of my tongue.

Stephen groaned. "If you keep that up I'll be forced to kiss you. One kiss will lead to another, and you know what will happen then, don't you?" He glanced around us, at the trees with the sun slanting through their branches. "We were lucky no one happened by; we can't take too many chances."

I came alert to our surroundings, to the risk we'd taken. Never once had it occurred to me we might be observed; I'd been too engrossed in Stephen.

"I had a devil of a time trying to follow you," he told me. "If I hadn't remembered Alsie's shortcut through the cypress hedge, I might never have found you." He bit into his apple half. "Good," he said, smiling at me, "but you taste better."

A pang of pure joy pierced me. I loved him so much at that moment it was all I could do not to throw my arms around him and try to show him exactly how much he meant to me. Instead, I took a bite of my half. The sweet apple juice pleased my tongue, but I knew nothing and no one would ever again please me as much as Stephen.

This wonderful interlude in the grove was only the beginning of our happiness, I assured myself. Now that we'd declared our love to each other, the future stretched ahead, bright and shining, as warm and life-giving as the sun overhead.

Stephen and I walked hand in hand to the cypress hedge. "I'll go the long way round," he told me.

I nodded, wanting to keep what we shared a secret for the time being. I eased through the opening and, as I stood up on the other side, the sun vanished as mist shrouded the grounds of Sea

178

Cliff House. I shrugged off my moment of unease, reminding myself that the sun still existed, even though temporarily invisible. We might have to conceal our love for awhile but, like the sun, it would always exist, bright and shining.

It wasn't until I was alone in my room that I realized not one word had been said about marriage. He couldn't, I immediately told myself. Not so soon after Cecile's death. It would be wrong. Especially since I'd been involved in the tragedy.

I still felt I was to blame, but after what had happened between us, I knew my guilt wouldn't stop me from being with Stephen as much as possible. I couldn't stay away from him; I'd been foolish to try.

For days I floated on invisible clouds. Every time I saw Stephen, I grinned so idiotically that anyone watching must have thought me demented. Though we had no chance to be alone for any length of time, we found a moment here and there—a quick kiss in the upstairs hall, a longer embrace in the library. It wasn't enough. I lived for the following Thursday, when Alisette would be visiting Margaret again.

Before then, Sonia guessed what had happened between us.

"It's written all over you, Esma," she told me Tuesday night in the privacy of my room. "You've gone and done it."

I pressed my hands to my burning face.

"No good trying to hide it from me," she insisted. "I knew you was a goner from the moment he kissed you that first night he came home. After that he meant to have you and, poor innocent that you are, you didn't stand a chance."

"We're in love," I protested, upset at how she degraded the beautiful hours Stephen and I had spent under the pines. "It wasn't tawdry at all."

She half-smiled. "You never think it is, your first time. Well, I wish you more luck than I ever had with my men, but I got to warn you to be careful. For one thing, I don't think Mrs. Peter would approve."

I wasn't sure she would, either. While she liked me enough to encourage me to view Gerald as a possible husband, her own son would be different. Especially so soon after Cecile's death. And quite possibly, as an orphan of unknown parentage, I wouldn't be considered suitable enough to ever marry a Nikolai. I decided I must be very careful indeed.

Unfortunately, the next morning, when Stephen came up behind me on the back stairs and caught me around the waist, I forgot all my good intentions. It wasn't until Mrs. Yates loudly cleared her throat that I had any notion she was watching us from the top of the stairs.

Under her stern eye, even Stephen looked abashed. "I came to tell you I'm riding into town, Esma," he said. "I'll talk to you later this evening." He glanced at Mrs. Yates. "And you, too."

"Yes, Captain," she said grimly.

He clattered down the stairs and was gone. I had no choice but to climb up to where Mrs. Yates waited.

"How long has this been going on?" she demanded.

"Nothing's been going on." I disliked lying, but Stephen and I were none of her business.

"I must say I'm surprised at you. And shocked. It won't do, Esma Drake. Either you promise to end such sinfulness here and now, or I'll go straight to Mrs. Peter."

How can anything so wonderful be a sin? I wanted to cry. I love him, I can't give him up. I looked away from her, biting my lip.

"Look here, what you're doing is worse than you realize," Mrs. Yates went on. "It's wrong. A sin against God and man. You must stop."

Nothing she could say would ever convince me my love for Stephen and his for me was wrong. I looked at her defiantly.

"Very well, I'll speak to Mrs. Peter," she said.

"No!" I cried, afraid of what might happen then. "Wait, I'll promise. At least until you listen to what the captain has to say."

"That's not much of a promise. But I'll go this far—I'll wait until after I talk to him before saying anything to Mrs. Peter."

The rest of the morning passed in a blur of activity. Though I went through the motions of teaching Alisette her numbers, I was hardly aware of whether her answers were right or wrong. After she settled in for her nap, I sat in my rocker, Sister Samara's Bible in my lap for comfort, but I was too agitated to attempt to read any of the verses.

"Stephen and I haven't sinned," I whispered. "We haven't." But doubts assailed me, as troubling and persistent as stinging gnats.

Whatever the Bible might have to say about it, I well knew Sister Samara would agree with Mrs. Yates and not with me. What Stephen and I had done went against all I'd been taught, and yet I didn't feel sinful. Or repentant. Nor did I think for one moment I'd been tempted by the devil and fallen. Stephen and I loved one another. What happened in the pine grove was wonderful and loving, not a sin. Not tawdry, as Sonia tried to tell me. Not wrong. Not, as Mrs. Yates insisted, "worse than I knew."

When Alisette woke, I suggested we go to the library for a geography lesson with the globe. The door was ajar, and I was about to push it open and enter when I heard an unfamiliar voice from inside. I hesitated.

"I tell ye I don't mean to go to me Maker with this on me conscience—how dare ye call me a liar? A dying man don't lie, and that's the truth." It was a man's voice, old and cracked.

"I simply don't understand why you waited so many years," Gerald said.

Alisette pushed past me and, before I could stop her, sailed into the library. I had no choice but to follow her in. Mrs. Peter was also there, perched on the edge of a leather settee.

"We want to use the globe," Alisette announced.

"Some other time," Gerald told her. "We're busy at the moment."

She tilted her head to stare curiously at the stranger, an ill-clad old man with a ragged white beard and a large red nose. His clothes, though sadly stained and tattered, marked him as a sailor. He stood by the desk, with his cap in his hands, facing Gerald.

"Run along, Alisette," Mrs. Peter ordered. I took the child's hand to lead her from the room.

As I started for the door, Gerald said, "Wait, Miss Drake." Turning to Mrs. Peter, he said, "In view of what Floyd Rogers has told us, don't you think Esma ought to be here?"

Mrs. Peter shifted uneasily, clearly upset. "I'm afraid you're right. Take Alisette to Mrs. Yates, Esma, and then join us."

I cajoled Alisette from her pouting by promising a surprise when I was free and left her with Mrs. Yates, all the while wondering why on earth my presence was wanted in the library. When I returned, the old man was speaking and Mrs. Peter motioned me to take a seat beside her.

"I ain't no liar," Mr. Rogers muttered. "Don't take kindly to being named one, I don't."

"I didn't say you were." Gerald sounded weary, as though he'd repeated the assurance more than once. "Would you mind telling your story one more time so we understand everything clearly?"

"Like I said, 'twas thirteen years ago this month we got a big blow from the north," Floyd Rogers began. "Never saw waves to beat the ones that day."

"That was the day we lost my husband's first ship, *Sea Bear*," Mrs. Peter said. "I remember the storm well. I should, we all very nearly perished, Stephen and Peter and I. Poor little Estelle—" She broke off, clenching her hands in her lap.

For a moment all I could think of was Alisette's doll, and then I recalled who she'd named the doll after—Estelle Marie Nikolai, lost at sea. Mrs. Peter's daughter and Stephen's sister, drowned in the storm that spared the others, the very storm the old seaman described.

"Ye being seafarers, ye know 'bout flotsam and jetsam and how the sea casts 'em on the shore during a storm. Me, I scouted the sand after that blow was over, looking for what I could use." He glared at Gerald. "Nothing wrong with that, be there?"

"No, nothing," Gerald soothed. "Please go on."

I realized as I watched him weave on his feet, that the old man had been drinking. Why were both Gerald and Mrs. Peter so intent on the words of a drunken old sailor? And why insist that I listen?

"Sometimes I found what I druther not," Floyd Rogers continued. "Dead men, their clothes stiff with salt. So I thought at first she was a dead 'un, too, the little tyke. Only she weren't. Blue with cold she were and scarce breathing, but alive for all that. I took her up, I did, and toted her to me cart, wrapped me blanket 'round her, and whupped up

183

me old mule. I feared she'd die afore I could get help for her, what with me old mule being so slow. Came to a farm, I did, and I persuaded the farmer to get out his buggy and tote the tyke to the sisters. So that's where we brung her."

"You mean the Sisters of Charity Orphanage near Fort Bragg," Gerald said, glancing at me.

"'S what I told ye the first time. I was living thereabouts, then. Like I said, I brung the tyke to the sisters but I took something from 'round her neck. A sin, I knows it now, knew it then. But a man needs what he needs, and so I took the gold locket she wore, the very one I gave ye when I come in, with them initials on it. I meant to sell the locket for the money but, when the time come, I only parted with the gold chain it hung on. Me conscience made me keep back the locket. I never sold it, that I didn't. All these years it's been with me, been my bad luck for I never had any good."

"Why bring the locket to us now?"

"Take a look at me and ye see a dying man. I confessed me years of sins to the priest and when he hears 'bout the locket, he says, 'Take it to the orphanage and find the rightful owner.' Well, I tried. The sisters told me the little gal me and the farmer handed over to 'em thirteen years ago growed up and left and were working at a place called Sea Cliff House. Took me awhile to get here, but here I am, and ye've got the locket. That's all I've got to say. Never thought I have to say it twice and get called a liar for me trouble. If ye don't mind, I'll be going."

"Wait, Mr. Rogers," Mrs. Peter said.

"No, missus, I can't rightly do that. I told all I knows, and it's time to go."

"Gerald, please give him some money," she said.

Wavering on his feet, the old man held up his

184

hand. "I won't take yer money, missus. I done what I had to, and I don't want payment. Good day to ye." Without another word, he turned and staggered to the door.

Gerald followed him, protesting. We heard the front door open and close. A few moments later Gerald returned to the library.

"Mr. Rogers couldn't be persuaded to stay," he told Mrs. Peter. "I'm sorry you had to be subjected to this, but when he handed me the locket I thought I'd better have you come and listen to his story."

"You did the right thing." She took a deep breath, obviously fortifying herself. "Give me the locket, Gerald."

"The initials are EMN," he said as he placed a small heart-shaped locket in her hand, the gold as bright as new. "The N is larger and in the middle as is the custom."

"Yes, I feel the initials quite clearly." Mrs. Peter's voice quivered as she traced the outside of the locket with her finger. "It's Estelle's locket, beyond a doubt."

I sat stunned, unable to speak, desperately trying to make sense of what I'd heard. Estelle Marie Nikolai was the half-drowned child the old man had found on the beach and brought to the orphanage after stealing her locket. Estelle was the child who grew up there and came to Sea Cliff House.

But I was Esma Drake. It couldn't be true that Esma was Estelle Nikolai. That I was Estelle. Could it?

Sister Samara's words echoed in my mind. "We named you Esma because you babbled the word over and over when you were delirious with pneumonia. Drake, I chose myself."

Esma. A small child, sick with fever, trying to

185

say Estelle Marie? And the nightmares of green water, of drowning—were those a legacy of being shipwrecked?

"You have two moles, don't you, Esma?" Mrs. Peter asked and went on without waiting for me to agree or to deny it. "Let me describe them. They're under your left collarbone and the larger one is above the smaller."

I swallowed, my hand going to my throat. I tried to speak and could not. All I could do was nod, and I knew Mrs. Peter couldn't see that.

"She says she has the moles," Gerald announced.

"Do you mind if I touch them?" Mrs. Peter asked.

I forgot about Gerald watching, forgot everything but Mrs. Peter and myself, for I did have two moles under my left collarbone, as Stephen had discovered. Fingers trembling, I undid several buttons of my bodice.

Lightly, delicately, her hand skimmed over my throat and down to touch the skin beneath my collarbone and trace the outlines of the two moles.

"Those who are dead are alive," she whispered.

Recalling the time on the promontory with her, I shivered. Captain Peter's message!

Withdrawing her hand, she flung her arms around me, hugging me with all her strength. "My little Estelle," she said, her voice choked. "My dear daughter miraculously restored to me." She held me away and caressed my face while tears streamed down her cheeks. "Peter told me, but I didn't understand. His message meant you weren't dead, had never drowned, but lived."

Though I felt her touch and heard her words, everything seemed to be happening to someone else, not to me. I sat numbly, dumbly, unable to come to terms with what was happening. It couldn't be true, I must be dreaming. Automati-

186

cally, I rebuttoned my bodice; at the moment I wasn't capable of anything else.

"My dear Mrs. Peter," Gerald said, "I'm so happy for you. And for you too, Esma—that is, Estelle. Miss Nikolai."

"No," I protested weakly. "Esma's my name."

Mrs. Peter—my mother?—patted my hand. "We'll go on calling you Esma, dear, if that's what you prefer." She dried her tears with a lace-edged handkerchief. "I only wish my beloved Peter could have lived to see this day."

My mother. I'd been an orphan too long to be able to believe I had a mother. Was it possible I really did?

"I can't believe it's true," I said in a small voice.

"But it is," Gerald assured me. "The old man's story, the locket, and your moles prove you are Estelle Nikolai come home at last to those who love you."

Those. The word echoed ominously in my mind, stirring a beginning dread. If I was Estelle, then Mrs. Peter was my mother. But she had two children, Estelle and Stephen. As this simple truth filtered through my numbness, my hand flew to my mouth to hold back my agonized cry.

Dear God, Stephen was my brother!

Chapter 12

I hoped to avoid the predinner gathering in the parlor that evening by going in to dinner after Mrs. Peter—no, my mother. Would I ever grow used to calling her that?—Gerald and Stephen had entered the dining room. I had to face Stephen sooner or later, but I needed to put it off as long as possible.

I stood in front of my mirror, staring at the stranger—Estelle, not Esma—in the glass and wondering how I could manage to swallow even one morsel of food. How I wished I could have had supper with Alisette and not have had to go downstairs at all.

Alisette had been thrilled to discover I was her aunt. "Alexandria knew you were all the time," she insisted. "That's what she meant about always trusting Estelle—she meant you."

For her good-night story, Alisette begged me to tell her again how the old sailor had found a half-drowned child on the sand, not understanding how the story unsettled me. I'd been glad when she finally fell asleep.

I was somewhat disappointed to see my same image in the glass, even though I hadn't really expected the change from an orphan to a person with a family would magically alter my appearance. I still looked like plain Esma Drake. As I thought perhaps I'd have been better off to remain Esma Drake in name as well as looks, someone tapped on the door.

"Come in."

Sonia entered. "Miss Estelle." She spoke formally, but her eyes were bright with speculation. "Your mother asked me to tell you they're waiting for you in the parlor."

I tried to gather my pride and sail past her as though I'd been raised all my life as Estelle Nikolai, but I could not. All the servants had heard the strange story of how I'd come to be revealed as a Nikolai. How many also suspected what had happened between Stephen and me? Sonia, for one, knew.

"Oh, Sonia, what am I going to do?" Desperation edged my words.

She crossed to me and put an arm around my shoulders. "'Twasn't any fault of yours," she said in a low tone. "Or his, neither. Hold your head up high and don't let on anything's wrong. Pretend it never happened."

"I can't."

"Seems to me you got to." She squeezed my shoulders, turned me so I faced the door, and gave me a little shove. "Go on, you can do it."

Katherine—I still couldn't think of her as my mother—Gerald, and Mrs. Yates were in the parlor. And Stephen. My brief glance at him told me he was as upset as I.

"My dear," Katherine said when I greeted her, "we are celebrating tonight in your honor. Gerald, would you assist Mrs. Yates and open the champagne?"

I never in my life had seen champagne, much less tasted it. The bubbles tickled my nose and I fought to keep from sneezing.

"To Estelle," Gerald proposed, raising his glass. "The lost is found."

Stephen, I noticed from the corner of my eye, barely touched his glass to his lips. I avoided looking at him directly, though he seemed to be staring at me.

"It does seem odd," he said, "that this old seaman waited so long before coming forward."

Gerald nodded. "My exact thought. But apparently Mr. Rogers is in ill health and believes he's dying."

"What does it matter?" Katherine asked. "Our dear little girl is returned to us at last. Your father tried to tell me she was alive, Stephen, but I was too dense to interpret the message correctly."

"And what *was* the message?" he asked.

To my own amazement I intoned, "The alive are dead and the dead alive."

"Then *you* heard the words?" Stephen asked me after a moment.

"No, oh, no," I said hastily, wishing I'd kept my mouth shut. I still couldn't look at him directly.

"Esma was with me and I told her what the message was," Katherine put in. "Your father's spirit speaks only to me."

"The alive are dead and the dead alive." In Stephen's mouth the words were bleak and chilling. "It seems you've interpreted only half the message."

Katherine waved her hand. "The most important part, dear boy. I can scarcely credit my great good fortune in having my little girl returned to me. I'm sure you're equally happy to regain your sister, Stephen."

"I notice you still call her Esma." His comment neatly avoided a direct answer.

"Only because she prefers it." Katherine smiled

at him. "I shouldn't care to suddenly be called by a name other than Katherine, and I'm certain you'd have trouble answering to a different name than Stephen."

When he didn't reply, I risked a glance, and his desolate expression tore at my heart.

"Esma or Estelle," Gerald put in, "Miss Nikolai has come into her own, and that's a cause for celebration." He raised his glass again. "Cheers!"

Stephen didn't seem to have heard him because he continued to stare into his glass as if seeking a message among the bubbles.

I was relieved when Mrs. Yates announced dinner was ready to be served. By pushing the food around on my plate and swallowing an occasional bite, I managed to counterfeit eating.

"I've spoken to Mrs. Yates about a different room for you, Esma," Katherine told me as Sonia cleared the plates away from serving dessert. "I don't think the ivory room is quite—"

"Please, I'd rather stay where I am," I said. "Alisette would be lost without me across the hall from her, and I do enjoy looking down on the roses from my room."

Katherine nodded. "I shan't insist. Though I do believe we must find a governess for Alisette. She mustn't command all your time, Esma."

"I enjoy her so," I said. "I'd be most unhappy if we couldn't continue on together."

"We'll see." Katherine spoke mildly but I'd come to understand it was difficult to deter her from what she meant to do. Sooner or later, there'd be a governess, and I'd be Aunt Esma, one of the family but no longer Alisette's companion.

"I've remembered something interesting," Katherine went on. "That rag doll Alisette is so fond of was once yours, Esma. You were so attached to the doll that you cried yourself sick

191

after it got left behind when we boarded that ill-fated ship. I'm surprised you've forgotten."

"I don't recall anything before the orphanage," I said, repeating what I'd told Katherine and Gerald earlier. "Nothing at all." As I spoke, it occurred to me how odd it was that both Stephen and I couldn't remember our pasts. Since he was older when he was injured he had, of course, forgotten far more than I.

"What's your first memory from the orphanage?" Gerald asked.

"Sister Samara feeding me broth, coaxing me to take just one more spoonful."

"Perhaps you're fortunate not to remember the shipwreck," he said.

Not wishing to reveal that I did relive my near drowning in the recurrent nightmares I'd had for thirteen years, I murmured an agreement.

"Because of this amnesia, Stephen doesn't remember that terrible night, either." Katherine patted Stephen's hand. "You tried to save your little sister, but she was swept from your arms."

Stephen's strained face took on a grim look. "A memory loss can be convenient," he said. He didn't so much as glance my way, but I felt the words were directed at me.

Did he think it would be easy for me to forget how terribly we'd sinned? As Mrs. Yates had said earlier in the day, a sin against God and man. It was almost as though she'd known we were brother and sister.

But, of course, no one had. Not until the old sailor came to Gerald with the locket.

Somehow the meal ended and, after accompanying Katherine up the stairs, I escaped to my room without having to speak to either Gerald or Stephen. I still wasn't able to bring myself to call

Katherine "Mother" but, because I knew it would please her, I made up my mind to try, beginning first thing in the morning.

I had trouble getting to sleep and, for the first time in weeks, dreamed of drowning. I was roused, my heart pounding in terror. I gradually calmed, only to recall how Stephen had once heard me cry out in my nightmare and had come into my room to comfort me.

How was I to forget all that has passed between us? How could I go on living in the same house with him and not remember every time I saw him how we'd come together in sweet passion? Sinful passion.

"I must," I whispered. "I have no choice."

But it was a long time before I slept again.

I woke with a start to broad daylight with the rag doll on my pillow and Alisette bouncing on my bed.

"Are you going to sleep late every day now that you're my aunt and not Miss Drake?" she asked.

"I still feel like Miss Drake inside," I told her, sitting up, "so I expect I'll usually wake early." I touched the rag doll's yellow yarn hair. "Your grandmother says that when I was a little girl, she was my doll. My favorite doll."

Alisette studied me for a long moment. "You can have your doll back if you want," she said finally.

I hugged her to me. "Thank you, but I want you to keep Estelle; she's yours now."

Alisette smiled in relief. "Do I have to change her name 'cause yours is Estelle, too?"

I shook my head. "She's Estelle, I'm Aunt Esma."

"Aunt Esma." Alisette said the words slowly. "I'm glad you're not Miss Drake any more 'cause if

193

you're a Nikolai, like me, you won't ever leave Sea Cliff House, and we'll be together for ever and ever."

"For a long time, at any rate," I said, concealing my shiver at the thought of never leaving Sea Cliff House.

"How would you like to have a picnic lunch?" I asked her, deciding I needed to get away from everyone for awhile. Everyone except Alisette. Her welcome presence diverted me from thoughts of Stephen.

"Can we go to the pine grove?" she asked.

"May we," I corrected, trying to ignore the stab of pain her words evoked. Knowing I'd have to revisit the grove sometime, I took a deep breath and added, "The answer is yes."

I took care to choose another location within the grove. After scolding us, the bluejay entertained us by swooping down for the crumbs we scattered and, between him and Alisette's chatter, I managed to keep the tears away. We played tag on the way home and arrived at the back door breathless.

"Did you have any little girls to play with when you were Estelle and lived at Sea Cliff House?" Alisette asked.

"I don't know. I can't remember that time."

"Oh. Like Papa. I hope I never forget *anything.*"

I couldn't tell her there were some things best forgotten.

On Friday, my mother asked me to walk with her to the promontory. "I want your father to know I understood what he was trying to tell me," she said, "but there's another reason why I want you with me. I heard his message so clearly when you accompanied me before, and I hope having you there will prove helpful again."

194

Concealing my reluctance, I agreed to do anything I could to help.

As we left the house, Katherine took my arm. "I'm sure you realized Gerald and Stephen and I had a meeting in the library yesterday. I wouldn't want you to think we were excluding you from family business, but the truth is it didn't occur to me to ask you to be present until we were through. It shan't happen again. As a Nikolai you have the right to voice your opinion in all family matters."

"I didn't feel excluded," I said truthfully. "Since I know so little about the Nikolai businesses, I don't even *have* opinions."

"This, though, you do know about. Mr. Ferguson sent a report from San Francisco on his charting of the sea currents and on his study of our cliffs. I find no fault with his conclusions or his estimate of the cost to protect Sea Cliff House, nor did Gerald or Stephen. Where they disagreed was on whether or not to go ahead with what Mr. Ferguson recommends—a massive breakwater to take the brunt of the waves and multiple steel rods driven into the rock face all along the cliffs to reduce their crumbling."

Looking out at the multitude of white-capped waves rolling shoreward, I said, "It seems to me the breakwater would have to be awfully long and high to give any real protection."

Katherine beamed at me. "You're absolutely right. Unfortunately, extensive also means expensive. Stephen tells me we can't afford to do it. Not and pay for the new ship Mr. Bendixsen is building for us in his shipyard."

I recalled Stephen poring over the account books about the mill. I hadn't heard about the new ship.

"Gerald argues that the money's there," she

went on, "but offers no opinion on what we should do. The final decision will be up to me. I intend to ask Peter what to do and abide by his decision."

I glanced at her in amazement. Did she really believe her dead husband—my father—would advise her? I wished I had some tiny memory of him from the past to treasure so I wouldn't have to think of him as bones resting on the sea floor.

"I sense your disapproval," Katherine said. "Try to understand, Esma. Whatever his faults while he lived, Peter loved me, and our love transcends death."

I found the sentiment beautiful but had difficulty accepting the idea of spirits speaking to the living, so I said nothing.

Though I'd overcome my fear of the sea to some extent, I was by no means comfortable walking so close to the edge of the cliffs, and my heart began a panicky beating when we stepped onto the rocky promontory. As I had the one other time I'd come here, I fastened my eyes on Katherine so as not to see the waves.

She was awe-inspiring, standing tall and straight as she gazed out to sea, her hooded black cape billowing behind her in the wind. I might not have always agreed with Katherine, but I sincerely admired her.

An eternity seemed to pass while I waited with her, the roar of the sea in my ears, spume dampening my cheek as the waves crashed repeatedly on the rock face. I ventured a quick look to my right, saw white water reaching more than halfway up the cliff and hurriedly averted my gaze to the quieter waters of the tiny cove to my left where Cecile's body had been found. I froze in horror at what I saw.

No, I told myself desperately, it's not Cecile

come back to haunt you. That body sprawled on the sand can't be hers; you saw her buried.

As my terror ebbed a bit, I was able to recognize that the body wore men's clothes.

"Peter spoke to me," Katherine said. "I'm not entirely certain what—"

"M-mother!" I gasped, clutching at her arm. "There's a dead man in the cove."

"Dear God!" she exclaimed. "When will it end? Can you see who he is?"

"No."

We hurried back to the house with our grisly news. Armin and Stephen set off with a rope, and I tried not to picture them climbing down to the cove to retrieve the drowned man and haul him to the top.

Less than an hour later, they were back. Gerald, Katherine, and I heard that the drowned man was the old sailor, Floyd Rogers.

"It looks as though he fell from the top of the cliff," Stephen said.

Another accident like Cecile's, I thought with a shudder.

"Armin says it's well-known around town that Rogers was a heavy drinker," Stephen added.

Gerald nodded. "The man was certainly three sheets to the wind when he came here with the locket."

I agreed, recalling how Mr. Rogers had staggered from the library. Terrible as it was, at least his death could be nothing more than a tragic accident.

"The poor man must have fallen on his way back to town from Sea Cliff House." Katherine frowned. "But whatever was he doing near the cliffs?"

"When a man's had too much to drink," Gerald said, "there's no accounting for his actions."

"I'll testify to that." Stephen spoke through clenched teeth, causing his words to take on a personal meaning. I wondered what had befallen him that he remembered with such distress. Had he been drinking in Hong Kong on the night he was so badly injured?

"Besides," Gerald went on, "it had gotten a bit misty by the time Rogers left."

"He told us he was going to meet his Maker," Katherine said. "It brings home how close we all are to death every day of our lives."

I put my hand on her shoulder to comfort her, and she covered it with her own.

"Death was the substance of Peter's message, as well," she went on. "Doom," he told me. "Doom and death." She paused and took a deep breath. "I've decided to leave Sea Cliff House."

I drew in my breath in surprise. "Leave?"

"Yes, Esma, we'll be moving into Eureka as soon as I arrange for a suitable house in town. I hope you don't mind."

"No," I said fervently. "Oh, no."

"And you, Stephen?" Katherine asked.

"I'll be off to the Orient as soon as the new sails are ready," he said. "By next month at the latest. So it matters little where I live in the meantime. In any case, Captain Peter left Sea Cliff House to you."

Involuntarily, my hand went to my heart. Stephen would be sailing away on *Sea Dragon*. Would he ever return?

Katherine turned to Gerald. "Have you any comment?" she asked him.

"My offer still holds."

"Offer?" Stephen's voice was harsh.

Gerald's smile was, I thought, a bit smug. "Why, yes, I've made an offer—a longstanding

198

one—to buy Sea Cliff House if your mother ever decides to sell."

"Buy the house?" Stephen asked incredulously. "The Nikolai house?"

"Why not?" Gerald's smile faded; his tone was challenging.

"I truly believe Gerald loves the place as much as your father did," Katherine said to Stephen. "Sea Cliff House will be in good hands."

"You actually intend to sell the house to him, then," Stephen said flatly.

"Yes. I'd about made up my mind before Esma and I walked to the promontory. Alisette needs to mingle with children her own age. Living in town will provide many opportunities for her. And I—" she paused and smiled at Stephen. "It's time I mingled with my peers as well. While it's true this could be done without moving, I believe we'll all be happier in another house. Your father thinks so, too."

How Katherine deduced that from a message such as "Doom and death," I couldn't fathom.

"And think of your sister," Katherine went on. "We must see she's introduced properly, and I'll have a far easier time doing that in a smaller house, where Mrs. Yates, Sonia, Molly, and Armin will be more than adequate help. In this huge old place, they can barely keep up with the day-to-day chores, even though we live quietly. A ball held here, for instance, would be quite beyond their combined efforts."

Stephen looked directly at me, his lips twisted into a cynical smile. "Is that what you want, Esma, balls and parties?"

I fought for and found enough composure to say tartly, "Since I've never been to a ball or a party, how do I know?"

199

"I must confess," Katherine said, "that, with the aid of Mrs. Plains, I've already selected the place in town I want. The house is fortuitously vacant at the moment, and the price is most reasonable. I've instructed Mr. Tisch, our attorney, to draw up the necessary papers."

Both Gerald and Stephen stared at her as though they couldn't believe their ears. Apparently I'd come to know my mother a bit better than either of them, for her news didn't shock me. Katherine loved surprises.

"You gave no inkling of this when we discussed Mr. Ferguson's report," Stephen said.

"I'm sorry to have deceived you." Katherine didn't sound sorry. "This is a move I've been considering for a long, long time. Mr. Ferguson's report had nothing to do with it one way or the other, except to further my resolve. If I must invest money, it won't be to protect Sea Cliff House, it will be to buy another."

"But Sea Cliff has been in the Nikolai family from the time it was built," Stephen protested. "Are you quite sure you wish to sell it?"

Katherine nodded.

There was a moment of silence, then Gerald said, "Getting back to poor Mr. Rogers. Since I was the one he first spoke to, I'll be glad to go into town now with Armin when he brings in the body so I can report all we know to the authorities."

"A distasteful task, but necessary, I fear," Katherine said. "Thank you, Gerald."

Stephen would have followed Gerald from the library, but his mother stopped him. "Please wait a moment, Stephen, I have an announcement to make before you go."

He turned back and sat on the edge of the desk, his arms folded.

"Mr. Tisch is also revising my will to include

Esma." Katherine smiled at me.

I bit my lip, knowing she would not be dissuaded and wondering if Stephen would resent the inclusion.

"That's fine," he told her. "Esma deserves her share as much as I deserve mine." Why did I think I heard a tinge of mockery in the words?

"I knew you'd approve." Rising, Katherine started toward the door. I accompanied her, intending to go upstairs with her, but she laid a restraining hand on my arm. "Don't bother coming with me—I'm going to speak to Mrs. Yates about the move to Eureka. She'll need time to get used to the idea."

Stephen opened the door for her, and when I would have followed her out, he caught my arm. A moment later he'd closed the door behind his mother, shutting the two of us in the library. My heart thudded in apprehension.

"It's past time we talked." His voice was cold.

I raised my chin. "I see nothing to discuss. There's nothing either of us can say that will change what has happened."

"You got what you wanted, the Nikolai name. You'll eventually get what's left of the Nikolai money as well. You've done right well for a poor, bereft orphan, haven't you?"

"None of it was my doing," I protested hotly. "I never dreamed when I came to Sea Cliff House that I'd ever been here before."

He stared at me contemptuously. "I said it once and I'll say it again—amnesia's mighty convenient, isn't it?"

I glared at him, anger simmering inside me. Was he implying he didn't believe I was Estelle Nikolai? I could hardly believe it myself, but the evidence seemed conclusive. "Do you resent Katherine putting me in her will?" I asked. "Is that what's bothering you?"

"Katherine," he muttered. "Why not say 'our mother'?"

I winced. Not that I'd forgotten we were brother and sister—how could I?—but the sneer in his voice cut me to the quick.

"I don't care to continue this conversation," I said, turning away and reaching for the door handle.

He caught my hand, crushing it in his as he whirled me to face him.

Too close, we were too close, my rapid heart-beat warned. But when I tried to pull free, he didn't release me. His gaze held mine as firmly as his hand gripped mine, and I thought for a moment I saw pain as well as anger in his green eyes.

"Esma, give it up," he said softly.

I couldn't speak or even struggle to free myself, all I could do was look at him, powerless under the force of his gaze.

"God damn it!" he cried, "Why did you have to ruin everything?" Sliding his hand up my arm, he pulled me toward him.

Before I could think what to do, the library door swung open, and Alisette ran into the room. Stephen immediately let me go, and I stepped back.

"I thought you'd never come out so I came in," she said. "Rosie said the old sailor fell off the cliff and drowned like Mama. Did he?"

"I'm afraid so," Stephen said.

"Rosie says that makes two. She says there'll be another 'cause accidents always come in threes. Do you think there'll be three, Papa?"

Stephen glanced at me. "Do you, Esma?"

I swallowed, suddenly fearful. If there were to be a third victim, wouldn't that suggest the two other deaths were *not* accidents? That someone had deliberately pushed both Cecile and Floyd Rogers into the sea to drown?

Logic belatedly came to my rescue. Cecile and the old sailor had no connection whatsoever. There was no reason for anyone to kill them both. Why should there be a third accident?

"Rosie's just repeating a superstition," I told Alisette firmly, wishing the cook would keep her mouth shut when Alisette was in the kitchen. "Accidents don't come in threes any more than blessings do."

Without another word to Stephen, I put an arm around Alisette's shoulders and led her from the library.

Later that night, Sonia came to my room. "I hear you found the body," she said.

I hugged myself, shivering. "I don't care to be reminded."

"Funny the old man should drown so soon after he brought back the locket, wasn't it?" She moved closer to the rocker where I sat and lowered her voice. "He didn't drown that same day like they're saying, though, 'cause I saw him the next day coming from the old ruins."

I wasn't certain whether to believe her or not. "Where were you?" I asked. "You can't see the old ruins from the house."

"You can if you're in the tower. You can see clear to Eureka from there."

"The tower!"

"Yeah. Mrs. Peter took it in her head to have the tower cleaned after all these years." She shifted her shoulders uneasily. "It's sure spooky up there."

Spooky was the right word—the tower had frightened me the one and only time I'd been inside it.

"What would Mr. Rogers be doing at the old church?" I asked.

203

Sonia smiled thinly. "My guess is meeting someone, just like Cecile used to. Only not for the same reason."

"Who?"

"If you mean Rogers, I'm not sure. If you mean Cecile, it was men. Sometimes Gerald, sometimes Armin."

I had known about Gerald, but Armin?

Sonia laughed. "You ought to see your face. Some women are like that, Cecile for one, didn't you know? Any man will do."

Armin. I'd seen him near the cliffs the day Cecile fell. Had they quarreled? Had he accused me of pushing her in an effort to conceal his own guilt?

And now Floyd Rogers was dead. Was it Armin he'd met? Why? And had the old sailor accidentally fallen or was he pushed?

I was afraid of the answers.

Chapter 13

Alisette, usually one of the first to hear—or over-hear—what was going on, didn't learn of her grandmother's proposed move to Eureka until after lunch the next day.

"Is it true we have to move?" she asked as she ran into my room.

I stopped tidying my hair in front of the mirror and turned to her. "Yes. Your grandmother has found a lovely house near the bay and—"

"I won't go!" Alisette cried. "I'm a Nikolai and Nikolais have always lived at Sea Cliff House. Nobody can make me leave."

I was taken aback. Though this was the only home she'd ever known, I'd had no idea she was so attached to the gloomy old place. Aware that there was no reasoning with her when she was set on something, I sought for a roundabout way to convince her the move would benefit her as well as the rest of us.

"Why do you wish to stay?" I asked.

"I don't want to leave Alexandria all alone in the graveyard 'cause she'll get lonesome."

Though it went against what I believed best for her, under the circumstances I decided to compromise. "Your grandmother isn't selling the

205

cemetery and the old church, just Sea Cliff House and its grounds," I told her. "Mr. Callich is buying the house, and he wouldn't mind if we came to visit Alexandria." I smiled. "He might even offer us tea."

"Uncle Gerald's going to stay here?" she asked. I nodded.

"Then I'll live with him," she announced triumphantly.

"Do you think that's fair to your papa and your grandmother? Think how they'll miss you."

Her brows drew together. "I don't care. Grandma and Papa didn't ask *me* if I wanted them to sell my house."

"Actually Sea Cliff House belongs to your grandmother, not your father."

"My mama told me that someday the house would belong to me. Now it never will. Never." Her voice broke on the last word, and she burst into tears.

I lifted her into my arms and sat in the rocker, holding her close. "You'll get used to living in Eureka," I promised. "You can play with Margaret Plains and meet other little girls, too."

"I don't want to," she sobbed. "I want to stay here."

I rocked with her nestled against me. "Going to a new place is always a little scary," I murmured soothingly. "I was terribly frightened about leaving the orphanage to come to Sea Cliff House."

As I hoped, this distracted her. Pulling away so she could look into my face, she said, "Were you honestly, truly scared?"

I wiped her wet face with my handkerchief. "Oh my yes. Don't you remember how I thought the round windows were like eyes staring down at me accusingly?"

She nodded. "Papa said he sort of thought so, too. But they're not really scary, they're just windows." She shifted position to lean her head against my shoulder. "That was when Papa first came home and we walked in the garden. He gave you and me both a rose, and we kept them and pressed them in a book. Only you got scratched by a thorn from yours, and I didn't."

I'd never forget how Stephen had blotted the blood from my palm with his handkerchief. *"In some of the South Sea Islands,"* he'd said, *"there's a belief that if you let anyone have even one drop of your blood, that person gains power over you forever."*

I closed my eyes briefly against the pain in my heart. How could I change what I felt for him? I knew I must, but how?

"I guess I have to live where Papa is," Alisette said. She clutched my hand. "You'll be there, too, won't you?"

"Heavens, yes. *I* don't want to stay on here with your Uncle Gerald."

"He isn't really my uncle, you know."

"I realize that."

"Mama used to kiss him a lot before Papa came home."

I decided the best policy was to ignore what she'd said.

Alisette interlaced her fingers with mine. "Once Mama told Uncle Gerald that even if Papa never came home she wouldn't marry him, 'cause he'd never have enough money. Uncle Gerald laughed and told her she might be surprised 'bout the money, but she wasn't the one he wanted to marry anyway."

As I searched for a change of subject, Alisette went on. "How come you don't have any rings? Mama had lots. I have my baby ring, only my fingers got too big to wear it anymore. Even Sonia's got a ring. It's Mr. Ferguson's, and she wears it round her neck on a chain. I saw her kissing Mr. Ferguson once. Before that she used to kiss Uncle Gerald sometimes."

"I think we have time for one game before your nap," I said hastily, my tone falsely bright. "Would you like to play tic-tac-toe?"

Alisette frowned. "Even though you're my Aunt Esma now you *still* sound like Miss Postern sometimes."

We settled for tic-tac-toe. Though I feared her worry over moving to Eureka might unsettle her, she fell asleep quickly. When she woke from her nap, to my relief she seemed to have forgotten her upset over the prospect of leaving Sea Cliff House. Not once during the following week did she mention the move, so I concluded she'd decided to accept the inevitable.

By Saturday, Katherine had sorted through what she wished to take with us to Eureka and what she intended to leave for Gerald. All the massive furniture and some of the other pieces would stay behind.

"What I'm leaving was bought for Sea Cliff House, and I feel it ought to remain. Besides, I prefer more delicate furniture." She smiled at me. "What fun I'll have furnishing the new house."

It was obvious she was enjoying herself. As for me, I couldn't wait for the move. The house in Eureka would be a new beginning for me, one I badly needed. I'd try my best to leave behind what had happened between Stephen and me. Perhaps, just perhaps, after a time away from Sea Cliff House, I might be able to forget.

Stephen no longer stayed at the house during the day. He was aboard *Sea Dragon*, I supposed, readying her for the journey to the Orient. I saw

208

him at dinner, but he scarcely spoke a word to me and rarely even glanced my way. Yet, when we were in the same room, I had to force myself to concentrate hard on whatever I was doing—even eating was a chore in his disturbing presence. I hated to think of him sailing away, but I knew it was best for both of us.

After dinner on Saturday evening, Katherine invited me to her suite to discuss, she said, how I'd like my room in the Eureka house furnished.

When we were settled comfortably, I told her what I really wanted was the contents of the Ivory Room transferred to the other house. "I feel at home with that lovely Chinese furniture," I said.

"Whatever you wish, dear."

We sat for a few moments in silence, and I couldn't help but notice she seemed distracted. "Is anything wrong?" I asked.

"I'm terribly worried about Stephen. About him sailing. I dare not ask him to stay—the Nikolai men are seafarers, one and all."

"Why are you so worried?"

"I've had another message from your father," she said. "I went to the promontory to tell him we were leaving Sea Cliff House, as he wished us to do. Then I mentioned that Stephen would be sailing in a few weeks. Do you know what Peter told me?"

I shook my head, controlling my aversion to having anything at all to do with spirit messages.

"'With me,' Peter said. 'With me.'" Katherine covered her eyes with her hand. "I'm afraid, afraid of what he means. Does his message foreshadow Stephen's death? Will *Sea Dragon* sink and Stephen drown? What else can 'with me' mean but that soon Stephen will be at the bottom of the sea with his father?"

A prickle of dread raised the hair on my nape.

"Oh, no!" I exclaimed. "No, it can't mean he'll drown. Not Stephen!"

Katherine sighed. "What else am I to think?" She reached for my hand and held it tightly between hers. "Don't *you* leave me, Esma. I couldn't bear to lose both of you."

"I'm not going away," I assured her. "Wherever you and Alisette are is my home."

Later, walking to my room, I tried to stop thinking about the meaning of Captain Peter's fearful message by reminding myself that, despite the fact he was my father, I didn't believe that the dead spoke to the living. What Katherine actually heard in her mind must be only an echo of her own fears.

On Thursday of the following week, I was invited to accompany Alisette and Katherine to tea at the Plains home. Afterwards, leaving Alisette in the care of Margaret's grandmother, my mother and I walked the four blocks to the house where, in a matter of days, we'd be living. It was my first good look at the place, though I'd seen it several times from the carriage window.

The wooden siding had been newly painted and the house gleamed in the sunlight, white and bright and shining. Though smaller than the mansion we were leaving, it was a generous size, three stories with a cupola on top facing the bay.

The dining room's oriel windows looked onto a garden smaller than the one at Sea Cliff House, but every bit as beautiful, with a rose arbor and a gold-fish pond. Alisette would be happy about the pond; she could still sail her boats.

Inside, the house smelled of paint and varnish and wallpaper paste since all the rooms had been redecorated according to Katherine's instructions. She'd chosen the colors while relying on me as to proper shades and the patterns of the paper. I'd been nervous about my choices, but the results dazzled me.

"It's beautiful," I murmured.

"I'm glad you like it," Katherine said. "I think we'll be happy here. If only Stephen—" She bit her lip and said no more.

"He'll come back from this journey the same as he returned from the others," I said firmly, praying my words would prove to be prophetic.

"I'd like to go down to his ship," Katherine said after a moment. "I believe I'm up to walking a few more blocks."

With her hand on my arm for guidance, we left the house and made our way to the docks. As usual, I was torn between wanting to see Stephen and dreading meeting him. I couldn't help but recall my first visit to *Sea Dragon*—how happy I'd been then. How miserable I was now.

"Tell me when you catch sight of her," Katherine ordered. When I did, she said, "I haven't seen *Sea Dragon* in years. Describe her to me, please."

"The three masts are bare of sail," I began, trying to remember the words I'd learned from Alisette and Stephen. "She flies the red and gold Nikolai colors behind her bowsprit and the stars and stripes from the stern mast. Her brass fittings shine in the sun and so does the gilt dragon on her prow. She's a ship of which to be proud." My voice rose as in my imagination I pictured *Sea Dragon* flying before the wind with her sails unfurled and billowing. "She's magnificent!"

"Yes, she's all of that and more," Stephen spoke from my left. I whirled to face him.

"Stephen!" Katherine exclaimed, turning toward him while I tried to regain my equilibrium.

"I saw you walking this way and came to meet

you," he told her. But he looked at me.

"I'd like to go aboard," she said.

"I'd be honored by your presence on my ship." He spoke to her but kept his eyes on me. "Will you also come aboard, Esma?"

"I—yes, thank you," I stammered.

Once we were on the ship's main deck, I was so intent on Stephen that at first I didn't notice how the relatively short walk had exhausted Katherine. I finally realized she was leaning quite heavily on me, something she never did.

"Are you all right?" I asked her, alarmed by how ashen she looked.

"I'm a wee bit tired," she admitted.

"Stephen, she needs to sit down," I said, and he immediately called for a chair. Moments later a sailor ran up with a wooden and canvas contraption that unfolded into a sort of lounge chair.

Katherine sat down, leaning her head back against the canvas and closing her eyes. "I'll be fine after a little rest," she assured us.

"I'll send a man for the carriage," Stephen said to me. "Where is it—at the Plainses'?"

I nodded, and he went off while I stood beside my mother, watching her anxiously. She seemed to be breathing a bit easier, but her color remained pale. By the time Stephen returned, she'd fallen into a doze. When he started to speak, I put my finger to my lips and moved from her side to stand by the rail. He followed me.

"Has she been ill?" he asked in a low tone, his eyes on Katherine.

"Not that I know of." I glanced toward her, but she hadn't moved.

"I don't think she's seen a doctor since I've been home," he said. "Maybe she should, but not that idiot March who used to take care of Alsie. I'll see what I can arrange."

212

"I wish you would. I'm worried about her."

His gaze shifted to me and he studied me for a long moment. "You're such a mass of contradictions I can't be sure what's genuine and what's put on."

I stared at him indignantly. Was he implying I was only pretending to care about Katherine? Before I could put together a scathing reply, he spoke again.

"How do you really feel about the move to town?"

"Relieved," I said honestly, not adding that I was equally relieved to have the subject changed. "I've never been fond of Sea Cliff House. Alsie isn't too happy, though."

"She hasn't said a word about being unhappy to me."

"I think she's become resigned to the move. At first she considered remaining behind to live with Gerald, but then she decided she'd rather live where you were, even if it wasn't Sea Cliff House."

Stephen looked across the water toward the Humboldt Peninsula, the strip of land between the bay and the ocean. "If I could, I'd take Alsie with me when I sail," he said slowly. "I'll miss her."

"Not half as much as she'll miss you." Or I'll miss you, I added silently.

"I hate leaving her behind. I hate leaving!" He slammed his fist down on the rail. "I swear that if I'd known beforehand what would happen, I'd never have brought *Sea Dragon* across the bar into Humboldt Bay. Never!"

Would I have come to Sea Cliff House if I'd known? I sighed. It was too late for such a question. He'd crossed the bar into the bay and I'd gotten off the stage and into the Nikolai carriage: both of us on our way to a meeting that would

213

eventually leave the two of us devastated.

"I need to talk to you in private," he said. "This isn't the time or place for what I have to say."

"No." I whispered the word, afraid to be alone with him, afraid of myself.

"Yes. And soon."

I left him abruptly, returning to Katherine's side, but I feared it wouldn't be as easy to avoid the meeting. Not with Stephen so determined.

By the time Armin clattered onto the docks with the carriage, Katherine was awake and looking somewhat better. Stephen helped her from the ship and lifted her into the carriage.

"I mean to ask a doctor to see you," he told her, "and I expect no argument."

"Perhaps you're right," she said. "As long as it's not that old fool March."

Her ready agreement alarmed me more than a refusal would have. If Katherine was so easily persuaded to be examined by a doctor, then she must believe something more than mere exhaustion was wrong with her.

Dr. Landers, a stocky, youngish man with a full black beard, arrived just before dinner. I'd wanted to sit with Katherine, but she'd refused to let me remain in her bedroom, saying all she needed was a bit of sleep. After showing the doctor to her suite, I retreated as far as the west-wing gallery, not wanting to appear to be eavesdropping by waiting outside her door. I wandered from picture to picture, while Alexi's green gaze, so like Stephen's, seemed to follow me from his portrait.

If you're one of us, he seemed to be saying, *then behave like a Nikolai. Properly.*

"You're a fine one to talk," I muttered, staring at his painted face.

According to what Katherine had told me, the Nikolais were a respected Russian family, friends

214

over the years with more than one czar. Two seafaring half brothers, Alexi and Sergei, established themselves in a Russian community on the California coast while fur trading with the native Alaskans. The small settlement, now called Fort Ross, prospered for a time.

As a result of an agreement with Mexico in 1841, Czar Nikolai ordered all Russian citizens to leave California and come home. Alexi, determined never to return to Russia, quarreled with his older half brother who was equally determined to obey the czar's command.

Secretly appropriating the partnership money and the Nikolai fur-trading ship, Alexi fled from Fort Ross, sailing up the California coast where he put in at the then-unknown and unnamed Humboldt Bay, successfully avoiding the dangers of the bar. He'd been surprised to find a deserted Russian church on the headlands.

Sergei never forgave Alexi's desertion and treachery. He returned to Russia and became a ship's captain, but his Nikolai branch hadn't proved as successful as Alexi's.

"Some would call you a thief," I told the portrait. Alexi's painted smile didn't falter, and his green eyes glinted as wickedly as ever.

"Rebel is a kinder word for Alexi," Stephen said from behind me. "But thief will do."

I pressed my hands to my heart in a futile attempt to quiet its sudden wild beat. Not turning, keeping my gaze on the portrait, I said, "You look enough like Alexi to pass for him."

His harsh and bitter laughter startled me into glancing at him.

"We Nikolais share certain traits." Reaching a hand to my hair, he fingered a curling strand that had escaped from the confining tortoiseshell comb. "Dark curls, for one. I've no doubt you have

215

Nikolai blood. But then, so does Armin. It's common knowledge Captain Peter bedded local women—who knows how many bastards he sired? For that matter, I've heard old Alexi did the same. A few drops of Nikolai blood doesn't make you Estelle Marie Nikolai. You're a fraud, and you know it."

I clenched my fists, gritting my teeth to hold back the angry words. I would not lower myself to reply to his absurd accusation. To back up the old seaman's story, there'd been the proof of the locket and my moles—how could I not be Estelle?

He caught my shoulder and turned me so I faced him. I immediately shrugged free of his hold.

"You and that old sot Rogers conspired to defraud Katherine Nikolai," he accused. "How you obtained the locket, I don't know—maybe it washed up on the beach. Why did Rogers have to die? Because he drank too much and talked too much? And how did he really die, Esma?"

I stared at him in horror. "Are you implying I killed Mr. Rogers?" I asked incredulously.

"I wouldn't go quite that far. There could be yet another conspirator involved."

"Armin, perhaps?" Ice edged my words. "Or another as yet unidentified by-blow of your father's? I notice you never refer to him as your father. Are you ashamed of him?"

"When have I heard you call Katherine 'Mother'?" he countered.

I bit my lip. "I'm not used to having a mother." Then, angry because he'd forced me to defend myself, I lashed out at him again. "Why can't you accept me for what I am?"

His hands clamped down on my shoulders. "You're so damn plausible. Plausible enough to take anyone in. God knows you took me in with your feigned innocence." He shook me so hard one

216

of my combs flew from my hair. "Damn you, Esma, damn, damn—" He stopped shaking me, stopped speaking. What might have been a sob convulsed him. "Damn you," he repeated hoarsely, "why can't I hate you?"

Before I realized what he meant to do, I was in his arms, and his mouth covered mine. My traitorous body responded by pressing closer to him as his kiss ignited a smoldering fire within me.

No! I told myself. You must not! Using every ounce of willpower I possessed, I broke free, pushing him away. "How can you?" I cried. "I'm your sister!"

We stared at one another for a long moment. I don't know what would have happened if we hadn't heard a door close along the corridor.

"The doctor," I said breathlessly.

Stephen turned away from me, and we both waited.

Dr. Landers was blunt. "Your mother has a serious heart condition," he said. "I've prescribed tincture of foxglove, but she's not to overdo, no, indeed. I stressed rest and moderation, in addition to the medicine, but Mrs. Nikolai is a determined woman and not easily convinced." He fixed his attention on me. "You must take good care of her. As for you, sir," he switched his gaze to Stephen, "you must persuade your mother that rest is essential to her health."

Almost in unison, Stephen and I assured the doctor we'd do all we could.

"Then I leave her in good hands," he said with a quick nod of his head. He instructed me as to how many drops of the tincture I was to measure for her and took himself off.

I started for Katherine's suite, but Stephen grasped my arm. "I'm warning you," he said grimly. "I don't expect her to die."

217

I glared at him. How could he think for a moment I'd do anything to harm Katherine? "She's my mother as much as she is yours," I snapped.

His smile was mocking. "Quite possibly."

His words left me in confusion. One moment he was accusing me of planning to kill Katherine, and the next he was admitting I might be Estelle after all. If that *was* what he meant. I wasn't sure about anything he said.

Freeing myself from his grasp, I turned my back to him and, head held high, marched along the corridor to Katherine's suite.

I found her propped on pillows in her bed, wearing a lacy robe in a dark shade of pink. I'd never before seen her in any other color besides black. Though she looked drawn and tired, the pink became her.

"Sit here," she said, patting the bed. When I obeyed, she took my hand in hers. "I suppose Dr. Landers told you about my heart," she continued. "He seems competent enough but, no matter what he says, you're not to worry. You see, Peter will warn me when my time is near and so far he has not."

"Dr. Landers thinks you'll be all right if you take your medicine and don't overdo," I said, not commenting on the prospect of spirit messages from my father. "I intend to take good care of you."

She smiled and stroked my hand. "You're mothering me. It seems only yesterday you were a baby in my arms. I used to rock you in an old carpet rocker that's now stored in the attic. You wouldn't remember, even if you could, because you were so very young, but I used to sing a Russian folk lullaby to you that I learned from my mother, a song she'd learned from her mother. In

English it means something like, "Lullaby, my child, my baby, lullaby."

Katherine began to hum, then sing:

> *"Bhayu bhayushki bhayu*
> *Bhayu detochke moyu—bhayu . . ."*

I tensed, listening to the oddly familiar words. Nonsense words, I'd always thought. But they weren't, they weren't at all. The words were Russian, that's why I hadn't understood them. Though I'd repeatedly told myself I had to be Estelle, deep in my heart I hadn't believed it until that moment.

I began to sing along with her:

> *"Bhayu bhayushki bhayu*
> *Bhayu detochke moyu—bhayu . . ."*

"You do remember!" Katherine exclaimed delightedly.

I was so choked up I couldn't speak. She really and truly *was* my mother. Blinking back tears, I leaned over and kissed her cheek.

I heard a noise. Stephen stood in the open doorway, staring at us, his eyes wide with shock. I had no idea how long he'd been there. A moment later, he spun on his heel and was gone.

Chapter 14

The following evening Stephen didn't appear for dinner. Nor, I heard from Katherine the next morning when I went to her suite to measure the drops of her heart medicine, had he come home at all. "He said good-bye to me early yesterday morning," she told me, "because he wanted to remain aboard *Sea Dragon* while the lumber was being stowed."

My heart turned over. If the ship was taking on cargo, Stephen must be ready to sail. Why was he leaving early? To avoid seeing me again?

Controlling my agitation, I said, "I thought his sailing date was the end of next week."

"He intends to make a run to San Francisco to test the new mast and sails before he sets forth for the Orient. The cargo of lumber will be sold in San Francisco and *Sea Dragon* will return to Eureka to correct any problems they might have with the mast or sails. I thoroughly approve of his caution. Especially in view of your father's last message to me."

Relief flooded through me. Stephen would be back in a matter of days, and I'd have my chance to say good-bye before he left again, perhaps for years. Though separation was the only solution to our problem, I hated to see him go.

"Have the movers come yet?" Katherine asked. "I do believe I feel well enough to ride to the Eureka house and supervise the men when they unload the boxes."

We weren't moving completely into the other house today, merely sending the packed boxes and small pieces of furniture. Nevertheless, it would be several wagonloads. My mother and Alisette shared certain traits—stubbornness being one. If confronted too bluntly, Katherine would insist on going, and I didn't believe she should. I chose an oblique approach to deter her.

"There's no need for you to ride into Eureka," I said, "unless you don't trust me to oversee the movers."

"Why, of course I trust you, dear. You're a most capable young woman. But I can't just loll around all the time, can I?"

"You can always help Mrs. Yates keep an eye on the loading from here." That, I felt, wouldn't be nearly so strenuous as the ride, plus remaining in an incompletely furnished house for hours on end telling the moving men where to put the various packed boxes and the odds and ends of furniture.

"What about Alisette? Will you leave her with me? You'll never be able to watch her and the movers, too."

"I'll manage, Mother. I think she should get used to the new house, so I'll take her with me. I'll find tasks for her. If Alisette thinks she's helping she can be very good."

After leaving my mother, I started for the kitchen where I'd left Alisette helping Rosie make an angel food cake, but Sonia intercepted me in the foyer.

221

"I've been watching for you," she said in a low tone, glancing nervously around. "Look, would you do me a favor?"

"If I can."

"You're going into town, right?"

I nodded.

"Take me with you, please." Her eyes, wide and frightened, pleaded with me.

Though I didn't understand why she was afraid, I saw no reason not to give her a ride into Eureka. In fact, Sonia would be a help.

"I'll be glad to have you with me," I told her. "Two pair of eyes will be better than one when trying to watch Alisette and cope with the movers at the same time."

She lowered her gaze to her clenched hands. "Would you please say you told me to go with you if anyone asks?"

Though somewhat taken aback at her odd request, I agreed.

Sonia then followed me into the kitchen. She continued to dog my footsteps while Alisette and I got ready to go. When Armin pulled up in the carriage, Sonia hastily retrieved her hat, a jacket, and a shawl-wrapped bundle from a chest in the foyer.

"What's that?" Alisette asked, pointing to the bundle.

"Something I'm taking into town for your grandmother," Sonia told her.

Alisette accepted the explanation, but I was positive Sonia was lying, and I wondered why. As I lifted Alisette into the carriage, the moving men's wagon rattled into the drive. Sonia jumped into the carriage and huddled into a corner as though trying to hide, leaving me the last to climb in. She said not a word all the way into Eureka.

We'd barely arrived at the new house—we weren't even to the door yet—when Mrs. Plains's personal maid, Thelma, came hurrying along the wooden sidewalk.

"Miss Nikolai, I'm to ask if Miss Alisette will come to play with Miss Margaret," she said. "And Mrs. Plains invites you both to lunch."

I accepted, telling Thelma to thank Mrs. Plains for her kind offer. Alisette went off with her willingly enough.

"I'll show you through the house before the moving men arrive," I told Sonia, starting up the steps to the porch.

"I don't have time," she said, her eyes on the Nikolai carriage. Together we watched Armin turn a corner and the carriage disappear from view.

"What's wrong, Sonia?" I asked.

She looked furtively around, finally climbing the steps to join me on the porch. "I'm going to San Francisco to meet Jock Ferguson," she said. "He asked me to come, and so I am."

Not wishing to embarrass her, I forbore asking her if marriage was a part of the offer. "I hope you know what you're doing," I commented.

"Anything's better than getting shoved off a cliff."

"What on earth are you talking about?"

"Rosie told God's truth when she said accidents come in threes. I don't mean to be the third."

I was totally confused. "But why would you be?"

"I know too much." She leaned closer, dropping her voice. "I didn't tell you everything, didn't tell you I saw that old sailor, Rogers, long before he ever brought that locket to the house. I was taking a walk on my half day, and I heard voices in the church ruins. I went and hid and pretty soon I saw Rogers come out of the church. Cecile saw him, too, 'cause she was on her way to meet who-

223

ever was still in the church. She walked right past the old sailor."

Sonia looked meaningfully at me. "You know what happened to Cecile. You know what happened to Rogers. Well, it won't happen to me!"

I stared at her. "Who *was* the other person in the church?"

She shrugged. "I got my notions, but I'm keeping 'em to myself. It's safer." She reached and hugged me. "You be careful, Miss Estelle."

I watched her hurry down the steps and along the plank sidewalk toward the docks. It wasn't until she was almost out of sight that it occurred to me she might be planning to sail on *Sea Dragon*. If Stephen hadn't already left. With this in mind, I went into the house and climbed to the third floor where I looked from a window in the cupola toward the bay.

Sea Dragon was still moored at the wharf, but I noticed a tugboat making its way toward the ship, and I remembered what Stephen had told Alisette and me when we visited his ship: "Ships need piloting in and out of Humboldt Bay to get safely around the bar. The best pilot I ever saw is Hans Buhne and his tug *Mary Ann*."

I stood watching the ship until the movers arrived. By then she'd begun to cast off her lines, getting ready to sail.

Directing the men here and there, upstairs and down, left me no time for thinking of anything else. It wasn't until they rode off in the wagon for the next load that I was able to return to the cupola. *Mary Ann* with *Sea Dragon* in tow was well out into the bay.

"Good-bye, Stephen," I murmured, relieved that it wasn't a final good-bye. "Return safely."

I was about to turn away when a moving figure below caught my attention, a child running toward the docks. The girl, her dark hair flying loose behind her, wore a gray dress and no coat or hat.

Dear God, it was Alisette!

Had she also watched from a high window at the Plainses and seen *Sea Dragon* pull away from the dock? I realized with dismay she might not have heard that her father was only sailing as far as San Francisco and be thinking he was leaving on his voyage to the Orient. The poor child must feel her papa had deserted her, but what did she hope to do at the dock? The ship was gone.

Catching up my skirts, I rushed down the two flights of stairs and through the front door, anxious to be with her on the dock so I could relieve her mind. By the time I reached the plank sidewalk, she was out of sight. I ran as fast as I could.

"Alisette!" I called. "Alisette, wait!"

I was breathless when I reached the section of the dock where *Sea Dragon* had been moored. There'd been no sign of Alisette on the way, and she was nowhere in sight now. In fact, no one was in the immediate vicinity. All the activity was farther along the wharf where another ship was being loaded.

Glancing across the bay, I saw *Sea Dragon* nearing the bar. I also spotted a small rowboat bobbing in the water not far from the docks. To my horror, a small figure crouched inside the boat. Alisette!

She'd taken the boat in a desperate attempt to reach her father on *Sea Dragon*!

With no thought in my mind except rescuing her, I hurried down a rickety ladder to where another rowboat rocked in the waves lapping against the pilings. I climbed in awkwardly and fumbled with the rope holding the boat to the post until at last it came loose. Shoving with an oar, as I'd seen Stephen do, I pushed away from the dock.

Rowing, I discovered very quickly, looked easier than it was. My frantic attempts at first only turned me in a circle. Finally I mastered enough skill to go in the direction I wanted, but my progress was slow and difficult and the gap between my boat and Alisette's didn't seem to narrow. She still was making no attempt to use her oars, and her boat drifted with the current.

"I'm coming, Alisette!" I cried. "Hold on!"

Inch by painful inch, I closed the gap between us, praying with each awkward stroke I took that she'd remain huddled in the bottom of the boat and not stand up and topple over the side. I thanked God for the relatively calm water of the bay.

I was dimly aware of shouts from shore and the hooting of a steam whistle, but I didn't look anywhere except at my goal—Alisette's boat. It seemed to take forever before the prow of my boat scraped against the side of hers. I'd made it!

Now all I had to do was lift her from her boat into mine and row back to the dock.

"Alisette," I said. "Sit up."

She didn't move, remaining curled into a ball on the bottom of the boat.

Was she hurt? "Alisette!" I cried in alarm, rising to my feet and reaching for her.

My boat rocked ominously. Standing, I realized, had been a serious mistake. Frantically, I tried to stop the rocking and sit down, but it was too late. I screamed as I felt myself toppling and then cold green water closed over my head.

Panic-stricken, I fought my way to the surface and tried to grasp the side of a boat, but both had drifted beyond my reach. My wild splashing was futile; I went under again, my wet clothes and the

226

pull of the sea dragging me down and down.

Down to the bottom of the wild green sea.

I was surrounded by green. Water choked me. There was nothing but water—my nightmare come true. And suddenly I knew this was not the first time I'd struggled against drowning, not the first time that I'd fought the sea to stay alive. As my frenzied thrashing brought me once more to the surface, I remembered it all happening before— the desperate gasp for air, the terror when I couldn't stay on the surface, the despair when I sank despite my weakening efforts to stay afloat.

I was a child again, a terrified five year old all alone in the immensity of the ocean and, no matter how hard I tried to save myself, the merciless sea was far stronger than I.

I tried to call for my big brother Stephen to help me, but my mouth filled with water instead of air, drowning my voice. Green was all around me; I couldn't breathe. And then darkness blotted out the green, and I knew no more.

I floated in darkness. Voices making meaningless sounds came and went. Then hands began to push me this way and that, pummeling my back, hurting me, and I tried to protest, but I had no words. Suddenly I was very sick, liquid vomit spewing from my mouth. I wanted my mama, she'd make me feel better, but I couldn't open my eyes to find her.

I coughed and coughed, my throat raw from the bitter vomit until finally I could cough no more and began sinking back into the peaceful darkness.

"Esma!" a man called, over and over. But that wasn't my name, I was Estelle Marie. He couldn't coax me from the darkness with the wrong name.

But he wouldn't stop, and so I finally opened my eyes. A man's face swam before me, a man with

227

dark hair and a dark beard. He had green eyes like my brother Stephen. As my eyelids drooped shut once more, I frowned. It was the wrong face. The man should have light hair and blue eyes and no beard.

Fragments of memory drifted past: I'd been in the water and then I'd been sick, and when I opened my eyes a man was looking at me. A man with fair hair and blue eyes. A man I knew. He worked at Papa's mill. I tried to grasp the memory shards, but the darkness beckoned and I slipped into it once more.

The next face I saw was Katherine's.

"Thank God you're awake," she said fervently.

But I wasn't fully awake. Though I understood I was grown up and not five years old, confused memories of the past clogged my mind so that I couldn't think clearly. I turned my head and black button eyes stared blankly at me. My rag doll. No, not mine, it was Alisette's. Alisette had been in a boat, drifting in the bay, and I'd gone after her. . . .

"Alisette!" I tried to cry, but her name emerged as a hoarse cough.

Katherine correctly interpreted the discordant sound. "Alisette is fine, dear, she didn't even get wet. She insisted on leaving her doll in your bed to make you feel better."

Relieved, I sank into sleep. I don't know how much later I woke coughing. The lamp was lit, and a woman I didn't recognize hovered over me. When my spasm eased a bit, she offered me a dark liquid in a medicine spoon.

"I'm the nurse," she said. "Dr. Landers ordered this for your cough."

Obediently I swallowed the bad-tasting dose.

The next time I woke, daylight revealed a room

I'd never seen before. I lay in an unfamiliar bed with a curved mahogany footboard, looking at wallpaper decored with yellow cabbage roses. I raised my head and the room spun for a moment, but when I persisted, easing onto one elbow, everything finally settled into place.

The nurse stood beside the bed. "You're not to get up," she said firmly. "Dr. Landers says you're just this far from having pneumonia." She measured a tiny space between her thumb and forefinger.

"Can't I sit up?" I asked plaintively. Catching sight of Thelma standing just inside the door with a tray of food, I realized I must be at the Plains house, though I had no idea how I'd gotten there. Or who'd rescued me from the waters of the bay.

The nurse propped two pillows against the headboard and helped me sit up. After handing me a damp cloth so I could wash my face and hands, she stepped aside, and Thelma arranged the tray in front of me.

I'd taken no more than two sips of a delicious beef broth before the door flew open and Alisette bounded in. "I heard you talking so I knew you woke up," she said, climbing onto the bed. Retrieving her doll from beside me, she hugged it to her breast. "Aunt Esma, I didn't mean to make you almost drown."

"I know you didn't, Alisette. But didn't you realize you might have drowned yourself?"

She looked down at the bedclothes. "Grandma scolded me already."

I brushed a strand of hair from her forehead. "I won't scold you. I'm just glad you're all right."

She raised her head and looked at me. "Papa should be scolded 'cause he didn't say good-bye to me. If he had, I'd have known he was only going away for a few days."

I concealed a smile. No scolding completely chastised Alisette.

"You're keeping your aunt from eating her lunch," the nurse said. "She needs to eat to get well."

Alisette's contrite expression made me say hastily, "I don't remember what happened after I fell in the water, Alisette. Why don't you tell me while I eat."

"I got scared in the boat," she said. "I heard you tell me you were coming and to sit up, only I couldn't, 'cause I was too afraid. People were hollering and boat whistles blowing. Then there was a big splash and you screamed, and I raised up and looked over the side of the boat, and you were in the water. So then I screamed, too. Pretty soon I couldn't see you anymore.

"After awhile Papa came in a big boat with lots of men rowing, and he lifted me into his boat, and then he took off his boots and his coat and dived in the water. He went under, and I couldn't see him either, and I was scared you both would drown. Only you didn't 'cause Papa found you and lifted you into the big boat, too. He put you over his knees, and the whole time the men rowed us to the docks Papa pushed on your back and water kept coming out of your mouth."

"I think I recall that part," I said, grimacing.

"Papa carried you into the mill, and he kept saying, 'Esma, Esma,' but you never answered. Finally he yelled, "She's alive!" and everyone cheered. By then Mrs. Plains had come looking for me, and she had them put you in her carriage and she brought both of us here to her house."

I vaguely recalled seeing a man's face and thinking it was the wrong face. It must have been

Stephen, but why would I believe his face was the wrong one?

"Where is your father now?" I asked.

"He had to get back on *Sea Dragon*, 'cause they had to go round the bar right then or wait a whole 'nother day."

So Stephen was on his way to San Francisco.

"Papa said he was looking through a spyglass trying to see our new house, and that's how come he saw me get in the boat. He said he'd already lowered the big boat off the ship when you began rowing out to me—that's how he got there so fast. So now Papa's saved you twice and me once."

"Yes," I said, "he has."

"I almost forgot. Papa said to tell you Sonia was aboard *Sea Dragon*." Alisette frowned. "Why did Sonia get to sail with Papa when I didn't?"

"Sonia's not coming back," I told her. "She's meeting Mr. Ferguson in San Francisco and staying there."

"Oh. Are they going to get married?"

"I hope so."

"Maybe he'll give her a ring she can wear on her finger 'stead of round her neck." She cocked her head as if listening. "That's our carriage 'cause the wheel squeaks." Sliding off the bed, she hurried to the window and looked down. "I was right. Grandma's here."

By the time my mother came into the room, Thelma had taken away the tray and I was brushing my hair. My mother came to the bedside, leaned down, and hugged me. "How are you feeling, dear?"

"I'm hardly even coughing. If I can persuade the nurse to let me, I plan to get up."

"Don't overdo."

231

"That's what I'm supposed to be saying to you!" I told her.

"Well, *I'm* better, too. I managed the move without once having a weak spell."

"I'm sorry I—"

She put a finger across my lips, stopping me. "I had plenty of help with the move. My dear friend Ida Plains found me a wonderful woman to be our maid—Loretta's her name, she's a widow in her forties. No more of these flighty young girls for me. You did know Sonia ran off without so much as a by-your-leave?"

"She begged a ride to San Francisco on *Sea Dragon* just before Stephen sailed," I said. "Mr. Ferguson sent for her." I had no intention of burdening my mother with all Sonia had told me.

"Good riddance. I never took to the girl. If Gerald hadn't recommended her I wouldn't have taken her on in the first place. In any case, I'm now living at the new house. When you're strong enough, you'll come there. Mrs. Yates and Loretta, with Molly helping, have done wonders getting everything into shape. And Rosie loves the new kitchen."

Realizing I'd never have to go back to Sea Cliff House again lightened my heart. "I'd like to go home right now," I said. "I know I could walk to and from the carriage."

Katherine, with her unerring sense of where a person was standing, looked toward the nurse. "In the morning, I think, Mrs. Walters," she said to her. "I'm sure Dr. Landers will approve." Turning back to me, my mother said, "You'll agree to wait until tomorrow morning, won't you, dear?"

While I did feel markedly improved, almost my old self, I knew I'd get nowhere arguing with her. "All right, I'll content myself with getting up and

232

sitting in a chair," I said firmly. And I refused to be dissuaded.

By evening I was strong enough to walk around without leaning on Mrs. Walter's arm. Though I thought having a nurse on hand throughout the night would be unnecessary, I was outvoted by her, my mother, and Mrs. Plains.

"We'll all feel so much easier with Mrs. Walters looking after you tonight," Mrs. Plains told me.

"I've been a burden to you—" I began.

"Nonsense. I was happy to be of help." She squeezed my mother's shoulders affectionately. "Katherine and I have been friends since we were girls. Many's the time she came to my assistance. It's only fair I have the chance to return the favor. With Alisette sleeping in Margaret's room, it was like the old days when Katherine and I giggled until way past our bedtime. As for you, Esma, though you're welcome to stay as long as you like, for your mother's sake I'm delighted at your rapid recovery."

Mrs. Walters did prove a blessing when she offered to wash my hair, still stiff with salt. Much as I hated to admit it, the procedure tired me and I was glad to crawl into bed for the night.

I fell asleep immediately.

A face hovered before me, hazy and indistinct as though separated from me by a veil of fog. "Who are you?" a man's voice asked. "What's your name?"

I tried to answer, but I didn't know my name. I didn't know who I was or where I was.

"She doesn't remember." A woman's voice this time. "She doesn't remember anything."

The face grew clearer, a man's face, a man I knew, if I could only recall who he was. Then it faded and was gone.

233

I tried desperately to speak, but only a mumble emerged. "Esma, Esma, Esma." The word made no sense to me. It certainly wasn't my name.

Suddenly the man's face reappeared, hovering disembodied above me, terrifying me. He didn't speak, but something about him was indescribably menacing. Knowing I must escape him or I was doomed, I slid from my bed and fled into a green-painted corridor whose thick green carpeting muffled my footsteps. I ran and ran down this endless green corridor, but I knew the face followed me, though I feared to look behind.

At last the green corridor came to an end, and I faced an ornately carved door with a large brass knob. The door was locked, but I carried the key. I was almost as frightened of what lay beyond the door as I was of the evil face, but I unlocked it and plunged through.

I stood in the kitchen at Sea Cliff House where Rosie, dressed in Katherine's long black hooded cape, stirred a cauldron over the fire.

"Beware," Rosie intoned, "beware. Listen. The bell tolls the death knell."

At the first toll I came awake, gasping. And listened while the bell chimed ominously two more times into the darkness.

A lamp flared. Someone bent over me. A woman. Mrs. Walters. "What's wrong?" she asked.

"The bell," I cried, still caught in the throes of my dream.

"Why, that's St. Bernard's bell tolling the hours. It's three o'clock in the morning."

I swallowed my fright. "I had a bad dream," I murmured.

"And no wonder, after what you've been through," she said.

I took a deep breath and let it out slowly.

"Would you mind leaving the lamp on low for the rest of the night?"

"Light can be a comfort," she agreed. "Are you sure you don't need anything else?"

I shook my head, closing my eyes to convince her I was all right. When I heard her moving off to her cot, I opened my eyes, staring up at the plastered ceiling, painted yellow to match the cabbage roses. As frightening as the dream had been, I tried to recall as much of it as I could for I felt the dream held an urgent message, a message I must decipher.

Otherwise I'd be helpless to avoid the terrible danger lying in wait for me.

Chapter 15

Once I was home with Katherine and Alisette, I recovered rapidly, soon regaining my normal good health. But my mind remained troubled as I pored over the bits and pieces of memories that had returned to me from that long-ago time before I found myself in the orphanage, wishing I could make sense of what I'd remembered. I didn't share these memories with my mother as I was certain they'd only upset her.

In fact, I told no one.

Alisette was settling in to our new home quite well, though she still mentioned Alexandria. She also missed having her pony close at hand. Since the stable at the back of the Eureka house could hold no more than the two carriage horses, Katherine had arranged for Bosun, the gray mare, and Sir Toby to be boarded on a nearby farm. Alisette and I could still ride but not as conveniently, and she grumbled about the long walk to the farm.

"Why can't Armin drive us today?" she asked Katherine one morning after we'd been in the new house a week.

"One reason is that Armin's not here at the moment," Katherine said. "Another reason is that

Mrs. Plains has invited you to Margaret's birthday party today. It's to be a surprise for Margaret."

Alisette immediately forgot about riding Sir Toby. "I've never been to a birthday party." Her voice was both excited and a bit apprehensive.

"I'll tell you about the first one I went to," Katherine said. "It was a party for Margaret's grandmother when she turned six. . . ."

Leaving Alisette raptly listening, I went to make sure she had a dress not only appropriate for the party but also clean. I found one, a dark blue velveteen, that I thought was a sober enough color for a child still in mourning. Unfortunately, a greasy stain marred the skirt.

I knew I didn't have enough time to try to clean the dress so, hoping Molly would be able to cover the stain somehow, I hurried to find her.

Mrs. Yates, Rosie, and Loretta shared the servants' quarters on the third floor of the house, but Molly and Armin had moved into two rooms above the stable. The rooms, while nice enough, weren't as spacious as their cottage on the grounds of Sea Cliff House.

Apparently hearing me climbing the outside steps, Molly opened the door before I reached the top. She invited me in, and I saw she'd placed a table near the window overlooking the garden. A half-finished gown lay on the table near her sewing box.

"Oh, Miss Estelle," she told me, "I'm at my wit's end." She wrung her hands, forgetting in her distress to ask me to sit down.

"Why, whatever's the matter?" I asked.

"He ain't home yet, and it's going on for ten o'clock. He ain't never before stayed away all the night and into the morning like this. You don't think something's happened to him, do you?"

I hadn't any idea where Armin might be.

Wanting to ease Molly's worry, I said, "Perhaps Mr. Callich asked him to help at Sea Cliff House, and he stayed in the cottage overnight."

She shook her head. "Ain't nothing left to sleep on in the cottage. Besides, Armin promised Mrs. Peter he'd fix that armoire first thing this morning. You know, the one the movers dropped and the leg broke off of."

Since I hadn't been present during most of the moving, I wasn't aware of a broken armoire.

Molly laid a trembling hand on my arm. "Rosie said as how accidents come in threes, and we had two already. I'm afeared it's him this time."

Rosie and her superstitions! I covered Molly's hand with mine. "Don't borrow trouble. If it will make you feel better, I'll walk to the mill and ask Mr. Callich if he's seen Armin."

"Would you, Miss Estelle? I'd be ever so grateful." As I turned away to leave, she asked, "What's that you're carrying?"

"It's a dress of Alisette's. She's invited to a party today, and this dress has a stain on the skirt. I don't want to bother you now, though. I'll find something else for her to wear."

"You may as well give it to me. It'll pass the time for me figuring what to do to hide the stain."

Leaving the dress with Molly, I returned to the house for my hat, gloves, and a jacket for the walk to the mill. I hadn't seen Gerald since my near drowning, though Katherine said he'd promised to drop by and visit us when we were settled. Even if he didn't know where Armin was, maybe he'd have some suggestions as to where he might be.

Gerald was not at the mill.

"Mr. Callich rode up to Sea Cliff House," one of the workers, an older man, told me. "Since he bought the place, he's like a child with a new toy."

I thanked him, said there was no message, and

left. I hated to tell poor Molly my effort was a failure, but what else could I do? If I decided to go to Sea Cliff House, I'd have to walk to the farm to get the mare for what would likely be a wild goose chase.

Sonia had told me Armin was a ladies' man, even hinting Cecile had fallen prey to him. Wasn't a new lady friend the probable explanation for him staying away all night? Understandably Molly wouldn't want to accept such an explanation.

But Sonia's words about leaving because she didn't mean to be the third victim kept running through my mind—both her words and the furtive way she'd left Sea Cliff House, as though afraid of someone there. Who?

Where *was* Armin?

With any luck, he'd have returned by the time I got back to the house.

He hadn't. Molly began to cry when I told her I had no news. Hugging herself and rocking back and forth, she sobbed, "He's dead, I just know he's dead."

Chilled by the intensity of her belief, I decided to ask Katherine what she thought.

"For some reason, Molly's convinced he's dead," I said to her.

"Armin's up at Sea Cliff House in all likelihood," she replied, "helping Gerald settle in the new horses he bought."

"Without asking permission from you? Or letting Molly know?"

Katherine shrugged. "He takes advantage of the fact he knows I feel an obligation to him. As for Molly—" She sighed. "He's not very kind to her, poor thing. The one person he does occasionally confide in is Mrs. Yates. We might ask her." Katherine reached for her call bell.

I'd all but forgotten Mrs. Yates was Armin's aunt.

As soon as Mrs. Yates came bustling into the room, Katherine told her how upset Molly was over Armin not coming home all night, nor yet today. "We thought you might have some idea where he is," Katherine finished.

"I'm sure I don't know," the housekeeper said calmly enough, though I noticed she was twisting her apron in her hands. "He said not a word to me."

Katherine thanked her, and she left.

"I suppose I ought to ride up to Sea Cliff House," I said reluctantly. "We do know Gerald's there and, if Armin isn't, Gerald might know his whereabouts."

"Absolutely not! I won't have you walking all the way to the farm and then making that long ride to Sea Cliff House," Katherine said firmly. "Not over Armin. Perhaps all of us, including Molly, are better off *not* knowing what he's up to."

Alisette rushed into the room. "My very favorite dress isn't in my room," she wailed. "The blue velvet. I wanted to wear it to the party. I looked and looked but it's gone."

"You take care of Alisette," my mother said. "I'll give some thought to what we ought to do about the other matter."

Alisette wouldn't be satisfied until she had her dress back, and so I returned to Molly's rooms above the stable to retrieve it and show Alisette why the dress would be impossible to wear to a party.

Molly called to me to come in. To my surprise, she'd stopped crying and was sitting by the table putting the finishing stitches into a midnight blue brocade panel with a tiny ivy leaf pattern that

240

she'd set over the stain into the skirt of Alisette's dress.

She looked up at me with red-rimmed eyes. "It's better working. Some better, anyhow. Sort of takes my mind off—" Her voice broke, and she reached for the wadded handkerchief on the table next to her.

"You've done a beautiful job with the dress," I told her. "It's more attractive than ever. You really are a talented seamstress."

She tried to smile but failed. "Here 'tis, then." She rose and handed me the dress.

"Thank you. Alisette will be most grateful." I looked at her brimming eyes and added, "We'll do what we can to find Armin, Molly."

"I know that. 'Tain't your fault, whatever's happened."

When I returned to the house, it was time to get Alisette ready for the party. As always, she hated having her hair brushed, but when she was finally buttoned into her refurbished favorite dress, with her hair neatly caught back by a blue ribbon, even she approved of her image in the mirror.

"Maybe I really *am* going to grow up to be beautiful," she said to me. "Papa says all the Nikolai women do."

"I never doubted you would for a minute," I assured her.

She turned to me. "*You're* a Nikolai woman," she said, as though the thought had just occurred to her.

I nodded.

Tilting her head one way and the other, she examined me. "You're not pretty like my mother was," she observed at last, "but I guess you must be beautiful 'cause I heard Papa tell you so once."

"You hear entirely too much for your own

241

good," I said, wondering where and when she'd overheard Stephen. I hoped that was all she'd heard.

"I can't help it if people talk when I'm around!"

At the moment, I hadn't the heart to lecture her about eavesdropping. Eager as she was to get to the party, I doubted she'd listen anyway.

I was returning from delivering Alisette to the Plains house and had just opened our front gate when a man called to me.

"Miss Nikolai!"

I stopped, turned, and saw what appeared to be one of the mill workers hurrying toward me.

When he reached the gate, he said, "Mr. Callich sent me here. He said I was to tell you that Armin Brown had a bad accident up at Sea Cliff House."

Dread jolted through me. "What happened?" I cried.

"Mr. Callich said a horse kicked Armin in the head and he—well, he's dead."

Irrationally, my first thought was that at least Armin hadn't fallen off the cliff. Almost immediately I was overcome with pity for Molly and sorrow that Armin had died. Though I hadn't liked or trusted him, I'd never wished him dead.

"Thank you for coming to tell us," I managed to say.

"Mr. Callich says you and your mother aren't to worry, he's taking care of everything."

I nodded. "Please let him know we appreciate that."

Once inside the gate, I hesitated. I really wanted to go to my mother, but I decided it was my duty to give Molly the sad news first. I did not look forward to the telling.

Oddly enough, Molly didn't break down completely, as I'd expected she might.

242

"I warned him he was getting into deep water," she said between sobs. "When he didn't come home last night, I knew in my heart he was dead."

I wondered what she meant. What did "getting into deep water" have to do with the horse kicking him? This was no time to question her, however. "I'll send Mrs. Yates over to be with you," I told her.

"*She* warned him, too," Molly said, "but he never listened to either of us."

"Warned him about what?" I asked, my curiosity overcoming my principles.

"He was up to something, wouldn't say what." She gazed at me from tear-dimmed eyes. "Well, it killed him, didn't it?"

"But his death was an accident," I reminded her.

She stared at me for a moment, then buried her face in her hands, sobbing and making me sorry I'd questioned her.

I went into the house by the back door, it being more convenient, and found my mother in the kitchen with Rosie, discussing the week's menu.

"Why, you're white as a ghost," Katherine said to me. "What on earth is the matter?"

I told her about Armin.

Before she could speak, Rosie exclaimed, "His was the third! Accidents always come in threes."

I shuddered, reminded of my nightmare where a witchlike Rosie had stirred a cauldron, all the while muttering about doom and death bells.

"I'll send Mrs. Yates to poor Molly immediately," my mother said. "It's thoughtful of Gerald to make the necessary arrangements, but then Gerald has always been thoughtful, even as a boy."

He came by the house late in the afternoon and was shown into the parlor, where Katherine and I joined him.

243

"I've taken care of most of the details," he told us, "but I wasn't sure if you wanted Armin buried in Myrtle Grove Cemetery or where."

"Oh, no, not there," Katherine said. "He belongs with the Nikolais in the family cemetery by the old Russian church. Peter would expect no less."

Gerald nodded slowly, as though he wasn't quite certain this was proper.

"The church and the graveyard *were* exempted from the sale of Sea Cliff House," she added, evidently sensing his hesitation.

"My dear Mrs. Peter, I wasn't objecting." Gerald's tone held a tinge of annoyance.

My mother's nod was brisk. "Good. Then it's settled. I would like to know, though, how this terrible accident happened."

"I can't help blaming myself," Gerald said. "If I hadn't asked Armin to put my new pair of matched bays into the stables for me, he'd be alive at this moment. I would have seen to the horses myself, but I had to make a trip up the Eel River to the mill's logging camp yesterday, so I asked Armin if he'd take delivery of the bays and see to it they were well settled in."

"You'd mentioned to me you were buying carriage horses," Katherine said, "so I suspected something of the sort when Armin didn't turn up this morning, though I didn't dream he'd been killed."

"We'll never know what spooked the horses." Gerald's tone was laced with regret. "Whatever it was, they went wild and turned on Armin. Since I didn't return to Eureka until early this morning, and the couple who'll be looking after me at Sea Cliff House haven't yet arrived from Santa Rosa, there was no one at the place. The poor man lay dead in the stables all night. I found him when I rode up late this morning."

"You can hardly blame yourself for an accident," I told him.

He smiled sadly. "You're kind, Miss Estelle, but I do."

For some reason, once he was satisfied I was truly a Nikolai, Gerald had taken to calling me Estelle, even though he knew I preferred Esma. Although the servants called me Miss Estelle, the family and my acquaintances used Esma, at my request. I wondered why Gerald did not.

"Would you like me to tell Molly how it happened?" Katherine asked him.

"I'd be grateful. While it's my responsibility, I hardly know the woman. I'm sure she'd be more comfortable with you."

As he took his leave, he said, "I trust the next time I come calling the occasion will be a happier one."

"We all pray that it will be," Katherine agreed.

As I bade him farewell, I wondered why I couldn't truly warm to Gerald. He was kind, helpful, and always proper. He'd long been a true friend to the Nikolais. It wasn't that I didn't like him exactly—or was it? And if I didn't, why didn't I? I could find no answers.

When I'd settled into bed that night, my chaotic thoughts kept sleep at bay. After Armin was buried, I sincerely hoped his would be the last funeral for a long time. It seemed there'd been nothing but deaths ever since I'd come to live with the Nikolais. Accidents all.

Or were they?

Sonia had fled to San Francisco because she didn't believe Cecile or Floyd Rogers had died accidentally. But surely Armin's death was a

245

genuine, if tragic, mishap.

I closed my eyes and his face appeared to me—Nikolai features, but coarser, his brown eyes cunning as a fox's. His hadn't been the face I'd seen when I was a five year old rescued from the sea. I blotted out Armin's face and tried to will myself to bring back the other, the face that hovered at the edges of my memory like a word almost on the tongue.

Who was the man who'd come to my bedside in the orphanage and asked my name? Somehow I couldn't convince myself the face and the voice had only been a figment of my delirium. Sister Samara might remember. I couldn't leave my mother to make the journey to Fort Bragg to visit the sister, but I *could* write her. I made up my mind to do that very thing in the morning. I'd been so remiss I hadn't even told her that I was really Estelle Marie Nikolai. How pleased she'd be at my good fortune in finding my family.

That settled, I sought sleep once more, but it proved elusive. My mother's voice echoed in my mind: "After the storm that scuttled *Sea Bear,* we searched the coast for any trace of you, asking questions in every town and hamlet."

Who was "we"? Surely not my mother. Stephen and my father? But she'd told me Captain Peter had almost immediately sailed off to the Orient on another Nikolai ship, *Sea Wolf,* and young Stephen had signed on *Sea Dragon,* the ship he'd eventually captain, as a deck hand, sailing to the Sandwich Islands.

Who *had* been sent to look for me? I must ask my mother. Not that I meant to tell her about the face and the voice. That was my concern for the time being.

I did wish I had someone to confide in, though.

246

Despite everything, if Stephen were here, he might be the one. I wondered when he'd return from San Francisco. Katherine had said in a week or ten days, and a week had already passed. I hadn't allowed myself to think about him or how I missed him. He'd be back only briefly, and then he'd be sailing far, far away. Who knew how long before he returned from his voyage to the Orient? I might as well get used to his absence. If I could. If I *ever* could.

Meanwhile there was another funeral to attend. Poor Molly would need support and sympathy.

I finally fell asleep and dreamed that Stephen stood on one side of a wide chasm and I stood on the other. Though we tried our best to bridge the impossible gap between us, everything failed. I woke with a heavy heart.

I was busy with Alisette all morning, and it wasn't until she napped that I had a chance to be alone with my mother.

"I hope you won't think I'm morbid," I began, "but I'm still trying to come to terms with what happened to me after *Sea Bear* foundered and went down."

"I think your interest is quite natural," she assured me.

"Since I know my father and brother sailed soon after *Sea Bear* was lost, I've been wondering who it was that you sent to try to find me."

"I thought I'd told you. It was Gerald, of course. He was so helpful and kind—I don't know what I'd have done without him at that time. Or since, for that matter."

Inside, I reeled with shock. Gerald! I did my best to keep a surface calm, not wishing to upset Katherine.

"But he didn't find me." I was amazed at how

247

normal my voice sounded.

"He searched down the coast as far as San Francisco. It didn't occur to him—or to me—that you might have been taken to an orphanage so far inland. Gerald was devastated when he had to return and tell me he'd failed."

I mustn't jump to false conclusions. Perhaps Gerald had actually never reached my orphanage, perhaps the man I so vaguely remembered had not been Gerald.

For the rest of the day, I had trouble paying attention to what went on around me because my mind churned with possibilities. What if the man who stood by my bed in the orphanage *had* been Gerald? On the other hand, what if the man I thought I recalled was nothing but a specter in a delirium dream?

That night I made a deliberate effort not to think about the past, silently saying the rosary over and over. I hoped the prayers might help my troubled mind and free me from the futile struggle to remember. Somewhere during the recital of the fourth rosary, I fell asleep.

Green water closed around me, choking me. I fought but to no avail, I was drowning. Green changed to black as dark as the pit, a seemingly endless darkness.

The next I knew I was cold, so very cold, cold and wet, I was lost, wandering in a strange place, and I was sick and couldn't find my mother.

Much, much later warmth cocooned me, gentle hands touched me. And there were voices. Women's voices. Then a man's, loud in my ears.

"What's your name?"

I couldn't answer, but after a struggle I opened my eyes and saw the man's face. His blue eyes looked into mine and, for an instant, before every-

thing I knew slipped away from me and was gone beyond recall, I recognized him. He worked in Papa's mill. . . .

I woke with a start and sat up in bed, my heart pounding. Gerald Callich! It was his face in my nightmare. But was it a true seeing or just a dream? I had no way of knowing. The only thing I was sure of was that sooner or later I'd have to confront Gerald about what I thought I remembered.

What about Floyd Rogers with his locket? Had he been my rescuer, as he claimed? He'd brought me to the sisters, he'd said. But Sister Samara had never mentioned an old sailor; she had said a farmer brought me to the orphanage. Mr. Rogers had mentioned a farmer but claimed to have gone with the man to the orphanage. Why hadn't the sister told me there were two men?

Making up my mind, I rose from the bed and padded to my teak writing table. Drawing a sheet of notepaper from the drawer, I uncapped the ink, picked up a pen, and began my long overdue letter to Sister Samara.

When I finished, I blotted the paper carefully, folded the letter, and slid it into an envelope. I'd carry the letter to the post office myself, first thing in the morning, and entrust it to Mr. Fred Axe, the postmaster, who'd send it on to its destination. If I knew Sister Samara, she'd write back immediately, answering each of my questions in detail. Perhaps after I read her reply, my nightmares would be over once and for all. I fervently hoped so.

As I rose from the chair, my door opened, and I started, frightened for a moment before I saw it was Alisette.

She slipped through the door and ran to me. I lifted her into my arms and, as she hugged me tightly, I could feel her trembling—and hear her

249

wheezing as well. I carried her to my bed and tucked her under the covers with me.

"Now we're nice and cozy," I said. "Did you have a bad dream?"

"He came after you," she said, clutching my arm. "I tried to warn you, but you couldn't hear me."

I held her close. "It was only a dream. Here I am safe and sound."

"It was the bad man," she said, not heeding my words. "The one who stole my doll and locked me in the tower." She shuddered. "He doesn't have any face!"

"Only a dream," I repeated, "only a dream. Listen to me sing the lullaby you like so well, the Russian lullaby that your grandmother used to sing to me when I was a little girl. Listen carefully to the words and in the morning I'll teach them to you and tell you what they mean."

As I sang the familiar and now meaningful words to Alisette, my own fears vanished like fog under a noonday sun. The feeling that I was one of a long line of women who'd passed on this simple lullaby to a child who would one day sing it to her own daughter comforted and thrilled me at the same time. I was carrying on a tradition; I'd been given a great gift—I knew who I was and I'd become part of a family.

This child and I shared the same blood, we were Nikolais. I decided then and there that no matter whether Stephen eventually remarried or not, I would never give up Alisette. I loved her. I'd take the place of her mother and raise her to the best of my ability.

Eventually Alisette's breathing eased; she relaxed in my arms and fell asleep. But it was not so easy for me. The thought of Stephen remarrying had lodged in my mind like a festering splinter that could not be eradicated.

How could I ever honestly welcome any wife of his? I sighed, knowing that if and when that day came, for everyone's sake, including mine, I'd have to pretend.

As for myself, I couldn't imagine any other man kissing me or making love to me—the very thought was distasteful. Stephen was forever prohibited to me, but that didn't mean I had to marry another. I simply wouldn't marry at all.

Ever.

Chapter 16

The sun shone for Armin's funeral, but that was the only brightness I found in the day. As I stood in the old Nikolai cemetery with the other mourners, uneasiness shrouded me like the fog that I'd so often seen drifting between the tombstones, not only because I had come to a place I dreaded, but because once again I was at the funeral of someone I didn't mourn.

Alisette held tightly to my hand. Neither Katherine nor I had wanted her to come, but Alisette had begged so insistently that her grandmother let her have her way. I glanced again at Alexandria's crypt and shuddered at the sight of the broken marble feet at its top, all that remained of the marble angel.

Alexandria was, of course, the reason Alisette had pleaded to come. She'd jumped from the carriage and rushed to the crypt as soon as we arrived. I started after her, but, before I reached the crypt, she turned away and ran to me with tears in her eyes. She hadn't said a word since, pressing close to me and clutching my hand as though afraid I'd somehow get away from her.

As Father Lynch intoned the familiar words, I

tried to comfort myself with the thought that Armin would be proud to know he was being laid to rest with the Nikolais, recognized as one of them in death as he never had been in life. Being Armin, though, he might well have sneered at the belated honor.

Had he been guilty of pushing Cecile over the cliff? I wondered. Or Floyd Rogers? If so, Armin had gone beyond the reach of any man's punishment; his sins were now between him and his Maker. If he'd loved anyone or anything, it was horses. How terrible to think he'd died because of a horse. Whatever he had or hadn't done, I couldn't think of his death as retribution.

The priest finished, made the sign of the cross, and the men began to lower the casket into the open grave while both Molly and Mrs. Yates wept.

"She's gone away," Alisette whispered.

Bewildered for a moment because I was still thinking of Armin, I finally realized she must have meant Alexandria. Or, rather, her spirit.

Whether I believed in spirits communing with the living or not, Alisette needed comforting. I crouched down beside her. "Don't be sad," I murmured. "Alexandria knows you don't need her any more."

Alisette looked at me with such trust in her eyes that I felt mine mist over. "Is that why she left?"

I nodded. "She's gone back to heaven," I said firmly.

The small knot of mourners was disbanding. People drifted away from the grave. Mrs. Yates supported Molly with one arm around her waist. I walked Alisette to our carriage, driven by the adolescent son of the Plainses' driver, and waited there for Katherine. She soon arrived, assisted by Gerald who helped the three of us into the carriage before

253

turning back to speak to Father Lynch.

We'd no sooner gotten underway than Alisette said to her grandmother, "Has Grandpa Peter's spirit gone back to heaven like Alexandria's?"

Katherine pressed Alisette's hand. "I've told him not to expect me on the promontory any more," she said at last, "so perhaps he *will* rest more quietly."

"I miss Alexandria," Alisette said plaintively.

"It was time for her to go." Katherine's voice was gentle.

Alisette sighed. "I guess so. Anyway, I'm glad she won't be lonesome all alone in the graveyard."

I couldn't help but wonder if my mother wouldn't also miss her "messages" from my father. At the same time, I was as glad she'd stopped listening for them as I was that Alisette had given up Alexandria.

It was a relief to return to our home in Eureka, a place so much brighter than Sea Cliff House, a place where no unhappy memories lurked. I immediately climbed to the third floor to look from the cupola window toward the bay for any sign of *Sea Dragon*. I saw none.

I don't know how many times during the rest of the day I returned to the cupola to look again and again toward the bay with the same disappointing result. Even though I must welcome him home as a brother, I longed for Stephen's return with all my heart.

When I tucked Alisette into bed that night, she echoed my own thoughts. "I miss Papa so," she told me. "*Sea Dragon*'s been gone eight days 'cause I counted them. Tomorrow's Saturday. Do you think he'll be back tomorrow?"

"I hope so. But, remember, your grandmother said it might be ten days. Tomorrow's only nine."

"I can't wait for ten. I want him to come tomorrow!"

"We all do, but we must wait."

She sighed, then brightened as a new idea took hold. "Will you take me to Mr. Benediction's tomorrow to look at the new ship he's building for us?"

"Mr. Benedixsen," I corrected.

"Can we go there? You haven't even seen the new ship 'cause you weren't with Papa and me. Papa said he's going to name her after me—*Sea Maiden*. He told me maiden means little girl. I can hardly wait till she's launched. Papa 'zplained about launching—it's when the ship slides into the water."

"I've never seen a ship launched," I admitted. "I'm sure it's a marvelous sight to behold."

"Papa told me he watched a Chinese ship launched once. In China they call ships 'junks.' Did you know that?"

I hated to spoil her fun by saying I did know, so I avoided a direct answer. "How interesting. Tell me more."

"Well," she said importantly, "first they kill a chicken and two goats and two pigs. I don't know why, 'zactly. Anyway, they beat gongs like the little one I have, only theirs are real big and make lots of noise. The China people believe there really are sea dragons, so they throw a special kind of paper into the sea and shout and guns go off and the gongs beat real loud when the ship slides into the water. Papa says you never heard such noise." Her animated expression faded, and she began to pout again. "I wish *I* could go with Papa to China and see them launch a junk."

I wished I could, too.

"Shall I tell you the story of Princess Auria?" I

255

asked, to distract the both of us. It was her favorite.

She nodded and I began. When I neared the end of the tale, I saw her eyes drooping shut and lowered my voice. She was sound asleep at the finish.

To my surprise, when I went downstairs to dinner, I found Gerald in the parlor having sherry with Katherine.

"I've invited Gerald to dinner," she said. "Just think, his new servants haven't yet arrived, and he's rattling around in Sea Cliff House all by himself."

I concealed a shiver at the thought of being alone in that gloomy old place. "When were you expecting them?" I asked.

"The stage was delayed," he said. "I'm sure they'll arrive tomorrow. I do appreciate the dinner invitation, but actually I came by to invite you both for a ride in my new carriage tomorrow afternoon. I thought we might take a turn in the country."

"I have an appointment with an old friend," Katherine said, "but it would do Esma a world of good to relax and enjoy a ride in the country."

This was the first I'd heard of any such appointment, and I wondered if Katherine could possibly be trying to arrange things so Gerald and I would be alone. It wouldn't be her first attempt to matchmake between Gerald and me. My immediate impulse was to excuse myself, but after a moment's reflection I decided it might be the perfect chance to ask him a few questions about his search for five-year-old Estelle.

"Thank you, I'd like to go," I told him.

We avoided the topic of Armin at dinner and spoke of less distressing subjects.

"A new play will be presented at Russ House,

256

beginning next week," Gerald said. "*Octaroon*, I believe it's called. Perhaps I shall have the honor of escorting you both to the theater, if we may set a date."

"I'll think about it. Thank you for the kind offer," I said evasively when Katherine looked to me for a response. I didn't wish to be courted by Gerald, nor by any other man.

But, all in all, the evening passed pleasantly enough, though by the time Gerald took his leave I felt quite worn out from parrying future invitations.

"It doesn't do to be too coy," Katherine chided gently when we were alone.

I said lightly, "I imagine Gerald isn't the only eligible bachelor in Eureka."

Katherine smiled. "Of course not, dear girl. I suppose I favor him because, with Stephen away so long, Gerald became almost like a son to me."

"I understand," I told her, "but I must do my own choosing."

She laid her hand on my arm. "You mustn't let me try to run your life."

"You'd never do that." Impulsively, I hugged her. "I'm so happy you're my mother."

Tears brightened her eyes. "No one could be happier than I."

In the morning Alisette begged to be taken to the docks. "Maybe someone there knows when *Sea Dragon* will be in," she insisted.

Since Gerald wasn't coming by for me until after lunch, and the morning was fair, I gave in to her pleading, trying to to admit to myself that I was as eager as she for word of Stephen's return.

The dock workers we encountered at first were all busy loading or unloading ships, so I refused to allow Alisette to bother them. She finally pointed

257

at a gray-bearded man wearing a red knitted cap who sat at the end of a jetty with his back to the dockside bustle.

"*He's* not busy," Alisette said.

"I think he's fishing," I cautioned.

"That's not busy." She tugged at me. "He won't mind if we talk to him."

I held tightly to her hand as we walked out onto the jetty, still not quite easy with water on both sides of me. As we approached the bearded man, he turned to look at us, and I saw by his wrinkled face he was even older than I'd thought.

"Hello, I'm Alisette Nikolai," Alisette announced. "What's your name?"

He smiled at her. "So ye be a Nikolai. I can see it in your face, that I can." He glanced at me. "And ye be another, I'll wager."

I nodded.

He turned his attention to Alisette. "I knew your grandfather, old Peter, I did. Sailed on his ships once or twice afore I took to fishing."

"Grandpa Peter's on the bottom of the sea," she said soberly.

"So he be. Many's the good man who rests there."

"You didn't tell me your name," she reminded him.

"Ye can call me Uncle Oscar, how's that?"

"All right. Uncle Oscar, my papa's the captain of *Sea Dragon*, sailing home from San Francisco. Have you heard when she'll be in?"

He looked across the bay, squinted at the sun, hidden behind thin clouds at the moment, then wet his forefinger with his tongue and held it up to the wind. "Hmm," he said. "From the southeast. Could be a blow coming. If your papa's a good captain he's either flying afore the wind to make it

258

over the bar afore the wind shifts, or he's planning to lie up in a safe cove and wait her out."

Alisette wet her own forefinger and held it up. "What happens if the wind shifts?"

"Some of the worst winter storms start with the wind in the southeast, then she shifts to the southwest and finally to the northwest. Makes for an ugly cross sea. Few's the captain who care to weather such a sea. 'Course, once they make the bay they're safe enough, but during bad weather, all ships are bar bound, can't get in or out of the bay.

"Ye see, Humboldt Bay's shaped like a pear with its stem toward the ocean. It runs nigh onto twenty miles to the northeast and twenty miles to the southeast, making her landlocked 'cept for the channel. Them's the safest kind of bays." He pointed. "Lookee there, the tug's on her way across to bring in a ship now."

We waited anxiously, straining our eyes for a glimpse of the ship outside the bar, but long before we could see more than its masts, Oscar dashed our hopes by sayng, "She's a barkentine, can't be *Sea Dragon*. Most likely *C.L. Taylor*, she's due in today."

Interesting as it was to watch the tiny tug maneuver the much larger barkentine around the bar, Alisette and I were too disappointed to give it our full attention.

"I hope Papa doesn't get bar bound," Alisette said.

"He's a Nikolai, ain't he?" Oscar asked. "Nikolais make good captains, so don't ye worry none."

His words cheered Alisette. As she and I walked home, though, I couldn't help remembering that my father was also a Nikolai and by all accounts a good captain, but it hadn't saved him from leaving

259

his bones at the bottom of the sea.

Some time after lunch, when Gerald came by with his matched bays hitched to his new carriage, there was still no sign of *Sea Dragon*. On the other hand, the weather hadn't changed, so perhaps old Oscar was wrong about a storm coming.

"We'll drive toward Ferndale," Gerald told me after assisting me into the carriage, sitting himself beside me, and taking up the reins. "There are a good many prosperous farms on the way. Have you ever seen Spanish merino sheep?"

"I've never so much as heard of them," I said.

"A Mr. Roberts imported some. They have a remarkably heavy fleece that makes very fine white wool. He's said to be doing well with his merinos."

Preoccupied with my own worries, I nodded, only half my mind on Gerald's conversation. I was barely aware of the farms we passed with their windmills turning in the wind and their fields lying fallow. Occasionally an orchard of leafless apple or pear trees caught my eye, making me wish it were spring and the trees in bloom. But it wasn't spring, it was November.

Would there be a "blow" as Oscar called it and, if so, would *Sea Dragon* make it safely home? I couldn't bear it if anything happened to Stephen.

"Will it storm today, do you think?" I asked, unable to hold the question back.

Gerald didn't appear to be startled by my abrupt change of subject. "I doubt it," he said. "Today's most pleasant for November, by and large."

"An old sailor on the docks was talking to Alisette and me," I said, "and he predicted a storm. 'A big blow,' he called it. Alisette is anxious about her father coming safely around the bar into the bay."

260

"The bar is tricky to navigate in the best of weather," he agreed. "That sand spit is as wide as a mile in some places, and the channel through it is a tricky run. But with Buhne piloting, the captain's chances are good. Of course, in bad weather things are different." He smiled. "But then we don't have bad weather today, do we?"

"My mother told me how my grandfather steered his ship safely past the bar and into the bay, long before Mr. Buhne and his tug. She says Alexi's ship was the first to enter the bay since the early Russian fur hunters who built the church, then abandoned it."

Gerald nodded. "I've always believed those Russian sea-otter hunters were told of the bay and its sand bar by the Eskimos with whom they traded. No doubt you've heard how Captain Alexi came by his ship in the first place—he simply took it. Old Alexi was an acquisitive man, and what he acquired he hung onto. I'm sure he's turning in his grave over Sea Cliff House going out of the family. The only way to placate Alexi is for you to marry me so a Nikolai will live once more on the property."

Was he serious? I stared at him, speechless, and he laughed, reaching over to pat my gloved hand.

"I have wonderful plans for Sea Cliff House," he went on. "I'll soon arrange for construction of the breakwater, and then I'll begin remodeling the house itself. I promise you'll be pleased with my changes, Estelle."

"I prefer being called Esma," I said, deciding to make no comment about his offhand marriage proposal—if, indeed, that's what it was.

"Your name is Estelle," he said rebukingly.

"I realize that, but—"

He continued as though I hadn't spoken. "Ever

261

since I was a boy I've dreamed of someday being master of Sea Cliff House. Now I am. Master." He savored the word on his tongue. "Have you any idea what that means to me?"

I shook my head, a bit disquieted by a side of Gerald I'd never seen before.

He nodded. "That's because no Nikolai would ever tell you what really happened to my father. He owned the mill, you know, but he needed money for expansion and Peter Nikolai had the money, so Peter became his partner.

"The Nikolais are all acquisitive—downright greedy—and they don't care who gets trampled underfoot in the process of amassing money. What Alexi did to his half brother Sergei, your father did to my father. He stole from him. One day they shared the mill equally and the next, by some weaselly process of law, Peter was the sole owner.

"Oh, they'll tell you my father drank and didn't run the place properly, but it's hogwash. Peter Nikolai stole the mill from him, and that's the truth. When my father realized what had happened, he went after Peter. I'll admit he'd had a bit to drink at the time; what man wouldn't, under the circumstances? Some say he tried to bury an ivory-handled Malayan kris in your father's heart. My mother never believed he actually had the kris in his possession, but, whatever did happen during their fight, Peter struck my father over the head with a belaying pin, causing him to have a stroke."

I drew in my breath, dismayed. No one had mentioned a word of this to me before. I couldn't help but wonder if the odd dagger I'd seen Gerald with was his father's kris.

"My father didn't die immediately," Gerald went on. "Oh, no, he lingered for months before passing on, causing my mother untold anguish as

262

well as back-breaking care, for we had no money. The scandal and his illness were an indirect cause of her own death two years later.

"Before my mother died, the *Sea Bear* foundered and you were lost. Peter then sailed off in *Sea Wolf* and never came back. Retribution caught up with him—he went down with his ship. Katherine came to our aid, offering me work so I could support my mother and myself. After my mother died, Katherine invited me to move into Sea Cliff House. Katherine believes in justice, but then she wasn't born a Nikolai, she merely married into the family."

He patted my hand again. "You, Estelle, are like your mother, even though Nikolai blood runs in your veins."

I didn't quite know how to take this. Nor was I sure that Gerald hadn't told me a somewhat skewed story of his father's tragic end. Nevertheless, some of it must be true, and it made me unhappy to think my father might have been less than honest.

"I'm sorry about your parents," I said, feeling my words were inadequate.

"In my place, most men would have planned revenge." His blue eyes gleamed with a strange light.

For some reason, I thought of the blue eyes in the face I remembered from my childhood delirium, and I knew I had to ask him now if he were that man.

"Gerald, I've remembered a bit from my early days in the orphanage," I began.

"Have you now. That's interesting." His voice was even, his face showed nothing.

"I recall a man bending over me, asking me my name."

263

"And what did you tell him?"

"I couldn't answer. I was too sick, and my memory wasn't clear."

"Your memory wasn't clear? Then how do you remember the man?"

I bit my lip, hating to admit I couldn't be positive. Avoiding a direct answer, I said, "My mother tells me she sent you to search for me as far down the coast as San Francisco."

He nodded. "I didn't think to go inland as far as Fort Bragg. I'm sorry now that it never occurred to me. How much easier your life would have been if I had."

His words sounded sincere, and yet, for no reason I could put my finger on, I couldn't quite bring myself to believe him.

"Later," I said, "when you came to my orphanage looking for a girl to be Alisette's nurse, what did the sisters tell you about my past?"

"Nothing. I didn't ask, I'm afraid, since we were all sure Estelle had drowned many years before. All I was interested in at that time was finding an intelligent, capable girl to be trained to care for a sickly and difficult child."

I remained silent, though I was by no means satisfied.

"Estelle," he said, "look at me."

I did, and his blue eyes, seemingly as guileless as a child's, gazed directly into mine.

"Do you actually suspect me of finding you at that orphanage when you were five and deliberately not identifying you and taking you home to Sea Cliff House?"

Did I? I wasn't sure but, with him gazing into my eyes, it was hard to imagine Gerald committing such a wicked act.

"I—I can't believe you'd be so—so evil," I stammered.

"Evil?" He frowned. "Evil?"

I nodded. "Surely no one but an evil person would deliberately keep a child from her loving parents."

"I hadn't thought of it as evil. Still, perhaps you're right. But consider, Estelle. Floyd Rogers came to me with the initialed locket. If I were this evil person, wouldn't I have kept the locket, gotten rid of the old sailor, and never mentioned a word of his story to the Nikolais, you included?"

"Mr. Rogers *did* have a fatal accident," I reminded him.

"After the fact, not before. And, if you'll recall, the wretched old man was a drunk who stumbled and fell to his death." He smiled. "Enough of such talk. We must look to the future. I've invited you to enjoy the day, not to worry and fret over a past that can never be altered. It's enough that you've finally taken your rightful place as a Nikolai. I'm proud to have had even a tiny part in restoring you to your mother, however belatedly."

Everything he said was true. Why did I keep trying to blame Gerald for vile deeds he hadn't committed?

I forced a smile. "I suppose I've been adversely affected by the terrible events of these past few months."

"We all were. It's been a frightening time."

"Oh, yes. Sonia was frightened enough to run off to San Francisco because she feared having an accident befall her." As soon as the words were out, I longed to call them back. What had possessed me to bring up Sonia?

Gerald was mute for long moments. "I assume Katherine has mentioned to you that, before I came to live at Sea Cliff House, Sonia was my housekeeper."

"Yes, she did. And that you asked her to take

265

Sonia on as a maid."

"True." He sighed. "My dear Estelle, at this moment I wish you weren't quite so innocent. I really don't know how to put this. The appetites of men and of women differ. I am a man and, at one time, Sonia was a bit more than my housekeeper. Do you understand what I mean?"

Because Sonia had all but spelled it out to me, I understood perfectly. "Yes," I murmured.

"All women aren't alike, either," he went on. "Sonia—well, she has appetites unusual for a woman. In a word, it makes no difference to her what man's bed she shares. In San Francisco, no doubt it will be Jock Ferguson's and that's why she ran off."

What he said had some truth, but it wasn't the entire truth. I shook my head. "Sonia was afraid of someone. She wouldn't tell me who—I thought it was Armin."

And I had, but now Armin was dead. Kicked by a horse. Another accident.

"Unlucky as it is to speak ill of the dead, Armin was an unsavory lout, no question about it. The world's a better place without him."

I was liking this new side of Gerald less and less.

"I'm beginning to feel rather fatigued," I said, though the truth was I'd had enough of his company. "Perhaps you should think about turning back."

"Why, of course, Estelle. Your well-being is my first consideration."

Why did I think I detected a tinge of mockery in his voice?

I must have been wrong for, without delay, he turned the horses into a nearby farm drive and, making a circle, came back onto the road heading toward Eureka.

"I'd hoped to picnic with you by a stream near

here," he said, "but that can wait for another time."

I could think of few things I'd rather do than picnic with Gerald.

"I think you'll approve of my new servants," he went on.

"Have they arrived, then?" I asked, thankful for a change of subject.

"I think I mentioned they're a couple. Sven and Hannah Holmsberg—Swedes, I believe. I'm planning to let them have the cottage after I hire a maid and a cook. For the present, Sven and Hannah will do all the work."

"You seem to have everything well planned."

He smiled, more to himself than at me. "Oh, yes, *very* well planned. I've been planning for years."

How uncomfortable he made me! I'd be more than happy to get home.

"I know you'll be pleased with my projected renovations for Sea Cliff House, Estelle."

"No doubt," I murmured politely, not caring one way or the other what he did to that gloomy old mansion. It might have been my ancestral home, but, since I hadn't grown up there, my only feeling about the place was relief that I didn't have to live in it any longer.

"I will consult you about the furnishings, it's only right."

"I'm no expert on furnishing a house," I said hastily. "Katherine is far more experienced."

"But for me your likes and dislikes are the ones that count."

I glanced at him from the corner of my eye. Why on earth would he say something like that?

An uneasy silence fell. I could think of nothing to say, and Gerald appeared wrapped in his own thoughts. I hoped he'd remain that way for the rest of the ride home. I only wished I'd asked him to turn around earlier.

It was some time before I noticed we didn't seem to be passing the same farms we'd gone by while driving into the country. "I don't recognize the scenery," I said tentatively.

"We're returning by a different route."

Now that I thought about it, I did recall a fork in the road a mile or so back. While I was glancing about, attempting to get my bearings, the day darkened. Looking at the sky, I saw clouds covering the sun. A few minutes later, a brisk chill breeze sprang up, coming, I thought, from the southwest instead of the southeast, as it had earlier.

What was it Oscar had told us on the jetty? In the winter, a wind first from the southeast, then the southwest, and, finally, from the northwest meant a bad blow. The wind had made its first change of direction. Would there be another?

And where was *Sea Dragon?* I prayed she and her captain were already safe inside the bar.

How comforting it would be to have him home again, no matter how short his stay. I'd be content just to know he and I were under the same roof. Well, perhaps *content* was the wrong word—having Stephen nearby still sent my pulses pounding. But I'd also be reassured by his presence.

Preoccupied by my thoughts of Stephen's safety, it took me some time to realize the carriage had slowed and was climbing a steep hill. Taken aback, I sat up straighter and stared about me. The other road had been quite level.

Though the town of Eureka nestled under a bluff, the land on which it was built was very flat, and this plateau extended some miles to the east. The greatest rise was to the south, where the cliffs rose—the site Alexi Nikolai had chosen for his house.

268

"Are we on the right road?" I asked Gerald.

"Of course."

It took me a minute or two to realize I might have posed the wrong question.

"But are we on the road to Eureka?" I persisted.

He turned to me, and his smile chilled me to the marrow.

"Naturally not," he said. "Don't you remember? I told you I was bringing you to Sea Cliff House."

Chapter 17

I stared at Gerald as the carriage crested a hill. Beyond him in the distance I could see the pointed dome of the old Russian church and the tower of Sea Cliff House.

"No," I whispered, "no."

"Come, come, Estelle," Gerald said. "You should be happy to be returning to your family's mansion."

Gathering my wits, I looked him straight in the eye. "Take me home to Eureka this minute, Gerald," I commanded. "It's getting late and the wind's rising. Katherine will be worried about me."

"She needn't worry; you're with me. And we'll soon be home—at Sea Cliff House." He spoke as though reasoning with a fractious child.

His words and the strange look in his eyes frightened me. I didn't know this Gerald at all; I was with a total stranger.

"I don't want to go to Sea Cliff House." I tried to speak calmly. "I wish to go to *my* home."

"But Sea Cliff House *is* your home, Estelle."

I swallowed. Had he lost his reason? What was I to do? Every revolution of the carriage wheels was bringing me closer to that gloomy old mansion I'd been so happy to leave.

A growing fear drove me to desperation. "If you don't immediately turn back toward Eureka," I cried, "I swear I'll leap from the carriage and make my own way to town." I started to rise from my seat.

His hand circled my wrist, pulling me down again and holding me fast at his side. "You'll do as I say."

I struggled to free myself, but he merely tightened his grip, crushing my wrist bones together until I gasped with pain.

"You're hurting me!" I exclaimed indignantly.

"Sit still and I won't have need to. You're behaving very childishly, Estelle."

I stopped struggling, and the pain in my wrist eased as he loosened his hold. "Be reasonable, Gerald," I begged. "Why do you insist on taking me to a place where you know I don't want to go? What can you possibly gain by it? I don't understand."

"Perhaps you'll understand better when I tell you I've been preparing you to be mistress of Sea Cliff House since you were five years old."

I gaped at him. He couldn't be serious!

"F-five years old?" I stammered.

"I had to make certain you didn't regain your memory but as soon as I was sure you wouldn't, then I was the only one who knew who you were, the only one who knew Estelle Marie Nikolai was still alive. It's been a long wait while you grew up, but well worth it."

I could hardly take in what he told me. My head whirled with confusion. "Then it *was* you I saw bending over me in my delirium," I finally accused.

He nodded. "You called me evil, but I'm not, I'm merely a man who makes long-range plans.

271

Since it was more than a year after *Sea Bear* was wrecked before Katherine would allow anyone to enter poor little lost Estelle's room, I found it a simple matter to slip in and take an initialed locket which I concealed until the day I'd need to use it as proof. Katherine never discovered what I'd done. And, after thirteen years, who could say whether little Estelle had been wearing the locket or not when she was lost at sea?"

My free hand went to my throat as though searching for the locket. "Are you saying I wasn't wearing that locket?" My voice rose. "That Floyd Rogers's story was a hoax?"

Gerald laughed. "Old Rogers himself was a hoax. I was careful to choose a man who could tell a good tale, drunk or sober. You and Katherine hung on his every word."

"You're mad," I whispered.

He shook his head. "Madmen don't make careful plans. Wait until you find what's in store for you at Sea Cliff House, Estelle."

"You can force me to go there with you now," I said heatedly, "but nothing will make me stay!"

"I have my own methods of persuasion, as you'll discover."

I hid my shudder of distaste and tried to comfort myself with the thought that at least I wouldn't be alone at the mansion with him. While I'd never met his new servants, I hoped to be able to enlist their help. What were their names again? Sven and Hannah, as I recalled.

The day had darkened noticeably, and the wind's icy breath blew chillingly through the carriage. I wasn't sure, but I believed the wind's direction had shifted once more—to the northwest. Oscar's prediction of a big blow appeared to be a true one. I huddled in on myself, shivering, unnerved not only by my plight but by the possibility Stephen's ship might be at sea, in danger from the coming storm.

It began to rain, wind-borne drops slanting in at us as Gerald whipped up the horses. Though I'd rather the shelter would be anyplace but at Sea Cliff House, I soon found myself longing to get under a roof, away from the wet and the cold sea wind. I made no complaint when Gerald, after driving the carriage into the stables, lifted me from the seat and pulled me with him toward Sea Cliff House.

I thought he'd enter by the more convenient back door, but he did not, forcing me to walk with him around to the front even as rain pelted us, and the freezing wind blew my hat from my head despite the pins holding it on. I could scarcely hear the crash of the waves against the cliffs above the howl of the wind, and I gasped with relief when we reached the steps to the porch. He pushed open the front door and, unexpectedly sweeping me off my feet, carried me across the threshold into the darkness of the foyer.

"I'm not your bride!" I snapped as he set me on my feet, retaining his hold on my wrist.

"Not yet."

"Never!"

He chuckled. "You're a Nikolai, all right. Fighters, one and all. It will make my victory all the sweeter."

I looked around, wondering why not a single lamp was lit. From the chill, I was certain no welcoming fires burned on any of the hearths, either.

At best, Sea Cliff House was gloomy. In the darkness of the storm I could barely make out the outline of the furniture and could not see Gerald's face well enough to know his expression. Though perhaps that was just as well.

"Why haven't your servants lit the lamps?" I asked.

"You mean Sven and Hannah?"

"Yes, of course." I spoke impatiently, as much annoyed with Gerald as afraid of him. How dare he treat me like this?

"They can't," he said.

"Whyever not?"

"Because they're not in the house."

My heart sank. He must have given them the cottage, after all. Somehow I must get away from him and reach the cottage. Meanwhile, I'd best hold fast to my anger to keep my fear at bay.

"I don't enjoy stumbling around in darkness," I said crossly. "If you'll release me, *I'll* light a lamp or two."

"I'd rather we both tended to the lamps."

Holding me fast by the wrist, he led me into the music room where the two of us, using one free hand apiece, awkwardly lit the lamp on a table near the door. I was glad for the light, but the lamp's red shade cast what I felt to be an unpleasant glow.

Like hellfire, I thought, a frisson rippling along my spine.

Katherine had taken her grand piano to Eureka, but a small one, a baby grand, sat in its place. With a nod toward its gleaming dark wood and ivory keys, Gerald said, "My mother's. Sit down and play, Estelle."

"I'm not musically talented," I protested. It was not modesty but the truth.

"I'm sure you were taught to play. It was one of the requirements when I paid the sisters for your education."

I bit my lip, at last understanding why Sister Samara had insisted I keep trying to master the piano when it had become clear to both of us that I'd never play well.

"You must learn," she'd told me when I'd asked her what was the use of continuing. "It's a skill you'll someday be required to demonstrate."

"My mother favored Mozart." Gerald forced me down on the piano bench, released my wrist, and handed me sheets of music from a cabinet next to the piano. Realizing I had no choice, I leafed through them and, discovering a waltz by Strauss I might be able to stumble through, placed it before me on the music rack and set the others aside.

Gerald stood close behind me, too close to allow me to flee successfully. Knowing I must convince him to move away, I removed my gloves slowly. Shivering exaggeratedly, I hugged myself.

"How can you expect me to play when I'm half frozen?" I demanded. "What kind of welcome is this? The fire isn't even lit."

He reached past me, swept a paisley shawl from the piano top, and draped it over my shoulders. "We'll have a fire later," he said. "Play."

In the dim reddish light, I squinted at the notes before me and, for the first time, read the title of the Strauss piece: "The Blue Danube Waltz."

As I haltingly began to play, I couldn't help remembering the first time I'd heard this melody— on Katherine's music box, wound by Alisette. I recalled how we'd danced as I tried to distract Alisette from fretting over what might have happened to her mother.

The music box had still been tinkling when Katherine opened the door to summon us into her sitting room and tell us that Cecile had fallen over the cliff and was dead.

But she hadn't fallen, she'd been pushed to her death—I was sure of it now.

275

Unable to go on, I brought my hands down hard on the keys, ending the mockery of my playing with a discordant crash. "Who pushed Cecile over the cliff?" I cried, while the notes on the sheet music danced before my eyes.

"Though I heard Armin accuse you," Gerald said calmly, "I've always believed her fall was accidental."

I didn't dare turn to face him, because he still stood too close. "I know it wasn't an accident," I said firmly, determined not to lose my nerve. "Armin pushed her, didn't he?"

Gerald sighed. "Armin was always too impulsive. I'm afraid his rashness led to his own death under the hooves of my horses."

I couldn't stand to keep my back to him any longer, so I slid to the end of the bench, rose, and faced him. "You've known all along Armin deliberately killed Cecile, haven't you?"

He shrugged. "What difference does it make? She's dead."

I took a deep breath, trying to control any sign of revulsion at his callousness. "Yes, she's as dead as Floyd Rogers. Did Armin push him, too?"

"I told you Armin was rash. He acted without thinking. But it was through his actions that I came to appreciate how very permanent a solution death was." He took my hand. "This is far too morbid a subject for a happy occasion. Come, I'll show you what I plan for the parlor."

"I don't want to know!" I cried. "I want to go home."

"How many times must I tell you—you *are* home." He pulled me after him, lifting the red-shaded lamp to light the way into the parlor. "Now that I'm master of Sea Cliff House, I intend you to be its mistress. We'll be married as soon as possible, you and I."

"I will never marry you." I spoke through clenched teeth.

"One way or the other, you will. I haven't planned all this to no avail." He smiled at me, the red glow of the lamp making his smile seem inexpressibly sinister. "Think of Katherine's shock when she discovers you've spent the night alone with me here. Your reputation will be irrevocably ruined, and you'll have no choice but to marry me."

"I won't stay!"

"You've forgotten the storm. Even if I'd allow you to leave—and I've no intention of it—you'd never reach Eureka with a gale like this blowing." He strode across the foyer to the front door and flung it open.

Wind rushed into the house so violently it swept a vase from an ornamental table, sending it crashing to the floor. The prisms of the chandelier tinkled wildly against one another, and the lamp in his hand, despite its protective chimney, flickered. My hair blew about my face, temporarily blinding me while Gerald struggled to force the door closed once more.

"Care to venture into that?" he asked when he finally shut out the gale.

Even through the closed door, I could hear the roar of the storm—the wind, the rain, the waves pounding against the cliffs—and I knew that trying to get to town was not only impossible but might well prove fatal.

"I'll spend the night in the cottage with your servants if I must," I said haughtily.

He threw back his head and laughed, the sound echoing throughout the foyer. "My dear, Estelle, there are no servants in the cottage any more than there are in the house. Sven and Hannah have yet to arrive."

277

Dear God, I was truly alone with Gerald! Fighting off panic, I said defiantly, "I'll tell Katherine the truth. That you lured me here and forced me to remain overnight."

He pulled me into the parlor. "I don't think so. Not after what's yet in store. The evening's barely begun. I have plans for tonight, Estelle, plans that include you."

He set the lamp on a table, then, without warning, he pulled me against him and brought his mouth down hard on mine.

His kiss repelled me, bringing bile to my throat. I struggled desperately to free myself from his unwelcome embrace. Since he was far stronger than I, though I managed to turn my face to one side, he kept me an unwilling prisoner in his arms.

"A Callich pitted against a Nikolai once more," he said in my ear. "God, how I've longed for this day! Fight all you want, Estelle, it'll make the Callich victory and my revenge all the sweeter."

"Let me go, Gerald," I pleaded. "No matter what, I'll never marry you. Never!"

"You'll soon have no choice," he repeated.

Only then did I fully realize that he meant to force himself on me, to lie with me as though we were already married. Nausea churned my stomach while terror speeded my heart.

"I'm patient," he whispered, "I plan far ahead. I planned all along to revenge myself on the Nikolais for what they did to my father. And I've succeeded. I have their houe, and soon I'll have their daughter as well."

No! I vowed. Not as long as I was able to fight. But he was stronger than I. Brains, not brawn was my only chance.

"I thought you meant to show me how you planned to renovate the downstairs, Gerald." I was amazed at the evenness of my voice. "Why don't

278

you? I'm eager to know what you mean to do."

At first I thought he wouldn't let me go, but finally he released me, though he kept hold of my arm. "You're right," he said, breathing heavily. "The finale belongs after the overture."

What I needed was a weapon, something to disable Gerald long enough for me to get away. While the storm confined me inside, Sea Cliff House was a large mansion with many nooks and crannies where I could hide. With luck, I might even find doors with keys in them and be able to lock myself in. If I kept my weapon with me, I could defend myself against him again and again, if need be.

Quite openly, I glanced around the parlor: after all, he wanted me to look. Doing my best to ignore the sinister effect of the shadows lurking in the corners, I pulled the paisley shawl closer around me as best I could with one hand.

"I rather like this room as it is," I said, praying my voice wouldn't quiver. My gaze fastened on the fireplace tools and singled out the poker—heavy enough to strike a damaging blow but not too heavy for me to lift. I had to get to it somehow. "We could use more light," I told him. "And a fire."

"We won't be in here long enough for a fire," he said, dashing my hopes.

"Was the fireplace one of the things you planned to change?" To my amazement, my desperation didn't sound in my voice.

"The fireplace? I hadn't thought about it. It's Italian marble, you know."

"I've never really cared for marble," I said. "Especially after that angel so narrowly missed me at the cemetery. I suppose that was Armin's work, too?"

"A damn fool thing to do!" Anger edged Gerald's words. "Between them, he and Cecile

279

might well have killed you. She was a real bitch with no scruples whatever, and she had poor taste as well. Armin was little better than an animal for all his Nikolai blood."

I thought of Sonia's hints that Cecile had taken Armin as a lover. But she'd suggested Gerald had been Cecile's lover as well.

"Poor taste?" I said, raising my eyebrows. "Sonia told me Cecile was as interested in you as she was in Armin."

He stared at me blankly for a long moment. "Sonia talks too much," he said finally. "It's just as well she left when she did."

Something about his words sent an icy stab through me. Was it Gerald who Sonia had feared would harm her?

"I—I think Sonia was afraid of you," I said.

He brushed Sonia sway with a wave of his hand, and I hurriedly returned to my main purpose, getting closer to the poker.

"I'd like to look at that Italian marble, if you don't mind." I gestured toward the fireplace. "As I recall, there's an unsightly crack on the left." Actually the crack was hairline and barely noticeable, but I hoped the mention of an imperfection would catch Gerald's interest.

"Show me," he commanded, grabbing the lamp and pulling me toward the fireplace.

I pointed to the crack. As his attention fixed on the marble, I shifted position so my skirts blocked my free hand—my left—and stealthily reached for the cast-iron poker. When my hand closed around its brass handle, I took a deep breath and carefully eased it from the holder, praying the poker wouldn't clang betrayingly against the metal.

"Strange, I never noticed that crack before," he said, holding the lamp closer and higher. "I won't have cracked marble in my parlor fireplace. Sea Cliff House must be perfect in every way. Perfect!"

280

The poker came free at last, and I knew it was now or never. I lifted the poker and swung it as hard as I could at Gerald's head, but my left-handed swing was awkward, and I missed. Glass shattered as the iron hit the lamp, knocking it from his hand. He swore and let go of my wrist. The last I saw as I turned to run was fire streaking along the carpet, following the trail of oil spewed from the lamp.

I knew I hadn't hurt Gerald, much less disabled him. Unfortunately, I'd dropped the poker and didn't dare pause to recover my weapon, but at least I'd gained my freedom. I meant to keep it.

Plunging through the flame-lit darkness, I raced up the stairs, knowing if there were to be any doors with the keys in them, they'd be on the second floor.

As I pounded up the broad staircase, I thought I felt the house shiver around me, but I had no time to think why. I must find a hiding place, somewhere that Gerald would never think of looking. Where?

The third-floor attic over the west wing! Praying the door wasn't locked, I ran on. The darkness upstairs was complete, so I had to fumble along the corridor until my seeking fingers touched the attic door. My luck held and the door yielded when I frantically grasped the knob. I closed it behind me and forced myself to tread cautiously and carefully as I ascended lest I alert Gerald to my destination.

At the top, hands outstretched, I inched toward the trunk I remembered, the trunk with the brass eagle on the lid. How well I remembered the day Alisette and I found the rag doll in that trunk, the one to which she claimed Alexandria had led her—my doll, though I didn't have any recollection of it, even now.

Despite my outstretched hands, I almost fell

281

over the trunk. Dropping to my knees, I opened the lid and feverishly removed most of the contents, being careful to pile them behind the trunk. As I lifted the sheathed sword from the trunk, it pulled loose from the ancient, tattered leather scabbard and clanked against the side of the trunk. I froze, sword in hand, listening. Had Gerald heard the noise?

Long moments passed without any sign of pursuit, and I finally decided he had not. I laid the sword carefully on the pile of clothes behind the trunk, climbed inside, curled up and closed the lid, assuring myself that Gerald would never find me—not shut inside a trunk in the attic.

Almost immediately, doubts assailed me. If he did think to look here, I was trapped. Why hadn't I thought to keep the sword inside the trunk with me? I didn't know the proper handling of a sword, but, even if I had, I wasn't at all sure I'd be able to bring myself to use it against him. Swinging a poker was one thing, slashing someone with a sword was another.

Then I remembered the flames crawling along the carpet in the parlor. What if the house caught on fire? Trapped here in the attic, I wouldn't stand a chance of escaping. And, enclosed as I was inside a trunk, I wouldn't even smell smoke until too late.

Don't panic, I told myself firmly. Stay put. Gerald will never allow Sea Cliff House to burn. He'll make certain the fire's out before he comes after you. You're safe where you are; he'll never find you.

But, I realized, even if he didn't find me I had gained no more than a temporary respite. Hidden in the trunk was far from being safe at home in Eureka. As soon as the storm eased, I'd be forced to try to get away from Sea Cliff House. That might not be soon—even in the trunk I could hear the hammer of rain slamming against the roof and the wolf howl of the wind.

As time passed, my thoughts drifted from my predicament to the past. As I'd suspected, Armin had been responsible for the deaths of Cecile and Floyd Rogers, Gerald had said so. Then it occurred to me that I was accepting the word of a man who'd already proved to me he was not only devious but a liar. Wrapped in the shawl and enclosed in the trunk, I was warm for the first time since entering Sea Cliff House, but even so a chill shook me.

Was Gerald also a murderer? There was only his word that Armin was the guilty man. Or, come to think of it, that Armin had been trampled to death by a horse. Since I could no longer accept Gerald's word, I didn't know what to believe.

If only Stephen were here to save me, but he was not. For all I knew, he might be in danger himself, struggling through stormy seas in his ship. And even if he'd sailed safely past the bar before the gale struck, he'd have no idea where I was, no notion of the menace that stalked me through Sea Cliff House.

No one would come to my rescue. I had to save myself. How? I huddled in the trunk, trying to think what to do next. The trunk quivered now and then, frightening me, for I knew the attic floor must be shaking from the fury of the storm. Dare I remain in the attic?

I had no idea how much time had passed when I heard, faint and faraway, a voice calling, "Estelle! Estelle!"

For an instant hope bloomed, to be nipped in the bud when I realized only Gerald would call me Estelle.

I held my breath. If I could hear him, it must

283

mean he was near the attic door—perhaps he even had it open! Still, he couldn't know where I was. I was safe as long as I didn't move or make a sound.

"Estelle!" he called. "Please listen. Listen to me, you'll die if you don't."

Alarmed, I slowly and quietly eased the trunk lid up an inch in order to better hear what he was saying.

"Estelle," he warned. "The house is afire. I can't put it out. You'll burn to death if you're upstairs. Listen to me. There's not much time left. Save yourself!"

As I tried to make up my mind whether he was telling the truth or using a ruse to make me reveal my hiding place, I thought I smelled smoke. Frightened, I pushed the trunk lid open fully and sat up.

Yes, I *did* smell smoke! Remembering the flames in the parlor, I could well believe Sea Cliff House was on fire. Gerald was right. If I remained in the attic, I'd be trapped and die. Perhaps it was already too late to escape.

Panic sent me scrambling from the trunk and stumbling through the darkness toward the stairs. I all but fell down them in my hurry. At the bottom, I found the attic door open and the pungent stench of smoke stronger. I groped toward the back stairs, careless of how much noise I made in my rush to escape the fire.

Suddenly, unseen hands grabbed me, fastening on my shoulders in a grip I couldn't break. I gasped. Gerald!

"Let me go," I cried. "The fire—"

"The fire's no more than a bunch of smoldering rags," he interrupted. "I burned them to smoke you out. You're clever, the Nikolais all are, but not as clever as Gerald Callich." He chuckled triumphantly.

284

As he shifted his grip to grasp my wrist once more, my shoulders slumped in defeat. He'd outsmarted me, and I wouldn't find it easy to escape him again. He began to pull me with him toward, I thought, the front stairs, though I couldn't be sure.

The blackness now shrouding Sea Cliff House was more than storm gloom, and I knew night must have fallen. Where was he taking me? Somewhere a loose shutter banged against the siding, and the floor shivered under our feet as though the house were prey being shaken in the wolf-wind's teeth. I wondered how it could survive under the onslaught.

"While I was searching for you, I decided on the most appropriate spot," Gerald said, riveting my attention on him once more. "Since you're the Nikolai princess, I think the tower's the place, don't you?"

I remained obstinately silent.

"Yes, the tower's certainly appropriate for what I have in mind," he went on. "And, just in case you're still considering ways to disable me, keep in mind that I'm now appropriately armed. I brought my father's ivory-handled kris with me. You've seen the kris before, haven't you?"

"Yes," I whispered, the image of the deadly Malayan dagger with its wavy, sharp blade coming clearly to my mind.

"Never think I won't use the kris if necessary," he murmured almost caressingly. "Not to kill you, oh, no, never that, my bride-to-be. But remember the kris can wound as well as kill. I don't *want* to hurt you, but, if I have to, my dear, I will."

I believed him, and his threat banished whatever resistance I had left. I was helpless.

Chapter 18

Gerald didn't appear to notice the terrible shuddering running through the house as he forced me ahead of him up the spiral stairs of the tower. I had found the tower unpleasant enough in daylight, but in darkness it was frightful. With the raging storm attacking the tower and a madman behind me, in my terror I could hardly drag myself from one step to the next.

I tried to force my mind to work. If I was to escape from Gerald, I could not allow panic to overwhelm me. Was there anything in the tower I might use as a weapon against him? Desperately, I struggled to recall every detail of the tower: padded window seats, a brass telescope, a small brass table, and a round Oriental rug. I shook my head in despair. There was nothing.

My heart thudded against my chest—doom, doom, doom each frantic beat seemed to tell me. You're doomed, doomed, doomed.

Unexpectedly, I reached the top of the stairs and stumbled forward onto my knees. Gerald's hand gripped my shoulder and yanked me upright. I could hear his harsh breathing in my ear and cringed away. In a moment he'd be forcing himself on me. I had to think of something to stop him, but what?

I blurted out the first thing that came into my mind. "You haven't yet told me how you were able to buy Sea Cliff House. I remember Stephen seemed surprised you had the money."

Gerald laughed as he pulled me with him until we bumped against a window seat. "Do sit down, my dear Estelle, while I explain."

I did as he ordered, glad of even a few moments reprieve. He sat beside me, and I tensed. Had I gained anything, after all? Other than holding my hand firmly in his, though, he didn't touch me.

"Katherine had no head for business," he said, "so I took care to make myself indispensable to her. Fortune favored me, keeping Stephen at sea for so long. Since he wasn't here, Katherine left all business matters to me. She had no idea I was siphoning off most of the Nikolai profits for myself. It wasn't thievery—far from it! I merely appropriated the money they'd stolen from my father years before. I find it fittingly ironic that, in a sense, I used Nikolai money to buy Sea Cliff House."

I prayed he'd never stop talking. To encourage him, I asked, "But did no one suspect?"

"I took care they did not. Katherine trusted me. Cecile, on the other hand, trusted no one, but she soon was hopelessly infatuated with me. I know *her* kind. I brought her to heel and kept her there by treating her with a mixture of assumed affection and contempt. I had everything under my control when I introduced you into the household. All would have continued to go well if Stephen hadn't come home."

Despite my perilous circumstances, his sordid tale of betrayal fascinated me. "Surely you knew

287

Stephen would return one day," I said.

"I'd rather hoped *Sea Dragon* had joined the other Nikolai ships at the bottom of the sea—and Stephen with her. But come home he did, to my regret, though I'll admit his amnesia was a pleasant surprise, because it meant he'd have trouble discovering how I'd doctored the books. On the other hand, his arrival brought a new problem when Cecile became jealous of you.

"She couldn't bear to see any other woman admired by a man. Any attention I paid to you, however slight, annoyed her. When it became clear to her that Stephen preferred you to her—another irony, though I was the only one who could appreciate it—she became impossible to reason with."

Gerald, by concealing my true identity, was also partly to blame for what had happened between Stephen and me. How callous of him to dismiss as ironic what, in truth, had been a tragedy as far as Stephen and I were concerned. But I couldn't allow myself to be distracted by my feelings; I needed all my wits about me. I had to keep Gerald talking as long as I could.

"I knew Cecile hated me," I said. "When I wasn't hurt by the falling angel, she took more drastic action: she pushed me over the cliff. Alisette saw her."

"Stephen proved useful that one time, he saved your life. If you'd fallen to your death, all my plans would have been for naught. I was furious with Cecile, but I kept my head and did nothing while I tried to think of a plan to draw her and Stephen closer. Once she got him in her bed, I was certain her jealousy of you would diminish, if not cease. If Alisette were missing, I told myself, their anxiety over their daughter should unite them. Unfortunately, you found her too quickly."

"You were the bad man who locked her in the

tower!" I shivered, knowing I was as helpless as Alisette had been. He'd shown no mercy to an innocent child; I could expect none.

"No, no, Armin abducted her." Gerald was clearly upset that I'd accuse him. "All I did was suggest it to Armin. When locking Alisette in the tower failed in its purpose, I pointed out to Armin how Cecile was endangering my plan by trying to get rid of you. If anything happened to you, I told him, everything was off, including the money he anticipated getting."

It took me a moment to digest this. "You mean Armin was your accomplice all along?"

"Of course not." Gerald's voice was annoyed. "I didn't need any assistance, and, if I had, I never would have chosen a lout like him. Our involuntary association began when he took one look at you and guessed who you were. Blood calling to blood, I suppose. Anyway, he came to me with his suspicions, and I had to promise him money to keep him quiet. I planned to reveal who you were in my own time and in my own way."

"But you did use Armin," I said slowly, beginning to see how diabolically Gerald had controlled Armin. "You told him to get rid of Cecile, didn't you?"

"I merely suggested we'd both be safer without her. Especially after he told me she'd seen old Rogers meet me—before he officially came to deliver the locket." Gerald spread his hands. "How was I to know Armin would be so violent?"

My skin crawled. I could hardly bear to go on talking to such a monster. But I feared what would happen if I lapsed into silence. "Floyd Rogers drank. I suppose he talked too much when in his cups," I said. "Did you suggest to Armin that he—?" I couldn't go on.

"Armin acted on his own after seeing Rogers

289

come back to the house to demand more money from me." Gerald chuckled. "Like all the Nikolais, Armin was greedy. He didn't want to share my money with anyone else."

The pieces were dropping into place for me, creating a hideous picture. "Sonia saw Mr. Rogers leaving the old church," I told Gerald. "It must have been you he met there."

"I trust Sonia will have the good sense to remain in San Francisco." His words were edged with menace.

He would have killed her if she hadn't gone, I was suddenly sure of it, as Sonia, who knew Gerald well, feared he would. I shuddered.

"None of this can be proved, of course," Gerald reminded me. "Armin, the murderer, is dead himself."

How convenient for Gerald. Too convenient? I thought so. It would have been relatively easy for him to render Armin unconscious by a blow or by offering him drugged brandy or whiskey. With no one but the two of them at Sea Cliff House, Gerald would have had little trouble making Armin's death look like an accident.

As I opened my mouth to accuse him, a particularly vicious gust of wind rocked the tower so violently I slid off the window seat onto the floor. Gerald lost my hand momentarily but grabbed my arm before I could even think of fleeing down the stairs.

"We've wasted enough time," he said, pulling me to my feet. "I didn't bring you to the tower to talk. We'll have more than enough time to talk later."

I knew why he'd brought me. Bracing myself so the swaying of the tower in the wind wouldn't make me fall against Gerald, I sought frantically for a way to stop him. The only weapon I had was words.

"I'm surprised you didn't bring me to the old church," I said tartly. "Wouldn't that have been a more appropriate place to take a Nikolai bride?"

He laughed. "I'm delighted to find you have a sense of humor, Estelle. So few women do." He started to draw me to him.

Mentioning the church had reminded me of the Nikolai legend, or was it a curse? Could I use it? I had nothing to lose by trying.

"Listen!" I pitched my voice high and shrill. "Listen, do you hear that?"

"It's only the wind."

"No, no, I hear the sound above the wind. It's a bell. A bell tolling. Oh, surely you must hear the tolling!"

"I hear nothing but the wind and the waves."

"I wasn't thinking. You're not a Nikolai. Of course you wouldn't hear the bell. It's tolling, I tell you. Sea Cliff House is doomed!"

As if to underline my words, there came an ominous cracking sound from below, and the tower shook violently, flinging me sideways. Gerald fell across me, pinning me to the window seat.

"How convenient," he said in my ear. "Even the storm is on my side."

"The bell—" I gasped, struggling to rise.

"No bell is tolling, and none will," Gerald said, shifting position so he could gather me into his arms. "Either you're lying to try to distract me, or you're mistaken in what you think you hear. The tolling bell is nothing but a myth. As a matter of fact, the old church bell's clapper is rusted to the inside of the bell—it can't ring. Sea Cliff House will withstand this storm as it has so many in the

291

past. And as it will withstand every storm in the future."

I fought to sit up, but he pressed me down onto the window seat, his body half covering me while his lips sought mine. I twisted my face to the side. He chuckled.

"Shy, Estelle? I'll take care of that." With his hand clamped to my jaw, he forced my face toward him. "That's better." His open mouth covered mine.

Nausea gagged me. I couldn't bear his kiss. To think of being forced to endure more than the kiss terrorized me.

"I'm sorry we don't have a light," he murmured hoarsely. "I'd like to watch you while I make you mine."

My stomach heaved, and bitter bile burned my throat. "Whatever you do to me, I'll never be yours!" I cried. "Never!"

The wind's shriek matched my own as it battered against the tower. Then there came a brief lull in the storm, and something slammed downstairs.

"The front door!" I gasped, more from hope than belief. "Someone came in."

"Wishful thinking," Gerald muttered, but he raised his head and shoulders to listen.

I twisted my body as hard and fast as I could, shoving against him with my knees. Taken off balance by my sudden move, he slid off the window seat onto the floor, dragging me with him.

I wrenched free of his hold, scrambled to my hands and knees, and groped for the stairs, fearing that at any moment I'd feel his arms closing around me once again.

"Estelle," he warned, "I still have the kris."

The thought of the Malay dagger made me

whimper in fright as I scuttled across the shuddering floor. Just as my hand closed on the iron rail of the spiral stairs, he grabbed my foot. Screaming, I kicked him as hard as I could with my other foot. He swore, his grip loosening enough as I yanked my foot free. I flung myself at the stairs, half falling down them as the steps pitched and yawed beneath me like a boat tossed in wild seas.

I threw open the door at the bottom and, heedless of the pitch darkness, raced toward the front stairs, too terrified to worry about slamming into a wall. Suddenly I ran full tilt into something that reeled backwards. Arms came around me and I shrieked in terror.

Gerald!

"Esma?" Stephen's voice.

I went weak-kneed with relief, clinging to him for a long moment, unable to speak. I couldn't imagine how he came to be here, but I thanked God he was. Then I remembered Gerald and his kris.

"He's got a knife, a dagger," I babbled, pulling away from Stephen. "We've got to get out of here. Hurry!"

"Gerald?" Stephen demanded.

"Yes, Gerald. He's mad. Oh, please hurry." I tugged at Stephen's hand, urging him toward where I hoped the stairs were.

Stephen hesitated, then came with me, and together we stumbled through the darkness until, when I banged into the open attic door, I realized with dismay we'd passed the stairs.

At that moment, light flared behind us. Gerald had lit one of the wall sconces near the head of the stairs. He stood with one hand on the bannister railing, the other holding the unsheathed kris. Its wavy blade gleamed wickedly.

"You're trapped, Stephen," he called. "I control

the stairs, and there's no way out through the west wing. I had the foresight to bring the Callich kris, but I see you've forgotten the Nikolai belaying pin." He laughed. "The odds are with me this time."

As Stephen shoved me behind him, I remembered the old Russian sword from the trunk in the attic. *He'd* know what to do with it.

I pulled Stephen's head down to whisper in his ear, "I'll get you something better than a belaying pin."

Leaving him in the hall, I flew up the attic stairs and across to the trunk, paying no attention when I banged my shins on unseen obstacles. Grasping the hilt of the heavy sword, I started down the stairs, only to find Stephen halfway up them, his back to me. I gasped when I saw Gerald at the bottom, the blade of his kris menacing Stephen.

Hurriedly, I thrust the sword into Stephen's hand. He hefted it, then slashed the blade through the space between him and Gerald.

"What's that you were saying about odds, Callich?" he asked.

His words were all but drowned by a tremendous crash from the west wing. The entire house jolted, tossing us from one side to the other of the narrow staircase. I was thrown backwards against the steps. I struggled to my feet and, horrified, saw Stephen sprawled headfirst on the lower stairs, the sword gone from his hand. Gerald stood over him, dagger upraised.

"No!" I screamed and lunged for the sword.

My fingers grasped the hilt and, with both hands, I brought up the sword blade just as Gerald's arm swept down. The kris clanged against the sword. Gerald drew back. I was afraid to swing the sword, lest I injure Stephen as he scrambled to his feet.

294

By the time I handed Stephen the sword again, Gerald had disappeared. We hurried down the rest of the attic stairs and saw him racing down the front staircase.

"We've got him on the run," I said hopefully.

"I doubt it. He's full of tricks. Stay behind me."

I followed Stephen, and we'd reached the top of the staircase before Gerald reappeared, coming from the library. He stopped and pointed something at us.

"The bastard!" Stephen exclaimed. "Look out, Esma, he's got a gun."

Stephen yanked me forward, past the stairs, sword upraised. The gun cracked twice, and then the blade of the sword smashed into the glass chimney of the wall sconce, plunging us into darkness.

We raced for the back stairs, ran down their narrow curving steps, and stopped short at the door. Stephen cursed.

"He's locked it." He flung his weight against the door once, twice, three times, but the solid wood didn't give. Since we had no choice, we rushed back up the stairs.

As long as we were in darkness, Gerald had no advantage. Perhaps we could slip by him, I thought, and get to the front staircase.

My hopes were dashed by a flare of light— Gerald had lit another wall lamp. He saw us, turned, and took aim. Quickly, Stephen pulled me into one of the bedrooms and slammed the door, muttering that there was no key. He handed me the sword, stumbled to the windows, and flung them both open.

Mercilessly, the storm invaded the room, wild wind and driving rain. As we crouched to one side of the door, waiting for Gerald in the darkness, the wind flung breakables to the floor. Carrying the reek of the sea, it swirled cold and wet around us. Above its howl, even though we were in the east wing, I could hear the surging smash of waves against the cliffs. I thought I heard something else, too, very faintly, and the hair rose on my nape. I gripped Stephen's arm, afraid to speak lest my words make it true.

He put his hand briefly over mine, and I took heart at his touch.

The door flew open. As Stephen had intended, Gerald was momentarily halted by the blast of the wind as it whipped past him and down the corridor. The light flickered and dimmed, grew bright again, flickered, and snuffed out—no match for the storm.

Stephen dived at Gerald. I couldn't see the struggle, but I knew Stephen, crouched, would have struck Gerald, bowling him backwards. I edged into the corridor, my back to the wall, the sword hilt clenched in my hand, wishing I knew what was happening. The wind blowing my hair into a tangle reminded me it would be futile to try to light a lamp. Besides, as long as Gerald had the gun I was afraid of light anyway.

What was happening? Had Stephen disarmed Gerald? Who was winning? I bit my lip in agonized anxiety.

The gun roared—at my feet, it seemed—and I gasped. "Stephen?" I quavered.

Someone grunted. There was a thud as of a fist hitting flesh, but Stephen didn't answer.

Finally I could bear the suspense no longer. I had to *see*. Knowing Mrs. Yates's storage closet was next to the back stairs, I groped along the wall until I reached what I thought was the right door. Though Mrs. Yates was no longer there, I thought it likely extra upstairs supplies were still stored in the same place.

I opened the door, set the sword to one side, and fumbled along the shelves until I found a tin of matches and an old-fashioned candle holder with a protective chimney. Using the door to shield the flame from the wind, I struck a match, lit the candle, and quickly thrust the chimney over its wavering light.

Closing the door, I held up the candle—taking care to protect it from the wind with my body—and peered along the corridor. Gerald and Stephen grappled on the hall carpet in a confusion of arms and legs. Between them and me lay a dark object. The gun!

I ran and picked it up, backing away from the struggling men. I'd never had a gun in my hands before, and this one was both larger and heavier than I expected. It was a revolver—a Colt, I'd heard them called. Could I use it if I had to? I had no doubt I was physically able to point the barrel and pull the trigger, even if I had to use both hands, but could I do that knowing I might kill a man?

I'd do anything in the world to save Stephen, I told myself firmly while my candle wavered and flickered. But I knew in my heart that, as much as I loathed and despised Gerald, I'd never be able to deliberately kill another human being.

Under those circumstances, keeping the gun with me wasn't safe. If Gerald got the chance, he'd be able to wrench it away from me and, God knew, *he* had no scruples about killing.

Who was winning? I couldn't tell. Making up my mind, I opened the door of another bedroom, set the light inside, and ran to the first room where the windows were still open. Braving the blast of the wind, I flung the revolver into the storm. When I left the room, I used all my strength to force the door closed behind me to shut away the worst of the wind.

When I retrieved my candle, it burned with a steadier flame. By its flickering light, I saw the two men were between me and the front staircase. Stephen was sitting astride Gerald, pummeling him. Winning. But then I noticed one of Gerald's hands snaking toward his pocket, and I feared for whatever he was reaching meant trouble for Stephen.

"Stephen, watch out!" I cried at the same moment that Gerald pulled the kris from his pocket and freed it from its sheath.

He stabbed at Stephen. Stephen swore and rolled free of him, blood dripping from his arm as he got to his feet. I stood frozen. How badly was he wounded?

"The sword!" he shouted to me, his eyes searching the floor.

I didn't have it. Where had I left the sword? I asked myself frantically. In the bedroom? No, I didn't think so.

Gerald rose, kris in hand, and looked quickly about, his gaze also sweeping along the floor. I realized they both were looking for the gun. If only I hadn't thrown it away, I could give it to Stephen.

But Gerald didn't know what I'd done with the gun. Could I make him afraid to come after us with the kris by pretending I had the gun? If he couldn't see it, I doubted Gerald would believe me.

"Where's the damn sword?" Stephen demanded.

Where *was* it? Suddenly remembering, I turned and bolted for the supply closet.

"No, you don't," Gerald cried and pounded after me.

Stephen flung himself at Gerald, tackling him so that they both crashed to the floor. I grabbed the sword hilt, ready to hand it to Stephen, but they were once again rolling about on the carpet, Stephen gripping Gerald's right wrist, trying to prevent him from using the kris.

What use was the sword to me? Even if it didn't take all my strength to lift the heavy blade up over my head, I'd never find an opening to disable Gerald—if I could bring myself to thrust a sword blade into him once I did.

I circled them warily, watching for a chance to do something—anything—to get rid of the deadly kris. At last Stephen pinned Gerald's right arm to the floor. Taking a deep breath, with both hands I lifted the sword, point down, and jabbed the blade into Gerald's hand. He screamed and dropped the kris, blood staining his fingers.

Though sickened by what I'd done, I knew I must retrieve the kris. With the sword point I flicked the dagger far enough from the struggling men so I could safely pick it up. Inadvertently, I exerted too much force and the Malay dagger skimmed over the carpet, slipped between the bannisters, and dropped into the darkness of the foyer below.

As I stood immobilized, the sword clenched in both my hands, wondering what to do, I heard the sound again, a sound that made my eyes widen in horror. Mixed with the noise of the wind and the waves came the unmistakable toll of a bell.

I swallowed, numb with fear. Impossible or not, I heard a bell tolling, and there was only one church bell close enough to Sea Cliff House to be heard over the storm.

The house shuddered, and something crashed below. I felt the floor shake under my feet as though the house, too, had heard the bell and knew its time had come.

"Stephen!" I screamed. "Listen! The church bell's tolling for Sea Cliff House!"

Intent on pummeling Gerald, he paid no heed. The bell continued to ring its warning, paralyzing me with fright.

Suddenly plaster crumbled overhead, big chunks breaking away and dropping into the corridor around the fighting men.

"The house is falling around us!" I shouted. "Listen to the bell!"

Stephen broke free of Gerald and stood for a moment, covered in white plaster dust, shaking his head as though dazed. Gerald, too, stumbled to his feet, his clothes as white as Stephen's. They stared at one another.

"I hear a bell ringing," Stephen said as much to Gerald as to me. "I don't know what it means, but we'd better all get the hell out of here—the whole damn place is collapsing."

"No!" Gerald cried. "You're lying. I hear no bell. Sea Cliff House will stand forever!"

Stephen turned from him and hurried to me. Taking the sword from my hand, he urged me down the staircase, stopping halfway and turning to look at Gerald, still standing in the hall. I looked, too. As we watched, Gerald turned, opened the tower door, and walked through it, disappearing from our view as he climbed the stairs. A vast shaking, like that of an earthquake, ran through the house, and the tower door slammed shut.

The bell continued to toll.

Chapter 19

Stephen and I hurried down the shaking front staircase, ducking our heads to avoid the broken glass showering onto us from shattered prisms of the swaying chandelier. When we reached the foyer, I saw the paisley shawl on the floor and scooped it up. I started for the front door, but Stephen pulled me to the left, and I followed him toward the kitchen and the back door.

There was a tremendous crash behind us. I glanced over my shoulder to see the chandelier smash onto the floor in a great welter of glass. Even as I shuddered at our narrow escape, the dim light from upstairs snuffed out, and we were forced to slow our pace, groping through darkness.

Bombarded by falling plaster and startled by crash after crash, we stumbled toward the back door. I shivered. Would the house collapse on us before we managed to escape? The creaking of the dying house and the shattering of glass and china drowned any sound of the bell. But I had heard it tolling, and so had Stephen. I no longer doubted Sea Cliff House was doomed.

Gerald had climbed to the tower. Would he have time to flee before the house collapsed beneath him? I wondered if he were sane enough to even

301

realize his danger. Or, perhaps, like a captain going down with his ship, Gerald meant to stay with the house, no matter what.

It seemed an eternity before we reached the kitchen and staggered across the quaking floor amidst the clamor of falling pots and pans. We hadn't reached the back door when Stephen stopped.

"What's the matter?" I asked apprehensively.

"Left my slicker on a chair," he muttered. "Where—oh, here it is."

Then we were at the door. I couldn't understand what took him so long to open it until he swore.

"Damn! The key must have fallen out of my pocket during the scuffle. I had locked the door behind me."

My heart sank. What now? Return to the front door? Could we possibly get there before the house came down around our heads?

"Don't move," Stephen ordered. "I'll try a window."

In the darkness I couldn't see what he was doing, but after a few moments I heard glass shatter and the fury of the storm blasted into the room.

"The windows were all jammed," he told me. "I had to break a pane. I'll climb through, then lift you out. Here, put on my slicker. There may be splinters of glass left in the window frame."

Reluctant to abandon the shawl, I quickly folded it, tied it around my waist, and slid into the sailor's oilskins. Several minutes later, we both stood outside the house, battered by the wind and deluged by rain.

Stephen grasped my hand. "Run for the stables," he commanded.

If he hadn't pulled me along, I doubt if I could have made headway through the swirling, howling gale. As it was, we'd barely reached the gate in

302

the wall separating the stables from the gardens when a terrible roar made us pause and look back. In the darkness and the storm, it was impossible to see what was happening, but I feared it marked the end of Sea Cliff House.

"She's going," Stephen shouted and thrust me through the gate as the ground heaved under our feet.

He all but dragged me the rest of the way into the stables and slammed the door shut behind us. Guided by the stamping, snorting horses, we reached the carriage.

"I lost my lantern in the storm," Stephen said, "but there ought to be another in here." I heard the carriage creak as he climbed in.

A match flared, then the welcome glow of a lantern lit the interior of the stables. The matched bays were still hitched to the carriage.

"I took a moment to toss blankets over the poor beasts," Stephen said as he started to unbuckle their harnesses. "I didn't dare stop long enough to unhitch them, not after what Sonia told me the day I left San Francisco."

Sonia! What *had* she told him? I opened my mouth to ask, then seeing how skittish the horses were, I postponed my question. We were safe for the moment, and the horses needed care more than I needed to know what had brought him to my rescue. Easing off the heavy oilskins, I moved slowly and carefully to the front of the horses, speaking in a soothing monotone to try to calm them so Stephen would have an easier time unhitching them.

Between the two of us, we urged the bays into separate stalls and fed them. Stephen then unsaddled Bosun, who was tied to a post, and tended to him.

"For awhile there I didn't think Bosun would

303

make it through the gale," he said, stroking the chestnut's nose affectionately. "He's a wonder."

I eyed Stephen's bloodstained sleeve. "It's time I took a look at your arm," I said firmly.

At my insistence, he stripped off his soaked jacket and shirt. When I found that the several-inch gash on his right forearm had stopped bleeding and had already crusted over, I breathed easier. I'd unearthed a couple of clean cloths in the tack room, so I bound one of them over the shallow wound, doing my best not to look at his naked chest. Merely touching him made my heart pound shamelessly.

He used the second cloth to dry his dripping hair and wrapped a horse blanket around his shoulders. The oilskins had kept me quite dry, and now I huddled into the paisley shawl for warmth.

"Shall we sit in the carriage?" he asked.

"No!" I exclaimed. "I'd rather sit on the bare stable floor, dirty as it is, than ever get into Gerald's carriage again."

After glancing around, he walked to a ladder and pointed upward. "There's hay in the loft. If I spread a blanket over it, we'd be fairly comfortable."

I put my hand on his arm. "What about Gerald?"

His hand covered mine. "No one will ever have to worry about Gerald Callich again, Esma. When we felt the ground tremble under us at the gate, that was part of the cliff breaking away and falling into the sea, taking the house with it—just what Jock Ferguson's report warned might happen. Gerald didn't have time to escape; he couldn't possibly have survived."

I swallowed. "The cliff broke off? Are you sure?"

He nodded. "If you'll listen carefully, you can hear the sound of the waves slamming against the

304

rock face quite clearly, even with the storm. That's because the stables are much closer to the edge than they used to be."

I bit my lip as I listened. He was right. "But are we safe here?" I asked apprehensively.

"The storm's lessening. I think the damage has been done." He half-smiled. "Besides, the Nikolai curse didn't mention the stables being demolished."

"You heard the bell, too!"

He nodded. "I heard the tolling."

"Gerald said the clapper was frozen to the inside by rust, so it couldn't ring."

"This gale's enough to send any bell to clanging, rusted clapper or not."

"You don't believe a Nikolai spirit tolled the bell?"

He shrugged. "Who knows? All sailors are superstitious. Even captains. Neither I nor any of my men ever whistle aboard ship since we might whistle up a gale like this one."

Taking his hand from mine, he slid an arm around my shoulders. "You're shivering, Esma. Come on, let's climb into the loft. If need be we can burrow into the hay for warmth."

I hitched up my skirts and climbed the ladder with Stephen close behind. He spread a blanket on the hay and, after we were sitting side by side, draped another one over us both. With the dim light of the lantern below filtering up to the loft, it seemed almost cozy.

Cold and tired as I was, my breath came faster from Stephen's nearness. I clenched my hands, determined he must never know I couldn't put him from my heart.

"What did Sonia tell you in San Francisco?" I asked.

"She hardly said a word to me on the trip south, but the day before *Sea Dragon* was scheduled to sail back to Eureka, Jock Ferguson brought her down to the docks. 'My wife has something to tell you,' he says."

Mr. Ferguson had married Sonia after all, I thought, pleased she'd at last found a man she could trust.

"Sonia took some time coming to the point," Stephen went on, "but she finally got around to warning me Callich wasn't to be trusted, that he'd secretly met the old sailor, Rogers, at the ruins both before and after Rogers came to the house with the locket. 'If you ask me,' Sonia said, 'he's got his eye on Miss Estelle. I wish I'd told her everything.'"

"I wish she had, too," I said fervently.

"I questioned Sonia, and she eventually admitted she left Eureka in a hurry, because she was afraid Callich would kill her. 'I know too much, I'd've been another fatal accident,' she insisted.

"I wasn't quite sure exactly what Callich was up to, but I feared for you. After going over the account books and asking questions at the mill, I suspected that he'd been embezzling from the Nikolais for years and doctoring the books. Now here was Sonia accusing him of conspiring with old Rogers and of murder. What did he have in mind for you? I set sail immediately, praying I wouldn't be too late."

"Oh, Stephen," I said, "thank God you came home."

He took my hand, holding it in both of his. Wrong or right, I couldn't help hoping he'd hold it forever.

"We were the last ship to make it past the bar before the storm broke," he said. "When I reached the house and heard from Katherine that you'd gone for a ride in the country with Gerald, I didn't like the idea. It never occurred to me you might be

306

in any real danger, though—not until the wind rose and you didn't come home. Then, somehow, I knew he'd brought you to Sea Cliff House for some twisted purpose of his own.

"I saddled Bosun, but the storm hit us when we were only halfway here—a big blow. If Bosun hadn't known the road so well we might not have made it." He brushed a strand of damp hair from my forehead. "Poor Esma, you've had a terrible time of it."

I longed to lay my head on his shoulder, but of course I did nothing of the kind. "Gerald must have been insane," I said. "He found me in the orphanage thirteen years ago and never told my parents, planning even then to use me to exact revenge on the Nikolais. Today he brought me here against my will, insisting I was to be his bride, even though I told him I'd never marry him."

Stephen muttered under his breath.

"He did embezzle Nikolai money," I continued, "and used his ill-gotten gains to buy Sea Cliff House. He'd vowed revenge on the Nikolais as long ago as when Captain Peter and his father quarreled. He blamed the Nikolais for his father's death—and his mother's, too. As for me, he only wanted to marry me because I *was* a Nikolai. When I refused, he tried to—to—" I broke off, shuddering as I relived the dreadful moments when I'd been trapped in Gerald's embrace and feared I'd never break free.

"A real bastard!" After a pause, Stephen laughed harshly. "Coming from me, that's like the pot calling the kettle black. Callich wasn't a bastard by birth but by nature. I qualify both ways. I'm exactly what I once accused you of being—a Nikolai bastard.

"I know you're really Estella Marie, the daughter of Katherine and Peter, I knew it from the

307

moment I heard you sing that Russian lullaby with Katherine. I'm sorry I hurt you by accusing you of lying and by calling you names." He lifted my hand to his lips. "You're exactly what you seem to be—a beautiful, sweet, honest young woman. And a true Nikolai."

"But," I protested, confused by his words and shaken by the feel of his lips on my hand, "but you're a true Nikolai, too."

"I carry the blood, but I'm no child of Peter and Katherine. I'm not even a bastard son of Peter's."

"But you—you're Stephen," I stammered. "How can you not be when everyone recognized you?"

"Remember my amnesia? That was to cover the fact I didn't recognize any of *you.* How could I? My name is Marcus Alexander, bastard son of Peter's distant cousin, Marcus Nikolai—from the Russian branch of the family. He met my mother when he was in port in San Francisco. My first name is my father's, my last my mother's—Marcus Alexander. My mother died when I was a child."

I gaped at him, unable to believe my ears. "If you're not Stephen," I said slowly, "then where *is* Stephen?"

He hunched forward, wrapping his arms about his knees. "Let me tell you how it came about. I met Stephen Nikolai for the first time on the docks in Hong Kong when *Sea Dragon* and my ship—I was first mate—were moored side by side. The minute we set eyes on one another, we were struck by our likeness to each other. Why, we might have been twins."

"Alexi," I murmured. "You look like Captain Alexi."

"Then Stephen did, too. He invited me out on the town with him, and we had a few drinks. Sometime during the evening, he decided it would be a lark to exchange clothes and identity papers

308

and see if any of our shipmates knew the difference. He insisted on having a barber cut my hair so it matched his and trim his beard to match mine. It all was harmless enough and nothing more should have come of it. Unfortunately, later that night, after we had a lot more to drink in some questionable places, we found ourselves in a brawl. I remember crouching back to back with Stephen, standing off a bunch of cutthroats. The next I knew, I woke up in a hospital with a stranger bending over me.

"'Thank the Lord you're awake, Captain Nikolai,' he said. I tried to tell him who I was, but I couldn't move or speak—a result of my head injury. It was several more days before the paralysis lifted, and by then I'd been told by the man—*Sea Dragon*'s first mate—that my new friend Marcus Alexander had been killed in the fight, his ship had sailed, and he would be buried at sea."

"How awful," I whispered.

He sighed. "Think of it, Esma. There I was, a bastard with little enough of my own, suddenly elevated to captain of a ship. A Nikolai ship! Tempted, I put off setting things right until it was too late. Once I went aboard *Sea Dragon* as Captain Nikolai, I coveted that ship, wanted her for my own, wanted what my father had denied me by making me a bastard. I reasoned that no one would be hurt. My mother was dead, and Stephen's family would be spared the grief of knowing he was at the bottom of the sea. You know the rest. I pretended amnesia, and the crew accepted me, which gave me confidence the family also would.

"Even then it took me almost two years to gain enough courage to sail back to California and face Stephen's family. He'd told me he was married and

309

that his wife was pregnant when he sailed from Eureka. We were together such a short time that I knew little more about to whom I was coming home, though I learned from the crew that his father was dead but not his mother.

"As I rode Bosun from the docks to Sea Cliff House, I told myself I couldn't continue the masquerade. I would, I vowed, tell the family the truth the moment I walked through the front door. Instead, when I came into the foyer, I saw you with Alisette and fell in love with you on the spot—my wife, as I thought. Everything else fled from my mind but you. Then I kissed you and was lost. If I told who I was, I'd forfeit you. By the time I discovered you weren't my wife, it was too late to be honest."

"I can't get over the fact you're not Stephen," I said wonderingly.

He turned to me and took my hands. "Believe me, I'm not Stephen. How I longed to tell you who I really was after we were together in the pines. And then came the revelation that you were Estelle, Stephen's sister. I could see what agony you suffered, believing we were brother and sister, and it tore me apart. I almost confessed the truth to you then. I would have, if I hadn't convinced myself you were an imposter and not really Estelle. My anger prevented me from thinking straight."

"You're not my brother," I whispered. My heart soared, free of the load of guilt I'd carried for all those weeks.

"As near as I can determine our kinship, we're distant cousins. Don't forget Alexi and Sergei were only half brothers to begin with—they had different mothers. So Alexi's son, Peter, and Sergei's son, Marcus, were half first cousins, once removed."

Joy sang through me. Distant cousins. Not the

310

same thing as brother and sister—not the same thing, at all, at all.

"Oh, Stephen," I began and paused. "Marcus?" The name was strange on my tongue. "Marcus," I repeated firmly. It was his name, and I would use it.

He smiled ruefully. "Say it as much as you wish, Esma. You don't know how I yearned to hear you call me by my real name. Do you despise me for what I've done? Appropriating a dead man's name, his ship, and his family?"

"I could never hate you," I murmured. "Perhaps what you did wasn't right, but if you hadn't pretended to be Stephen Nikolai, we'd never have met."

He put an arm around my shoulders, and I sighed happily and leaned against him. "I'd made up my mind to tell Katherine the truth when I returned from San Francisco," he said. "I haven't yet, but I will."

I recalled how my mother had told me that, despite her hands and her ears telling her Stephen stood before her, she felt he was a stranger. "I think in her heart she already knows you're not her son," I said.

"And, thank God, I'm not your brother," he murmured, pulling me closer. "I've wanted to hold you like this so many times. Unfortunately, though I knew there was nothing preventing me, you didn't."

"I was so miserable," I confessed.

"No longer," he whispered against my lips. "No longer."

His kiss wiped away all the tears I'd shed, erased the ugly memory of Gerald's unwelcome embrace, and warmed me from head to toe. As we clung together, my world narrowed to the hayloft, enclosed in Marcus Alexander's arms. I scarcely heard the storm outside for the storm within me.

"My love," he murmured. "My only love."

Though now I wasn't a complete novice to love-making, I seemed to feel the marvel of each kiss, each caress for the first time. There was no sense of familiarity, just wonder and joy as, our garments thrown aside, we lay flesh to flesh, his heart beating against mine.

"I love you, Marcus Alexander," I told him. "I have from the moment you first kissed me."

"Esma, my beautiful Esma, I can't believe you're really here in my arms."

He trailed kisses along my throat to my breasts, enmeshing me in a net of glorious sensation. I tangled my fingers in his dark curls, savoring my right to hold him and caress him. If I were his, he was also mine. We belonged to one another; we had from the beginning. It had never been wrong for me to love Marcus. Cecile had never been his wife any more than I had ever been his sister.

Though we'd traveled a dark and dangerous path to reach this moment, we'd overcome all obstacles. I would never doubt our love again.

He rose above me, and then we were one, sailing the wild seas of rapture together, caught in a storm of passion that carried us far from the world into our own paradise.

Later, as we lay in each other's arms under a blanket, Marcus plucked a piece of hay from my hair. "Poor Esma," he said, smiling. "First pine needles, now straw. Will I never get you into a proper bed?"

"As long as you're with me, I don't care."

His smiled faded. "That's the trouble—I may not be with you for long. Though I mean to tell Katherine all that happened between Stephen and me, she's pretty well stuck with Marcus Alexander as captain of *Sea Dragon* unless she wants to postpone the voyage to the Orient indefinitely. And she can't very well do that because what with the new ship being built, she'll need the profit from the trip to keep Nikolai Shipping afloat."

I'd forgotten all about the Orient trip, forgotten he'd be sailing away from me in less than a week. Tears stung my eyes. How could I bear to have him go?

"Marcus," I whispered, pressing against him. "Hold me, Marcus."

He pulled me close. "Now that I have a reason to return," he murmured, *"Sea Dragon* will make the fastest run in history."

He kissed me, and my tears dried in the warmth surging anew through me. I forgot about everything except the magic of our love.

Chapter 20

On a sunny morning in mid-May, I stood beside my mare and Sir Toby near the ruins of the old church. The storm had spared the bell tower, though the bell itself had fallen into the rubble. No one had disturbed it since. For my part, I felt I'd rather not know whether or not the clapper was still rusted to the inside of the bell. If there were such things as spirits on earth, may they rest in peace.

I had brought my mother's hooded black cloak along for good luck. I lifted it from the mare's saddlebag and, as I unfolded it, I remembered how frightened I'd been just over a year ago when I first saw her standing on the promontory, wearing the cloak.

My fear had been from ignorance. As I'd soon discovered, she was a warm, generous, and understanding woman. As she'd proved when she listened to Marcus Alexander's explanation of how and why he'd allowed himself to pass for Stephen Nikolai. I recalled that time as though it were yesterday.

Marcus had stood before her, looking as apprehensive as an accused man before a judge. He'd

314

told her everything, not sparing or excusing himself.

"Do sit down," she said when he finished, gesturing to the other half of the settee. "I may not be able to see you, but it makes me nervous to have you looming over me."

When Marcus, his expression strained, eased down beside her, she ran her fingertips gently over his face. "So like and yet not the same," she murmured. "I think I've known from the first you weren't my son, but I wanted so much to believe you were Stephen."

Katherine sighed and wiped a tear from her eye with a lace-edged handkerchief. "Peter knew, of course, and he tried to tell me. Twice." She turned to me. "You recall the messages, Esma."

"Yes." How could I ever forget?

The alive are dead and the dead alive. Foretelling what Marcus had just confessed—that he was an imposter. And, later, the second message, *With me, with me.* Stephen had been with his father for a long time.

Had those prophetic words really come from my father's spirit or from Katherine's own mind?

"No doubt the pretense has taken as much of a toll on you as any one of us," Katherine told Marcus.

"I know you can never forgive me," he said.

She clasped his hand between hers. "Let's not speak of forgiveness. You've done your best to be my son and Alisette's father. Though I've lost Stephen, I still have you, and so does Alisette. As for Esma—" She paused for a moment before continuing. "Since I've lost my sight, I've become more acutely tuned to the feelings of those around me. I've known from the first day you came to us, Marcus, that you and Esma were falling in love.

Given the circumstances at that time, nothing could come of it, of course. I believed you were Stephen, and he had a wife already.

"After Cecile's fatal accident, I hoped, after time passed, perhaps the two of you might find happiness together. Then, later, when we learned Esma was my daughter and Stephen's sister how my heart ached for you two. But now—" She smiled.

I stared at her, taken aback. My mother had known all along!

"I have as much to be forgiven for as you, Marcus," Katherine went on. "I was truly blind to Gerald's perfidy. I wanted to believe him, and so I did. I cringe when I think of how I unwittingly placed Esma in such terrible, terrible danger."

I rose from my seat by the fireplace and knelt beside her. "Gerald fooled everyone, Mother. He'd been doing it for years. How could you have known?"

She released Marcus's hand to pat mine. "At least Marcus arrived in time to rescue you from that scoundrel." She straightened. "You might ask Loretta to bring us tea," she told me.

Since the call bell was within her reach, I realized she wanted to be left alone with Marcus, and so I did as she bade me, taking care not to return too soon.

That evening, when Marcus and I took a stroll in the garden, he told me how Katherine had surprised him by offering to give *Sea Dragon* to him.

"You'll have to earn her, of course," Katherine had added. "Before the ship becomes yours, I'll expect Captain Alexander to make a successful trip to the Orient—with the profits to be mine."

"That's a more-than-generous offer," he told her. "You can't know what it will mean to have *Sea Dragon* for my own—really my ship."

"Ah, but you forget I married one Nikolai man,

316

and I bore another. Nikolai men are seafarers, and you are a Nikolai, whatever you choose to call yourself."

He pressed her hand to his lips. "You treat me like a son, Katherine," he said. "I wish you *were* my mother, my own died when I was so young I scarcely knew her."

"In that case, perhaps once you return to Eureka, you'll see your way clear to accepting me as your mother-in-law." Katherine had smiled as she spoke, but her tone made it evident she meant what she said.

After repeating her words to me, Marcus drew me into his arms in the dubious privacy of the rose arbor. I nestled against him, no longer caring if anyone saw us. I didn't care if all of Eureka knew we were in love.

"How can Katherine be my mother-in-law unless you marry me?" he asked softly. "Will you?"

I happily agreed, and we sealed our betrothal with a long, lingering kiss.

My only regret from that moment until now had been the long wait, without him, until our wedding day. Since Katherine had specified we were to wait until *Sea Dragon*'s return, we'd both felt we must abide by her wishes.

Alisette's reappearance at my side shook me from my reverie. "I put the blue cornflowers on Mama's grave," she said. "Then I took one of the roses we picked for Grandma and put it on Alexandria's grave. You don't think Grandma will mind, do you?"

"No, she'll understand." I blinked back tears. How I missed my mother!

She'd died quietly, in her sleep, less than a month before. Oddly enough, on the eve of her death, she'd told me my father had spoken to her

317

that day, telling her he'd see her soon.

I was glad she hadn't suffered but, oh, how I wished she was still here.

Alisette's hand crept into mine. "Don't be sad about Grandma," she urged. "She's happy to be with Grandpa." She tugged at my hand. "It's time to go look."

I slipped on my mother's cloak and took Alisette's hand again. As we walked slowly toward the cliff edge, now no more than fifteen yards from the church ruins, I remembered, as I always did when I came here, the terrible night when Sea Cliff House had slid into the sea with Gerald trapped inside. I had never been able to mourn his death.

"I just know I won't remember," Alisette said.

"Remember what?"

"Not to say Papa 'stead of Uncle Marcus."

I laughed. "He won't care. I really do believe he thinks of himself as your papa anyway."

She brightened. "Then I'll call him Papa."

The waves crashed against the rockface below us, reminding me of the sea's destructiveness. But I was a Nikolai, and I no longer lived in fear of the sea. Still, I held tightly to Alisette's hand as we stood near the cliff edge, peering out to sea.

I'd come here every fair day since the month began, either alone or, if she wasn't having lessons from Margaret's governess, with Alisette. Though the promontory was gone, crashing into the ocean during that stormy night, I could see farther out to sea from these highlands than from any other place.

Like Katherine a year earlier, I was waiting and watching for *Sea Dragon*.

"There she is!" Alisette cried, pointing to a three master heading up the coast.

"I hope so," I said fervently, "but we can't count on it." The ship was too far away for us to discern any details, and I'd been disappointed many times already.

"I know so." Her tone was smug. "That's *Sea Dragon*."

I opened my mouth to ask her how and closed it again without speaking. If she were receiving spirit messages again, I didn't wish to hear about it.

"Don't you want to know who told me?" she asked.

Reluctantly, I nodded.

"Uncle Oscar."

For a moment I couldn't recall who Uncle Oscar might be. Then I remembered the old sailor we'd met on the jetty the day of the storm.

"Yesterday Margaret and I were playing in her yard," Alisette said, "and he walked past, so I said hello and he stopped. I asked him if he'd heard any word of *Sea Dragon*, and he said he had."

"Why didn't you tell me right away?"

"'Cause I wanted to surprise you. Uncle Oscar told me he heard she'd been sighted off San Francisco two days ago, and he figured she was due to cross the bar late today."

I shaded my eyes with my hand and stared at the far-off ship, her sails full and white against the bright blue of the sky.

"You and Papa are going to get married right away, aren't you?" Alisette asked. "'Cause then we can sail with him when *Sea Dragon* makes her next voyage."

I stared at her. "Sail with him? What gave you that idea?"

"Papa told me the day he left. He said it was our secret, but I guess I can tell you now 'cause he's almost here. He's going to have his cabin changed so there's a tiny place for me to sleep, separate from you and him, and the three of us will live on the

319

ship so we don't have to say good-bye any more. Won't that be fun?"

Never to be parted from Marcus? I couldn't imagine anything I wanted more.

"When we sail to China, maybe we'll get to see a junk being launched," she said. "I can hardly wait."

I murmured agreement, but the launching of Chinese junks wasn't for what *I* yearned.

"And Papa said when you have babies I can help take care of them," Alisette added.

I blinked, taken aback. Babies? Then I smiled. Of course we'd have children, Marcus and I. My heart melted at the thought of singing the Russian lullaby to a baby son with black curls and green eyes, a future sea captain.

We watched the ship sail closer, until at last I saw the gold and red Nikolai colors flying. "It really is *Sea Dragon!*" I cried.

"I told you," Alisette said. "Now you won't have to cry any more—we're going to be happy forever and ever."

And so we would be, I thought as we mounted and began the ride back to Eureka to welcome Captain Marcus Alexander, the man we both loved.